SPRING BREAK

* available from Severn House

SPRING BREAK

A Daniel Jacobus Mystery

Gerald Elias

Severn House Large Print
London & New York

This first large print edition published 2018
in Great Britain and the USA by
SEVERN HOUSE PUBLISHERS LTD of
Eardley House, 4 Uxbridge Street, London W8 7SY.
First world regular print edition published 2017 by
Severn House Publishers Ltd.

British Library Cataloguing in Publication Data
A CIP catalogue record for this title is available from the British
Library.

ISBN-13: 9780727893307

Severn House Publishers support the Forest Stewardship Council™
[FSC™], the leading international forest certification organisation. All
our titles that are printed on FSC certified paper carry the FSC logo.

Typeset by Palimpsest Book Production Ltd.,
Falkirk, Stirlingshire, Scotland.
Printed and bound in Great Britain by
T J International, Padstow, Cornwall.

Dedicated to music students, especially female ones, because it's hard enough to learn to play the violin.

Springtime is upon us.
The birds rejoice with festive song and
gentle breezes caress the murmuring
brook.
Thunderstorms, those harbingers of
Spring, roar, casting their dark mantle
over heaven.
Then they die away to silence, and the
birds take up their charming songs once
more.

On the flower-strewn meadow, with leafy
branches rustling overhead,
The goatherd sleeps, his faithful dog
beside him.

Stirred by the festive tones of rustic pipes,
Nymphs and shepherds lightly dance
beneath the verdant canopy of spring.

Sonnet by Antonio Vivaldi for
his violin concerto,
'Spring,' from the Four Seasons
(Translation by David Cowley
and Gerald Elias)

Prologue

The faculty meeting had been hastily called and began in some disarray, as they so often did. It was gaveled to order by the committee's chair, Charles Hedge, dean of the acclaimed Kinderhoek Conservatory of Music in bucolic Cornwall County, New York. All the faculty knew was that it had something to do with the 'Going for Baroque' festival, the conservatory's annual gala three-week series of artistic and fund-raising events capped off by the Vivaldi by Twilight concert.

'What's this all about, Hedge?' Harold Handy, Professor of Music History, asked. A longtime conservatory professor and esteemed music historian, Handy's two-volume textbook, *The Essentials of Western Music*, was a standard on every reputable music school's reading list. 'Don't we have enough meetings already?'

'More than enough, I should say,' added Sybil Baker-Hulme, in a rare display of collegial agreement. Professor of Advanced Musicology and Baroque Studies, Baker-Hulme, formerly of the Royal Academy of Music in London, was the foremost British authority on the Baroque period and commanded an impressive and authoritative listing of scholarly publications.

'Isaac Stern has cancelled,' Hedge said tersely,

1

and let the broad implications of that uncharacteristically succinct statement register with the faculty committee.

'What do you mean, "cancelled"?' asked Bronislaw Tawroszewicz, Director of Chamber Orchestras. A native of Warsaw and a graduate of the Paris Conservatoire, he had trained as a violinist but found his true passion on the collegiate podium, where he could assert his authoritarian instincts without restraint. The youngest and only untenured faculty member at the meeting, Tawroszewicz had the thinnest résumé, which, given that he was barely ten years older than his students, was only to be expected.

'Just that, Bronislaw.' Hedge concealed his impatience no more successfully than a skunk disguising its scent. 'His manager called and said Mr Stern would not be able to attend.'

'Not very good form to cancel two days before an engagement,' said Dante Millefiori, Professor of Orchestral Studies. Tall and magisterial, Millefiori had built the orchestra program in his own image: a surfeit of flair but, critics said, wanting of depth. The orchestra toured domestically and internationally on an almost annual basis but was rarely invited back. Millefiori had been hoping to corral Stern to read through a concerto or two with the symphony orchestra in order for him to show off his conducting skills, which he felt had so far been underappreciated by the concert world.

'What was the reason?' Handy asked.

'None given,' Hedge replied. 'Probably something else came up. Who knows? Maybe another of Stern's PR trips to China. But his manager did ask if his visit might be rescheduled.'

Could that be a hopeful sign? It seemed to lift the weight of the room. But not for long.

'Rescheduled when?' asked Elwood Dunster, Professor of Violin. Dunster was the elder statesman of the string faculty, one of the few remaining professors connected to the conservatory's historical and philanthropic roots.

'Next year.'

Whatever optimism remained abruptly evaporated.

'So, what is your suggestion?' Tawroszewicz asked, after an extended silence. 'We can't cancel "Going for Baroque." It's tradition. Right?'

'It's more than simple tradition, Bronislaw. We were going to kick off "Going for Baroque" with Stern's masterclass and participation at the symposium. It would have been a major recruiting tool for next year and would have demonstrated to our prospective donors how worthy our conservatory is of the eight-figure gift we've been trying to convince them to give us. So I'm going to turn your question around, if I may, to your distinguished colleagues. What are *your* suggestions?'

'Can't we just do without him?' Baker-Hulme asked. 'After all, what does Isaac Stern know about Baroque music, anyway?'

'That's not really the point, though,' Dunster said. 'Stern is more famous in the music world – the general world, really – than all of us put together. He's a great violinist, teacher, humanitarian, what have you. At this point, his absence would almost speak louder than his presence.'

General mumbling seemed to indicate agreement.

'What about Rostropovich?' Tawroszewicz asked. 'He's as famous as Stern – more even – and Gorbachev is coming back to New York this weekend. Timing is great.'

The mumbling was replaced by a distinct buzz.

'And if elephants could fly,' Baker-Hulme said. 'Isn't that what Americans say?'

'What does that mean?' Tawroszewicz asked.

'What she's saying,' Millefiori answered, 'is that the likelihood of getting someone of the stature of Mstislav Rostropovich on a year's notice, let alone a day's, is less than nil.'

'Well, it's all moot,' Hedge intervened. 'We, in fact, reached out to Rostropovich's agent, among others, even before we engaged Stern. The invitation was politely declined. Any more brilliant ideas?'

'I know I'm not full-time faculty, but may I make a suggestion?' Yumi Shinagawa, Adjunct Professor of Violin, asked.

'Be our guest.'

'What if we invited Daniel Jacobus?'

'That old blind violin teacher? The curmudgeon?' Millefiori asked with some astonishment.

'Jacobus?' Baker-Hulme asked, seconding Millefiori. 'Why, he's a mere instrumentalist, and hardly even that anymore, from what I've heard. What might he have to contribute?'

'I can assure you,' Yumi responded, somewhat

4

defensively, 'when I studied with Daniel Jacobus, I learned more about Baroque music than from all of the music history classes I ever took, maybe because he put as much emphasis on the "music" as on the "Baroque."'

'No need to be testy, my dear,' Hedge said. 'Sybil's point, that we do want our guest panelist to be well-read, is a valid one.'

'Daniel Jacobus might not be as famous as Stern,' Yumi said, 'but he has a very strong reputation.'

Jacobus had gained notoriety as a brutally honest and astutely perceptive musician and teacher, which had earned him the respect and admiration of his peers. It had also earned their envy and enmity, and not only in regard to music. Though Jacobus savored nothing more than being left alone, he had ironically come to be thought of as a busybody, because no matter where he went he had an uncanny knack of dredging up trouble. The result was that Daniel Jacobus was a revered, yet isolated, icon.

'Yes, a strongly *unsavory* reputation,' Millefiori replied. 'He might know his music, but from what I've heard, his teaching methods would be frowned upon by the National Association of Schools of Music. May I remind everyone that we depend upon the good graces of NASM for our accreditation?'

'If I may say, Dante,' Handy replied, 'I think you're putting the cart before the horse. We're here to teach music, not kiss the posterior of a distant bureaucracy. If Mr Jacobus has a fresh approach to things, isn't that something we'd want? If nothing else, it might un-stuffify the atmosphere around here.'

'I don't know,' Tawroszewicz said. 'I heard about this Jacobus. I heard he sticks his nose into other people's business. Everywhere he goes, it ends up trouble.'

'Why, Bronto, have you something to hide?' Baker-Hulme said.

Tawroszewicz blanched.

Emboldened by some chuckling among the faculty, Baker-Hulme continued. 'I've changed my mind, Charles, and withdraw my objection. I think it would be delightful to have Mr Jacobus among us, even if *some others* think he is a pariah. I just have one question for dear Yumi.'

'Yes?' Yumi asked.

'Mr Jacobus is still alive, isn't he?'

This time there was general laughter.

'Yes,' Yumi replied. 'Alive. And kicking.'

The committee got up to leave.

'Wait a second,' Handy said. 'How do we know Jacobus will accept the invitation?'

'Don't worry,' Shinagawa replied. 'He's a born teacher. I know he'll jump at the opportunity.'

'Are you kidding?' Jacobus indeed jumped, almost knocking over his chair when Yumi made her pitch. 'Sorry. I'm not into group masturbation.'

'But, Jake,' Yumi said.

'"But, Jake?" "But, Jake?"' Jacobus mimicked Yumi. 'But what? The answer is no. N-O. Whose move is it?' Jacobus said to Nathaniel.

'Mine, I think,' Nathaniel said. And as he had done countless times, he took Jacobus's right hand in his left and placed Jacobus's index finger on the checker that Nathaniel intended to move, and they moved it together. Years ago, to accommodate Jacobus's blindness, Nathaniel had filed the red checkers roughly into squares so that Jacobus would know which were his. That way Jacobus could "picture" the board with his fingers as the game developed.

With the move, Jacobus and Nathaniel began their fourth game of the day. Jacobus had won the first game, but Nathaniel won the second and third handily, leaving Jacobus testy. So it was not a propitious moment for Yumi's arrival at Nathaniel's apartment.

'Jake, I have some great news!' Yumi had said after letting herself in with the extra key Nathaniel had given her.

'Bush was telling the truth when he said "No new taxes"?' Jacobus had quipped.

'Better. You've been invited to give a master-class at Kinderhoek!'

'So, what's the great news?' he'd responded.

'And you're going to be the featured guest on at the Baroque symposium panel!'

It was that prospect which had prompted Jacobus's somewhat callous remark about communal self-arousal.

Jacobus supposed he should be proud of his former student, now an esteemed, albeit part-time, adjunct professor at the Kinderhoek Conservatory. The school's administration was capitalizing on her rising celebrity as a market-able commodity to attract the best students. One of their most successful recruiting taglines had become, 'And you may be interested to know that Yumi Shinagawa is now on our faculty,' as if she was a BMW offered as a bonus to a vacation package. Her part-time status was not due to any second-rate aspect of her musicianship, but because her primary position, as concertmaster of the renowned orchestra Harmonium, in New York City, restricted her to a once or twice weekly hour-and-a-half commute to Kinderhoek to teach her studio of nine budding prodigies.

Whereas Yumi's career trajectory was on a steep ascent, Jacobus's life had recently hit rock bottom. He had been rendered homeless the past winter when an arsonist had burned down his house in the Berkshire hills of Massachusetts. He'd moved in with Nathaniel Williams, his closest friend, at his ample apartment on West 96th Street in New York until the construction of his new house was completed. That Jacobus and Williams had formed such a long-lasting bond of friendship was as unlikely as it was unbreakable: Jacobus, an atheistic Jew, a teenage refugee from prewar Germany. Acerbic. Opinionated. Impatient. Nathaniel, an imposingly large, congenial, polite African American from Kentucky. A common love of music, of integrity, and of good food had greased the wheels that drove their friendship. But even the closest of friends can endure each other only so long in a confined space, especially two who had lived alone for so long they had become irrevocably set in their own eccentric ways.

'Come on, Jake,' Nathaniel intervened. 'You

haven't even gotten your fiddle out for the past two months. A little stimulation will do you good.'

'As I said, I'm not into masturbation.'

Jacobus further argued that he had tired of the world pitying blind people rather than treating them as equals and fully expected the conservatory would be no exception. He refrained from admitting aloud another reason. He was feeling more tired than usual. That age might be beginning to creep up on him. He did not want to cause Yumi any concern about his health. Besides, listening to someone else drone on about their health was the most boring subject he could think of. He hoped he had put the issue of the invitation to rest, but Yumi persevered, politely arguing that the pedagogical insights he could offer were unique and valuable.

Unbeknownst to Jacobus, the impetus for Yumi suggesting he be invited to Kinderhoek had originated with Nathaniel, who a week earlier had pleaded with her: 'He's gone past frayin' me around my edges. Now he's getting my insides.'

'Jake, let's admit it,' Yumi concluded. 'You're no spring chicken. Chances are you might kick off tomorrow. Who knows how many more opportunities you'll have to change so many young people's lives?'

Jacobus laughed.

'I'm impressed with your unsweetened logic,' Jacobus conceded. 'Let me think about it. I want to finish my game.'

'Sure. And, not that it has to do with anything, but I brought you your favorite cheese Danish,' Yumi said.

9

'And coffee?'

'Of course.'

'The way I like it?'

'Boiled to sludge.'

'Uh-huh.'

If Jacobus's victory in the fourth game was in part the result of Nathaniel discreetly allowing himself be outmaneuvered, it served the greater good.

'OK,' Jacobus said. 'I'll do it.'

One

News of the symposium's last-minute replacement created quite a buzz at the Kinderhoek Conservatory, even more so, in a certain way, than if Isaac Stern had not cancelled. As great as he was, Stern was a known quantity and had given a masterclass at the conservatory the year before. Jacobus, on the other hand, had an unpolished aura steeped in conflict and mystery. His arrival on campus aroused as much curiosity among the faculty as among the students. Yumi checked him in to his accommodations at the Campus Inn and then, after a brief rest and a dry hamburger, walked him to the Hiram Feldstein Auditorium of the Dolly Cooney Performance Building, the venue for the symposium.

The auditorium was filled to the brim with students, faculty, staff, and potential donors. Baroque music – or more accurately, the performance of Baroque music – had become a hot-button topic in the cloistered world of classical music in recent years, and Charles Hedge, emceeing the discussion, sought to capitalize on the passionate debate as a means to fatten the school's endowment. Backstage, Jacobus was cursorily introduced to the other three panelists, with whom he exchanged

11

vague and meaningless pleasantries. Escorted by a young co-ed, they slalomed through pots of seasonal tulips, hyacinths, and daffodils decorating the stage. Jacobus stumbled upon one of them, was caught from falling by the young lady, and heard someone in the wings mutter, 'Already?'

Jacobus and the other three panelists sat at a linen-draped table in the center of the stage, where they waited for the event to begin. Jacobus shifted his behind in an uncomfortable classroom chair. *How had she done it?* he asked himself for the umpteenth time. How had Yumi sweet-talked him into being a panelist for this damned symposium?

Additional spring flowers had been positioned in the middle of the table, dividing him and Bronislaw Tawroszewicz – the other applied, or performing, musician – who were seated on the right side of the table, from the pair of academic musicians, Sybil Baker-Hulme and Harold Handy, on the left. The seating arrangement reflected the subtle though profound division between performers and scholars, which had persisted ever since someone first banged a log with a stick and someone else tried to explain why, and which continued to be a dubious hallmark of advanced music conservatories.

Yumi had given Jacobus the rundown on the other panelists. That he had never heard of them was more his fault than theirs, as blindness reduced Jacobus's interest in keeping current with music pedagogy. Even so, he'd never had much patience for reading about music. He learned

12

from listening and playing and not from people writing about it.

Yumi had also prepped Jacobus with the ground rules for the discussion. Starting with Baker-Hulme, each panelist would present their opening perspectives on the topic at hand. That would be followed by written questions from the audience passed up to Dean Hedge. Each speaker was provided a microphone and a glass of water, and the three who were not blind had written notes spread out before them.

Jacobus collected his thoughts while Hedge, at the podium, annoyingly preoccupied himself with testing and retesting his microphone with snippets of prepared comments while waiting for the final attendees to cram into the auditorium. At the appropriate moment, Hedge cleared his throat into his microphone. He welcomed the packed assemblage to the 'Going for Baroque' curtain-raiser and expressed the heartfelt view that 'if all performances were so well attended, classical music would be declared alive and well!' The response, by design, was an affirmative roar. He then introduced each guest, reading down their substantial résumés. Finishing, Hedge invited everyone upon the conclusion of the symposium 'at nine o'clock or dawn, whichever comes first,' to a light reception in the lobby where they could 'interface' with the guest speakers.

'And now, ladies and gentlemen,' Hedge concluded, 'let's give a proud Kinderhoek welcome to our esteemed panelists.'

Not able to take a visual cue from the other panelists, and not having been in this position before, Jacobus was clueless how to respond. Should he wave? Should he bow? Should he smile? He could draw upon his memory to recall which facial muscles were necessary to simulate a smile. But any response he could think of seemed presumptuous, so he simply sat there. If they assumed he was being antisocial, so be it, there was nothing he could do about it.

When the applause died down, Professor Baker-Hulme spoke into her microphone, expressing her delight at being so warmly received. She then commenced her presentation with the same moral certitude that had created the British Empire, or so it seemed to Jacobus.

'After the death of Johann Sebastian Bach in 1750,' she began, 'the music of the Baroque became, to paraphrase Handel's *Messiah*, "rejected and despised." It was repudiated by a new generation of more frivolous popular taste, which inaccurately deemed the Baroque's inherently contrapuntal nature as too academic and too intellectual. With few exceptions, the aesthetic of the Classical and Romantic eras, and well into the twentieth century, turned a deaf ear to the vast musical treasury that had lasted for one hundred and fifty years from the time of Claudio Monteverdi in the early 1600s.'

Perfect Queen-of-England enunciation, Jacobus thought. From there he began to extrapolate: Middle-aged. Prosperous. Confident. Wears nice clothes even at a picnic. Hair in place even when it's a mess. 'I'm more famous than you' kind of voice. For Jacobus, the mental exercise had become so ingrained over the decades since the onset of

14

his blindness he was no longer aware it was even an exercise.

'The early twentieth century brought us a false renaissance of Baroque music,' Baker-Hulme continued, 'starting with the *faux* Baroque compositions of Stravinsky and Respighi, and followed by the misguided attempts to "improve" Baroque music by basting it with thick-as-molasses monstrosities like Leopold Stokowski's arrangement of the Bach Toccata and Fugue in D minor.'

Baker-Hulme recited the word 'monstrosities' with such flair that the audience had no choice but to agree with the absurdity of the idea and laughed en chorus. 'I refer to these abominations as *nefarious* Baroque,' she said. She went on to recount how true scholarship – with her at the helm – had brought Baroque music back from the brink of the abyss and concluded her statement with upbeat affirmation, sounding not unlike Margaret Thatcher addressing Parliament.

'As the result of decades of intense scholarship, with our understanding of historically informed performance, we can now recreate the musical glory of the Baroque era exactly as audiences of the period heard it! The way it was *meant* to sound!'

Jacobus could hear seats slapping against seat backs, as the audience rose to its feet in applause. After they resettled, he heard Dean Hedge step to the microphone, take a deep breath, and speak the single word: 'Next,' drawing a unanimous guffaw.

'I have great admiration for my esteemed colleague's scholarship,' Professor Harold Handy began. Handy's famous monotone, Yumi had told

15

Jacobus, had earned him the mixed reputation of possessing a lively intellect and wry wit but of being a tedious lecturer. 'And I have no question as to the veracity of her words. I would simply like to present a broader perspective, if I may.'

So far she was right about the tedious lecturer, Jacobus thought. Handy would rush through a sentence and then pause at great length before commencing the next, as if each was a newly conceived and separate thought.

Handy cleared his throat, which, Jacobus soon noted, was his habit prior to making what he thought was an *essential point*. Maybe no one else noticed it because they were looking at Handy as well as listening to him. Jacobus simply found it annoying.

'That term, "historically informed performance," that Sybil used. It's a fairly new one. I don't know who coined it – I'm not sure anyone does – nor how it is determined whose performance is historically informed and whose is not. Unlike cancer warning labels on cigarette packs, there are no universally accepted standards for informedness. Unlike most clubs, which require certain qualifications for membership, "historically informed" musicians are solely self-appointed.'

I'm starting to like this guy, Jacobus thought. *Let him clear his throat all he wants.*

'"Historically informed" means, I suppose, that the performers have read some of the books and, like the children's game of telephone, have passed around some of the tales about how music was performed at the time it was written. In some cases – for instance in regard to vibrato on string instruments – historically informed performers contradict the historical record. Why, you may ask. Who knows? Maybe it's because they like being different. Sometimes these H.I. folks play on instruments of similar construction to those used when the music was first performed; even, for a twisted logic difficult to fathom, when those instruments, like the French horn, are painfully inferior to modern instruments.'

Handy cleared his throat.

'The clear, and I believe intended, inference of the "historically informed" self-label is that anyone not fortunate to be so dubbed must thereby be historically *un*informed. Club membership denied.

'In the end, the only absolute essential is what the performance means to the listener. The *listener*. Though I cannot be certain, I suspect Bach or Mozart would agree with that, and if that's what you take away from your listening experiences, then that's as informed as anyone needs to be. Thank you.'

The symposium was turning out to be more entertaining than Jacobus had expected. Harold Handy had just thrown down a gantlet. Of that, Jacobus was certain, though the audience seemed unsure, as their response was perhaps slightly less enthusiastic than for Sybil Baker-Hulme. The tension between the two academics was palpable, even from Jacobus's end of the table.

'You can *talk* about music,' Bronislaw Tawroszewicz began, interrupting Jacobus's musing. 'But the people don't buy tickets to hear talk. They buy tickets to hear music.

'Most important thing is sound. Big sound.

17

Beautiful sound. We have great instruments. Why not use them? Use full bow! Use vibrato! Why not? When I conduct chamber orchestra we play with energy. We make thirty musicians sound like sixty, not fifteen. Like Harold says.'

Though it was by no means certain to Jacobus that this was what Harold had actually meant, it was clear Tawroszewicz was attempting to stake out different territory from Baker-Hulme, even if that territory was at the boundary of acceptable contemporary practice.

Tawroszewicz then proceeded to list all the great conductors and musicians, with their historic pedigrees, with whom he had worked from the time he had emerged from the cradle. They included many who Jacobus had only heard about by reputation, as they had been trapped behind the recently dismantled Iron Curtain. But the litany also included many he had never heard of, and as the list lengthened like an afternoon shadow, Jacobus unsuccessfully stifled a yawn, which did not go undetected by the speaker next to him.

'In old days, the instruments made a bad sound and the bows were weak,' Tawroszewicz resumed, finally circling back to the subject. 'Why should we try to play like that? That's not how *we* learn to play the violin or the viola or cello.'

'Oh, please, Bronislaw!' Sybil Baker-Hulme interrupted with some heat.

'Down, girl!' Hedge said, seeking to lower the temperature.

'But really!' she continued. 'Bronislaw doesn't know the difference between Bach and Brahms, let alone Bach and Boccherini. It all sounds like day-old porridge when he conducts.'

Jacobus was happily awake again.

'Sybil,' Hedge intervened, 'you will certainly have the opportunity to make your points in the Q and A. What do you say we let Bronto finish having his say?'

'If he must,' Sybil said and sighed.

'All I say is,' Tawroszewicz said, 'why should we always play vegetarian? Sometimes there is meat.'

The pregnancy of the ensuing pause finally gave birth to the awareness that Tawroszewicz was finished.

'Thank you, Bronislaw,' Dean Hedge said, eliciting modest applause.

'Now I would like to turn to our special guest, Daniel Jacobus, for what will undoubtedly be a unique perspective.'

Jacobus reminded himself once more of Yumi's final entreaty before he went onstage: 'Jake, promise me you won't piss people off.'

Jacobus's decades of teaching had taken place in the privacy of his living room. One teacher, one student. With the anticipatory silence, he now felt hundreds of eyes drilling into him, blind though he was. And unlike a performance, he had neither the composer's voice *with* which to speak, nor his violin *through* which to speak. Suddenly, his lips were parched. He felt for the glass of water, took a sip, and then fumbled for the microphone. In the heat of the moment he neglected to feel its dimensions and brought it too close to his mouth. When he said, 'The first thing,' it almost deafened the entire audience, and several people yelled out, 'Turn it down!' Some laughed. How the hell had he let Yumi talk him into this? He moved the microphone an inch farther away.

'The first thing to remember,' he started again, 'is that ninety percent of the music they composed then, as now, was crap.'

The audience must have felt this new perspective was either irreverent or refreshing, because it elicited a definite buzz. That didn't surprise Jacobus, though it hadn't been his goal. He was just telling the truth. He imagined Sybil Baker-Hulme already beginning to harrumph, but he thought he heard Handy chuckle.

Suddenly there was a cry. Or was it a shout? Whatever it was, it was muffled and short-lived. And it seemed to have come from over Jacobus's right shoulder, but too distant to have been onstage. Backstage, perhaps. Was someone already protesting his point of view? His choice of words? A disgruntled student who hadn't managed to get a seat and needed to advertise his backbench status? It could have been a her, not a him, but it had come and gone so quickly that Jacobus, focused on his message, couldn't categorize it. It was probably nothing, but it unsettled the audience sufficiently for Hedge to feel the need to bring the gathering back into focus.

'Ladies and gentlemen,' he said from his podium. 'We all know of Mr Jacobus's reputation for provocative ideas. But let's at least offer him a chance to *pro*voke before we *e*voke, shall we? Mr Jacobus, you were saying something about *crap*?'

If nothing else, Jacobus thought, Hedge knew how to work a crowd.

'Yes,' Jacobus said. 'What I was saying is that being a musician wasn't an obsession or a religious calling. That's the Hollywood version. It was a job. A craft, like a mason or a butcher. You made a living. When the boss said, "The Grand Poobah is coming for dinner tonight. We need two hours of music," you wrote two hours of music or you were out on the street. Composers scrawled music as quickly as possible using stock formulas with predictable results. It was generally intended to be very easy to play, partly because most musicians weren't particularly good, and also because the music had to be copied by hand at breakneck speed – meaning it was filled with mistakes. And there simply was no time to rehearse adequately. So, performances by most orchestras in those days were probably on the level of a bad high school these days.

'One problem with all this talking about how people played during this period of music or that period of music is that it assumes two things: first, that there have actually been such things as periods of music; and second, that there was one right way and any other way was wrong. You remember that Broadway show, *My Fair Lady*? Remember what's-his-name? The lead fella?'

Someone shouted out, 'Rex Harrison.' Another, 'Henry Higgins.'

Jacobus took a sip of water. His voice was already getting hoarse. He would wrap things up quickly.

'Thank you. Henry Higgins. Remember how

21

he could identify a dozen distinct accents within London alone? Well, just think of Italy in the eighteenth century. Think of the geography. You go from your village, over the hill to the next valley – which in those days took eight hours, not eight minutes, so you almost never went – and you can't understand a single word of your own *paesanos*. Why not? Because they speak a different language! Not a different accent. Not a different dialect. They spoke a different goddamn language! Given those circumstances, you really think there would be a single style to play music?

'You might be thinking I sound like I disagree with Professor Baker-Hulme, or maybe with Professor Handy, or maybe with Professor Tawroszewicz. But I don't, really. There certainly was a style, and we do need the scholarship, we do need the investigation, and we do need the careful analysis because there are some general things to deduce about Baroque performance that we can be pretty sure about. But we also do need to understand that style isn't what makes a performance memorable. Imagination. Creativity. The style's just the framework. And ultimately it comes down to the very same thing that every Baroque musician of his era and every musician since then had to consider day-in, day-out, whether he was playing for a queen or in the local beer hall. You can sum that up in two words: good taste.'

A small contingent cheered. Perhaps they were students who believed, mistakenly, that Jacobus had just liberated them from having to study their music history books. But the overall audience response was decidedly mixed. Jacobus was not surprised. He had found from experience that it made people uncomfortable to be confronted with having to take responsibility for their own decisions. And maybe they were right, because he had also found from experience that their decisions were generally wrong. At least there hadn't been any further outbursts, he thought, and took another sip of water.

Two

'And here's our first question,' Hedge said after thanking the panelists for their insightful observations. 'It's from a student, Charles Nobis, who writes he's a sophomore in the voice department and likes Baroque music. His question, which he'd like Professor Handy to address, is, "If we didn't have historically informed performance, wouldn't that be a bad thing?" Good question, and thank you, Charles, for "voicing" it.'

Harold Handy cleared his throat. Jacobus, fatigued, hoped it would be a short answer.

'Certainly we must inform ourselves of the history,' Handy began. 'But precisely what period of time is the performance supposed to reflect? A given era? A given decade? A given year? The given day that the premiere took place? It would require a *month-by-month flow chart* to know how musicians played, as it changed constantly.' Without raising his voice, Handy over-enunciated 'month-by-month flow chart' to emphasize his point.

'One could make the case that historically informed performances are, in the best sense, ideal museum pieces, providing a *reasonable facsimile* of how things *might* have been done during a particular slice of time. But perhaps a more accurate, nonbiased moniker would be historically *restricted* or, taking a cue from Civil

War aficionados, who duplicate classic battles down to the last brass button, *reenacted*.'

'May I interject a word here,' Sybil Baker-Hulme said.

'I'm not finished replying to Mr Nobis's question,' Handy bristled. 'You'll get your turn.'

Jacobus took a handkerchief from his back pocket and, stifling a laugh, pretended to cough into it. 'Don't mind me,' he said, waving the handkerchief.

'One of the charges leveled at classical music for having a relatively small share of the vast entertainment market,' Handy continued, 'is that we're a "museum piece." But one major difference between art and music is that once a painting is hung on the wall, that's it. It doesn't change. In fact, every effort is made to prevent it from changing. To wit, heroically painstaking efforts to restore masterpieces like *The Last Supper* and *The Night Watch* to their original glory.'

Throat clearing.

'Music, on the other hand, is *always* changing, no matter what we try to do to understand and maintain its "authenticity." Concert halls and the cultural context of the folks inside them change dramatically over time: Thirty musicians playing Beethoven's Fifth are no longer going to shock you out of your seat. Instrumentalists tinker with their instruments and, from night to night, the performance changes: The oboist might be trying a new reed. The bass player might be invigorated by a New York Yankees victory.'

This drew a few chuckles.

'Or the Mets.'

Even more.

'Thank you. I've finished my answer.'

'May I respond now?' Baker-Hulme asked, almost imploringly.

'Not quite yet,' Hedge responded. 'It seems our next question is for Mr Jacobus, signed by someone simply named Alicia. She writes, "Aren't you being really harsh about the quality of music and performance in the Baroque era? It sounds like an exaggeration." Maybe that's why Alicia didn't write her last name! Mr Jacobus, it's all yours.'

'Harsh? Maybe,' Jacobus began. 'But I'm being diplomatic as hell compared to what Mozart and Beethoven had to say about general standards. You've got to remember in those days there was no TV. No movies. No radio. No recordings. At night it got dark. Instead of a ball game you could watch a pack of dogs trying to eviscerate a chained bear or go to a public lynching. Or you could go hear music or theater. If you really got desperate you could stay home and read the family Bible.

'The routine for composers was to get up in the morning and write a new piece for a dinner or private party that very evening. Baroque music, except for expensive operas, was rarely played more than once before it was tucked away forever, because audiences felt if something was performed a second time they were being cheated and would start throwing rotten vegetables.

'Yes, there were geniuses, especially in the halls of wealth and power, because that's where geniuses had to go if they wanted to get paid what they deserved. They followed the money. Vivaldi

26

at the Ospedale in Venice at the height of its republic. Corelli in Rome was subsidized by cardinals and popes. Couperin in Paris for King Louis. Bach in Cöthen with Prince Leopold. Handel in London for King George.

'Sure, some guys got those cushy jobs. The lucky few. But even for them their job status was lower on the totem pole than a butler or coachman. Most musicians went to work every day, rain or shine. Played in poorly lit rooms where they'd freeze their asses off in winter and swelter in summer. Worked all hours at the whim of the local potentate for only enough *grolschen* to go home at night to share some bread and cheese and a glass of beer with their wife and nineteen kids. Musicians' unions today wouldn't allow such conditions, and God bless 'em.

'Most musicians played on instruments that Tawroszewicz noted were no better than the playing conditions. Strings, made of pigs' intestines from the local butcher, were constantly out of tune and always breaking, especially without any kind of temperature control. Horsehair for bows came off the old gray mare. Their fiddles rattled around in little wooden coffins, so even if they were any good to begin with, a few years of commuting to work in the family oxcart would've knocked any quality they might've had out of them.

'And then there was the question of training. Some musicians had the advantage of learning from older masters, but in general if you made a mistake you got whacked on your head with Master's bow and thrown into a closet until you got it right.'

Jacobus paused. He suddenly lost his train of thought. He took a sip of water and then another until it came back. *Oh, yeah. Performance practice.* He needed a rest.

'Not to get too esoteric, but you also have to consider competing tuning systems during the Baroque period. Pythagorean, well-tempered, meantone-tempered, and equal-tempered. Enough to make you hot-tempered. What I'm saying is that most of the performances you would've heard during the Baroque period probably sounded like shit. So here's the punchline: If we really want to recreate the authentic Baroque sound are we willing to accept listening to bad music sounding terrible?'

The question was rhetorical, but Jacobus would not have minded someone arguing with him. There being only silence, he continued.

'Or do we want to play only the best Baroque music and make it sound a helluva lot better than it did then? And that requires making judgments. Or, in other words, using your brain.'

More applause than the first time around. Jacobus gathered they had finally realized he wasn't just bullshitting. But maybe he was. After all, what did he know? He wasn't there three hundred years ago. Though sometimes he felt like it.

'Thank you, Mr Jacobus,' Hedge said. 'Now, finally your turn, Professor Baker-Hulme.' Hedge flipped to the next question. 'And you'll be happy to know it's from the renowned composer of *Platonic Dialogues* and *Synchronos*, and coincidentally the devoted husband of Sybil Baker-Hulme. Our own Aaron Schlossberg!'

28

'Hello, dear!' Aaron Schlossberg shouted from the back of the hall, which got a big laugh.

'So happy you could make it,' Baker-Hulme replied into the microphone.

'Wouldn't miss it for the world!'

Once the general laughter died down, Hedge continued.

'This kind of family atmosphere,' he said in reverential tones, 'is what makes Kinderhoek unique. But enough propaganda. Here's the question. I'll read it verbatim, but remember, I'm just the messenger! Aaron writes, *Don't let Jacobus get away with it, dear! Tell us about the glories of the Ospedale!*'

Everyone, audience and panelists alike, laughed at both the question and Hedge's dramatic rendering. Even Jacobus smiled.

'Thank you, Aaron,' Baker-Hulme replied. 'I would be delighted. My dear husband has been kind enough to lob me a softball.

'The Ospedale della Pietà was a convent, orphanage, and music school in Venice, almost exclusively for *figlie*, girls, and was, in the words of Mr Jacobus, one of those rare, sought-after "cushy" institutions. Not all the students were orphans, nor even poor for that matter. Initially, and through the seventeenth century, the *ospedali* – there were four – provided training in sacred music. As the excellence of the Pietà's training grew, so did its reputation. It attracted the attention of the nobility, who sometimes enrolled their infants, legitimate or otherwise. Many of the concerts were arranged especially for important, wealthy visitors—'

'So in some ways things haven't changed all that much, have they?' Hedge interjected. More laughter.

'Quite,' Baker-Hulme replied. 'But unlike concerts these days, the young ladies, because of mores of modesty, were constrained to perform behind an iron lattice grille, like a wall, which served as protection from the prying glances of lecherous men. I'm not sure the modern woman would countenance such acts of subservience.'

The feminists in the audience applauded in agreement. One shouted, 'Right on!'

'La Pietà hired the best faculty in the city and promoted its high quality concerts. None other than the great Antonio Vivaldi was appointed a violin teacher in 1703 and served in various roles on and off until 1740. Much of his greatest music was written for performance at the Pietà.

'One would not imagine that life in an orphanage had much to offer, so it might surprise you that, for the young ladies, the status that came with being successful *figlie* was much coveted, and created incentive for excellence. Though most remained at the *ospedale* their entire lives, some were lavished with gifts from admirers, a few were permitted to marry and were even provided dowries, and many were offered vacations in villas on the Italian mainland.'

'I'll take that!' a young lady in the audience called out, much to everyone's delight.

'Yes,' Baker-Hulme continued, 'not bad for an abandoned infant.

'As you can imagine, the *ospedali's* activities provided countless commissions for local violin and other instrument makers, *liuter del loco*, not only for the manufacture of good instruments but also for the constant maintenance and repair of such instruments, to which the good Mr Jacobus has alluded.

'With the wealth of information we have gathered, we can now recreate – in the best sense, Professor Handy – the best performance practices of the best music – thank you, Mr Jacobus – and hopefully, one day Professor Tawroszewicz will take the trouble to avail himself of that end of the musical spectrum.'

She nailed all three of us in one sentence, Jacobus thought. *Not bad.*

'Sorry to have been so longwinded, but it was such a good question, dear!'

There were no questions for Professor Tawroszewicz, which was cause for a bit of embarrassment. But Hedge covered it up with aplomb, telling Tawroszewicz he was lucky to have gotten off so easy. Jacobus silently echoed his relief that the discussion was over. Hedge then thanked everyone for coming and directed everyone to the lobby for refreshments.

After five minutes of schmoozing at the reception, Jacobus was eager to leave. The small talk was as stale as the cheese and crackers. Alicia, the student whose question had been addressed to Jacobus, tried to engage him in conversation, but he was exhausted. His energy level had been on the wane, and he felt a desperate need to sleep. When she brought up the backstage shout during his spiel, he shrugged. Nothing had come of it, and he had no reason to disbelieve Hedge's assessment that it had simply been a prankster. Jacobus excused himself as politely as he could muster and sought out Yumi. She congratulated Jacobus both for the content of his presentation and style points – 'you didn't once call anyone an imbecile or *hysterically misinformed*' – which was as much of that tête-à-tête as he could endure. On their way out, he steered clear of an animated discussion between Sybil Baker-Hulme and Bronislaw Tawroszewicz, but it was impossible for him not to overhear one heated exchange:

'You might have learned something, Bronto, had you been at the Pietà.'

'Maybe. But your husband, he would not have liked being there,' he replied.

'Why on earth not?'

'He would not have liked the grille.'

Three

The situation in Feldstein Auditorium Thursday morning was reversed. Students were on the stage and Jacobus was sitting in the audience. Yumi had dropped him off there, putting him in the hands of Elwood Dunster. She then went off to teach, stranding him without an escape strategy from the two-and-a-half-hour Vivaldi rehearsal. Dunster had been assigned to shepherd Jacobus around the rolling campus located within walking distance of the hamlet of Kinnetonka Crossing. Jacobus would have preferred exploring on his own and expressed that opinion, but the administration had politely insisted that he be given 'the full red-carpet treatment.'

It was unseasonably warm for early spring, and the auditorium's air conditioning had not yet been activated for the semester. The cloying scent of student sweat radiated from the stage. Worse, Jacobus was already getting bored. The Kinderhoek Conservatory Chamber Orchestra was decent enough, Jacobus grudgingly accepted, as far as student orchestras went. But the conductor, Tawroszewicz, bore out what Sybil Baker-Hulme had more than hinted at the night before; he was neither historically informed nor particularly informed in any other way. Energy,

33

whether controlled or not, seemed to be his sole default.

The girl playing the solo in Vivaldi's violin concerto 'Spring' didn't have especially refined technique, nor did she have much sense of what passed for acceptable Baroque style these days, though that was a different discussion altogether. She had arrived late to the rehearsal and was struggling. Her name, Yumi had informed him, was Audrey Something. One of Dunster's students. His best, supposedly. Jacobus tried not to imagine Dunster's worst, but with Dunster sitting next to him, he kept his mouth shut. As Jacobus's own teacher, Dr Krovney, used to say about such students, 'She's played twelve years and is four years behind.' One thing was clear. She seemed to be giving it the old college try, even if the brook in Vivaldi's 'Spring' churned more than it murmured. With two weeks before the performance, at least there was still enough time to dredge the sediment.

Tawroszewicz abruptly interrupted Jacobus's daydreaming about music with a river theme – *The Moldau*, *Siegfried's Rhine Journey*, Beethoven's Sixth Symphony, 'Ol' Man River' – when he stopped the orchestra and reprimanded the students. He coarsely informed them that if he had played that meekly when he was a student they would have made him sew doilies for the rest of his life. 'Do *you* want to sew doilies for the rest of your lives?' There being no response other than a sullen silence, they began once again.

'What do you think, Mr Jacobus?' Dunster whispered into his ear.

'Eh? What do I think?' Jacobus sought quickly for positives. As a guest at the conservatory he didn't want to be critical of the man's best student. An 'esteemed' guest, they kept telling him, though by being esteemed he felt as if someone had fastened a target to the back of his shirt.

'I think Tawroszewicz doesn't want his side of beef served on doilies.'

'Clearly,' Dunster whispered, stifling a chuckle. 'But I meant about Audrey. What do you think of Audrey's playing?'

Bullseye.

'Hard worker. Potential.'

'Yes,' Dunster concurred.

'Sophomore?' Jacobus asked, immediately realizing it was as dangerous a question as asking a woman when her baby was due before finding out whether she was pregnant.

'Senior. She seems distracted. I think you being here made her nervous. More than usual, anyway.'

'Nervous type?'

'Hyper. Too much adrenaline. Competitive, too. Maybe because she's a Plain Jane, you know?'

'No. I don't know.'

'Pasty, acne, socially ill at ease. But she loves the violin.'

'It's a competitive field. Might be to her advantage, the competitive part,' Jacobus said, though he almost choked on his words saying it. For him, competition was the bane of music and the main reason he had distanced himself from the professional world. 'Young people should play *with* each other, not *against* each other,' had long been his mantra.

35

'She's really looking forward to playing at your masterclass,' Dunster said. 'I've tried my best with her, but no doubt your insights can fill in the gaps.'

Jacobus shrugged. Was there a bit of sarcasm there? No matter. He had already compiled a mental list of a dozen basic gaps in the girl's playing that needed addressing. If a six-year-old had that many gaps in her mouth, the tooth fairy would be filing for bankruptcy.

'I'll do what I can,' Jacobus said.

They listened to the little that remained of the rehearsal in silence. It went reasonably well, but Tawroszewicz's style, the way he treated both the music and the students, was outdated by anyone's standards. As Jacobus had made abundantly clear the night before, he was far from being an ardent proponent of historically informed performance. But neither should Vivaldi be played with Brahmsian opacity.

Whatever. He would be charitably evenhanded. *To each his own. That's what makes music great, after all.* But he didn't really believe that, either.

Tawroszewicz wrapped up the rehearsal, chastising the students a final time that if they did not live up to his high standards their lives would be worthless. He then excused them with a warning to practice harder over the spring break if they had any pride. The students disbanded with few words among them.

'I get the sense they don't like him very much,' Jacobus said.

'He's tough on them, but for some reason they seem to respect him for that,' Dunster said. 'He's always bragging about getting great student evaluations.'

'Come again?'

'Student evaluations.'

'That's what I thought you said. Don't you have that backwards? The teachers evaluate the students. Since when do students evaluate teachers?'

'Times have changed, Mr Jacobus,' Dunster said. 'Every semester the entire faculty is evaluated. It's one way the powers that be determine how well we're doing our jobs. We have to do them in order for the school to remain certified. Along with hours taught, numbers of students, of graduating seniors, student concert attendance, faculty performances. It all goes into the mix. If you don't get recertified, you're in deep doo-doo.'

Jacobus pondered the bizarre premise of students evaluating teachers and concluded that had his past students been given that license, he might have been sent to the electric chair. Many times. And those were from the ones he was nice to.

'Every faculty member, every semester, by every student?' he thought out loud. 'That's enough wasted paper to fill the Smithsonian.'

Dunster laughed.

'You certainly are behind the curve, Mr Jacobus. It's all computerized now. No muss, no fuss. Students write their comments and, click, it's stored forever. A little *too* easy, I think.'

'Meaning?'

'When you have to write with paper and pen you have to think beforehand about what you're writing or you're going to have an awfully messy sheet of paper. But on these computers, kids only think *after* they write. And sometimes not even then. Sometimes I wish they'd consider what they're writing for more than thirty seconds before they commit their opinions to eternity.'

It sounded like Dunster had been on the short end of the stick. Jacobus was sympathetic, regardless of how good or bad a teacher Dunster was. How could someone teach, constantly looking over his shoulder, constantly worried about displeasing a student for fear of losing his job?

He and Dunster left Feldstein Auditorium and walked along the winding, cobblestone path that led to the Campus Inn. He probed the path with his cane, tapping it to the left and to the right with the deftness of an insect's antenna.

'Do you worry about those evaluations, Dunster?' Jacobus asked.

'Me? No. Not at this point in my career. I give all my students an A, anyway. I figure if they're good they'll make it and if they're not, the A is something that'll make them happy. So the students don't give me a hard time.'

'You think that's what's most important? To keep students happy?'

'Why not? Don't you?'

'I figured, at a conservatory, the most important thing would be to make sure the next generation plays Bach as well as the last. Because if *they* don't, who will?'

'I suppose that's one way of looking at it.'

Though the scent of newly sprouted grass and the gossip of robins and chickadees were welcome changes from Nathaniel's Manhattan apartment, they reminded Jacobus of his demolished home in the woods. A distant Mozart C Major piano concerto floated toward him from a student's practice room somewhere, intermingled with the sweetness of freshly blooming peonies. Jacobus forced himself from his sudden nostalgia.

'You said, "at this point in my career." How long have you been on the faculty?' Jacobus asked Dunster, trying to think of something apropos to say.

'Would you believe forty-nine years?'

'Jesus Christ! You must be as old as I am.'

'I do think we're about the same age. I was studying with Galamian the same time you were with Krovney.'

'Really?' Jacobus was puzzled. Ivan Galamian had been the foremost violin pedagogue of his time, the teacher of many of the major artists on the concert circuit. Though Jacobus had never studied with him, he had read Galamian's books. Krovney's approach differed from Galamian in key fundamental ways, but Jacobus respected Galamian's ability to turn out generations of well-prepared, solid fiddle players. What Jacobus had heard in Audrey Something's playing was hardly representative of the Galamian school, but after forty-nine years and averaging – let's say – ten students a year . . . Well, how could one's teaching *not* get a little lax? He chose to refrain from commenting and changed the trajectory of the subject of Dunster's longevity.

'I was under the impression this school was started by a bunch of European Jewish lefties,' Jacobus said, 'and Elwood Dunster isn't exactly a Jewish name, unless it's Sephardic or something. No offense intended.'

Dunster's fabricated laugh made it evident he'd been quizzed on the issue more than once and that his mouth no longer needed the brain to spout out the words.

'That's what a lot of people think about the school,' Dunster said. 'But that's not exactly right. The Kinderhoek Conservatory was founded by Theodesia Lievenstock in 1935. Spinster. Last of the Lievenstock line. All the way back to the early Dutch colonists of the Hudson Valley in the 1600s. Spectacularly wealthy family. Vast landholdings. She had a heart of gold, but no heirs apparent, and more money than she knew what to do with. So she became a major philanthropist of the arts.

'In '31 Theodesia heard about the persecution of Jewish musicians – Dutch, Polish, and German – from one of her Amsterdam cousins. Decided to rescue enough of them to found a music colony. Called it the Kinderhoek Settlement. Means "children's corner" in Dutch.'

'Quaint.'

'Well, yes. But she meant well. The colony's original mission was to provide a safe haven. Just for the musicians and their families. Solace from all their tribulations. Theodesia paid for everything. She built cottages and cabins for them – nothing fancy – and provided them stipends to get by on. And you're right, it mostly comprised Jewish socialists.

'Word got around about the high quality of the music-making. Attracted other musicians from the region. Then the whole country. Like a magnet. It was so unpretentious. Music for music's sake. Unique. That added to its allure.

'Theodesia was a visionary as well as a philan-thropist. She saw the potential. She formed a board of trustees, which incorporated. What had been an unstructured music program became the Kinderhoek Conservatory of Music. As the years passed, many of the original Jewish families left. American apple pie WASPs like me started showing up. I grew up in the city, and this was much more pleasant. Gradually the community evolved ethnically—'

'Meaning, more Christians?'

'Yes, I suppose that's what it means. There are still some pockets of the original Jewish socialist personality, but the area's become pretty well gentrified.'

'Is this the original campus?'

'By no means,' Dunster replied. 'Those first settlement buildings were never intended to be permanent. They were scattered all over. They've all been torn down or were overgrown by the woods, as far as I know. Much of the current campus was built anywhere from ten to twenty years ago. That was when things started to get unhinged.'

'Unhinged?' Jacobus asked.

'As the conservatory grew in stature and scope, costs of running it – including the infrastructure – grew concomitantly. Lievenstock and her small group of trustee friends couldn't continue to foot the tab out of their pockets. After she passed, the financial situation became critical, even with

41

the money she had left in her estate. Tuition, which had always been free, became affordable only to a privileged few. It came to a point that budgetary concerns threatened the institution with extinction. The program shriveled. The only students were hippie children of well-to-do parents who preferred the conservatory's laissez-faire attitude to having to study for a serious degree at a real school.'

'And that's changed?'

'You bet. In 1983. Hiram Feldstein – a former violist – who was among the first Polish émigrés to the Kinderhoek Settlement, gave ten million dollars to the conservatory and promised ninety more.'

'Not bad for a commie musician. Sloughed off his socialist roots, did he?'

'He wasn't a particularly talented violist, but he had a genius for buying and selling parking lots in New York City. The only strings he attached to his gift were that the school had to be tuition-free and that the only consideration for acceptance into the program be merit.'

'A man after my own heart.'

'Overnight, the conservatory went from being on life support to being one of the most sought-after programs in the country. And that applied to faculty as well as to the students. Much to everyone's dismay, Hiram went and dropped dead of a heart attack on us a few years back and now our good dean, Charles Hedge, has been lobbying Hiram's two children for the ninety million.'

'I thought you said he promised.'

'All word of mouth and a handshake. I was a

friend of Hiram's and helped bring the parties together. It was a done deal.'

'But the *kinder* aren't so convinced?'

'No, and I might not be, either, if someone told me I had to cough up that amount of change.'

'Wasn't it in his will?'

'That's the problem. There was no bequest because he thought it wasn't necessary, having already promised it. So that's why Charles has been courting the Feldstein offspring. By the way, I invited them to your masterclass and they're coming to hear Audrey play "Spring."'

'I never knew my masterclasses were so valuable. How badly does the school need the dough?' Jacobus asked.

'With all the students on free tuition and free room and board, we have to have an alternative revenue stream. Right now our faculty is chock-full of renowned composers, theorists, musicologists, and elite performers. They get paid premium rates. If we can't pay them and have to lay them off, we'll soon be somewhere between back on life support and dying of a heart attack.'

Jacobus thought of Yumi, his former student, and her weekly treks from the city. But not all performers lived in New York.

'How do you keep great performers on the faculty when they're out performing?'

'That's been the hardest part. You can imagine their concert schedules. A hundred, hundred and fifty concerts a year. You can't expect them to maintain a regular campus presence.'

'"Maintain a regular campus presence." Translated into English, you mean they make for great PR on the brochure, but they're sighted as often as a California condor?'

'Maybe, but I have to admit, we've got a top faculty who've attracted some pretty talented kids.'

'Sounds idyllic,' Jacobus said. 'Must be totally unlike other music schools dedicated to professional training that I'm familiar with.'

'In what sense?'

'People getting along with each other.'

'Now you're putting words in my mouth.'

They arrived at the inn.

'Need help getting to your room?' Dunster asked.

'I think I can make it on my own. Thanks.'

'By the way, are you going to Aaron Schlossberg's spring equinox party tonight?'

'Party? No. Not if I can avoid it.'

'You should go,' Dunster said. 'He's had a soiree every equinox since he joined the faculty. And with tomorrow being the last day before spring break, everyone gets to gorge and work it off over the vacation. I'll be there, holding hands with Eve and Eli Feldstein. The food at the spring ones is especially good.'

'Better than his music, I hope.'

'There, there, Mr Jacobus! Aaron Schlossberg is considered one of the great composers of our time.'

'Which puts him on the rung just below Dittersdorf for *all* time.'

'You're not a fan of contemporary music?'

'I'm not a fan of bad music, old or new. I have very eclectic tastes in the music I dislike.

Random squeaks and squawks somehow don't do it for me.'

'My student you heard playing "Spring" earlier? Audrey Rollins? She's big into new music and is playing in the premiere of one of Aaron's new chamber pieces. *Synthesis III*.'

The title alone made Jacobus cringe. *What ever happened to 'Symphony,' 'Sonata,' and 'Concerto'?* It was as if the composer felt a need to convince the listener that the piece was something special and couldn't count on the music alone to do it. Presumably there had been a *Synthesis I* and a *Synthesis II*, though that was by no means a given. In any event, Jacobus was not discomfited at not having heard any of the series.

'When's she playing it?' he asked.

'May fifth. It's on her graduation recital. Would you be free?'

'May fifth? Nah. I think I'll need a colonoscopy that day.'

'I take your point, Mr Jacobus, and don't necessarily disagree with you. It's just that when you're on the faculty of a music school, some things are best left unsaid. See you tonight?'

'Well, maybe.'

'Everyone will be there. They're dying to meet you up close and personal.'

'Well, then maybe not.'

Four

'Jake, we're going to be late,' Yumi called from outside the bathroom door.

'I'm still on the can!' Jacobus shouted back. The very notion of being confined among an assemblage of self-absorbed academic musicians and being expected to engage in hoity-toity conversation of little to no consequence had thrown Jacobus's bowels into open rebellion.

'How much longer?' she asked.

'Who the hell knows? What do you expect me to do when nature calls?'

'Tell her this is not a convenient time and you'll call back. We have to go.'

'OK, but it's your car.'

It did Jacobus's stomach no favors when Yumi veered off the paved road onto Sylvan Hollow Road, the pocked dirt lane that led to the modernistic manse of Aaron Schlossberg and Sybil Baker-Hulme, nestled in the woods five miles from campus. As the car jolted along the corduroy road, he closed his window to barricade himself from the noise.

'Do me a favor and try not to hit a tree,' Jacobus groused as the car went over another pothole.

'I'm doing my best. Camaros aren't built for off-roading. What's with your stomach, anyway?' Yumi asked.

'Must've been the mystery meat they served me in the cafeteria before the rehearsal.'

'Well, you'll enjoy Aaron's food.'

'So I'm told. What's it all about?'

'You've heard of farm to table?'

'Is that like hoof to mouth?'

'Never mind. Aaron does *forest* to table. He's a renowned forager and hunter – written books about it – and a gourmet cook. Maybe you've heard of his book, *Wild Living*?'

'Hot dogs with mayo?'

'Don't be silly. You can't imagine the kinds of things he comes up with.'

'Yes, I can. That's what worries me. How much farther?'

'We're almost there. Thanks to your uncooperative digestive tract holding us up, a lot of people will already be there. We'll have to park a little farther away and walk. Is that OK with you?'

'Whatever. Tell me about this shindig. Is this par for the course?'

'Why do you ask?'

'The impression I got from Dunster is that this school is something special.'

Yumi pulled the car onto the left shoulder as far as she safely could next to the trees, and judged she had left enough room on the road for another car to squeeze through. She was able to squirm out her door and went around and helped Jacobus out of his side.

'I haven't been teaching here very long, but it does seem different from your typical music school.'

'So it doesn't have your typical rivalry between academic and performance divisions of the faculty? Or cutthroat competition for talented students among performance teachers? Or conflicts over budget and curriculum between administrators and faculty?' The tightening in Jacobus's stomach returned, if it had ever left. 'Or festering jealousy between faculty who are full-time, "dedicated" teachers versus those more illustrious teachers – like yourself – who are primarily performers? Or—'

'Jake, you are so cynical!'

'What makes you say that?'

Jacobus felt his ribs elbowed but not hard enough to hurt.

'These are nice people,' Yumi said. 'And I've told them such good things about you.'

'You've just shot your credibility to hell.'

He felt another jolt.

'Just behave yourself,' she said.

As they approached the house, the raspy chatter of blue jays darting through the woods and more distant caws of crows soaring above it gradually merged with and were overtaken by a low hum of human conversation, the clinking of china, and the occasional shout of orders to hired wait staff. A virtuoso catbird on a branch caustically impersonated the sound of them all.

Jacobus, with Yumi on his arm – or rather, he on Yumi's – poked his way forward with his cane, stumbling from time to time, Yumi catching him, as the dirt path changed to crushed stone, then to flagstone, then to polished concrete. It was something a person with sight would have had no difficulty traversing, but to Jacobus it was yet one more adventure into the unknown.

It had been the opposite in his old house. In his yard he had known where every root and stone laid in wait to trip the infrequent visitor to his ill-maintained homestead. Inside, he could adroitly navigate the clutter of his living room, strewn with dust-covered music, records, and a maze of music stands, chairs, and paraphernalia of indecipherable origin, while his friends stumbled about, even with the lights on. Though the memory of those patterns would be with him forever, all that was now gone.

'Almost there,' Yumi whispered encouragingly into Jacobus's ear. 'Sybil's at the door, welcoming visitors.'

The reception line crawled along, giving Jacobus ample time to second-guess his decision to come.

'Dearest Yumi!' The unmistakable voice from the symposium. Imperious yet charming. 'So wonderful to see you here,' Sybil Baker-Hulme said, perhaps even meaning it. 'And the extraordinary Daniel Jacobus!'

'Must be a different Daniel Jacobus,' he said. He extended his hand, which was received firmly.

'You're far too modest,' she rebuked him, graciously. 'I'm so looking forward to picking your brain later on, but as I must man the battle stations and welcome guests at the moment, I will ask the lovely Yumi to accompany her handsome escort through the house to the veranda where Aaron awaits to pour him a glass of excellent Chardonnay.'

Jacobus nodded and went to move on, but Baker-Hulme didn't relinquish her grip on his hand.

'I really mean that,' she whispered. 'I have something to talk to you about that I think you'll find interesting.'

'I can't wait,' Jacobus said, extricating his hand from Sybil's clutch. She seemed to be trying too hard.

Yumi ushered him into the house.

'Harold!' Jacobus heard Sybil say from over his shoulder, the surprise in her voice thinly veiled. 'You've actually come! Your appetite got the better of your convictions?'

With all the other conversation going on, Jacobus couldn't make out Harold Handy's response, but supposed it would be his typical monotone.

The interior was spacious, constructed of reverberant materials. It might have been well-designed for chamber music, but for conversation the acoustics were impossible for even the keen-eared Jacobus to decipher all but snippets of competing small talk. He did hear his name bandied about as Yumi escorted him through the room. And did he detect the occasional upward inflection, as in, 'so *that's* Daniel Jacobus?' Apparently not everyone had gone to the symposium. He also took note of an emphasized word or phrase here and there, out of context but appropriate for the event and the demographics: 'delicious as always,' 'commencement,' 'tenure track,' 'exceptional,' 'musical,' 'GPA,' 'scholarship,' 'sabbatical.' And others less so: 'outrageous,' 'fired,' 'mockery.'

Smells were equally intriguing. Of course there were the usual ones – perfume, body odor, dry cleaning, tobacco – which Jacobus shelved off into one part of his brain. He concentrated more on the abundance of savory and pungent aromas. Grilled meats, exotic marinades, fresh herbs and spices. Normally he would have started drooling, but his appetite was mysteriously in abeyance.

They crossed into another room. Quieter. Smells no longer of food but of leather, old paper, cigars. A library.

'Here comes Charlie,' Yumi said.

'Charlie?'

'Charles Hedge, the dean. Last night's moderator. The faculty calls him Dean the Bean, as in bean counter. He's always smiling. Just smile back.'

'I'm getting tired being nice.'

'Yes, I can tell.'

'Mr Jacobus! You made it!' Hedge said with guileless Midwestern sincerity.

'I suppose.'

A brotherly pat on the back.

'Great job last night. Injected a little spice! Livened things up! Kinderhoek is all about diversity of views.'

'So I'm—'

'We are so looking forward to your masterclass tomorrow. What a way to finish before spring break!'

'Well—'

'How did you like Feldstein Hall?'

'Not—'

'We just had it totally retrofitted. A million

dollars. And a new Steinway. Aren't the acoustics great?'

'Yes, great. Great! Best I've ever heard.'

'We got the money from our Feldstein endowment. The building itself was endowed by Dolly Cooney.'

Hedge enunciated Dolly and Cooney with special care.

'Am I supposed to be impressed by that name?'

'You don't know Dolly? The founder of the Venerable Bead chain? She's a Kinderhoek alum. When she was a clarinet student she started making handmade beads to help pay her tuition. That was back in the day when they still had to pay tuition. Who'd guess she'd be a genius at marketing beads? Who'd guess *anyone* would be? Lucky for her because, between you and me, she would never've made it as a clarinetist. Lucky for us, too. Dolly still lives here and is on our board. She comes to all our concerts. She's a real kick in the pants. You'll love her.'

'I'm sure I will.'

'Well, I'm talking your ear off. You go have a great time. I've got to go spread the cheer. See you tomorrow at the masterclass. I'm hoping we might establish a precedent with this, maybe call it our Distinguished Artist Master Class Series.'

'Whatever you say.'

'We'd attach a donor's name to it, of course.'

'Of course.'

'But I feel our chances are pretty darn good of getting a six-figure gift for it. It's doable. What do you think?'

'Yes. Doable.'

'And if things go well, you can count on coming back, maybe coach quartets? Hey, let's talk.'

'Sure. Just one question, Hedge.'

'Yes?'

'That cry at the symposium? I say something that hurt someone's feelings?'

Hedge paused.

'Nothing to worry about, Mr Jacobus. Total false alarm. Just the usual student hijinks.'

Hedge patted Jacobus on the back and was gone. Back into the fray in the living room.

'Looks like you're a big hit,' Yumi said.

Jacobus shrugged. The tip of his cane clicked against an impediment on the floor. He slid his cane along it. The floor track for the sliding door to the veranda. He stepped over it and was outside again. The change to the fresh evening air, warm and moist, was a welcome relief from the cramped herd inside. Only a few people mingled in the tranquil dusk. The chirp of crickets and warble of wood thrushes painfully reminded him of the home he no longer had, but at least it was quieter out here.

'Ah, Mr Jacobus!'

Cancel that. Jacobus recognized the voice of the audience questioner.

'Schlossberg.'

'Yes, it is I. Lord of this manor. We didn't have a chance to meet at the symposium. Wonderful, wonderful talk. Wonderful for the kids.'

Schlossberg's voice, deep and authoritative, was at the same time mellifluous and disarming. A combination of Leonard Bernstein and Barry

White, whose recordings Nathaniel forced him to listen to.

'The Lady Sybil has instructed me to ply you with our finest vintage.'

The alcohol that Jacobus detected on Schlossberg's breath explained the slight slurring he almost convincingly concealed.

'And how about a glass for my ward, the fair Yumi?' Jacobus asked.

'I'll pass, Jake,' Yumi said. 'I just saw Tallulah inside.'

Jacobus understood the nuance of Yumi's speech patterns as intimately as a Bach sonata. She was more intent on leaving than on actually going somewhere specific.

'Who's Tallulah?' he asked anyway.

'Tallulah Dominguez. She's chair of the piano division. We're playing a recital together at the end of the semester and we have to figure out when we're going to rehearse. I want to catch her while I've got the chance. Back in a while.'

'Women,' Schlossberg said when Yumi was out of earshot. 'Can't live with 'em. Can't live without 'em. But mainly, can't live with 'em. Here, have a glass.'

Jacobus could think of no appropriate response, so he muttered a few random syllables. Schlossberg poured wine into Jacobus's glass, spilling some onto his hand. Jacobus heard him pour more into his own glass, then put the bottle down with a thud.

'A toast!' Schlossberg exclaimed. 'To spring!'

'Mud in your eye,' Jacobus said, and took a

sip. It was nicely chilled. Slightly fruity but dry. Perfect for the season.

'Did you know, my dear friend, that the goddess Cybele was the mother of all mother goddesses?'

'Now I do.'

'Well, believe it! In ancient Rome, the followers of Cybele believed she had a consort named Attis who was born via a virgin birth.'

'Go figure.'

'He died.'

'Poor guy.'

'So you say. So you say. But what you don't know is that poor old Attis was resurrected each year during the vernal equinox. So I say, here's to dear Sybil. Here's to spring. Here's to the vernal equinox, which bestows life and fertility to the land. At least for the immediate future.'

'Well said,' said Jacobus, wishing he were playing checkers with Nathaniel.

'I'd show you around the hallowed premises,' Schlossberg said, unselfconsciously emitting a low, rumbling belch, 'but that wouldn't really float your boat, would it? So how about I give you a seat here and bring you a plate of goodies? We can chat when I get back.'

'Fine.'

From his deck chair, a comfortable folding wooden one with a cushion, Jacobus had his back to the woods. The conversation inside the house was directly in front of him and the sounds of the forest behind him. He stood up, turned around, and felt for the veranda's railing. He rotated the chair one-hundred-eighty degrees and pulled it close to the railing. He sat back down, confident he had minimized the chances anyone would bother him.

'Hey!'

That was clearly meant for someone else.

'Hey there!'

'Are you talking to me?' Jacobus asked.

'Mr Jacobus?'

'You Tallulah?'

'No!' Nervous laughter. 'I'm Audrey.'

'Audrey?'

'Audrey Rollins. At the rehearsal today. I played the Vivaldi solo.'

She spoke in explosive clusters of syllables.

'Ah, yes. Dunster's student.'

Her voice was too filled with pent-up energy for him to endure for any length of time. Jacobus sipped his wine and turned away, but sensing the girl hovering in place, concluded his tactic wasn't about to succeed.

'Didn't know students were invited to this shindig,' he said, conceding defeat.

More laughter. Nervous laughter. He always wondered what was behind laughter in response to nothing that was funny. It generally hid something.

'I'm not a guest. Some students were hired to wait tables and clean shit up.'

'Shit?'

'Plates and glasses and stuff.'

'Oh, that kind of shit. How'd you get hired? You take classes from Baker-Hulme?'

'No! I mean, Aaron's my chamber music coach . . . So what did you think?'

'About what?'

'About how I played the Vivaldi.'

Jacobus was disinclined to give a lesson, especially one that was so seriously needed.

'I understand you're playing in the masterclass tomorrow.'

'Yeah! I'm really nervous.' Apparently believing that was the wrong thing to say, she quickly corrected herself. 'But I'm really excited!'

'Let's talk about it tomorrow.'

'OK.' Slightly deflated. 'But I want to practice before the class so if you could tell me . . .'

This girl was not to be denied. Better to get her off his back sooner than later if he was going to enjoy some peace and quiet.

'All right. First off, you play with a lot of energy. That's good. But, number one, you're not controlling it, so your tone is raw, and it's throwing off your intonation. So just calm yourself down a bit. Don't overplay.'

'Cool!'

'Whatever. Number two, for Baroque music your energy needs to be more horizontal and less vertical. You're pressing too hard with the bow, so you're not getting the clarity and transparency you need for the music to come alive. Too opaque.

'Third, way too many accents. You accented virtually every beat in the melody in the first movement. Whack whack whack whack whack. That's not a melody. It's an assault. Bad enough if you only accented the first and third beats. Better yet if you just put some emphasis only on occasional downbeats.'

57

'Wow. That's great! I can't wait to tell Professor Dunster.'

'Actually, better if you didn't, honey.'

'I suppose. Anything else?'

'You're a glutton for punishment, aren't you?' he said.

Again the nervous laugh. 'What do you mean?' she asked.

Jacobus had just given her some general technical advice. Maybe something more poetic would be enough for her to leave him alone.

'Nothing. All right. One more thing. What's the name of this concerto?'

'"Spring." I think.'

'You *think*?'

'Yeah. "Spring." I'm sure. Definitely.'

'So it has to be light. Right? And joyful. Springtime! Just imagine. Winter was long and cold and dreary. In your parlance, it sucked. Now you get to go outside in the sun and play again. You have to make it sound like that.'

'Cool!'

'You know the sonnet Vivaldi wrote?'

'Yeah!' Pride was swelling. '"Springtime is upon us—"'

'No, no, no!' Jacobus barked. 'He wrote no such thing. Vivaldi was Italian. He no *speaka da English*. What he wrote was, *"Giunt' è la Primavera e festosetti la Salutan gl' Augei con lieto canto, e i fonti allo Spirar de' Zeffiretti con dolce mormorio Scorrono intanto."* Etcetera. There's music in them words. "Springtime is upon us" sounds like a post-apocalyptic novel for fourth-graders.'

58

'Boss!' Audrey said. 'I'll memorize the whole—'

'Audrey!' It was the voice of Aaron Schlossberg. 'Entrapped yet another victim with your dogged curiosity?'

'Sorry.' The energy in her voice dissipated like morning fog.

'Why don't you and Lucien go clean up poor Elwood's mess? The dear professor seems no longer capable of carrying on a conversation and holding a plate of food simultaneously. Time for you and that boyfriend of yours' – heavy emphasis on 'boy,' Jacobus noted – 'to earn your keep.'

She went off without a further word.

'Don't mind her,' Schlossberg continued.

'She called you Aaron.'

'That is my name, I believe.'

'But she called Dunster, her violin teacher, Professor Dunster.'

'Times are changing. Elwood is definitely old school.'

Jacobus didn't care what students called him as long as they played their scales in tune.

'I brought you some tasty morsels,' Schlossberg said. 'Tell me what you think.'

As Jacobus received the plate from Schlossberg, their hands touched. Jacobus, who had imagined Schlossberg as being tall and slender by the quality of his voice, was surprised at how thick, almost swollen, his fingers were.

'Got a fork?' Jacobus asked.

'Unnecessary. It's on a skewer.'

Jacobus found one end of a short wooden skewer and, after first poking himself in the cheek with the pointed end, put it in his mouth. In a temporary state of denial about his unsettled stomach, he pulled off a small chunk of meat with his teeth. Different, tender. Unusual sauce – sweet and savory at the same time. Delicious.

'Rabbit?' he guessed.

'Close! You've got a better sense of taste than most. Squirrel. Marinated with Eastern Red Cedar berries. Not really a cedar. It's a juniper. *Juniperus virginiana.*'

'You hunt squirrels?'

'Vice versa. They hunt me. They get in the attic, so I trap them. But, hey, why waste good squirrel? Right?'

'They told me you're an expert forager. But they forgot to mention you're also a born exterminator.'

'Who knew? Right? But I must concede that wandering through the woods does beat banging one's head on the attic rafters. Being in the woods gives me inspiration. You hear that murmuring brook back there? That not only provides me with a year-round watercress supply, it was my stimulus for my *Landscapes IV*. Love of nature. Like Beethoven.'

'You've got chutzpah,' Jacobus said. 'Even Brahms knew he was no Beethoven.'

'Hey, growing up as a little runt in Brooklyn you need a little chutzpah to get where I am now.'

'And exactly where is that? To paraphrase our recent vice-presidential candidate, "I served with Beethoven. I knew Beethoven. Beethoven was a friend of mine. Schlossberg, you're no Ludwig Beethoven."'

Applause.

'Well said, Jacobus,' Schlossberg said, laughing. 'You should've run for VP. You probably would've done better. But you must admit, they lambasted Beethoven's music in his day no less than mine is now. Even more in some critical circles.'

'On the other hand, Beethoven was also the most renowned composer of his day.'

'Ditto here, if I may say so without incriminating myself. Now try this.'

Jacobus felt another plate pressed into his hand. He was having a hard time disliking Schlossberg regardless of what he felt about the man's music and his ego.

'You'll need a fork for this one,' Schlossberg said. 'I'll give you a hint. It ain't spinach.'

Steamed greens of some sort.

'Garlic in it.'

'Good start. Wild garlic scapes,' said Schlossberg.

'You did all the cooking?'

'Yes, sir! Dame Sybil took care of all the rest. She's such a detail person. Allows me to devote my full attentions to the kitchen.'

Jacobus let the flavors linger in his mouth.

'Chicory!'

'Very good, Jacobus! *Cichorium intybus*. You're the only one to get it right. How do you know chicory?'

'A friend of mine, Nathaniel Williams, he's from the South. Cooks with it. But there's something else too, right?'

'Yes.'

'You've got my goat.'

'Well, you'll be pleased to know that goats

love it, too. Stinging nettle. *Urtica dioica.* Of course, when you cook it, it takes the sting out. It was traditionally eaten to treat all kinds of disorders – kidneys, urinary tract and gastrointestinal tract, skin, cardiovascular system, flu, rheumatism, gout. You name it. Ready for one more?'

Jacobus's stomach had been threatening to rebel after the first bite of skewered squirrel. Now the mutiny was close at hand.

'I better not,' he said.

'But I insist!' Schlossberg insisted. 'You'll love it. I won't even make you guess. Chanterelle mushrooms, *Cantharellus cibarius*, picked fresh this afternoon, sautéed in butter and wild sage.'

'You eat like this all the time?'

'My doc tells me I'm not supposed to. Diabetes. But since I don't tell him, I'll live forever. Like Attis. With the wonder of modern medicine, all I have to do is poke myself in the thigh with a needle from time to time and I eat and drink what I want. And most of what I want is in my own backyard. Other than paying a regular visit to the wine store, you can survive quite happily without ever having to set foot in Price Saver. Better, in fact.'

'Only if you can pick me some Folgers out in your woods here.'

'Here, take this plate,' Schlossberg said. 'There's someone over there I want to introduce you to. Back in a sec.'

Jacobus, his stomach in turmoil, counted to ten before extending the plate over the side of the veranda and, as inconspicuously as possible,

62

committed the *Cantharellus cibarius* to the shrubbery below. Schlossberg returned shortly thereafter, accompanied by someone emitting an overpowering dosage of English Leather cologne, which did nothing for Jacobus's digestion.

'Finished already?' Schlossberg asked.

'Love that wild sage,' Jacobus said.

'Me, too. Well, let me formally introduce you to another sage, my young colleague, Bronislaw Tawroszewicz. You ducked out of the reception so fast last night you didn't have a chance to chat. Call him Mr T. Everyone does. This is his fourth year at Kinderhoek and he's up for tenure at the end of the semester.'

'How do you do, Mr Jacobus?' said Tawroszewicz. 'I saw you again at the rehearsal this afternoon. What did you think?'

Why was everyone always asking for an opinion he didn't want to give?

'Great music.'

'Yes, I agree. And orchestra?'

'Coming along.'

'Yes. I know how you mean. You try different things. But sometimes intimidation is the only way to get it out of those kids. I'm young, but I'm old school, like you. That's how I learned. European style.'

'Well, Mr T,' Jacobus said. 'Being tough is only half the story.'

'And what is the other half?'

'Having something intelligent to say.'

A pause, seemingly uncomfortable for Tawroszewicz, perfectly fine for Jacobus for whom sound was an uninvited interruption between silences.

'Well, Bronislaw must be saying a lot of intelligent things,' Schlossberg broke in, 'because he's doing wonders with the group, and the kids love him. He's just a big teddy bear.'

Teddy bear? What did that mean? Stocky? Hairy? In need of a shave? Jacobus sometimes gained insight into appearances even when he would rather not.

'They give me the highest evaluations,' Tawroszewicz added, as if students' opinions provided irrefutable empirical evidence.

'So your tenure's in the bag,' Jacobus said, disinclined to argue whether Tawroszewicz was qualified or not.

'There're always some naysayers,' Schlossberg said. 'As you well know. You've been around academia. I'd bet there were even some who would second-guess *your* qualifications.'

'Don't be ridiculous, Aaron.' It was the unmistakable voice of Aaron's better half, Sybil Baker-Hulme, with paint-peeling disdain. 'To put Bronislaw's name in the same sentence as Mr Jacobus's is akin to your curious tendency to insert yours in the same sentence as Beethoven. Why don't you partners-in-crime go off on an opossum hunt while Mr Jacobus and I have a scholarly chat?'

'I couldn't think of a better idea myself, dear,' Schlossberg said. 'In fact, dear, there's deer in the dining room. While we feast on venison, I'm sure Jacobus would like nothing better than to hear your opinions on whether Rameau began his trills on the top note upon attaining puberty.'

Sybil Baker-Hulme placed a cautionary hand on Jacobus's thigh as if to prevent him from saying something untoward. Since he had nothing to say, untoward or otherwise, the gesture was superfluous. Maybe, on the other hand, she was indicating to him, 'I told you so.'

As soon as the two men disappeared into the dining room, Sybil piped up.

'I'll never understand what Aaron sees in that cretin,' she said. 'Aaron has more than his share of faults, but complete absence of musical intelligence isn't one of them.'

'The kids love Mr T. He told me so himself.'

'You wouldn't know that from the scowls on their faces.'

'Professionals-in-training?'

'Perhaps so,' Sybil laughed. 'But his music-making, especially the Baroque, is so, so . . .'

'Crude?'

'Precisely.'

'There's more than one way to play Baroque music.'

'No doubt, Mr Jacobus. There are in fact several historically appropriate ways. But there are an infinite number of ways to play it wrong, and Mr T has a patent on all of them.'

It was Jacobus's turn to laugh.

'By any chance,' she continued, 'did he tell you the two of us will be collaborating – and I use that word in the broadest sense – on the performance of "Spring" on the Vivaldi by Twilight concert?' Sybil Baker-Hulme obviously assumed Jacobus's answer was 'no' since she didn't bother to wait for his response.

'Yes,' she said. 'I am going to narrate Vivaldi's sonnet as a prelude to each movement and then will hold my nose while they play. But here's my surprise: One would guess that I would recite in the Italian—'

'But you're doing it in English?' Jacobus asked. He was indeed surprised. English would be the sensible thing to do. He had told Audrey Rollins that the sonnet was in Italian, but Audrey was the performer, not the audience. The audience would benefit from understanding the text and how it related to the music. Having heard Baker-Hulme at the symposium, however, he had gathered audience comprehension would take a back seat to authenticity.

'Heavens, no, Mr Jacobus!' she replied. 'English! How proletarian. I shall narrate in eighteenth-century Venetian dialect, the language of the great playwrights Carlo Gozzi and Carlo Goldoni; the language in which it would have been spoken in Vivaldi's day and place.'

So not even modern day Italians would understand it, Jacobus thought.

'You said you had something interesting you wanted to talk to me about?' he asked.

'This is presumptuous of me, I know,' Sybil said. 'But have you read my new book by any chance?'

'Which book is that?'

'*The Emergence of Mezzo Piano in the Late Baroque and Its Implications for European Society*. It received a glowing review in *Early*

Music Journal: "Dr Baker-Hulme's voluminous tome offers heretofore unknown insights into how growing artistic freedom" – the first inclusion of mezzo piano in mid-eighteenth-century scores – "rocked the very foundations of the aristocratic power structure of central France and Germany.'"

Jacobus, desperately not wanting to betray his promise to Yumi to behave himself, grasped hastily for a polite reply.

'I couldn't find the Braille edition,' he replied. That should put him on safe ground. 'Might it be coming out in Braille by any chance?' he asked.

'Sadly not.'

'Damn!'

'But I would be happy to read to you some of its more salient points.' Maybe he had been too convincing. 'Sometime soon, perhaps?'

'Let us say sometime,' Jacobus replied.

'How long will you be with us? Will you be staying over spring break?'

'Just until after the masterclass tomorrow.'

'Well, bugger that!' Sybil said, to Jacobus's surprise.

'But Hedge said they might want me back sometime in the future,' he said. 'We'll see.'

'I would also love to show you an original manuscript I have by Domenico Scarlatti of a harpsichord sonata in F major. It might quite possibly be the first written mezzo piano in all of music history! But of course you wouldn't be able to see it, would you? I would be happy to let you touch it, however. You can literally feel the history! It's in the library.'

Jacobus gulped the remainder of the wine in his glass.

'I would love that,' he said. 'Could you please get me some more wine?'

He extended the empty glass.

'Delighted.'

As soon as she was gone, Jacobus grabbed his cane. With his hand on the railing, he shuffled his way to the steps that descended into the woods with the alacrity of a sighted man half his age.

The air had cooled considerably, indicating to him that the sun had set, so he hoped that with only a few steps he would be hidden from Sybil's view. Jacobus tapped his cane both forward and sideways. The forward taps enabled him to determine safe passage along the spongy forest floor – first grassy and then leaf- and moss-covered – without walking into a tree or boulder, or tripping on a root, or falling into a furrow. The sideways taps first made contact with annoying, thorny brambles that grabbed at his cane. Then came a grove of birches, but their trunks were of insufficient width to provide protection from another stifling lecture on eighteenth-century performance practice. Jacobus probed deeper into the woods, tapping trees with the virtuosity of a jazz drummer. He finally encountered several potential candidates, ringing his cane around their trunks to determine their circumference. From the bark's rough texture, he guessed they were maples and hid behind the broadest of them. The sudden exertion, combined with the wine and rich food, had winded him, but gradually his breathing slowed and he found himself relishing the respite from humanity and his anonymity in the forest.

Above the muffled conversation emanating from Schlossberg's house, a single thrush called. Though he could not see it, Jacobus knew it as a harbinger of the descending darkness of night. Yes, he would be well hidden. A bee buzzed by, behind schedule as it looped its way back to its hive. Then it was gone and the thrush, too, after a time, fell silent. Jacobus inhaled the moist evening air, redolent of pine and humus. He waited, hoping Sybil had given up on him and had corralled another victim. The longer he waited, the more he would like to have remained in that spot, lulled by its tranquility. He dozed for a time, he didn't know for how long – it could have been a half hour or more, as it was getting chilly – suddenly realizing Yumi might be trying to find him. He was about to hurry back to the veranda when he heard a new sound. Off in the woods, leaves were slowly, quietly being tramped upon. A squirrel? Too big. Four legs? A deer, perhaps, returning to its shelter before nocturnal predators commenced their night job. Jacobus listened with growing interest. No, it wasn't a deer. That was for sure. Deer can't talk.

Five

The phone rang and rang, waking Jacobus. *Where am I?* Jacobus asked himself. *Not Nathaniel's. Ah, yes. Motel room. Campus Inn.* He had drunk too much at the party. He had wandered back from the woods. Yumi had driven him back to the inn and tucked him into bed. That much he could recall. He felt for the phone on the bedside table.

'Yeah?'

'Hello, Mr Jacobus?'

'Speaking.'

'This is Sybil. Sybil Baker-Hulme?'

Jacobus didn't respond. He started to remember. He was in no mood to hear about how mezzo piano had overturned the world order.

'Mr Jacobus?'

'What time is it?'

'About ten a.m.'

Jesus, he thought. Yes, too much wine.

'I just wanted to find out if you were all right.'

'Of course I am. I just overslept.'

'I'm so relieved. It was pretty nasty. Dante Millefiori was just released from hospital.'

'Who's Dante Millie Flory and what are you talking about?'

'He's our orchestra conductor.'

'So you want me to send him a get well card?

70

"Can't wait to see you back on the podium real soon?"'

'Mr Jacobus, I'm talking about the food poisoning.'

'What food poisoning?'

'You haven't heard? Some of our party guests contracted severe stomach poisoning. Tanner Evans – he's a theory professor – and Dante actually spent the night in the infirmary. Even Aaron has been laid low with symptoms. He feels terribly about the whole fiasco, in more ways than one, as you can imagine.'

Jacobus imagined which of Schlossberg's epicurean delights had caused it. *Poetic justice,* he thought. *That's what you deserve when you compare yourself to Beethoven.* The only thing the two composers had in common was suffering from acute digestive ailments.

'Everyone is expected to make a full recovery, but I just wanted to find out if you had caught it like the others.'

'I guess not. The squirrel wasn't FDA approved?'

'No, it wasn't the squirrel. That was my guess, too. It was the mushrooms. Did you eat them?'

Jacobus recalled tossing them over the side of the veranda.

'I passed.'

'Lucky for you. Aaron said they were chanterelles, but they turned out to be poisonous lookalikes called jack-o'-lanterns. They only cause gastric problems for a couple of days, but obviously those can be rather severe. I've also been wearing a path to the loo and am only now finally feeling myself.'

'I thought your better half was supposed to be an expert in these things.'

'He is, and he insists that there were no jack-o'-lanterns in the mix.'

'How can he be so sure?'

'He said there are plenty of telltale signs that any mycologist would know, including that jack-o'-lanterns glow in the dark, of all things!'

'Obviously.'

'Obviously?'

'Why else call them jack-o'-lanterns?'

'You're very astute.'

'Thank you. You'd think only a blind person would have missed that,' Jacobus groused. 'But how did everyone else?'

'It's because you have to take them quickly from the light into the dark, where they exhibit a ghastly, pale green glow. Aaron insisted he took all the chanterelles into the cellar and turned out the lights just to make doubly sure. But you've met him. Do you think he'd ever admit to a mistake?'

'If he's so sure, how does he figure the mushrooms got onto the menu?'

'We don't know! It's a complete mystery. But all's well that ends well, I suppose.'

'That assumes one very basic thing.'

'What's that, Mr Jacobus?'

'That it's ended.'

After Jacobus checked out of the motel, Yumi picked him up and drove him to the Feldstein Auditorium for his masterclass. When it was over he would return with her to New York. Mission accomplished.

'Please try to be nice to the students,' Yumi whispered to him as she escorted him onstage. She guided him to the lone chair near the edge of the stage. In the middle was a music stand for the students, and next to the stand was the piano for the accompanist.

'Nice?' he replied. 'What does nice have to do with anything?'

'Please, Jake. Just do it for me.'

'OK. But don't forget, there's no "i" in nice.'

'Yes there is.'

'Shit. Never was good at spelling. You think that's why "nice" isn't in my vocabulary?'

Jacobus had told them in advance, no names. He didn't want to know if the students were boys or girls, fat or skinny, tall or short, American or Asian or Martian. He just wanted to hear them play. But of course after a few minutes of listening he could tell all of those things. He couldn't help it. If their bow strokes didn't give them away, then their fingerings did, or their tone production, or their interpretation (or lack thereof). Or just the way they walked onto the stage. He wasn't always right. But almost always.

He could tell right off the bat the first student was Yumi's. No surprise. She – it was a she, he guessed correctly – played the Mendelssohn Violin Concerto, one of the first things he'd taught Yumi when she had studied with him. *Jesus! How many years was it already?* Even so, this new kid was using some of the same fingerings and bowings he had hashed out with Yumi. Jacobus was not one to be dogmatic about such things. Everyone had different hands, different body types, and different temperaments. If a student's independent choices were well-considered and fit the music, so much the better. The one thing he *was* dogmatic about was that the student must *think*. His teacher, Dr Krovney, used to say, 'You can train a monkey to play a musical instrument, but a monkey cannot play *music!*'

What he liked about this student was that she had some ideas of her own, and some of those actually made sense. But even when they didn't, as was the case with her overly aggressive octaves at the bottom of the first page, she played with conviction. Jacobus almost smiled.

Not only did Jacobus know the student was one of Yumi's, he also could determine exactly which one it must be. Weeks ago, Yumi had told him about her. She was a special case. Mia Cheng was her name. She had a father who was a successful businessman and a mother whose sole goal in life had been to bear a child and see to the realization of their dream that the child would become a musical genius. Mrs Cheng dutifully gave birth to a daughter, perfectly healthy except for a deformity in her left hand, rendering a future as a performer impossible. They gave the baby to a distant overseas cousin who was unable to conceive and proceeded to forget about her. Then came Mia, who, with two fully functional hands, was groomed from birth to satisfy their dreams. The irony was that Mia, upon making two discoveries – that she had an abandoned sister and that there might be a life outside playing the violin – legally disowned her parents. From the very first note Jacobus could hear it all. This young

74

lady played with talent fueled by anger, engaged in combat.

The audience of students and faculty applauded Mia when she dashed off the prestissimo coda of the first movement. The positive response seemed refreshingly sincere, enthusiastic rather than merely polite. That was good. It was possible there were a handful of students present who were more capable, but not many. Though most of them probably admired the performance, there were always a few who might have been envious, even – inappropriately – dismissive, jealous they hadn't had the opportunity to perform. They'd talk afterwards with great self-assurance about how they would have done it better, how Mia had no idea what she was doing, and that so-and-so's recording was so much better. Typical student behavior. And, as Jacobus reminded himself, professionals were simply grown-up students who got paid.

He didn't have much to say to Mia Cheng. Mendelssohn had written *allegro molto appassionato* at the beginning of the concerto, but she had gone beyond passion and had attacked the music with venom, as if she wanted to conquer it rather than form a healthy alliance with it. Nevertheless, he had faith in Yumi's ability to 'make the rough places plain,' to quote Handel's *Messiah*. He quizzed Mia on all the ground-breaking aspects of the concerto that had made it the crowning achievement of the nineteenth-century violin concerto, as much to enlighten the students in the gallery as to gauge her level of preparation. She knew all the answers. Clearly,

Yumi had made similar demands upon her student as Jacobus had made of Yumi. He experienced a moment of pride, not for the two young and younger ladies in his thoughts but for himself, and for that lapse he immediately chastised himself.

He offered Mia Cheng some insights into ways to tie her individual ideas into her understanding of the concerto's structure, to make her interpretation a more unified whole, and had her repeat a few passages that had been technically accurate but musically unconvincing. He also made some suggestions about how she might better integrate her interpretation with the orchestral accompaniment.

Of course, for a masterclass there's no orchestra but merely the reduction of the orchestral score into a piano part. A Miss Lisette Broder was the staff accompanist, and Jacobus judged her first-rate at her job. The ease with which she adjusted to Mia Cheng's playing suggested she had played the accompaniments for years and knew the violin repertoire better than the students themselves. Her playing was so eminently pliable that Jacobus had no doubt she could adapt to whatever bizarre idiosyncrasies a student might concoct. No pianist begins training with aspirations of becoming an accompanist, especially of students. They picture themselves onstage as a soloist performing Beethoven, Schubert, Chopin, and Liszt. The work of staff accompanists is tedious and unfulfilling, never in the limelight. For the most part, their presence is hardly even noticed, unless they make a muck of things. So Jacobus appreciated how this one fit like a glove to Mia's playing, never forcing her out of her comfort zone.

For that reason, Jacobus reminded Mia that playing with a full orchestra wouldn't be so easy. 'It's a little harder for the *Queen Mary* to change course than for a speed boat,' he said, 'so be damn sure you're pointing the music in the right direction.'

'Yes, Maestro,' she replied.

When he finished with his comments, he excused her from the stage. There was more applause from the audience. For whom, he wasn't sure.

The next student walked onstage. Broder, the accompanist, began the piece, which Jacobus recognized from the first three languorous notes as the famous Violin Sonata in A Major by the nineteenth-century Franco-Belgian Romantic composer, Cesar Franck. A challenging piece technically, yes; more so musically, especially for a student. Even before the student began, Jacobus knew exactly how the kid was going to play because Broder's tempo was too slow, and he knew that she wouldn't have taken such a tempo unless she had been instructed to do so.

Acceding to Yumi's wishes, he forced himself to be patient, clenching and unclenching his fists, and allowed the student to play the whole first movement without interruption. But his exercise in restraint had the opposite effect. Rather than calming himself down, Jacobus only became more irritated. Clearly, the student had not paid a lick of attention to Franck's own explicit indications how he wanted the music to be played.

The student was simply mimicking some recording he had heard, and was not doing a very good job at that, either.

The student stopped at the end of the movement. Jacobus said, 'Don't look at the music for a minute. Look at me and tell me what tempo Franck asks for at the beginning of the piece.'

'Umm. *Adagio*?'

A boy's voice. Cocky.

'Now look at it.'

'Ah! *Allegretto ben moderato.*'

'*Allegretto*. So why did you play it so slow?'

'I'm not sure.'

'You're not sure. Here's another question, sonny. What does dolce mean?'

'Not sure of that, either,' he said, trying to make his response sound humorous.

Be nice, Jacobus reminded himself. *Be nice*.

'Not sure. Well, let's take a look at the music, shall we? How many times does Franck write dolce in the first movement?'

'The whole thing?'

'It's all of two pages, if I recall.'

After a brief silence, 'Does *dolcissimo* count?'

'Yes, *dolcissimo* counts.'

Another silence. Apparently, counting was a challenging task.

'Seven,' he said, finally.

'So Franck writes *dolce* seven times within four minutes of music. That suggests he thought it was important. And you don't know what it means.'

The silence was uncomfortable.

'One last question. Franck writes the infrequently

78

used term *con calore* one time only. That also suggests he considered it important. Can you tell me what that means?'

'With color?'

'Sorry, son. Guesses don't count, especially when they're wrong. *Con calore* means with heat or, in common parlance, passionately. Three strikes and you're out. Come back next time when you've given this music one iota of thought. Next.'

There was some rumbling from the gallery, a few stifled gasps, and even a bit of the same kind of nervous laughter one sometimes hears when news spreads about an untimely death. But if they didn't understand the lesson he had just given – a lesson, in Jacobus's mind, that was more valuable than picking apart meaningless details – that was their problem.

Jacobus hoped the next student would be better. He'd never had the capacity to tolerate apathy as an excuse for being ill-prepared, and would not pretend it was acceptable in front of a crowd of aspiring musicians. That kind of hypocrisy drove him mad. What would happen to music if the very people playing it didn't give a rat's ass? Maybe it had already been happening.

Ah! The audience is quieting. Jacobus tried to turn his thoughts away from the darkness. A student tuned to the piano and started to play. The Mozart Concerto in D Major that the youthful composer wrote when he was nineteen. Jacobus knew how unreasonable it was make comparisons with the performer who was about the same age, but still . . .

Then a performance of the virtuoso Introduction and Rondo Capriccioso by Camille Saint-Säens that was spirited but contained fistfuls of wrong notes and rhythms.

Finally, Vivaldi's 'Spring.' It was that girl, Audrey, who had prodded him for his guidance the night before. *Let's see how much she retained.* Jacobus sat back and self-consciously folded his arms. In the past he would have quite naturally folded them around his violin, but he hadn't brought it with him. Since moving into Nathaniel's apartment he hadn't practiced much and was more out of shape than usual. Any point of erudition he would have tried to reinforce by demonstrating on the violin, however valid, would have been negated by his own rusty execution.

With Audrey, he was disappointed in his hopes if not in his expectations, which he had learned in a lifetime of dealing with humanity were impossible to underestimate. Audrey had evidently spurned his advice about the accents, playing lightly, and everything else he had mentioned. Whether that was by intention or inattention, the playing was even rougher than at the rehearsal the day before. There were inexplicable inconsistencies between her and Broder, the pianist. From time to time Audrey played loudly when Broder played softly, and vice versa. Some of her notes didn't jibe with the harmonies that Broder played on the piano. Jacobus was perplexed. She had seemed so enthusiastic. He decided he'd cut her as much slack as he could to bring her along. After all, he had promised

Yumi, and for some reason, he liked the kid. He let her play all three movements, mainly because it took him that amount of time to compose what he would say.

When she finished the applause was polite and subdued.

'OK, dear,' he said, after it quickly subsided. 'First of all, you've got to be on the same page as your accompanist. It definitely is a solo for violin, but it also has to be a team effort. It's your job to sort out the notes and dynamics and make sure the feelings are mutual.'

'I played what was in my part,' Audrey argued. 'It's what I've always been playing.'

Before Jacobus could begin his lecture on using one's ears as well as one's eyes, Lisette Broder spoke up.

'*Mea culpa*,' she said. 'We've been rehearsing from the Ricordi edition, but I seem to have lost my part, so I had to borrow a different one at the last minute. It's an early, hand-written edition and apparently has a lot of mistakes in it.'

Broder sounded distraught. Clearly she took pride in her accompanying ability and now had to eat crow in public.

'Well,' said Jacobus, 'that clears up one mystery. But who knows what's a mistake and what Vivaldi intended? After two-hundred-fifty years our listener's ears have changed as well. The Ricordi edition is perfectly acceptable, though one could just as easily conjecture that it's the Ricordi edition that has the mistakes. Sometimes there's really no way to tell for sure, and that's one of the challenges of playing Baroque music.

81

You have to make a lot more of your own decisions.'

Ah, a teaching moment!

'But let's look at this concerto with what we know Vivaldi intended to portray. We've got bird calls, gentle breezes, a murmuring brook, and thunderstorms in the first movement. In the Largo we've got a goatherd with his faithful dog sleeping beside him in a meadow. In the last movement we have nymphs and shepherds roused into dance by the intoxicating music of rustic pipes. Those are all pretty vivid images and Vivaldi translated all of them into notes. We have to figure out how to play those notes to recreate the images.'

'That's what I tried to do,' Audrey said.

'Well, let's try them again, one at a time.'

They went back to the beginning, and Jacobus did his best to extract some semblance of character out of Audrey's playing. The result was inexplicably unsatisfactory, yet Jacobus patiently persevered. He stopped her in the middle of a thunderstorm that was lackluster as a morning drizzle.

'Try beginning those thirty-second notes with the bow on the string to get the articulation clearer. We want it to sound like thunder and lightning, not just cloudy with a chance of rain.'

'That's not how my teacher told me,' Audrey said.

Ah! The standard counterpunch of the petulant student. How many times had Jacobus heard that one? He had even gotten it from Yumi when she'd arrived from Japan and first started studying

82

with him. He had heard it so many times over the years his response was almost memorized.

'If I told you to do it the same way as your teacher, what would the point be of me being here? The idea of a masterclass is to get different perspectives. That's one of the things that makes music great. Try it out here. If you like it, fine. If not' – and here Jacobus thought charitably about Dunster – 'do it the way your teacher told you.'

'This is really tiring,' she said.

'Well, suck it up, buttercup. I'm about a century older than you and can manage enough energy to put my bow on the string.'

'I really don't like men,' Audrey said.

There was an audible gasp from the audience.

'Me, neither,' Jacobus responded, to relieved laughter. They thought he was trying to break the ice. They were wrong. He did not abide insolence, whether there was an 'i' in it or not.

'And I don't care much for women, either,' he added.

A rumble of confusion. How to interpret his comment?

'I really don't like being badgered,' Audrey said. 'I think I've had enough.'

'Suit yourself.'

Her departing footsteps echoed in the silence of the acoustically excellent Feldstein Auditorium.

Six

Yumi almost shoved Jacobus into the passenger seat of her Camaro.

'I can't believe you did that,' she said, and slammed the door shut.

He heard her tramp around the car with agitated footsteps and slide into the driver's seat.

'I can't believe you did that,' she repeated.

'I heard you the first time. What can't you believe?'

'"Suck it up, buttercup," for one.'

She turned on the ignition and over-revved the engine. The car lurched forward with a screech. If not for his seatbelt, Jacobus might have gone through the windshield.

'What's so bad about that?'

'It's not only insulting and demeaning. It's sexist.'

'Sexist?'

'Yes, sexist. Don't you realize when you call women things like buttercup, or honey, or sweetheart, you objectify them? You reinforce the stereotype of women as subservient and helpless? It's comments like that that make men think they can do whatever they want.'

'You're accusing me of abuse?' Jacobus asked. He couldn't decide if he was more dumbfounded or outraged.

'No. Not you. But it leads to it.'

They drove for several minutes in uneasy silence. Jacobus couldn't let it go. *Yumi just didn't get it.* He would explain.

'Something's wrong with that kid,' he said.

'Which kid? You humiliated two of them. Or don't you recall? And not just them! What about their teacher, Professor Dunster? You made it abundantly clear you think his teaching is inadequate. He's been a respected member of the faculty for decades.'

'So I've been told. By him.'

'And have you been told he's been responsible for getting major donors to support the scholarship fund? What if the Feldsteins were there? That's ninety-million dollars you might have just flushed down the toilet.'

'That's beside the point.'

'Well, it's not beside the point that you also humiliated *me*!'

'You! And just how did I do that?'

The car swerved unexpectedly.

'Careful,' Jacobus said.

'Don't tell me how to drive. You're not supposed to run over animals. Number one: I was the one who pushed so hard to get you invited to give the masterclass, so I now have to take responsibility for your behavior.'

'How? By committing hara-kiri?'

Jacobus realized immediately his comment was below the belt, but he was in no mood to concede any ground.

'I'll forget you said that, Jake,' Yumi responded, but Jacobus knew she never would. 'The second thing is,' she continued, 'by fawning over my

85

student and then trashing Elwood's, you made it seem you were playing favorites. Don't you understand how embarrassing that is to me?'

'Your kid was prepared. The others weren't.'

'Jake, they all played well! Yes, maybe there were shades of difference. But they're all just students! How dare you rake them over the coals like that!'

She's driving far too fast for a back road, Jacobus thought. They must be on the Taconic Parkway now. He hoped so.

'If I remember correctly,' he said, 'I was much tougher on you than I was to those kids this morning, and you've been thanking me for it ever since.'

'Jake, those were *private* lessons. This was *public*. Those kids were performing in front of their teachers and classmates. But of course you couldn't see that.'

That was the first time Yumi had ever cut him with a remark about his blindness. Jacobus was hurt, but in a way also relieved. Now they were even, and he speculated that she had insulted him intentionally for that purpose.

Two things troubled him deeply, though. Not for the first time, he wondered whether he was becoming a caricature of himself, so comfortable in his role of curmudgeon that he could no longer escape it. That he was now manufacturing scenarios, using other human beings as props, to enable him to play his role. *Tough but fair! The ancient, blind guru familiar with the wondrous mysteries of music. 'Do what I say and you shall go far, but if not, dire will be your fate!'*

Am I still an effective teacher, or is my bluster simply a tactic to massage my own ego? He had seen it often enough in other musicians – performers and teachers alike – and had always scoffed at their disingenuous pomposity. He was old, and by now he knew who he was. Or so he thought. *Could it be I'm someone else entirely but have constructed an impenetrable, false façade?*

He thought about his parents, exterminated in a World War II death camp. He thought about his brother who might have perished with them but who also might have escaped and, in fact, might still be alive. In any event he was never heard from again, and Jacobus would never know. Did *they* ever ask themselves the question, 'Who am I?' he wondered. Or was that question simply the machination of an addled, narcissistic brain with the luxury of too much time on its hands. Though he would not voice that particular concern with Yumi, he did speak about the other thing troubling him.

'The girl. Audrey.'

'What? What about her?'

It must have been a long time since he had said anything. The car was now stopping and starting. They must be nearing the city already.

'Something's wrong.'

'You intimidated her.'

'No, no. Last night she was eager. Everything I mentioned about the Vivaldi she just soaked up like a sponge. Bounding around like a puppy with a stick. I'm telling you, even I was looking forward to hearing her this morning.'

87

'That's quite an admission.'

'Take it for what it's worth. But something happened between last night and this morning. Night and day. Literally.'

Yumi took her time responding. Maybe she wasn't agreeing. But at least she was considering.

'Last night was a party,' she said. 'This morning she was on the spot. That's the difference. And you didn't help her.'

'I gave her the benefit of the doubt. I was patient. She wouldn't budge. Whatever was positive last night was negative this morning. She said, "I really don't like being badgered." Badgered? Kids don't talk like that. At least not spontaneously. It sounded like she'd practiced it. Something happened, Yumi. And I'm not trying to make excuses.'

'Is that a sign of remorse?'

'For what?'

'Never mind. Here we are.'

Yumi phoned up to Nathaniel's apartment, and Nathaniel came down to meet Jacobus on the street. Having anticipated their arrival, he had bought some bagels and lox from Shmeer Case on Columbus Avenue and invited the two of them up for a late afternoon lunch. Yumi declined politely but tersely, and drove off.

'What's the problem?' Nathaniel asked.

'What problem?' Jacobus responded.

Nathaniel knew Jacobus very well. Friends since college, long before Jacobus had lost his sight, they had played in a trio together after graduating for years of concert touring. Over time, Nathaniel bade farewell to the stresses of performing and of

88

being a black man in a predominantly Caucasian
field and utilized his musician's knowledge of
string instruments to become a highly reputed
consultant in the field of instrument and art fraud
Jacobus, after being stricken with sudden blind
ness on the eve of his audition for concertmast
of the Boston Symphony, had gone into seclusi
His orchestra career in a shambles, when he fin
reemerged he had determined to use his h
earned skills to teach others, thus beginning
legendary legacy as a pedagogue. Not unlike
individuals in other fields, Jacobus had acc
enemies and rivals alongside admirer
acolytes. Due to his indifference to p
correctness and his addiction to being
whether or not it hurt, as time went on th
leaned toward the former camp. That he
dragged into more than his share of murd
tigations – reluctantly, it must be sai
weighted the scales that much more.

Nathaniel understood Jacobus's u
idealism underneath his crustaceous e
also understood Jacobus's almost
inability to discuss any issue which
fragile inner sensitivity.

'Masterclass didn't go well?' Nat
slicing an onion bagel.

'It went fine,' Jacobus said. 'P
cheese.'

Nathaniel didn't ask any more
spent the evening comparing
mances of the Mendelssohn Oct
it was such a masterpiece it d
played it or how. It simply co

On Saturday, they planned to go for a walk in Central Park to enjoy the unseasonably warm weather, but instead of sunshine, morning thunderstorms rattled the windows of Nathaniel's apartment, followed by a persistent downpour. With time on their hands, Nathaniel set about working on his tax return and assisting Jacobus with his. Jacobus's wasn't very complicated as he received little in the way of Social Security benefits, and what income he did accrue was from increasingly rare private lessons and occasional masterclasses such as the disastrous one the day before. Nathaniel, with his contacts in the insurance industry, was able to obtain a substantial reimbursement for Jacobus's burned-down house by claiming that a lot of the accumulated junk that had been destroyed were priceless, irreplaceable antiques. Though some of them actually were – his eighteenth-century Gagliano violin being the prime example – most of his belongings would have been rejected by secondhand stores. In any event, the income from the insurance company wouldn't have to be claimed until the following year's return.

Much of Sunday was spent in their traditional manner. Over coffee, Nathaniel read sections of *Sunday New York Times* out loud, after which the two of them bemoaned the sorry state of the world, a therapeutic exercise which generally made Jacobus feel better. In the afternoons they listened to the radio broadcast of whatever opera the Met was performing and then talked about it. By the time they finished their critique, the

90

day, and the catharsis of dispensing with a week's worth of complaints, were over.

On Monday morning, Nathaniel left for an appointment for a consultation with an insurance company over a claim for a missing Fabergé egg, leaving Jacobus to his own devices. Over the years, Jacobus had become almost as familiar with Nathaniel's two-bedroom apartment as with his own house. He navigated the narrow corridor from bedroom to bathroom to kitchen, where he poured a cup of coffee from the Mr Coffee machine on the counter, and from there to the living room to listen to the radio news on the hour. Then back to the kitchen for more coffee and back to the living room for a repeat of the news.

By midday, claustrophobia began to set in. *How can a blind man be claustrophobic?* he asked himself. Yet confinement was driving him crazy. Even his gargantuan bulldog, Trotsky, had it better than this. They didn't allow dogs in Nathaniel's building, so Trotsky had to stay elsewhere until Jacobus's new house was built. The Millers, his neighbors in the Berkshires, were kind enough to take Trotsky in. According to their reports, the slobbering canine had made a successful transition, spending entire days on the porch, lying inert – the one thing he was expert at – and soaking up the salubrious spring sun.

Jacobus thought of his house in the Berkshires where he had lived for over thirty years. The square footage was probably less than Nathaniel's apartment and clutter-filled. But he had never felt hemmed in like this. He could always open the

91

door to the woods and the comforting silence. It was a silence softened by birds, breezes, and brooks, but even without sight he reveled in the sense of space. When he opened the door to Nathaniel's apartment, what was there? Another corridor, an elevator, a lobby, and then what? The grimy groans of an impersonal city as unseeing to him as he was to it.

Seven

It had been more than two months since Jacobus moved in with Nathaniel, and over a week since the disastrous masterclass. The adrenaline from the intensity of the moment had long since worn off, and the withdrawal left him listless and at loose ends. Jacobus was bored. And when he was bored he was intolerable, which might have been why Nathaniel was spending increasing amounts of time away from the apartment, consulting on cases.

'There's nothing to do around here,' Jacobus grumbled.

'Listen to some music,' Nathaniel said and turned his attention back to the *Times*.

'I've got Mendelssohn coming out my ass. I don't need any more music.'

'Listen to the news, then. Go for a walk. Make some coffee. Eat a sandwich.'

'Some friend.'

'My lord!' Nathaniel said. 'Shall I arrange a playdate for you? Or a babysitter?'

'Smug son of a—'

'All right! All right!' Nathaniel said. Jacobus heard him slap down the newspaper. 'I do declare! Would a game of checkers make you happy?'

93

'Happy? No. Modestly lessened sense of ennui? Yes.'

Nathaniel set up the board on a folding table between the two of them.

As Nathaniel was about to make his first move, Jacobus asked, 'What about some music?'

'Jake, I've never said this to you, but—'

'OK. Never mind. Just go.'

Nathaniel moved his checker with Jacobus's finger on it. Jacobus could have done it himself, since Nathaniel started out every game the same way. He released Jacobus's hand after making his move.

'It's strange,' Jacobus said.

'What do you mean? It's the same move as always.'

'No. Not that. Just that business about the mushrooms and that kid both happening at the same time.'

'Jake, let it go. You've been obsessing for a week. There's no connection. Some people got sick from bad mushrooms. And a hyper young lady got sick from you. You do have that effect, you know.'

'But Schlossberg was an expert. His wife said he went to great lengths to make sure the mushrooms were good. And the way he talked to the girl. There was something not right. Some innuendo I wasn't catching.'

'So what are you saying?'

'I don't know. Just that there was a connection.'

'You know what I think?' Nathaniel asked.

'You think I'm a doddering old fool who can't admit he was a prick to an eager student in front of her peers and who is just making excuses for his prickiositude.'

'Uh-huh. I couldn't've said it better. Your move. I'm getting the guacamole from the fridge.'

Jacobus grunted, a combination of acknowledgement and disapproval.

As the game proceeded, Jacobus gradually gained the upper hand. His ability to remember the location of all the pieces on the board was in part a fringe benefit of his training as a violinist memorizing dozens of concertos, sonatas, and concert pieces. At first he accomplished this in standard fashion, as most students do; then, after becoming blind, he was by necessity forced to memorize everything simply by the laborious process of listening over and over again.

'How do you remember where all my checkers are?' Nathaniel asked.

'Not hard when you only have three of them.'

There was a buzz on Nathaniel's intercom. Yumi was downstairs. Nathaniel buzzed her up. She hadn't spoken to Jacobus since unceremoniously dumping him off at the curb the week before. He prepared himself to be harangued and started planning parrying retorts.

Nathaniel went to the door when the bell rang. Jacobus remained seated at the table, considering his next move. He heard his two friends enter the living room.

'Schlossberg is dead,' Yumi said. Terse and tense.

If there was a pause in Jacobus's response, no one noticed it.

'King me!' he said, advancing his square checker to Nathaniel's end of the board.

'Is that all you have to say? This is terrible news!' Yumi said.

'No more terrible than anyone else who I hardly knew.'

'Jake, what's happened to you? Just because Aaron Schlossberg didn't have the honor of your profound friendship didn't mean he wasn't one of the most important people in the music world. You're heartless!'

'Am I?' Jacobus slammed down his doubled checker. 'Am I?' he repeated. 'Did you by any chance notice the beggar sitting on the curb outside Nathaniel's building? I can smell him a mile away. I've heard the rattle of his tin cup for years, rain or shine, winter or summer, and whatever I put in it he probably spends on booze. When he dies, which mercifully will be very soon, will that also be terrible news? Or is the death of someone who's not "one of the most important people in the music world" of less consequence? Tell me, are you going to mourn for *him*?'

'That's not the point,' Yumi said, but the wind in her sails had been reduced from gale force to a zephyr. 'I didn't know Schlossberg that well, either,' she conceded. 'And maybe he was on the pompous side. But he was a colleague on the faculty and he brought a lot of recognition to the conservatory. They said he would have been the next Philip Glass.'

'That's a motive for murder if I ever heard one.'

96

'It wasn't murder. He died of natural causes.'

'Burst swollen ego?'

'Not funny. Complications due to his diabetes.'

'Pass me some of that whack-a-moley,' Jacobus said to Nathaniel. He wasn't hungry but he was going to show them his opinion of dying of diabetes. 'Heavy on the chips.'

'You might be disappointed to know that guacamole is healthy,' Yumi said. 'Avocados have good cholesterol.'

'All cholesterol is good cholesterol. When did he die?'

'A janitor found him yesterday, but they think he died Thursday. In one of the prefab practice modules at the conservatory.'

'Didn't he have a studio in his house? What was he doing in a module?' Jacobus asked. 'I thought those were for students.'

'They think he must have been working on his latest opera. He was slumped over the piano. He had been working hard on it.'

'Didn't his good wife wonder where he was for all that time?'

'She said she assumed he was off in the woods on one of his foraging excursions. That he did it all the time, and since it was spring break—'

'Ah, his Beethoven reenactment. What opera was he working on, *The Life and Death of Me*?'

'*Anwar and Yitzhak.* It's about how Sadat and Rabin forged peace between Egypt and Israel only to be assassinated by their own people. The Met was going to premiere it next year.'

'Who's singing the role of Jimmy Carter? Pavarotti?'

'Can't you take anything seriously?' Nathaniel asked.

'Certainly. Have the police interrogated the fat lady to find out when she stopped singing?'

'You're ridiculous,' Yumi said, a little too indignantly. Jacobus perceived laughter about to bubble to the surface.

'Well, since no one's taken anything I've said about the mushrooms and the girl seriously, why should I bother to be otherwise?'

'This has nothing to do with any of that! Audrey is Audrey and Aaron is Aaron. And Sybil apologized to me about the mistake with the mushrooms just like she apologized to you and everyone else.'

'People got sick.'

'Yes, people got sick. They had bowel problems, just like you. But no one is worse for wear. Jake, didn't you hear me say Aaron died of natural causes? He had a serious diabetes problem and didn't take care of himself. It was just a matter of time.'

'All right. Whatever you say. I'm just a deluded old asshole who happens to see connections between—'

'I wouldn't say deluded,' Nathaniel chuckled.

Jacobus felt Yumi's arms around his shoulders.

'You're not *that* old, either,' she said.

'What would I do without friends like you two?'

'So I'm going to Kinderhoek to sit shivah with Sybil,' Yumi said.

Jacobus turned his head.

'Didn't realize sitting shivah was a Buddhist tradition,' he said.

'We Japanese are equal-opportunity mourners.'

'I was under the impression Schlossberg was a nonbeliever. And I'd place a large wager his wife ain't Chassidic.'

'There's still a Jewish community at Kinderhoek from the old days, and they're helping out. He's already been buried – his parents are Orthodox. They still live in Brooklyn and insisted on doing everything according to tradition.'

'Doesn't a wife usually have greater say over such things?'

'Tallulah told me that Sybil went along with it to get them out of her hair, even though she said he wanted to be cremated.'

'To have his ashes scattered throughout his beloved woods?'

'How did you know?'

'My sense of poetic injustice.'

'So, do you want to go with me or not?' Yumi asked.

That caught Jacobus by surprise.

'Didn't think you'd want to be seen with me. Especially up there.'

'Well, I don't really.'

'Then why do you want me to go?'

'You've got me thinking. Just in case.'

'In case of what?'

'In case you're right.'

Eight

Sunday, March 29

In times of tragedy, communities come together. Adversaries lay aside their animosities and embrace like long-lost brothers. Claws are retracted. Fangs are unbared. When, at eleven a.m. on the eleventh day of the eleventh month in 1918 the guns were silenced on the Western Front, implacable foes crawled out of their miserable trenches and shook hands. It's the human condition. Most of the time.

Sitting shivah, a centuries-old Jewish religious and cultural rite, was conceived as a comfort to the bereaved. Prayers are intoned. Food is served. Stories of happier times are told every day for a week-long period of mourning. For the devout, a garment is torn. On this occasion there was no need for a tailor.

Jacobus, in a white shirt, black tie, and gray yarmulke, sat next to a glassy-eyed whitefish. Nathaniel had loaned him the tie. Yumi had washed and ironed the shirt, having scavenged for it, unworn for years, from a closet Nathaniel had cleared for Jacobus's use. The yarmulke was provided upon arrival, courtesy of Congregation Beth Emanuel. Unlike the delicacies Jacobus had sampled on his previous visit, the whitefish had not been foraged from Schlossberg's woods.

Rather, it had been delivered from Bialy Stock in Kinnetonka Crossing in a carload of cold cuts and pastries, staples of a proper Jewish shivah. When he had arrived, Sybil was again greeting visitors, this time absent the high-spirited frivolity. She gave Jacobus a desultory hug, handed him the yarmulke with rabbinical solemnity, and told him to help himself to the food. He had mumbled something that he supposed sounded like condolences and propped the skullcap on top of what remained of his unruly, uncombed hair. As far as he was aware, it might have fallen off, but frankly he didn't care.

Yumi assembled a plate of food for Jacobus that she knew he would enjoy – pastrami, corned beef, thinly sliced beef tongue, Swiss cheese (available as it wasn't a strictly kosher affair), and a dab of liverwurst on a cracker. He hadn't been eating much lately, and she expressed the hope that the allure of high cholesterol, unhealthful food would restore his appetite. She told him she'd be back after 'doing a little schmoozing' and would replenish his plate with slices of lox, smoked sturgeon and sable, and a scoop of his new friend, the whitefish.

Jacobus, who always had two reasons for doing things, sat next to the smoked whitefish partly so he could easily help himself. He liked whitefish, one of God's miraculous, though expensive, creations. He considered having Nathaniel read the *Times* obits to him in the future so he could offer his condolences at shivahs more often.

He also sat next to the whitefish because it was strategically positioned. At the near end of the long tables of food, anyone who fed at the trough would have to pass him. Aware of his penchant for getting into trouble, he knew it would find him sooner or later, and his chosen location enhanced the likelihood it would be sooner.

Jacobus recalled that Sybil had exchanged piquant words with Harold Handy at the party the previous week and, wondering whether that was a one-time spat carried over from the symposium, mentioned that to Yumi.

'Oh, they've had a running feud for years,' she said. 'Harold thinks Sybil doesn't see the big picture, and Sybil calls Harold a dilettante and a shoddy researcher. Elwood told me she once said to him, "Harold might see the forest, but he wouldn't see a tree if one fell on him."'

'The English do have a way with words.'

'Yes. And as they say, ta-ta.' Yumi began to wander off.

'And don't forget a bialy!' he called after her. It was hard to find a good bialy anymore. Unlike bagels, which were ideal when topped with cream cheese, for some reason butter was the preferred spread for bialys. Also, whereas a bagel was perfectly fine either fresh or toasted, a toasted bialy ran a distant second to—

'Mr Jacobus?' said a female voice. Latin inflection.

'*Sí*, that's me.'

'Hello. I'm Tallulah Dominguez.'

The name didn't register at first.

'Yeah, yeah,' Jacobus said, finally remembering. 'You're the pianist performing with Yumi.'

'That's right. I'd like to introduce you to my

friend, Alonzo Sumter. He's head of the jazz department.'

Jacobus put his plate on his lap and extended his right hand. It was shaken twice, first by Dominguez, then by Sumter.

'In a relationship?' Jacobus asked.

'Yes! How could you know that?' Dominguez said.

'You're standing to his left and you shook my hand with your left hand. He shook my hand with his right. Why would that be? I'd guess it's because the two of you are holding hands – your right, his left. So, married or a relationship? I didn't feel a ring on either of your hands so I guessed relationship, though I can't be sure since a lot of musicians abstain from wearing rings because it could interfere with one's playing. That's why I asked.'

'Anything else you learned?' Sumter asked. His voice had a rich African American resonance, not much different from Nathaniel's, though a slightly higher register. Much younger, too.

'You play guitar?' Jacobus asked.

'Yes!' Sumter said, surprise in his voice. 'Do you know me?'

'No. Never heard of you. But you have long nails on your right hand, and there aren't too many other instruments where long nails are an advantage. I considered the possibility that you might be gay, but since gay people don't necessarily grow their nails any longer or shorter than anyone else and I already figured you had a relationship with the young lady, I concluded it was that you played guitar.'

'Cool!' Sumter said. 'Very cool. We were at your masterclass last week.'

'Oh?' Jacobus readied himself for the barrage.

'We thought your comments were right on,' Sumter said.

'Really.'

'Of course,' Dominguez continued. 'The standards here are going to hell. Everyone rests on their laurels—'

'And their asses,' Sumter interjected.

'No one cares anymore. The old guard—'

'No one?' Jacobus asked.

'Well, of course, *some* people care,' Dominguez replied. 'Alonzo is trying to build a jazz department here, and you would think he'd get some support. After all, not all great music is from DWEMs.'

'DWEMs?'

'Dead, white European males.'

'I see.'

'Alonzo applied for a Caldwell grant from the Conservatory for three years straight to have a Piazzolla festival. He wanted to do Piazzolla's Four Seasons along with Vivaldi's. Don't you think that's a great idea? They turned him down each time. And you know why?'

'No. Why?'

'Because,' Sumter said, 'the so-called experts on the committee who control the purse strings are the entrenched interests. Guys like Handy and Evans—'

'I know Handy. Haven't had the pleasure of Evans.'

'Theory department,' Dominguez said.

'Teaching about DWEMs?'

'See! You understand already,' she said. 'They have lost their passion, if they ever had it.'

'Dunster, too,' Sumter added.

Ah! Jacobus began to understand more clearly.

'Let me guess. He's on the grant committee, too.'

'Yes, he is,' Dominguez said. 'And that's why what you said at the class was so important. They don't insist their students study even the most elementary— Oh, I can't even talk about it, it gets me so upset.'

'If you don't hold those guys' feet to the fire,' Sumter added, 'this whole school will go down the tubes.'

'Time to get rid of some dead wood?' Jacobus postulated.

'They might not have told you this because they don't want it to get out, but Elwood has focal dystonia. He can't even play anymore, his hands shake so bad.'

Jacobus recalled Schlossberg at the party telling Audrey Rollins to clean up the mess that Dunster created when he had dropped his plate. He was sympathetic. When it came to playing an instrument, focal dystonia was worse than blindness.

'People have to retire sooner or later,' Sumter continued. 'Right?'

'For the good of the school,' Jacobus said, unsure if he was being sarcastic.

Jacobus heard a familiar voice in the background noise of conversation. It was a voice at once glib and pompous, and, like a busybody in-law one

105

hadn't seen for years, it was no longer totally unwelcome.

'Absolutely,' Dominguez replied.

'Excuse me, folks,' Jacobus said. 'But my hot pastrami is starting to congeal.'

'Of course,' Sumter said. 'It was a pleasure meeting someone . . .'

'Someone who understands,' Dominguez completed.

And then she kissed Jacobus on the cheek. Both cheeks! Maybe it was his lucky day.

Jacobus knew the voice in the crowd would find him eventually. He popped a thin slice of meat into his mouth not knowing exactly what it was. Tongue! As he swallowed it he conjectured that it tasted him while he was tasting it.

'Ah, Mr Jacobus! What a dubious pleasure to see you again.'

'Lilburn! I was just eating tongue. Apparently you've still got yours flapping around. I thought the *Times* put you out to pasture.'

'In a sense, Jacobus. But I must say, this grazing is not unpleasant in the least.'

'Help yourself, Lilburn, and then let's talk.'

Jacobus held out his plate.

'Throw a bialy on this for me. With butter.'

When Lilburn returned, he handed Jacobus his plate back and pulled up a chair.

'What took so long?' Jacobus asked.

'I fought hard for this bialy, Mr Jacobus. It was the last one, and I practically had to wrestle the rabbi for it.'

'That'll make it doubly enjoyable,' Jacobus said. 'So tell me, what brings you all the way from New York City to the bucolic hinterland?'

'The *Times* sent me here,' he said, 'to cover Schlossberg's funeral and do a retrospective piece.'

'I'm sure that'll sell a lot of papers.'

'Think what you might,' Lilburn said, 'but Aaron Schlossberg was on the verge of becoming a giant in the music world.'

'Among midgets, a child is a giant,' Jacobus replied.

'How literary of you, Jacobus! May I use that in my piece?'

'Only if you give me a free copy.'

'Some things don't change, do they?' Lilburn said.

'I want you to help me,' Jacobus said.

'Thus confirming my comment.'

'I'll remember you ever said that. This is what I need you to do: As you do your piece on the dearly departed demi-giant, I want you to ask around – discreetly – to find out as much as you can about how he died.'

'Complications from his diabetes. It was in all the papers.'

'So they say.'

'Do you have any reason to doubt that?'

Jacobus could sense Lilburn's antennae go up. Though he had been the well-researched if sometime patronizing music critic of the *Times* for decades, his hidden passion was for investigative journalism, and he had a nose for it. Jacobus explained his so far, modest qualms.

'I don't think there's anything there, Jacobus,'

Lilburn said, evidently disappointed. 'And once I finish this piece I have a looming deadline to complete my memoir.'

'Don't worry, Lilburn. I'll buy both copies. In the meantime, just do your Woodward and Bernstein thing and keep me abreast.'

'I suppose it won't do any harm, and maybe, as with Mozart's death, a bit of doubt over the cause of his demise will add some intrigue to the story.'

'You think the notion that Salieri poisoned Mozart has any legs?'

Lilburn laughed. 'I think that tall tale has been disproven time and again by the experts. You don't believe it, do you?'

'Not a bit. But as far as Aaron Schlossberg's concerned, let's not assume we know who the experts are.'

Nine

'Here comes Yumi,' Jacobus continued.

'Egad, Jacobus!' Lilburn said. 'How could you know that? With this crowd milling about, there's no way you could have heard her coming.'

'Would you believe me if I told you I can sense the aura of my dear former student, even when she's miles away? A karmic connection, as it were?'

'I wouldn't put it past you.'

'Don't be an idiot, Lilburn. It's that flowery soap she uses I smelled all the way up the Taconic Parkway. The damn stuff makes me wheeze. Karmic connection! Jesus, Lilburn.'

'Mr Lilburn!' Yumi said, joining them. 'So good to see you. You look a bit flushed. Are you feeling all right?'

'Ah, Miss Shinagawa!' Lilburn responded. 'No, I'm fine. Just fine. Your mentor was just explaining his . . . his . . .'

'No need to explain,' Yumi said. 'I can imagine. Can I get you a glass of wine?'

'No, thanks. Still on the wagon. Coffee would be wonderful, though.'

When Yumi returned with the coffee, she said, 'I never had a chance to thank you for your kind review.'

'Don't thank me,' Lilburn said. 'It was one of the best recordings of the Four Seasons I've heard in a long time.'

Jacobus intervened. 'Before you start kissing each other's asses, tell us what you found out about the party last week.'

Yumi hesitated.

'Don't worry,' Jacobus assured her. 'I've explained to Lilburn that I think things are even less kosher than the corned beef.'

'I wish I had something more interesting than the usual campus gossip to report.'

'I wish you did, too,' said Jacobus.

'I'd be interested, too,' Lilburn said. 'It might help fill out my *Times* piece.'

'Well, of course everyone was talking about the food poisoning last week,' Yumi said, 'trying to outdo each other with who had the worst symptoms.'

'Took away your appetite, did it?' Jacobus quipped.

'Yes. I can't look at food now without feeling queasy.'

'Your loss.'

'But everyone's recovered. So that's the good news.'

'What's the bad news?'

'Nothing out of the ordinary. There are two music theory teachers, Gunter Braun and Tanner Evans. They're at each other's throats, as always. Gunter is a Schenkerian and Tanner is a Pistonian.'

'Are they really?' Lilburn said thoughtfully. 'Yes, I at least know Walter Piston's work,' Lilburn said, 'because he was more of a composer. He taught at Harvard and only passed away ten or so years ago. He had some pretty famous students, like Bernstein and Carter.'

'Then you should know Heinrich Schenker was a German music theorist,' Jacobus answered for Yumi. 'My parents knew him, and it's possible I even met him when I was a kid. He developed a philosophy that music is primarily a melodic, linear phenomenon. He thought all tonal music was supported by a few basic harmonic pillars from which greater and greater contrapuntal detail emerges. Piston, on the other hand, had a more vertical approach to music theory. That music tended to follow harmonic chord patterns.'

'Yes, yes. Long ago, in a different life, when I was a music student we all studied Piston harmony. Numbering chords according to their relationships was homework from hell, but after a while that turned out to be helpful.'

'Apparently Gunter and Tanner don't share an inclusive viewpoint,' Jacobus said.

'I guess not,' Yumi laughed, 'but they have one thing in common. They both agree that performers are the dregs of the earth. That we're just car mechanics who don't understand anything about music. But they were very polite telling me so.'

'What else?' Jacobus asked.

'Not much. Dante Millefiori—'

'The conservatory orchestra conductor?' Lilburn asked.

'That's right,' Yumi replied. 'He was holding court with Sybil and Lisette Broder – the staff accompanist – and Connie Jean—'

'Who's Connie Jean?' Jacobus asked.

'Connie Jean Hawkins. She's Dean Hedge's secretary. She makes his appointments, files all the grades, and supervises all the scheduling. You can't get a room to rehearse in without going through Connie Jean.'

'What did she have to say?'

'Not much, because Dante did all the talking, as usual. Somehow he was able to go from complaining about spending the night in the hospital to proclaiming that if not for him, Aaron Schlossberg would never have become so famous.'

'Why does he think that?' Lilburn asked.

'Because Dante premiered a lot of Schlossberg's compositions and was able to take the conservatory orchestra on international tours, with Schlossberg's music on the programs.'

'I might think,' Lilburn interposed, 'that it was the other way round. That if not for Schlossberg's music, this Millefiori fellow would never have been able to get tour funding and would be a nonentity.'

'That's exactly what Sybil said. She was upset that Dante would be so arrogant on an occasion like this, while she's mourning her husband's death.'

'When all is said and done,' Lilburn said, 'he's nothing more than a student orchestra conductor!'

'You should have a talk with him then. He was saying that it takes more genius to conduct students than a professional orchestra, because—'

'Whatever,' Jacobus interrupted. 'It sounds like he's perfected his spiel. Give the man credit for the gift of self-promotion. He'd probably make more money as a motivational speaker than as a musician. But it doesn't sound like he'll benefit from Schlossberg's death whether he's the chicken or the egg. Was that other conductor,

Tawroszewicz, there with him? He and Sybil are as friendly with each other as a mongoose and a cobra.'

'I haven't seen him anywhere today. But that's not necessarily a big deal. Shivah goes on for a whole week.'

'Really, Rabbi Shinagawa? Remind me again when it was you received your ordination. Tell me, was there anyone else whose presence or absence might not be a big deal?'

'The only other people I spoke to were Dean Hedge, who was sitting in a group with Elwood Dunster, Dolly Cooney, and a man in a business suit who I didn't recognize.'

'Dunster, the violin professor, and Cooney of the Venerable Bead fortune?' Lilburn asked.

'Yes, that's right,' Yumi replied.

Jacobus could hear him scribbling on a pad.

'Horrid play on words, Venerable Bead,' Lilburn muttered. 'Surprised she ever made a dime.'

Yumi continued, 'They were all huddled together when I approached them and looked taken aback when they noticed me. But Dean Hedge was very polite and introduced me to Dolly Cooney, who I'd never met, and to the gentleman, who's the director of the local hospital and a conservatory trustee.'

'Did you catch his name?' Lilburn asked.

'A Dr Pine. Louis Pine.'

'Was he Schlossberg's doctor?' Jacobus asked.

'I asked him that. He gave me a big smile and said, no, he doesn't practice anymore. He just run things now, he said. They all thought that was very funny.'

'And the name of the hospital?' Lilburn asked.

Yumi laughed. 'That's an easy one to remember. The Dolly Cooney Medical Center.'

Jacobus stopped chewing his bialy. He said, 'Were there a man and a woman with them who might have looked like brother and sister?'

'You mean the Feldsteins?' Yumi asked.

'Yeah. Dunster said he had invited Eli and Eve, Hiram's progeny, for Hedge to shake down for ninety-million dollars.'

'No, they weren't with that group.'

'What do they look like?' Lilburn asked.

'Why do people always ask me that dumb question?' Jacobus said.

'Why do you assume people are talking to *you*?' Lilburn responded.

'I've never met them,' Yumi said, 'but I did see a couple here who were also at the masterclass. They were dressed like they were trying not to look rich and they did look pretty Jewish.' Yumi apparently realized she had just said something tactless, as she added, 'at least among us goyim.'

But Jacobus's thoughts had already drifted from ethnic profiling back to the group that Yumi had interrupted.

'I think we need to take this conversation outside. I know just the place.'

Jacobus led them to the stand of maples behind the veranda where he had hidden from Sybil Baker-Hulme the week before.

'Why all the cloak-and-dagger?' Lilburn asked. 'There are mosquitoes out here.'

Jacobus ignored him.

114

'What were they talking about?' Jacobus asked Yumi.

'The Feldsteins?'

'No, the Cooney cluster.'

'Mainly about how much Aaron Schlossberg would be missed. What a great man he was. How much he did for the conservatory. You know, things that would be appropriate for the occasion.'

'You mean the customary bullshit,' Jacobus said.

'Yes, that's accurate,' Yumi replied.

'I assume that's *after* they noticed you. Did you hear what were they talking about before that?'

'No. The sound is too live in that room. It's all a wash. All I can say is that they seemed . . . concerned about something.'

'The food poisoning incident,' Lilburn said. 'This Dr Pine is a doctor, after all. Maybe they're worried about medical expenses, or legal action. Or, perish the thought, maybe even about people's health!'

Jacobus heard Lilburn slap at a mosquito.

'Possible. But that's over and done with,' Jacobus said. 'The more recent incident is Aaron Schlossberg found dead slumped over a piano keyboard.'

It began to drizzle.

'I think we'd better go inside,' Lilburn said.

'You're some Boy Scout,' Jacobus said. 'OK.' They took a step toward the house.

'One second,' Jacobus said, stopping. 'You two do me a favor. Go a little bit more into the woods – fifty, a hundred feet. Tell me if you find a path.'

'Must we?' Lilburn protested.

'I'm sorry that you're not comfortable with the concept of outdoors, Lilburn, so let me ask in a way an urbanite would understand: Would you be kind enough to escort Yumi into the woods and protect her from the muggers hiding behind every tree?'

Yumi laughed.

'If you insist,' Lilburn said. 'But if I ruin my shoes, I'll bill you for them.'

'I'll give you mine.'

'No, thanks. I would first walk barefoot over hot coals.'

Jacobus heard Yumi and Lilburn move off into the woods, the former light-footed and nimble, the latter clumsy and lumbering. They returned in a few minutes. He heard Lilburn grunt when he tripped over a root, snapping twigs as he regained his balance.

'There's nothing there,' Yumi said.

'Did you see anything, Lilburn?' Jacobus asked.

Lilburn, panting, could offer no reply.

'Never mind,' Jacobus said.

'Does nothing mean something?' Yumi asked.

'It could.'

Ten

The drizzle intensified.

'Could we please continue our discussion else-where?' Lilburn pleaded. 'Preferably indoors?'

'There's a pub just off campus where all the music students hang out,' Yumi suggested. 'It's called Chops.'

Jacobus, Yumi, and Lilburn retraced their steps to the house, where they reiterated their condolences to Sybil Baker-Hulme. She thanked them for coming and squeezed Jacobus's hand. He handed her his soggy yarmulke.

Sunday normally would have been a busy day at Chops. The one day of the week the students were free of classes and concerts, if not of practicing, was usually bustling in the afternoon. But since classes didn't resume after the week-long spring break until Monday, the place was almost deserted. Jacobus heard a few young people chatting in a booth nearby, and instead of March Madness, a broadcast of *Live from Lincoln Center* came through loud and clear.

At the shivah feast, none of them were particularly hungry. Even so, when the waiter arrived for their order, Jacobus asked what was good on the menu.

'Chops,' the waiter replied.

They ordered coffee.

'So what's with all the hush-hush, Jacobus?'

Lilburn asked when they were seated. 'Why did we have to go out in the woods?'

'I was just thinking about that group Yumi encountered and what I've learned about them this past week. You've got Charles Hedge, the dean of the conservatory, who's obsessed with raising money and who's trying to get a ninety-million-dollar check from the Feldstein heirs or the conservatory will go kaput. You've got Elwood Dunster, the over-the-hill violin teacher whose sole *raison d'être* for remaining on the faculty seems to be that he's well connected with donors. Then you've got this Cooney gal who's bankrolled the conservatory and the hospital. And finally you've got the director of the hospital itself, Dr Pine, who says he likes to "run things."'

'So what's your point, Jacobus?' Lilburn asked.

'I don't have a point!' Jacobus barked. 'Why must I have a point? All I know is, it doesn't pass the smell test.'

'Are you suggesting some kind of conspiracy? There's nothing to suggest that. Some people got sick a week ago from food poisoning, and several days later a man who didn't take care of himself died of chronic diabetes. Sad, but hardly the stuff of—'

'And don't forget the girl!'

'The girl?'

'Audrey Rollins, the reluctant violin student. She was there, working at the party with her loverboy, Lucien. Then, the masterclass. Inexplicable attitude.'

'Jacobus!' Lilburn said. 'I'm surprised at you. You, of all people, know how headstrong and

118

vexing students can be – no offense intended, Miss Shinagawa. No doubt, the girl was out of her depth – clearly – and simply found a way out to protect herself that happened to make you feel bad. It has been the standard modus operandi for the recalcitrant prodigy since time immemorial.'

Jacobus noted that Yumi didn't jump to his defense. Then again, she didn't endorse Lilburn's opinion, either.

'Why did you ask Mr Lilburn and me to explore the woods?' Yumi asked.

Their coffees arrived. Jacobus kept his own counsel until the waiter left.

'Last week, in order to evade Sybil's musicological clutches, I hid in the woods. It was evening. I heard people walking, one of whom was talking. I suppose there could've been more than two, but it sounded like two. They couldn't have come from the veranda because they would have passed by me. If you had found a path coming from the house and going through the woods, I would have thought nothing of it. But since there was no path, it's curious that anyone would have gone that way at night.'

'Was it a man or woman talking?'

'Man.'

'You said you *suppose* there could have been two or more people,' Lilburn asked. 'But how can you be sure there was more than one?'

'Because I assume the man wasn't talking to himself. Any more intelligent questions?'

'I was going to ask if you heard what the man was saying, but perhaps I'll refrain.'

'You do that.'

'So what do we do next, Jake?' Yumi asked.

'It might not be a bad idea to find out who the janitor was that found Schlossberg's body in the practice room. I've got a few—'

'Someone's coming, Jacobus,' Lilburn interrupted. 'From the table in the corner. Perhaps we should change the subject for a moment. Weather or something.'

'Excuse me,' said a voice. Male, early twenties, *sotto voce* but slightly nervous.

'What do you think of the weather, son?' Jacobus asked him.

Yumi kicked Jacobus under the table.

'It's OK, I guess. A little rainy,' the young man answered, sounding confused. 'Kinda warm for the season. Why?'

'Never mind. What do you want?'

'I heard you talking about Aaron Schlossberg.'

'Are you a student at the conservatory?' Yumi asked.

'No, ma'am,' he said. 'CCCC.'

'Yes, yes, yes, yes?' Jacobus replied.

'Cornwall County Community College. We call it 4C. I'm in the medical assistant program. My name's Chase. Chase Anderson.'

'Isn't the college a bit far from here?' Yumi asked.

'Yeah. But I've got a work study at Cooney. To pay my tuition. I empty the trash cans and get rid of the used needles and change the sheets. Stuff like that.'

'So now that we know your bona fides,' Jacobus said, 'why were you eavesdropping on us?'

'I didn't mean to. Really! It's just so quiet today. I couldn't help it.'

'Jake, leave him alone,' Yumi said. 'What would you like to tell us, Chase?'

'I was there when Aaron Schlossberg was brought in. Man, it was not a pretty sight.'

'Thank you for confirming that he was dead,' Jacobus said. 'Now that he's buried I'm sure it will provide great comfort to his widow to know this.'

'Jake, let Chase talk,' Yumi said. 'Can you join us for coffee?'

'No, ma'am. Gotta get back to work. But I thought you should know something.'

'Go ahead,' Jacobus said. 'Ma'am said to let you talk.'

Yumi kicked him again. Harder.

'Well, it's just that they said Aaron Schlossberg died of complications from diabetes.'

'Is that not true?' Lilburn asked.

'Oh, yes. It's true,' Chase said. He hesitated.

'Chase, my boy,' Jacobus said. 'You've got something to tell us, spit it out. We won't bite you. Or at least, they won't.'

'Well,' said Chase, 'they weren't the kind of complications I've seen before.'

'No kidding. The guy was already dead for days.'

'Yes, I know. That's what makes it a little confusing. You see, they've got a dialysis unit at the hospital. So I've seen lots of patients with diabetes coming in for their treatments. Some of them two, three times a week, six hours each time. Some are in really bad shape and come to

121

the hospital in wheelchairs. I help get them in and out of their chairs and set them up in bed. I bring them magazines while they're connected to the dialysis machines and try to make them as comfortable as possible. I've seen a few of those same patients brought in to the ER unconscious. I've even seen them die. But none of them ever looked anything like Professor Schlossberg.'

'In what respect?' Jacobus asked.

'Professor Schlossberg was worse. Much, much worse.'

Jacobus became aware of Haydn's cheery String Quartet in D, Op. 76 no. 4 being played over the restaurant's PA system. *Ingenious composer*, he thought. To be so creative and so fresh with such an economy of material. To have elevated the string-quartet genre almost single-handedly – yes, with an assist from Mozart later on – and doing it while composing literally hundreds of other gems. One of the handful of composers who were rich, famous, *and* happy. Schlossberg had until so recently been one of those, and though, in Jacobus's opinion, Schlossberg wasn't fit to shine Haydn's shoes, the guy did have a following. And now he was dead and this kid, Chase, was taking it upon himself to tell them something that troubled him about it.

'Son,' Jacobus said, 'you said you're a student, right?'

'Yes, sir. At 4C.'

'Thank you for reminding me. Son, having taught many students over the years, and understanding how their minds work or do not work, I am compelled to ask my next question.'

'Yes, sir?'

'You tell us that a corpse looked worse than it should, as if maybe there are good-looking corpses? What do you base that on? What the hell do you really know? You're just a student.'

'Jake, please!' Yumi said.

'No, it's OK,' Chase said. 'You make a good point, sir. I'm not familiar with cadavers. All I can say is that his skin looked kind of blue and like he had a hard time dying. I know that's not much, but . . .' His voice trailed off.

Jacobus waited for more. With none forthcoming, he asked, 'Is that all you have to say?'

'You don't need to believe me. I just thought you might want to know.'

'Well, at least you're honest.'

Jacobus pondered for a moment.

'I tell you what, son. I'll give you a chance to back up your wildly speculative suspicions.'

'How's that, sir?'

'First, stop calling me "sir." I haven't been knighted. Yet. Now, it seems to me you have a knack for getting around the hospital.'

'Part of my job.'

'So I'm thinking it wouldn't look too out of the ordinary if you got your hands on, what do they call it, the coroner's report?'

'You mean the death certificate?'

'Whatever.'

'Jake,' Yumi said, 'that could get Chase in trouble. If he's caught doing something he shouldn't, he could lose his job and get kicked out of school.'

'Hey, don't worry about that!' Chase piped up. 'I'd like to give it a try. It was my mom who

123

wanted me to be a medical assistant. What I really want is to be a detective. I'll be really careful.'

Chase had the bit in his mouth, said goodbye, and ran off to fulfill his inner Philip Marlowe, but Jacobus wasn't sure where to go next. Yumi solved his problem for him.

'Tomorrow's my regular teaching day here,' she said, 'and it's the first day after spring break so I can't miss it. I'm thinking it's too late to drive back to the city if I'm just going to have to come back in the morning, so maybe you can go back to New York with Mr Lilburn.'

'Excuse me,' Lilburn said, 'but delighted as I would be to have Mr Jacobus accompany me, I, too, have to stay here in order to interview Schlossberg's colleagues for my piece.'

With little choice, Jacobus agreed to stay another night at the Campus Inn.

'It might break Nathaniel's heart, though,' he said.

Yumi offered to call Nathaniel with the change in plans. She assured Jacobus she would break the news gently and try to convince him it would all be for the better.

Eleven

The next morning, Yumi knocked on Jacobus's door at the inn and invited him to sit in on her half-dozen lessons – as long as he kept his comments to himself – to help him pass the time.

'You think they practiced over spring break?' he asked.

'They could be a little rusty,' Yumi conceded.

'Then I'll let you have fun on your own.'

At his request, Yumi dropped Jacobus off at Stuyvesant Hall, the music building where Schlossberg's body had been found. She asked him if he needed her to help show him around and he told her no, getting lost there was part of his plan. She pointedly did not ask what the rest of the plan was.

Once inside, Jacobus wandered aimlessly, not caring whether he was seen or not. He heard footsteps and chatter pass him in both directions. Some students asked if he needed assistance, but he consistently declined. He smelled coffee and heard multiple conversations at one end of the main foyer and assumed they emanated from a canteen or café. He went in the opposite direction.

The tip of Jacobus's cane slipped more than once on the corridor's linoleum floors. Others might have appreciated that they had been newly waxed over the vacation, but for him it was an annoying and potentially dangerous hindrance that only served to slow him down. Alternating his cane tapping from floor to wall like a windshield wiper, he came to a recess in the wall and found a doorknob. He entered a room, not knowing what it was.

'Can I help you?' a young man asked in a quiet voice.

'This the men's room?' Jacobus asked.

The young man laughed.

'Sorry, sir. You'll have to go to the end of the hallway for that. It's right before the elevator. This is the Lievenstock Music Library.'

'No kidding. You sure?'

'Yes, sir. I'm sure.'

'Damn. They must have given me wrong directions.'

Jacobus returned to the corridor and continued in the same direction he had been going, passing the men's room and the elevator, until reaching a heavy door. After shouldering it open, his tapping on the floor resonated with a metallic bling, putting him on the alert for a stairway. His tapping continued to click like a typewriter in the industrial-style stairwell as he trudged upward to determine how many stories the building had. Thankfully, only two. He was already winded. Next time, he decided, he would take the elevator.

He wandered along the second floor. Offices with little embossed plaques on their doors enabled Jacobus to read the names of professors with his fingers. He was amused to find that Professor Gunter Braun and Professor Tanner

126

Evans, the dueling theory teachers, had adjacent offices.

Jacobus returned to the stairwell and descended as far as the stairs would take him. The air was cooler than on the main floor. He heard the hum of the building's innards and concluded he was in the basement. His cane soon found the object of his search, the students' prefabricated practice modules. He was a student long before such things were invented, and never having taught at a music school, he had never been inside one. He put his ear against a thick glass door, and hearing only silence within, knocked. There being no response, he tugged it open, but only with great effort. The door was tightly fitted with thick gaskets, making the room impressively sound-proof. Entering, he extended his cane in all directions, finding that he could almost reach the sides of the small room with little more than a step or two in any direction. There was no piano in this one. Only a music stand that he discovered by knocking it over.

He left the room and continued down a wide corridor created by parallel lines of modules on either side of him. Some were large enough to fit a piano, which he determined by sliding the end of his cane along their width and length. As he went behind one of them, squirming in the narrow space between the back of the module and the concrete wall of the basement, his cane came in contact with a thick cable, lying snakelike on the floor. He slid his cane along it, which led to a fixture at the base of the module's exterior, which he tapped with his cane and received a metallic ping in response. Sliding his cane in the other direction led to a junction box in the basement wall. The cable clearly served as an electrical umbilical cord, providing power to illuminate and ventilate the module. He considered what the consequences would have been, both to the module and himself, had he tripped over the cable. Considering himself lucky he hadn't, he decided it would be smarter to restrict his exploration to the safety of the corridor, to which he backtracked. Passing by one module after another he imagined a line of aquariums, each with a different species of exotic, tropical fish in its own isolated little world: the solitary glimmering black Liszt Piano fish; a quintet of brilliantly golden Gabrieli Brass Canzoni fish; a shimmering pastel of Debussy Clair de Lune fish that floated effortlessly.

Having neglected to feel for switches in the previous module, Jacobus entered another. Inside, he found a pair of them next to the door. He turned the first one on and, as he expected, an internal fan, barely audible, started up. By making the modules soundproof, outside airflow was cut off, necessitating a ventilation system. Flipping the other switch, he heard a fluorescent light blink on and begin to hum. He then turned off the fan and waited for his body and the light, which was still on, to heat the room. Within a few minutes it was already stuffy.

Jacobus turned off the light and left the module. No doubt they were an effective and cost-efficient means to provide essential practice space for students. But they seemed so antiseptic and unnatural. So sterile. So uninspiring. So unmusical! Not the kind of place he imagined Schlossberg, the happy wanderer, would have wanted to visit, let alone die in. Jacobus retraced his path back upstairs to the main floor to pursue the next step of his plan. He heard a student walking in his direction.

'Excuse me, young lady,' Jacobus said. 'Where can I find the janitor?'

She told him to stay right there. She would find him and be back 'in a jiffy.'

A few steps away, she stopped.

'How did you know I wasn't a guy?' she asked.

'Footsteps. Scent. Swishy-swishy skirt. Even without those it's fifty-fifty, right?'

Three jiffies later, she returned.

Jacobus sniffed pine-scented cleanser.

'Mr Clean?' Jacobus asked.

'Sam Consiglio. At your service,' the janitor said.

'You wax these floors over spring break?'

'Yeah, that was me. I like to keep 'em nice and shiny.'

'You ain't kidding. Know where can I get a pair of ice skates?'

'Not in my job description. You need help walking?'

'I need help finding my hat,' Jacobus said. 'Seems I've lost it. I was wondering if anyone's turned it in.'

'What's it look like?'

'How would I know?' Jacobus guffawed, as if it were a punchline to an old joke. 'But there can't have been too many.'

'Nope. No one's turned anything in.'

'Maybe you could help me find it, then. I might've dropped it downstairs.'

Jacobus went back down to the basement with Consiglio.

'Many of these practice rooms?' Jacobus asked.

'Yep. Thirty.'

'Only thirty? With all these students? How does that work out?'

'They sign up for time slots on a sheet taped to each door. They're allowed up to three hours a day. Any more practicing they need, they've gotta go do it somewhere else. They're thinking of putting up a new building with more practice rooms, but that'll be at least another five or ten million the way things cost these days. Could you have left your hat inside a practice room?'

'Possible. I did go inside a piano room. Just wanted to play a few notes.'

'You a pianist?'

'Not really. I'd just heard there were some good pianos here.'

'I wouldn't go that far.'

'No? You mean someone waxed poetic as slippery as you waxed the floors?'

'That's a good one. You could say that. The pianos down here aren't so bad, but the students – they hammer them pretty hard. The Steinways are in the teachers' studios. They're the good ones. And of course, you've got the concert pianos over at the auditorium.'

'I heard that one of the profs died here last week.'

'Yeah. Aaron Schlossberg. We were on national news.'

Jacobus noted use of the word 'we.'

'What'd he teach?' Jacobus asked.

'He was a composer. Famous. I found him in Nineteen. Not a pretty sight. Something I'd like to forget about.'

'Must've been tough. Don't talk about it if you don't want to.'

Jacobus knew that was a sure way to get Consiglio to talk. Who wouldn't want to talk about finding a famous man dead?

'Nah, it's OK,' Consiglio said. 'The counselor told me it would be better for me if I do. They have free grief counseling here. Go figure. Me, getting grief counseling.'

'They say it can be helpful.'

'Hey, don't get me wrong. If it's free, I'll take it. But, between you and me and the wall, I'm not grieving. It's just that when you come across a dead body that's been sitting in an unventilated room for a few days . . .'

'Say no more.' Which of course meant, 'say more.'

When Consiglio didn't take the bait, Jacobus prompted, 'Heard he was composing his opera.'

'Decomposing, more like it. Sorry. That was just a joke.'

The punchline sounded rehearsed, as if he had been reciting it to anyone he could collar. He would probably never get any closer to fame.

Jacobus laughed.

'It's a good joke,' Jacobus said. So good that he had heard it every time a composer died in the last fifty years.

'Just out of curiosity,' Jacobus continued, 'how

come it took you a few days before you found him? Took that long for him to pass the smell test?'

'That's a good one, too. Nah. It being spring break, me and the wife went up to Mohonk resort for a little R & R. Up by New Paltz? You know where I'm talking? It's only an hour from here.'

'I think I've heard of it.'

'It's all we can afford on our salaries. No Bahamas for us. But it's close and it's really nice, you know?'

'So what brought you back? During spring break, I mean.'

'Overtime. I make time-and-a-quarter if I work over vacations. Anyway, the kids usually leave this building a mess and I figured I'd get a head start cleaning it up before they came back and junked it up again. I got more than I bargained for.'

'I'd say so,' Jacobus replied. 'So this Aaron Schlossberg was just sitting at the piano.'

Consiglio must have thought Jacobus, who was thinking out loud, was simply reaffirming the prevailing theory that Schlossberg had been composing when he died.

'Right,' Consiglio said.

'Can you show me Nineteen?' Jacobus asked. 'Maybe that's where I left my hat.'

'Sure. Why not? It's been all cleaned up. You can't smell nothing anymore.'

Consiglio escorted Jacobus into Nineteen. Jacobus sat at the piano, felt the keyboard, and plunked out a Bach Two-Part Invention to satisfy any lingering doubt Consiglio might have had about his honest intentions.

'Any sign of my hat here?' he asked.

Consiglio said no.

'Damn,' Jacobus said, with great conviction. 'So this is where it happened? Where Aaron Schlossberg died?' Jacobus asked, as if it was Abraham Lincoln's seat at the Ford Theater.

'Yep. Right where you're sitting.'

'Whoa!' Jacobus said and lifted his posterior off the bench. He continued to play, correcting the wrong notes, which were unintentional and frequent.

'And other than the shock of seeing a dead man, was there anything else out of the ordinary?'

'Can't say there was. The light was off so it was dark.'

'The fan, too?' Jacobus asked.

'Yeah. But to tell you the truth, I didn't spend more than about one second in the room. It gave me the creeps.'

'No kidding. So you went and called the cops?'

'Campus security. And they came and took care of everything else. Next time I saw the room he was gone. And the room was clean. Thank the Lord.'

'Amen,' Jacobus said. 'And what happened to the music?'

'What music?'

'The music on the piano. The music he was composing.'

'There wasn't no music.'

Twelve

'There you are!' said a woman's voice, imperiously. 'I've been looking everywhere for you.'

'And to whom do I owe the displeasure?' Jacobus asked.

'Connie Jean Hawkins. I am Dean Hedge's assistant. May I ask you a question?'

'By all means.'

'Just what do you think you are you doing here, Mr Jacobus?'

Jacobus remained silent.

'I repeat—'

'I heard you the first time.'

'And?'

'I said, you could ask a question. I didn't say I would answer it.'

'Dean Hedge wants to see you in his office. Now.'

Jacobus considered the response he would like to have delivered but balanced that against the likely detrimental effect it would have on Yumi's position on the faculty.

'Lead the way, Madame Defarge.' And to Consiglio, 'Thanks, Sam. If you find my hat, just ask Connie Jean to deliver it to me.'

The administration building was farther than Jacobus expected. As it was another pleasant day, and as he was not looking forward to what he anticipated would be a confrontation with Hedge, he dawdled, much to Connie Jean's growing irritation. Perhaps it was the afternoon warmth seeping into his old bones, or perhaps it was the scent of blossoming cherry trees, because contrary to Jacobus's natural inclination to use blunt force when seeking information, he decided a sunnier, more conciliatory tack might bear riper fruit.

'Sun feels good, doesn't it?' he said.

'Yes.'

'Must be nice to work here. Beautiful campus and all.'

'I've grown very attached to the conservatory.'

'I understand you're Hedge's main gatekeeper,' he said.

'If by that you mean I'm in charge of the day-to-day functioning of the conservatory, that would be correct.'

'I heard you do all the scheduling. Concerts, rehearsals. The works.'

'"Do" is not accurate. Coordinate would be accurate.'

'You get time to relax over spring break? Like the students and faculty? Great time of year.'

'Not on your life. I've had to finalize planning for all juries and senior recitals at the end of the semester. We've got our "Going Baroque" festival. And then there's summer session.'

'Juries?' Jacobus backtracked.

'The graduating students have end-of-year recitals. The non-graduating students have to perform the repertoire they've studied during the semester at faculty juries in their division to be allowed to continue in the program. It's a nightmare to schedule. Rounding up the faculty is like

135

herding cats, let alone getting hundreds of students signed up for fifteen minute slots without them trampling over each other.'

'So there was a lot going on during spring break?'

'Thankfully not. It's full speed ahead from the first week of January until then, so we don't book anything during breaks. It gives everyone, except me, a chance to decompress before the final sprint.'

'So campus was deserted last week?'

'Except for maintenance, yes. I had to coordinate that also. The physical plant gets worse every year. With our careful stewardship, we've extended life spans of some of these buildings beyond their expected obsolescence, but we're reaching a breaking point. Hopefully, we'll be getting the Feldstein money for the new construction we desperately need. In some of these old buildings we had leaks to patch up, and I had to call the—'

'So you're saying the buildings were locked up?'

'Essentially. Yes.'

'So what do you suppose Schlossberg was doing in a student practice room in a locked building?'

The ice returned.

'I have no idea.'

So much for the spring thaw.

There was no more conversation, except for 'This way, Mr Jacobus,' from time to time. Connie Jean made his name sound like an accusation.

They entered the Lievenstock Administration Building, originally Theodesia Lievenstock's family mansion. Connie Jean led Jacobus to the grand staircase centered in the marble foyer. Jacobus grasped a heavily varnished oak bannister, which splayed outward in a curve, and ascended. The tap of his cane echoed on polished stone steps. He imagined the portraits of three centuries of the Dutch Lievenstocks casting their dowdy and smug gaze down upon him. Connie Jean escorted him along a carpeted hallway and knocked on a solid oak door. Without waiting for a response, she opened it and the two of them entered.

'Please sit down, Mr Jacobus,' Charles Hedge said. It was a command rather than an invitation. Clearly, he was no longer the pat-'em-on-the-back happy camper.

Connie Jean led him to a chair and moved off to his left. The room was redolent of polished wood and fresh spring air entering through an open window. To Jacobus's right were a barely audible creak of a chair and the scent of an after-shave he recognized.

'Mr Jacobus,' Hedge said, 'I won't beat around the bush. This spring break has been a bad week. A disastrous week. First we had half our faculty taken ill. Then we had the tragedy of Aaron Schlossberg's death. And now this.'

'What "this" are you talking about?'

'When we invited you here to present a master-class, we did so with high expectations. And, may I add, the invitation was offered at the strong urging of your protégé, Yumi Shinagawa, who I'm sure you're aware has been one of our most esteemed adjunct faculty.' Hedge ominously elongated the 'has been.'

137

Hedge paused as if waiting for Jacobus to respond. But not having been asked a question, Jacobus remained silent. He wasn't going to snap at such obvious bait.

'What you may not know,' Hedge continued, 'is that the invitation was made over the objections of some others on the faculty who know your reputation of tearing down, rather than building up, students' self-esteem. Do you understand what I'm talking about?'

'Get to the point, Charlie. I've got a pedicure appointment and my toenails are starting to curl.'

'As you wish, Mr Jacobus. At your masterclass last week, you undermined the authority of Elwood Dunster, one of our most valued and senior violin professors, who, I clearly note, is a tenured faculty member, not merely an adjunct. You did so by contradicting his teachings in a condescending and destructive way. You—'

'Bullshit! How the hell could I know who the students' teachers were if I didn't even know the students' names? They could've—'

'Please, Mr Jacobus. Your protestations of innocence don't do your reputation justice. From what Ms Shinagawa has told us of your skills, you're able to tell the color of a violinist's shoelaces from the way they play vibrato. Do you really expect us to believe you had no idea who was playing?'

'All right. So what? I made the students aware of their shortcomings. That is something I would imagine Dunster does as well. At least he should. That's part of teaching. Not all of it, but part of it. Sure, you want to tell them when they do

138

something well. But if all you do is tell them how wonderful they are, they're not going to get better, are they? They won't know how.'

Jacobus sat back but decided there was more to be said.

'I've had some pretty decent students over the years, and I've had some pretty lousy ones, too. I tell all of them what the challenges are. How hard they're going to have to work to get to their goal, whatever that goal is. Sometimes the struggle is almost insurmountable, but the choice is theirs. If they're determined, I help however I can. But it's up to them. Yes, sometimes they get pissed off when I don't paint the rosy picture they want to see, but in the end I've gotten more "thank-yous" than "fuck-yous."'

'I haven't invited you here to listen to your offensive language or your defense of the pluses and minuses of your teaching philosophy, Mr Jacobus,' Hedge continued, though in Jacobus's mind that was exactly the conversation Hedge had prompted. 'Because in this case, the minuses have clearly prevailed.'

'If some egos have been bruised now,' Jacobus said, 'maybe they'll end up better musicians later.'

'No. Not maybe. Not at all is more like it. I told you last week that I had hoped your master-class would set a precedent. Well, it has, but not in the way I had anticipated. You see, Mr Jacobus, for the first time in the history of the Kinderhoek Conservatory a student has withdrawn from the program in midstream. Audrey Rollins, who was to graduate in two months' time, has dropped out. Because of you, Mr Jacobus, and you alone.

I thought you'd want to know. Do you know what this means?'

Since Jacobus didn't know what it meant, at least yet, he remained silent. Yumi had said Dean the Bean was always smiling. Jacobus had a feeling she was not entirely accurate.

Hedge went on. 'It means that a masterclass series is out the window for a very long time because the funding for it has been scared away. It means that we can no longer honestly state in our literature that Kinderhoek has a one-hundred-percent graduation rate. As it is, we might have to destroy and rewrite all of our brochures. That is not without its costs. Beyond that, though, think of what this has done to our fund-raising efforts! We were hoping to commence a capital campaign next year, and our perfect graduation record was going to be one of our main bullet points. It's something we've been proud of and which no other program can claim. And our major gift from the Feldstein family is now in jeopardy. You probably don't know about capital campaigns, but until you have at least a third of your resources already in hand, you're courting disaster.

'You've potentially cost us many millions of dollars, Mr Jacobus. Dollars that would have flowed into building a new practice facility, a state-of-the-art recording studio, purchasing new critical editions for the orchestras. I could go on.'

'No doubt,' Jacobus said.

'Ms Hawkins has a check for you for your participation last week. She will give it to you on your way out. Thank you for coming.'

Jacobus had no more to say. Actually, he did.

140

As he left the room, he turned his head toward where he had heard the chair creak, and whispered, 'Atta boy, Dunster.'

As they approached the stairway, Connie Jean pressed the envelope containing the check into Jacobus's right hand, requiring him to shift his cane to his left. Holding on to the bannister was a bit precarious with the envelope in his hand.

Two things had surprised him. It was not unexpected that Hedge would be annoyed at the result of the masterclass, but the level of his ire seemed disproportionate to Jacobus's alleged transgressions. Then again, Yumi had been as livid as he'd ever heard her after the class. Maybe his skin was getting thicker than he thought. Or maybe everyone else's was getting thinner.

The second thing was how cursorily Hedge had mentioned Schlossberg's death. Almost as if it were of little consequence. Maybe Hedge didn't think it was any of his business. But still.

And, yes, Jacobus thought, there was a third thing. Audrey Rollins's behavior. First, the enthusiasm. Then the recalcitrance. And then the sudden withdrawal from the school. There was something artificial about that.

He considered trying to find her to get an explanation. Surely the conservatory would have her address. But what were the chances that Connie Jean or Dunster would give him that information now?

Jacobus had counted nineteen steps going up the stairs, but in his musings on the way down he lost track. The lurch back into the present caused him to misstep. He grasped for the bannister, but because it was curved and polished, and because he had the damn check in his hand, his grip didn't hold. He began to stumble, and unaccustomed to holding his cane in his left hand, he was unable to regain his balance. At the last instant, he felt Connie Jean's hand on his back and he reached out to grab it but the angle was too awkward. Releasing the cane and the envelope so that he could use his hands to protect himself, Jacobus fell. He rolled to the bottom of the stairs, landing heavily on the marble floor. His cane clattered down after him.

'What's happened?' Charles Hedge called from the top of the stairs.

'Mr Jacobus has fallen. I think he's hurt,' Connie Jean said.

'Well, call the hospital. I suppose.'

Thirteen

He hadn't hit his head. That was the only body part for which he could make that claim, a conclusion his bruised body confirmed as he attempted to shift position in the hospital bed. He hadn't lost consciousness but wished he had. His ankle throbbed and his chest felt as if Nathaniel was standing on it. They took X-rays and gave him painkillers, which made him doze. When he awoke, they summoned a doctor to his room.

'Mr Jacobus, I'm Dr Simons. I've got some good news and some bad news for you,' he said.

'Just give me the good news and leave,' Jacobus replied.

'I'm glad to see you still have a sense of humor.'

'Who's joking?'

Unable to think of a response, Simons simply snorted.

'Amazingly enough,' Simons continued, 'X-rays revealed no broken bones. Bruised ribs, a badly sprained ankle. Plenty of black and blue. But that won't keep you laid up long.'

Jacobus replayed the entire stairway sequence over and over in his head.

Simons cleared his throat.

'You still here?' Jacobus asked.

'There's another thing.'

'I've missed lunch?'

'If only. Let me ask you a question, Mr Jacobus. Were you ever a smoker?'

'Cigarettes and salamis. My doc gave me a choice of quitting one of them.'

'I'll get straight to the point, Mr Jacobus. Chest X-rays picked up a not insignificant growth on your left lung. It could be totally benign. It might be something else. I would recommend we do a biopsy right—'

'No biopsy.'

'But in order to—'

'I said no biopsy.'

'It's just standard—'

'Are you deaf? No biopsy and if you violate doctor–patient confidentiality I'll get your license revoked. Not a word leaves this room. Do you understand?'

'If you insist.'

'I insist. Now give me some more pills and get the hell out of here.'

The next time he awoke, Yumi was at his side.

'Hey,' she said. 'Welcome back to the world. How are you feeling?'

'Like I've died and come back to shit.'

'Always accentuating the positive.' She handed him a glass of water, which he sipped, drooled some, choked on the rest, and handed back to her.

'What are you doing here?' he asked.

'I heard you'd been causing trouble again, so I cancelled the rest of my students and came over. Anything I can get you?' she asked.

'Scotch on the rocks.'

'Soon enough. Dr Simons said they just need to keep you overnight for observation and should be able to release you tomorrow, barring any unforeseen complications.'

'Is that all he said?'

'No.'

'What else?' Jacobus felt his bile rising.

'Since nothing was broken,' Yumi replied, 'he said it didn't matter whether you're in misery here or at home.'

Jacobus relaxed. 'That's comforting.'

'And that you won't be able to walk on your ankle for a while. They didn't think giving you crutches would be a good idea—'

'Why not?'

'They don't think you have the strength, and if you fell on it again you'd be out of commission for a long time.'

'Well, if you think I'm going to rot in bed—'

'They're giving you a wheelchair.'

Though Jacobus had been blind for decades it had only been in recent years he used a cane. And now he couldn't even walk. No eyes. No legs. And soon maybe no lungs. Jacobus considered how many more parts he could afford to lose before surrendering his independence. But he still had his ears. And his mouth, which he opened, protest perched on his lips.

'And before you say another word,' Yumi said, 'we're going to find someone to wheel you around until you're back on your feet.'

There was a knock at the door.

'Hey, Mr Jacobus, it's me. Chase Anderson. From Chops? Heard you were here, so I ducked out of the laundry room for a minute. How are we doing?'

145

'How the hell would I know how *we* are doing? *You* just walked in!'

Anderson laughed.

'That's just how they teach us. "How are we doing?" "Are we fasting today?" "Are we ready for some applesauce?" Hospital speak.'

'In that case,' Jacobus said, 'we would be doing a lot better had we not fallen down a staircase. Class dismissed.'

'No problemo, but I thought you might want to know I got hold of Professor Schlossberg's death certificate.'

'Then have a seat, young man,' Jacobus said, 'and test out your bedside manner. How did you manage that trick?'

'Simple. I asked to see it.'

'Ah. The direct approach. And?'

'I brought a copy. It looks a lot like my college loan form.'

'Such as?'

'Legal name, sex, social security number, age, date of birth, birthplace, address, father's name—'

'Young man, is there anything in the certificate that might be worth my few remaining moments on earth?'

'There's the cause of death and the manner of death.'

'What's the difference?' Yumi asked.

'Hey, I just learned that in class! Cause of death is the disease or injury that was responsible for the death, like if someone was stabbed in the heart or was in a car accident.'

'Or lung cancer?' Jacobus asked.

'Or lung cancer. Manner of death are the general circumstances. Lung cancer would be considered natural. Stabbed in the heart would probably be homicide. There's also suicide, accident, therapeutic complications – like if Mr Jacobus died of an infection from his sprained ankle. If they're not sure, they call it "pending investigation."'

'And what does Schlossberg's death certificate say?'

'The cause of death – that's number 32, Part 1a – says "immediate cause, renal and hepatic failure." Part 1b says "cirrhosis of the liver, advanced kidney disease." Part 1c says "complications due to diabetes." Y'see, it starts with the specific and gets more general. The manner of death – that's number 37 – the box checked is "natural."'

'So we were wrong, Jake,' Yumi said. 'Maybe we were just being overly suspicious.'

Jacobus appreciated Yumi's use of the word 'we.' In a way, he was relieved that there would be no mystery surrounding Schlossberg's death. He had had enough of the Kinderhoek Conservatory and was happy enough to get out alive.

'Probably, but not necessarily,' Chase said.

'Meaning?' Jacobus asked.

'Death certificates are issued real quick. They're mainly so that the family can bury their relatives and insurance companies can start processing claims. They don't always tell the whole story. At least that's what I learned in class.'

'Where does one get the "whole story"?' Jacobus asked. 'Or is that next semester?'

'I'd have to get the coroner's report for that,' Chase said. 'That might not be so easy.'

'But there wasn't any autopsy. He was six feet under before the bagels were even defrosted.'

'A coroner's report isn't an autopsy. In fact, a lot of coroners aren't even doctors. Coroners can be elected or appointed. Some are sheriffs or funeral home directors. And then there are the medical examiners, who usually are medical doctors but aren't necessarily forensic pathologists trained in death investigation. It's very confusing.'

'Think you can find the coroner's report?' Jacobus asked.

'I'll do my best. Fortunately, 4C spring break is this week so I'll have some time on my hands.'

Yumi had an idea.

'Would you like to make some extra cash during your break?' she asked.

'Are you kidding?' he said. 'How?'

'Pushing an old blind man around in a wheelchair.'

After Chase left, Yumi told Jacobus she needed to leave to reschedule her students. The conservatory required teachers to give each student fourteen hours of lessons per semester, and with the end of the year quickly approaching, along with juries and senior recitals, she was in danger of falling behind.

'How many did you end up teaching today?' Jacobus asked.

'Just two, including Mia Cheng, who you heard last week.'

'The Mendelssohn girl. With the mercenary parents.'

'Yes, that's the one.'

'Talented. A little kiss-ass, but talented. How did she do?'

'Today? Not very well. She's usually totally focused. Today she couldn't concentrate and had memory slips all over the place. Maybe it was the week off.'

That didn't sound like the MO of the student he had heard.

'Yeah. Maybe.'

Jacobus had a thought.

'She a friend of Dunster's student? The Rollins girl?'

'I think so. They were assigned to play a Haydn quartet together last semester. Why?'

'Might be worth a chat with her. Two violin students, strangely unhappy.'

'Lots of violin students are unhappy. Look at all of yours.'

'The reasons for that are perfectly reasonable. I said, *strangely* unhappy.'

There was a knock at the door.

'*Ye who enter*—,' Jacobus called out.

'Good God, Jacobus!' It was Lilburn, bursting in. 'What have you gotten yourself into this time?'

It was a thought-provoking question, for which Jacobus had no ready answer.

'Word is out that Hedge gave you the old heave-ho,' Lilburn continued.

'In more ways than one, maybe,' Jacobus said.

'What do you mean . . .? No, you can't think he intentionally pushed you down the stairs!'

149

'Not him. His harpy.'

'Connie Jean Hawkins?' Yumi asked. 'She wouldn't do anything like that.'

'No? She handed me my check in my right hand even though I was holding my cane with it and my left hand was free. Why did she do that? I wonder. When I lost my balance she did reach out to me, though to be very honest I'm not a hundred percent sure whether it was to rescue me or to give me a little nudge. I can't say it was intentional, but I can't say it was unintentional, either.'

'Jake,' Yumi said, 'I just can't imagine her doing that. Even I wouldn't have done something like that, and I've known you a lot longer.'

'Don't make me laugh,' Jacobus said. 'I'm too sore.'

'I suppose you're sore in more ways than one, also,' Lilburn said. 'As they say, no good deed goes unpunished.'

'News travels fast, eh?'

'Elwood Dunster couldn't restrain himself. That's how I found out you'd been raked over the coals. He's the last one I interviewed, but I suppose everyone on the faculty knows by now.'

'I suppose I won't be bestowed with an honorary doctorate in the foreseeable future. Did your interviewees provide any interesting morsels about Schlossberg?'

'He's already had two biographies written about him,' Lilburn said, 'so, if I may quip, most of his life is an open book.'

Neither Jacobus nor Yumi laughed. Lilburn cleared his throat and continued.

'Of course, I spoke to Sybil Baker-Hulme first. She has been the true stalwart in all this. Iron Lady Two, I call her. Not only is she in mourning for her husband, she told me the chamber music conductor, Tawroszewicz, is considering suing her for causing him gastric distress last week.'

'But those weren't her mushrooms. They were her husband's!' Yumi said. 'She had nothing to do with it.'

'Tell that to the lawyers,' Jacobus said. 'Maybe they'll understand the difference between a musicologist and a mycologist, though I doubt it. Did Tawroszewicz corroborate that?'

'I did interview him,' Lilburn said. 'There was clearly no love lost between him and Schlossberg.'

'You mean between him and Sybil,' corrected Jacobus.

'No, I mean Aaron Schlossberg. Tawroszewicz described Schlossberg as a "condescending bastard," quote unquote. He seems to feel that way about the entire academic side of the faculty, Sybil not excepting. I think maybe he was disgruntled that Schlossberg had composed a piece for just about everyone on the faculty except for him. I chalk it up to professional jealousy.'

Jacobus was not sure what to think. 'He and Schlossberg seemed pretty gruntled to me at the equinox party.'

'Maybe they were merely putting on a good face for the stranger in town.'

'Maybe. Anything else uninteresting you found out?' Jacobus asked.

'Not much. I did speak to Harold Handy, the music historian—'

'Another one who doesn't seem to like Sybil.'

'Yes. But he had great admiration for Schlossberg. Felt he had an excellent grasp of the relationship between the history and aesthetics of music, which informed his own compositions. He was greatly looking forward to *Anwar and Yitzhak*, which, alas, in all likelihood will never see the light of day.'

'Pity,' said Jacobus and almost believed it.

'What might be of interest to your particular inquiry,' Lilburn continued, 'was that Handy implied that Schlossberg's grasp was not only of music.'

'Meaning?'

'Meaning that Schlossberg wasn't averse to caressing young ladies' derrieres. Handy didn't come right out and say it, but the innuendo was quite clear. He had a gleam in his eye when he said that Schlossberg had a "hands-on approach" to teaching. I suspect he didn't want to state anything for the record that the Widow Sybil could later sue him for. Knowing their strained relationship, I could imagine that would be a real concern.'

There was a knock at the door.

'*Ye who enter—*,' Jacobus called out.

'How are we feeling?' a nurse asked.

A woman, and a young one, Jacobus guessed, whose voice was too cheery for his taste.

'Not sure,' Jacobus said. 'You'll have to feel me and then I'll feel you.'

'Jake,' Yumi said. 'That's disgusting.'

'That's OK,' the nurse said. 'I think Mr Jacobus is cute.'

'Now *that's* disgusting,' Jacobus said.

'I'll second that,' Lilburn said. 'I'm heading back to the city. I might be back up in a day or two. Call me if you need anything, Jacobus.'

Yumi also had to leave, as she had a Harmonium rehearsal the next morning.

'I'm sure you'll be in good hands with the nurse,' she said.

Fourteen

Tuesday, March 31

Jacobus had long since eschewed the tray of what the nurse referred to as breakfast, and still Chase Anderson had not arrived. A lilac-scented breeze wafting through his open window proclaimed a beautiful spring morning. He was antsy to get his ass out of bed and leave the hospital and dispel the dispiriting thoughts of cancer and the premonition of death that went with it. Death in itself didn't bother him a bit. How many times had he even yearned for it? But a long, slow death in a hospital? Chemo? Radiation? Hospital food? He would rather be hit by a train.

Under normal circumstances Jacobus would have taken that train back to New York City, but with his bum ankle it was more than impractical. He was trapped. Yumi's Harmonium schedule made it impossible for her to drive up to Kinnetonka Crossing, and Nathaniel's Volkswagen Rabbit was in its death throes at the mechanic's, duct tape notwithstanding. Lilburn offered Jacobus's sole hope. He had called Jacobus to tell him he was on his way back to campus to conduct more interviews and would be there at least overnight.

'Don't you have a deadline?' Jacobus had asked Lilburn.

'With a retrospective, my editor gives me some flexibility. Deadlines for the dead aren't nearly as pressing as concert reviews of living, breathing, curly-haired maestros.'

They arranged to meet at the inn that afternoon, and Jacobus would get a ride back to the city with him the next day.

Jacobus, cursing Anderson's tardiness, inched his body to the side of the bed. Leveraging most of his weight on his uninjured leg, he tested the waters with his sprained ankle, tightly wrapped with an Ace bandage. When his foot made contact with the ground, Jacobus howled in pain. There was a knock at the door.

'Are we still hurting?' the nurse asked, with a smiley, pouty voice, as if she were talking to a toddler.

'I'd say we're about ready to kill someone,' Jacobus said, through gritted teeth.

'Well, don't you worry. We'll be feeling better in a jiffy. Let's hop you into your wheelchair because there's someone special waiting for you in the lobby who can't wait to see you!'

'Are we ready to go?' Chase Anderson asked when Jacobus emerged from the elevator.

'One of us may not survive this day,' Jacobus said.

'Goodbye, Mr Jacobus,' the nurse said after he had been discharged. 'And don't forget our RICE.'

'Rice is going to get our ankle better?' he asked, thoroughly perplexed.

'R is for rest. We want to rest our ankle and not put any weight on it. I is for ice to keep down the swelling. C is for compression because we don't want our ligaments to stretch any more. And E is for—'

'Enough!'

Guided by Anderson, Jacobus bumped over the cobblestone campus paths in his wheelchair. He took a deep breath, inventing and testing a theory on the spot that if he made vigorous inhalation of fresh air a routine activity it would shrivel up 'the not insignificant growth' on his lung. The smell of freshly mown grass was accompanied by the whir of a well-oiled lawn mower, distant enough to not totally obscure the calls of a pair of robins much closer. As the birds' calls came from stationary points, Jacobus assumed they were perched in trees, which considering the unusually warm spring, would presumably be just bursting into leaf.

At first, Jacobus had lost sleep at the thought of giving up his independence to a wheelchair. But when all he had to do was tell Anderson where he wanted to go and Anderson did the rest, he decided having a full-time chauffeur was not so bad. No worries about stepping into oncoming traffic or dog shit, or tripping over ill-positioned shrubbery. He could use his brain to actually think instead of plotting where to place his next step.

'Stuyvesant Hall,' he barked. He had a couple of questions for Sam Consiglio, the janitor.

'You ever see that television show, *Ironsides*?' Chase asked.

'What kind of idiot question is that?' Jacobus asked, interrupted from his thoughts, the warm sun on his face, and his inhalation experiment.

'Sorry,' Anderson said. 'I keep forgetting you can't see. Anyway, Ironsides was this police detective who solved crimes from a wheelchair. I was thinking you're a lot like him.'

'Who played him? Olivier?'

'Who's Olivier? Raymond Burr.'

'Ah! Of Perry Mason fame. That show I was able to see. What makes you think we have a crime here?'

'Just you, really. But it's cool thinking there might be one.'

Jacobus shook his head and didn't bother to reply. Distant sprays of music gradually became louder as they approached Stuyvesant Hall. A few minutes later he felt himself being pushed up its inclined handicap ramp.

'Go right,' he said to Anderson. 'To the elevator.'

They descended into the basement. A muted cacophony from the practice rooms was a clear signal that spring break was ancient history. From among the various threads of Mozart, Chopin, Gershwin, and Debussy, played by pianos, clarinets, violins, and singers, came the familiar strains of Vivaldi's 'Spring.'

Jacobus's initial thought was that Hedge was wrong or had lied about Audrey Rollins dropping out. Then, straining his ears, he realized it was too good to be her playing. *Was it Yumi?* It sounded like her. He listened some more. *No.* It lacked the confident flexibility that a musician gains from years of experience. *It must be Yumi's student, Mia Something.*

'Take me to the Vivaldi,' Jacobus said to Anderson.

'Which one is that? I don't know much about music.'

'Do you at least know what a violin sounds like?' Jacobus asked in exasperation.

'Yeah. I guess.'

'How many do you hear right now?'

Jacobus waited.

'Two,' Anderson said, finally.

'Well, then, we have a fifty-fifty chance, don't we?'

At the second module they went to, Anderson had to knock hard on the glass door to get Mia's attention, as her back was to them and her concentration level high. When she did eventually open the door she first sounded pleased, then alarmed, at Jacobus's unexpected visit.

'Dr Jacobus!' she said. 'What happened to you?'

'Soccer injury. I heard you practicing.'

'I hope you weren't listening very long. I must sound terrible!'

Anderson wheeled Jacobus into the practice module. With the three of them, and Jacobus in his wheelchair, plus a baby grand piano and assorted music stands, the room was cramped. Jacobus told Chase Anderson he could go upstairs to the coffee shop. He would meet him there later.

After Anderson left, Jacobus said, 'First of all, I'm not a doctor. I just go to them more frequently than I care to. Secondly, the Vivaldi sounded very good, at least through a soundproof wall. What are you practicing it for?'

'Mr T asked me to play it with the chamber

orchestra when he heard that Audrey dropped out.'

'I'm glad you'll have a chance to perform it,' Jacobus said, 'but of course I'm troubled at the circumstances. Were you and Audrey friends?'

The enthusiasm that had filled Mia's voice was replaced with caution.

'We were friendly. I wouldn't say we were friends.'

'Are the two of you in the same dorm?'

'Dorm? No, Audrey lives off campus. With her boyfriend.'

'Do you know where?'

'No, why?'

'Not important. What instrument does the boyfriend play?'

'Oh, he doesn't go here. I never met him. Audrey just talked about him once in a while. I think he's a student somewhere.'

'Were you surprised Audrey dropped out so suddenly?'

'Yes and no.'

Before Jacobus could delve deeper in her ambivalent response, Mia continued on her own, as if she wanted to qualify her statement before Jacobus could press her on it.

'She's a little weird. You know? Hot and cold. Some days she could be really great, but other times she wouldn't even look you in the eye.'

'I heard she worked hard.'

'I suppose. We all work hard.'

'How did it come about that Mr T selected Audrey to play 'Spring'? She win a concerto competition?'

159

Jacobus knew that competitions could be crap-shoots. A mediocre musician could have a great day; a superlative one a horrible day. Judges could be, and often were, capricious and self-interested, especially when their own students were in the mix. From the little he'd heard of Audrey's playing, Jacobus was not expecting an affirmative answer to his question but would not have been surprised by one.

'No, there wasn't even any kind of competition or audition,' Mia said. Jacobus detected a shade of bitterness. Or was it something else more personal? Envy, perhaps. But now, at least, she had her golden opportunity, so maybe she was just trying to put any acrimony in the background and move on.

'Professor Schlossberg arranged that for her,' she added.

'Don't you mean her teacher, Dunster?'

'No. It was Professor Schlossberg.'

'What do you mean by "arranged it"?'

'He and Mr T have – had – this thing. I think he was giving Audrey one of his little rewards.'

'Which "he"?'

'Professor Schlossberg.'

'Rewarding her for what? For being willing to endure playing his piece, *Synergy Something*?'

'You mean *Synthesis III*,' Mia corrected. 'No, Audrey actually likes playing new music. She's one of the few. You just have to be able to figure out crazy rhythms and pretend you're really into it. And she has a lot of energy. I think she was thinking that was the direction she was going career-wise.'

'So what was the reward for?' Jacobus asked. 'What does Schlossberg have to do with the chamber orchestra?'

'I don't really know. It's none of my business.'

Jacobus didn't want to push too hard, though he suspected Mia knew more about it than she was admitting. But why should she open up to him? Almost a total stranger. A blind geriatric in a wheelchair. That would scare the shit out of any young person. The practice module was getting uncomfortably warm, even with the ventilation fan on. With its soundproofed walls and stale air, Jacobus imagined himself a priest in a confessional, though unfortified by the easy comfort of moral absolutes.

Jacobus revised his earlier mental image of the modules as fishbowls. They now seemed more like the controlled environment of an underground laboratory, where molds grew in test tubes. Young people spending five, six, eight hours a day slaving away in solitary confinement. For what? To make beautiful music? Not really. More to reach an arbitrary level of so-called 'perfection' or 'artistry' in order to sufficiently impress the adult inquisitor called 'the teacher.' That weekly make-or-break hour called 'a lesson.' At the mercy of the inquisitor whose snap judgment becomes the determinant for the remainder of that student's life. The student praying for crumbs of approval: 'You've done well,' could mean a career in the offing. And dreading the death sentence: 'You have no talent.'

Where does the unfortunate student go from a verdict like that? Back down into the catacombs, returning the next week to seek approval again? There's always next week. What would a student do for approval? What *wouldn't* a student do for approval? Where was the positive human interaction? Where was the music? Where was the sun?

'So when did you start working on 'Spring'?' Jacobus asked, not sure what direction the conversation was headed.

'I just started practicing it today. I haven't even told Ms Shinagawa yet.'

'You've played it before, then.'

'No. Never!'

'But I heard you using a lot of her fingerings and bowings.' Though Yumi hadn't studied Vivaldi's Four Seasons with him, Jacobus could still take credit for having taught her how to think about learning music like that, so in a way he was Mia's musical grandfather. He kept that thought to himself.

'Oh, I listened to her CD all last night!' Mia replied.

'When did you get the music, then?'

'Oh,' she laughed. 'I don't have the music. I memorized it while I listened to it.'

Jacobus was perplexed. Clearly this young lady was a serious talent. And dedicated. Her performance at the masterclass had made that obvious. One couldn't and shouldn't draw conclusions from a one-shot deal like a masterclass, because for all one knew, a student could have been practicing a given composition since he was in knickers. Granted, learning 'Spring' was not nearly the same challenge as a behemoth like the Brahms Concerto, but for a student to have essentially learned it

162

overnight, especially without the benefit of having the music, was a notable accomplishment. It made him wonder why she hadn't been invited to perform it in the first place and what had prompted the 'reward' to Audrey Rollins? Jacobus was all for democracy and giving everyone a chance, but there was no doubt who the superior musician was. He recalled what Yumi had told him of the stresses of Mia's psychologically harrowing upbringing. They must inevitably have left emotional scars. How could they not have? He could imagine she might have a personality that made her difficult to work with. So far, he hadn't sensed any such trait. But then again, he hardly knew her.

'You keep that up, young lady,' Jacobus said with false severity, 'and you'll make teachers obsolete.'

'God, I hope so,' Mia replied. 'No offense.'

Had he just been slapped in the face? If so, it was a rare occurrence for Jacobus to have been upbraided with such concise efficiency, especially by a student. Maybe he was starting to understand why she hadn't been selected to play the concerto. On the other hand, maybe it had come out differently than she meant. He would let it slide.

'Maybe you've got a point,' he responded. 'On the other hand, us vestigial organ grinders might still have something to contribute. You do know what this concerto is about?'

'Yes, I read all the program notes on the CD, with the sonnet and such. I memorized that, too.'

'I'm sure you did, but when I was listening to your playing, I was thinking, it's one thing to

163

understand what spring is about. It's another thing to embrace it so that when the audience is listening they feel sunny days and see green things bursting out of the ground. You don't want it to sound like you're in one of these solitary confinement rooms.'

'You mean like with Vivaldi's bird calls? They're kind of hokey, but I try to make them sound real, like Ms Shinagawa.'

'It's not enough to just sound like birds. Those are just technical tricks. You have to sound like "birds rejoicing with festive song," as Vivaldi wrote. Birds rejoicing they've survived, half-starved, through a freezing winter and are still alive to celebrate. Can you imagine how spring feels for a bird? To be on the brink of death and then feel the first warm sunrise? Knowing that it'll finally be able to poke its beak through the thawing ground and fill its empty gullet with a nice, juicy worm?'

'I never thought of spring quite that way,' Mia admitted.

'Me, neither,' Jacobus said, and they both laughed. 'But if you decide that's what the music's about, then you have to figure out how to do it with your hands. Never mind Sybil Baker-Hulme's exhortations for stylistic purity. It all starts with the decision to make spring sound joyful. And don't forget the adage,' he added, '"in spring a young man's fancy turns to love."'

'You got that from Vivaldi's bird calls?'

'Maybe that's a stretch.'

There was a silence. She probably wanted him to leave but was too polite to ask.

164

'I should let you practice,' he said.

'No, wait. I have a question for you.'

'Yes?'

'Isn't there also a part in "Spring" about thunderstorms?' Mia asked. 'They're also harbingers of spring, like the birds.'

'Yes,' he said. '"April showers bring May flowers."'

She persevered. 'But a thunderstorm is kind of the opposite, isn't it? It's angry and it's frightening. "Thunderstorms, those harbingers of spring, roar, casting their dark mantle over heaven."'

Jacobus wasn't sure where this was going.

'Yes, there's that, too. What's your point?'

'Only that if you compare bird calls to "a *young* man's fancy turning to *love*,"' Mia replied, 'then you'd have to say that with the thunderstorm part it's more like "an *old* man's fancy turning to *lechery*." Wouldn't you?'

Fifteen

What? Where did that come from? Is she talking about me? I'm an old man – no question about that – but lechery? What reason on earth does she have to fire that accusation at me? Is this another rumor about me that's spreading across the campus? Is it someone else?

Or was she simply being tongue-in-cheek, taking my own line of thought and extending it into absurdity? Does she understand my brand of humor, from Yumi perhaps, and inadvertently crossed a line? That was something I've done, myself, far too often. But out of the mouth of babes? Babes! He didn't even want to think about that double entendre. He didn't know what to think.

About to stammer out a garbled reply, he was saved by a tap on the glass door. It opened with a soft pop, breaking the stifling, vacuum-packed seal.

'Sorry to barge in.'

The voice of Lisette Broder, the accompanist at the masterclass.

'Mia and I have a rehearsal now,' she said. 'Apologies.'

'On my way out,' Jacobus said. He needed some air. Some time to think. Broder wheeled him backwards out of the practice room. Before the door closed he heard Mia call out, 'It was only a joke!'

166

He heard Broder play an A on the piano, to which Mia tuned her violin. They began their rehearsal. Jacobus suddenly realized he was helpless. When he was ambulatory, his feet and his cane provided all the information he needed to get where he wanted to go. But sitting in a wheelchair he had no feel for the ground. The muffled sounds emanating from the rows of practice modules gave him a confused sense of direction. He had no cellphone – even if he did he wouldn't know how to use it – so he had no way to contact Chase Anderson in the canteen. The situation was more aggravating than alarming. He knew that if he just remained in place someone would assist him sooner or later, but having to do so made him feel inadequate. Like an invalid. That was a condition he would not abide.

After straining his ears for half a minute or so, amid the subdued music and mechanical noises basements make, he discerned the whir of the elevator. He followed the sound toward the end of the corridor. Since he didn't know exactly in which straight line he should wheel himself, he twice bumped into modules and muttered apologies to students he might have disturbed. He finally found his destination.

He pressed the Braille-embossed up button on the elevator, barely able to reach it from his sitting position. His mind was still spinning. When he heard the doors open he rolled forward. Right into someone emerging from the elevator.

'Sorry,' he blabbered.

'Mr Jacobus. It's me. Sam. Sam Consiglio. At your service. Let me get the door for you.'

'Thanks, Sam,' Jacobus said.

Jacobus remembered his question for him.

'Sam, when you found Schlossberg, was the piano fallboard open or closed?'

'Closed,' Sam shouted as the elevator doors closed.

'Are you sure?' Jacobus hollered. The elevator was ascending.

He didn't hear the answer.

Jacobus emerged on the main floor. With his right hand outstretched so he wouldn't careen into anyone else and with his left on the wheel of his chair, he formed a bitter image of himself as the Heisman Trophy statue in a wheelchair. *Collegiate cripple of the year*, he thought. What had he gotten himself into?

Following the sounds of voices at the end of the main hall, he made a left turn and headed toward the public canteen for the students and faculty.

'Mr Jacobus!' It was that jazz player. *What was his name? Alonzo Something. Alonzo Sumting.*

'Mr Jacobus!' he repeated, much closer this time.

'Sumter!' Jacobus said. 'Alonzo Sumter.'

'I was on my way to look for you. Your assistant, Chase, said to give you a message. He said he had to go do an errand. Said he had an idea.'

'I've got an idea,' Jacobus said. 'One that he doesn't want to hear.'

Sumter invited Jacobus to join his coffee klatch while he awaited Anderson's return. With nothing better to do and no way to do it, Jacobus accepted. Sumter wheeled him in the direction of an animated conversation.

'But you can't discount all the good he's done over the years,' he heard someone say.

'Excuse me,' Sumter said. 'I've invited Mr Jacobus to join us.'

'Oh,' said the voice.

'Mr Jacobus, welcome,' said another. One he recognized. Tallulah Dominguez.

'Let me introduce you to two of our esteemed colleagues,' she said. 'Tanner Evans and Herman Braun. They're both on the theory faculty.' Dominguez pronounced the words 'theory faculty' with the same enthusiasm with which a Brahman would utter, 'Untouchables.'

'I was just saying, Mr Jacobus,' Evans continued, 'after all Elwood has done for the school—'

'You mean after all the money he's raised for Hedge,' Sumter interrupted.

'That's below the belt, Lon,' Evans said. 'Even if he'd never raised a cent, like you, this crusade against Elwood is unseemly. But I gather Mr Jacobus would take exception with that.'

Why does everyone think I have a vendetta against Dunster? Jacobus asked himself. *Dunster had a student who played poorly at my masterclass. Big deal! Dunster went to Hedge with his hurt feelings. Big deal! I once had a student who almost killed me. Now that was a big deal.* Before Jacobus could respond, someone else intervened.

'That's not fair, Tanner!' came the fourth voice, German-inflected, presumably Herman Braun. 'We know all the wonderful things Elwood's done, but there is a time that comes for everyone. That would be the case whether Mr Jacobus agreed with it or not.'

169

'And what Mr Jacobus said at the masterclass was one-hundred percent right,' Dominguez said, 'even though it might have upset a few people. Sometimes that's necessary.'

'That's not how your boyfriend felt when Elwood criticized *him*!' Evans said. '"All glamor and no substance," isn't that what he said? And Lon filed a grievance for that! And you say it's OK to hurt people's feelings?'

'That has nothing to do with it,' Sumter said.

'It doesn't in the least,' Dominguez agreed.

'Why not?'

'Because Elwood was wrong and Mr Jacobus was right,' she said. 'Look, Elwood is just . . . tired. He's got that tremor in his hands, so he can't play anymore. He hasn't shown up for the last two juries.'

'He was ill.'

'So he says.'

'And, besides,' Dominguez continued, not to be dissuaded, 'none of his students have done well in the concerto competitions. Shit, he hasn't had a top student for years.'

'We talk of hurting people's feelings!' Braun said. 'Of saying this or that. But that's not even the question. My dear Tanner, if we were graded on whether we hurt people's feelings, *none* of us would be here! It went beyond that. The young lady, Audrey Rollins, though not the top of her class, was Elwood's best student, and she dropped out. That's more than hurt feelings. The question is one of Elwoods's competence! And I say—'

Outnumbered three to one – Jacobus remained

doggedly neutral – Evans was putting up a tenacious fight.

'We do not know why the girl dropped out,' Evans said.

'Bah!'

'What do you say, Mr Jacobus?' It was Sumter.

Jacobus had hoped not to be drawn in. Where was that damn kid, Anderson, who was supposed to be his aide?

'I do have a few questions,' he said.

'Yes?' Braun asked.

'The first one is, can someone get me a cup of coffee? I can smell some sitting here on the table and it's driving me crazy.'

Dominguez offered to go and get it.

'Black!' Jacobus shouted after her.

'Regarding Elwood Dunster,' he remarked, 'I've got nothing against the guy at all.'

'That's not what we heard from Connie Jean,' Sumter said with a laugh.

'Then you heard wrong,' Jacobus responded, being far more polite than he would have with more familiar acquaintances. 'As far as I'm concerned he can keep teaching until he has both feet in the grave. What I don't understand is what's to be gained arguing about this. Doesn't he have tenure?'

There was a mumble of unanimous assent.

'So he really can't be fired in any event. Is that right?'

'Pretty much,' Evans admitted. 'Of course it's possible, but it's unlikely. And even if he were, there's a fairly ironclad grievance process. You'd practically have to rape a student to get fired, but

171

at our age we have a hard enough time just getting it up.

Again unanimity. This time laughter. At least they were starting to agree with each other. But after his interchange with Mia, this casual reference to rape made Jacobus uneasy.

'That's why Bronto is so hot to get tenure,' Sumter said. Again, full agreement.

'He wants a little nookie, too?' Braun declared with feigned innocence.

'Like they did 'in the old school'!' Evans said, imitating Tawroszewicz's East European accent.

Dominguez returned with the coffee. Jacobus took a sip and smacked his lips.

'I heard your little boy talk behind my back,' she said to the all-male gathering. 'This joking about sex with students is disgusting.'

The laughter subsided quickly.

'We didn't mean anything,' Evans said. 'As you say, we were just joking.'

'Well, don't. But in regard to Bronto's chances of getting tenure,' Dominguez said, 'they have gone down the toilet.'

'Why is that?' Jacobus asked.

'Because his big ally on the faculty was Aaron Schlossberg, and now that he's gone, the T in Mr T stands for toast.'

Yumi had said there had been a falling out between Schlossberg and Tawroszewicz, and he was about to repeat that but decided to keep his own counsel. Instead he asked, 'What about all those favorable evaluations he got from the students?'

'Yes, what about those evaluations?' Braun asked rhetorically. 'If there is anything we know about students it's that they say one thing and write another, assuming they know how to write at all. Or is it possible they were intimidated by him? If you talk to them, which I try to avoid at all costs – they will tell you Mr T is uniformly disliked. And that is one opinion I believe is shared between the students *and* the faculty.'

'Then why do you suppose Schlossberg backed him?' Jacobus asked.

'That was Aaron being Aaron,' Dominguez said. 'The iconoclast. He loved to throw his weight around. Big man on campus. The world famous artiste career-maker.'

From all four faculty members at the table, there ensued stories – 'I swear it's true!' – they had heard about Schlossberg's inexhaustible predilection for self-promotion, sometimes at the expense of unsuspecting lesser luminaries in the concert world. It was hard for Jacobus to know which were fact and which were tall tales. Maybe it didn't matter.

'Sounds like you've got no love lost,' Jacobus concluded.

'Well, I don't want to speak ill of the dead—'

'*Shh*!' said Sumter. 'Here comes Lisette.'

Dominguez whispered into Jacobus's ear. Her breath was warm and moist, and best of all smelled like coffee. He could feel her lips near his ear. It almost felt as if she were nuzzling him.

If only I were forty years younger.

'They say Lisette had a thing for Aaron,' she said. 'Unrequited love. As far as we know.'

173

They invited Broder to join them. The conversation returned to previous topics, though without the former heat and with nary a mention of Schlossberg. Broder had little to say except how busy she was with all the students preparing for their recitals and juries. Everyone cooed what an ideal accompanist she was.

Jacobus, impatient with the idle chatter, asked someone to phone Chase Anderson for him, but as it happened the boy was just rushing in to the cafeteria.

'Sorry I'm late, Mr J,' he said, breathlessly. 'But—'

'Never mind. Get me back to my room or I'll have you arrested for elder abuse. I've got witnesses.'

To the others he said, 'Been a pleasure.'

When they were outside, Jacobus asked, 'This better be good. You get the coroner's report?'

'Sorry. Turning out to be more difficult than I thought. Got some bureaucratic roadblocks there.'

'So what's the important errand you abandoned me for?'

'It's just as good. I think. When you were at Chops I heard you mention that violin student you're interested in had a boyfriend named Lucien. And since 4C is the biggest school in the county, I just trolled their online website to check student rosters and see if he might be enrolled there.'

'But we don't even know his last name.'

'We didn't, but I figured how many Luciens could there be? It took a little longer because I didn't have the last name, but turns out there's only one Lucien. Lucien Knotts.'

It made sense to Jacobus. Mia had told him that Audrey's boyfriend 'was a student somewhere.'

'What does he study?' Jacobus asked. 'He in your department?'

'Nah. He's a hospitality management major.'

'What's a hospitality major? He tells Grandma how to cut the cake?'

'Sort of. Restaurant business. Or hotels. Boring stuff like that.'

'There an address for Mr Hospitality?'

'Two thirty-four Steamboat Road. I know where that is. I bet we'll find that violin student there.'

They first went back to the inn to connect with Lilburn, but he was still out and about. Jacobus left a message at the desk for Lilburn: *Don't need a ride. Staying in the area. Call me.* As anxious as Jacobus was to leave Kinderhoek Conservatory, he felt it was important to seek closure with Audrey Rollins and to understand what had prompted her sudden about-face. If it had indeed been his fault – something he increasingly doubted – he wanted to set the record straight, if not make amends.

Next came the logistical problem of what to do with the wheelchair. Anderson drove a dilapidated AMC Gremlin with hardly enough room in the trunk to stash a wheel, let alone a wheelchair. They decided to leave the wheelchair at the inn. If it became necessary for Jacobus to walk, he could lean on Anderson. He took his cane with him for added stability, not that it would help a helluva lot.

175

Steamboat Road, a twenty-minute drive from Kinnetonka Crossing, paralleled the Hudson River. Though the potholed road wasn't more than fifty feet from the riverbank, there was so much overgrown brush and scrub forest between the road and river that the mile-wide Hudson was generally invisible. A short row of three- and four-story semi-occupied brick apartment buildings lining Steamboat Road, which included Knotts's address, was an unlikely sight in such a non-urban setting. The structures had seen better times during the nineteenth and into the twentieth centuries, when towns along the Hudson had used the river as a highway for transporting manufactured goods. Now the factories were gone and the main commercial use for the river was waste disposal. Some of the towns were beginning to reinvent themselves as historic tourist destinations, antique centers or, in Kinnetonka Crossing's case, by hitching its wagon to the music conservatory. Municipalities unable to make the transition vanished into the woodwork. But these particular apartments had seemed to be recovering from the worst times because, as Anderson described to Jacobus, the paint job appeared relatively recent, the windows had been replaced, and there were new solid wooden landings. Clearly, 4C's presence was having its own positive economic impact on the area.

Chase parked the car in front of 234 and advised Jacobus to 'chill' while he went to check if Audrey and Lucien were in. Jacobus turned on the radio and, shunning the unpalatable, preprogrammed rock-and-roll station whose bass line shook the car, turned the dial. He finally found WAMC-FM, which was in the midst of yet another fund drive. Giving up, he turned off the radio, lowered the window, and inhaled the not-particularly pleasant odor of the Hudson River on the warm, spring afternoon. Jacobus heard Anderson knock on the apartment door, ring the bell, and knock again. That folk singer who lived by the Hudson, Pete Seeger, had been knocking his head against the wall to get the government to force the river's corporate polluters to clean it up. Like the first generation at the Kinderhoek Settlement, Seeger had been a lefty. Maybe they had played music with each other. Seeger had stood up to the McCarthy inquisitors in the fifties. *Good luck to him cleaning up the river*, Jacobus thought. *He'll need it.*

A few minutes later Jacobus heard Anderson's returning footsteps, slower than before. They sounded resigned.

'They're gone,' Anderson said.

'So I gathered. Leave a note.'

'No. I mean I think they're really gone. For good. Their apartment was One-B, in the basement. I rang the buzzer and there was no answer, so I looked through the window.'

'Empty?'

'No. There's still furniture there.'

'So what makes you think they're gone?'

'It looks like a furnished apartment, like the one I'm living in. But there're no books or records or magazines. No clothes or food or personal stuff.'

'Violin?'

'Didn't see one.'

'Well, Sherlock, what do you propose we do?' Jacobus asked.

'The landlord's phone number was on the mailbox.'

'You've got a cellphone?'

'Yeah.'

'Call him.'

'Can't.'

'Why not?'

'No bars out here.'

'Why the hell do you need to go to a bar to make a damn phone call?'

'No! Not that kind of bar. Bars on the phone. There's no phone reception out here. We'll have to go into town.'

It was evening by the time they returned to the Campus Inn. Anderson retrieved the wheelchair from the hotel lobby, hoisted Jacobus, cursing, from the car into it, and wheeled him into the lobby. Jacobus called the Steamboat Road apartment landlord, who was surprised and aggravated to hear that his tenants might have cleared out. They had been paying their rent on time, he said, but he hadn't received any notice they were planning to leave, and they owed him next month's rent. No, he had no idea where the hell they might have absconded to, and requested to be informed when someone found out. Renting to students was 'a pain in the rectum,' he said. At least he had a month's rent as a security deposit, but it would be a bitch to find a new tenant with only six weeks left in the school year. He hung up energetically, as if that would solve his problem.

The desk clerk gave Jacobus a message that Martin Lilburn had called and wanted to know if Jacobus was interested in comparing notes over dinner at Chops. Jacobus, weighing his fatigue after a long day against the allure of dining with Lilburn and Anderson, had no difficulty declining the invitation. He did, however, have Anderson call Lilburn and arrange to meet for breakfast at eight o'clock, and told the desk he wanted a wake-up call at seven. Anderson wheeled Jacobus up the elevator and into his room. Before he left, Jacobus gave him a computer assignment to find out who Lucien Knotts's professors were. Maybe one of them would know why he had left and where he might have gone.

'Cool!' Anderson said. 'You'd make a good detective, too.'

Jacobus kicked the door shut. With his good foot.

Jacobus could think of any number of reasons why the two students had moved. Maybe they couldn't pay their rent. Maybe the boyfriend got a job somewhere so they both decided to drop out. Maybe he got her pregnant. Such things did happen. Maybe, maybe, maybe. He admitted to himself he was just pretending. He was considering those maybes only because he was troubled by what he really thought: that there was a link between the party where so many had gotten sick and the disappearance of Audrey Rollins and Lucien Knotts. The two of them were there, working, at that party. They could have been the same two people Jacobus had heard in the woods, though even if he heard Knotts's voice now, he still might not be sure. But what he was sure of was the disastrous masterclass the next day. And then Audrey Rollins dropped out and vanished.

Before he went to sleep he called Yumi and asked her to have a heart-to-heart with Mia Cheng. He sensed turbulence lurking beneath the surface with Cheng. Yumi, her teacher, would have more success unearthing it than he would. Jacobus was always bemused by the ease with which students confided in their teachers. How they always assumed the teacher had only their best interests at heart. How there was an assumed bond of trust that, curiously, was sometimes stronger than the bond that existed between the students and their own parents. He supposed that that was a good thing, for the most part. Depended on the teacher.

Jacobus lay cautiously on his back, inhaled deeply several times, and probed his chest. Finding nothing out of the ordinary, he speculated that the X-rays had been mistaken. Even so, he didn't sleep well.

Sixteen

Wednesday, April 1

The wake-up call came at seven, but without Chase Anderson to help Jacobus into his wheelchair. Jacobus tried again to put weight on his ankle, but the pain was still severe and, in any event, he wasn't sure where the hell the wheelchair was. He was not inclined to explore. Instead, he sat in his boxer shorts at the side of the bed and fumed.

Finally, there was a knock on the door, which, by agreement, Jacobus had left unlocked.

'Where the hell you been?'

'April Fools?' Anderson replied sheepishly.

'What time is it?'

'Quarter of eight, I think,' Anderson said. 'Sorry I'm late, but I got something for you.'

'Would it be a broken alarm clock?'

'Better, a folding wheelchair! I "borrowed" it from the hospital. We can go anywhere now.'

Jacobus thought about complimenting Anderson on his resourcefulness but wasn't in the mood yet.

'I also brought someone who might help with our investigation,' Anderson continued.

'*Our. Investigation!*' Jacobus said. 'For your information, there is no "investigation" and there is no "our." Got that? Who did you bring? I don't hear anybody with you.'

181

'Moshe Schneidermann. He was my professor for a medical ethics course I had to take last semester.'

'Medical ethics? What is it, a five-minute class?'

'No, it was really interesting. Professor Schneidermann is old, but he's really smart.'

'That's comforting. And how exactly do you suppose this Professor Schneidermann is going to help "our investigation"?'

'I think he might be able to help us get the coroner's report. He, like, knows everybody.'

Jacobus shrugged. Like the Jewish widow who spooned chicken soup into her deceased husband's mouth said, 'It vouldn't hoit.'

Anderson helped Jacobus wash up and dress and wheeled him into the lobby only slightly behind schedule.

'He's over there,' Anderson whispered.

'Thanks for pointing him out,' Jacobus replied. 'What would I do without you?'

Anderson brought the wheelchair to a stop.

'Mr Jacobus, I presume?' The voice was a little older and a lot more Jewish than his own.

'Schneidermann?' Jacobus asked.

'The same.'

'My young lackey here tells me you might be able to help us.'

'Maybe it would be possible. Maybe it would not.'

'What is that supposed to mean?'

'Just what it sounds like. The ethical considerations are complex.'

Anderson interrupted.

'I'll just call Mr Lilburn at Chops and tell him we'll be a little late.'

'You do that.'

After he left, Schneidermann said, 'A bright young man. I think we got along because we understood each other's persecution.'

'I'm not *that* hard on him,' Jacobus said.

Schneidermann laughed.

'Not that. Slavery. He understands what we, as Jews, have gone through for the past millennia, and I understand what his race has had to endure in this country.'

'What do you mean, "his race"?' Jacobus asked.

'He's Negro. Didn't you realize?'

He hadn't, having assumed from the name Chase Anderson that he was as lily white as Pat Boone. And unlike Alonzo Sumter's voice, Chase's sounded absolutely typical of rural New York. Jacobus brushed aside his oversight, but it provided a caution that jumping to conclusions based upon partial information could lead him down the wrong path.

'No matter. You said medical ethics are complex,' Jacobus said. 'From my experience, the only ethical complexity is who the doctor is going to overcharge: the patient or Blue Cross.'

Schneidermann wheezed out a laugh.

'Yes, it seems to have come down to that, hasn't it? But let me give you a couple of examples of how it might not be so easy.

'Let us say an old man, like you or me, needs a liver transplant and has been waiting a year for it. He's made his way to the top of the list and has only four or five months more to live if he doesn't get one. Miraculously, a liver becomes available. But let us say at the same time a young lady, full of life and potential, has been brought into the emergency room with a stab wound and will die within twenty-four hours without a transplant. Who gets the liver? Being Solomon in this case is not an option, by the way.'

Jacobus almost immediately said the woman but then thought, where is the dividing line? Age, sex, married or single? Who decides? Suddenly he wasn't so sure.

'And that's an easy one,' Schneidermann continued. 'What if a doctor offered you, Mr Jacobus, a pair of eyes that would enable you to see again? All the trees, all the beautiful paintings, all the smiling faces. All those things that have been cloaked in darkness for all these years. Would you take those eyes? Would you see all those things again? Think carefully.'

Jacobus considered his life since he had lost his sight. It had been a struggle. There had been endless challenges. Yet the world as he conceived it now didn't require the visual. His connection to sound, smell, and touch had deepened to such an extent that being able to see could, paradoxically, detract from the richness of his life.

'I detect some hesitation,' Schneidermann said, 'which means you are a thoughtful human being. Because you're also wondering what is the ethical dilemma here. Not necessarily yours, which is simply a question of balancing the pluses and minuses, but of the doctor, whose goal is to heal. Would a new pair of eyes heal you, Mr Jacobus, or would it tear your life apart?

'Which leads to the most difficult issue that confronts us: When to let a patient die. With the technology now available to us in medical science, we can keep many sick people alive indefinitely. That is a good thing, is it not? But what if someone's quality of life is vegetative – worse, intensely painful – as part of the bargain of staying alive? What if the patient begs the doctor to let him die? And what of the family's endless emotional and financial suffering? What then, Mr Jacobus? How does one decide? Ultimately, there is a time for us all, but when is the *right* time?'

Jacobus didn't care to discuss philosophy before breakfast. Or after breakfast, for that matter.

'That's what I want to find out,' Jacobus said. 'Chase said you might be able to get Aaron Schlossberg's coroner's report.'

'That is not possible.'

'You're a great help. Why the hell not?'

'Because there are no coroners in New York anymore. We have medical examiners.'

'Well, then the medical examiner's report.'

'That is not possible, either.'

'I don't want to sound like a broken record like you, professor, but why the hell not?'

'Because my recollection is that the newspapers said Aaron Schlossberg died of natural causes, which I presume they gathered from the death certificate. I understand from Chase Anderson that you've become acquainted with the certificate. Is that indeed what it said as to the manner of death?'

185

'Yes, that's what it said.'

'Then there would be no medical examiner's report. There would only be one if the death were ruled to be homicide, suicide, or otherwise suspicious.'

'But it is suspicious. It's damn suspicious!'

Jacobus explained the questionable circumstances surrounding Aaron Schlossberg's death. How all those people had gotten sick from mushroom poisoning. The mystery couple in the woods. Audrey Rollins's inexplicable behavior and disappearance. Schlossberg's body discovered in the practice room with no music on the piano, the keyboard closed, and the light and fan turned off.

'No one would use one of those rooms without turning those switches on,' Jacobus said.

'The only other possibility,' Schneidermann proffered, 'would have been if someone else had come *after* he died and turned them off.'

'And then left, leaving Schlossberg's body there to rot? Hardly worth considering.'

'I tend to agree.'

A new thought occurred to Jacobus.

'And if he was so damn sick,' Jacobus pursued, 'if he was so damn sick how did he get to the conservatory when his house was five miles away?'

What had been Jacobus's vague, uneasy conjectures were suddenly crystalizing. There was something terribly wrong with the picture.

'And even if he could have driven – which is highly unlikely – where was his damn car?'

The death certificate now seemed wholly

unsatisfactory, too tidy an answer to the questions that gnawed at him.

'Yes,' said Schneidermann. 'The death certificate is such an impersonal and simplistic end to a human being's existence, as if a life were no more than the completion of a form. It is cruel, is it not?' Schneidermann seemed to be thinking out loud. 'It is possible. But then again . . .'

'Chase said you have connections. Cut through the red tape.'

'Even if it were so, what are you suggesting be done?'

'Get Schlossberg's body exhumed.'

Schneidermann chuckled.

'I have read quite a bit about you, Mr Jacobus. You and I have much in common. More than you know. I, too, came to America because of the war. My parents, too, died in the Nazi camps. My interest in medical ethics came from living through that experience myself, though when I came here it was not in that capacity but as a musician. Like you. I played the clarinet. I was a teenager. Every week at the Theresienstadt concentration camp in Bohemia, where the Nazis showed the world how well they treated the Jews, I played the Mozart quintet and the Brahms quintet. While I played this music, phrase by beautiful phrase, my friends and family died. The more I played, the more they died. But at least they died having heard these most sublime compositions. And the Brahms especially, as you know, with its portents of sweet mortality. Some of the older people in the camp – the ones from Hamburg – had actually seen Brahms perform.

187

Did the music not provide them at least a modicum of comfort in their distress? Wasn't that a *good* thing? I wondered. Or was it? That is the question that drove me.

'I was among the first generation of musicians at the Kinderhoek Settlement. Theodesia Lievenstock was a kind woman who only meant well. I continued to play music, but the idea of being paid for it after Theresienstadt made me feel unclean. Like a vulgar whore. I could no longer tolerate the sight of my clarinet, and for many years could not listen to a note of music. Thankfully, that has changed.

'But the question of medical right and wrong consumed me. Because I had seen so much wrong I could hardly imagine there was any right. But there is, you see. Getting you a medical examiner's report after the fact would present some practical challenges – an exhumation and an autopsy – and some ethical questions – privacy rights, family rights, following the law, to name a few – but I think there is a greater good in what you are trying to accomplish. Am I morally right in saying that? I don't know. But let me make a few calls, innocently enough. Dr Pine and I have had over the years, let us say, a working relationship. He likes to pull strings. Perhaps I can pull his and make him think it is I who is the marionette. And I'm familiar, though less so, with Dr Dahl, the county medical examiner. Will that suit your purposes, Mr Jacobus?'

Jacobus had almost stopped listening after Schneidermann had mentioned the deaths of their parents. He was taken back to the time when he had been sent by his mother and father to the Juilliard School in New York, partly for his musical training, but more, he later realized, for his protection from the black tidal wave of Nazism. Music and two thousand miles of ocean had helped him block out the horror. For Schneidermann, the horror and the music were inextricably entwined.

'I asked, will that suit your purposes?' Schneidermann repeated.

'Yes,' Jacobus said, jolted back into the present. 'Yes. Of course. That will do very well. And when we're finished with this business, maybe then two old musicians might get together with three others over a bottle of wine and play some lovely chamber music.'

'Thank you for the invitation, Mr Jacobus,' Schneidermann replied. 'But no thank you.'

He also declined Jacobus's invitation to join them at Chops, declaring he was kosher. In any event, he wanted to stroll around the campus to relive the bittersweet memories of what was once the Kinderhoek Settlement. He wanted to hear young people playing music, joyfully.

Jacobus left Schneidermann at the inn and, with Anderson driving, arrived at Chops five minutes later and a half hour behind schedule for Lilburn. With school in session, the restaurant was much busier than on their previous visit. The frenetic Presto from Mozart's *Eine Kleine Nachtmusik* that played over the restaurant's PA made Jacobus feel even more rushed. Anderson spotted Lilburn in a corner booth.

Jacobus began to apologize for keeping him waiting.

'No need,' Lilburn said. 'I've devoted the extra time to attempting to untangle a veritable Gordian knot of conflicting interests I've heard since yesterday. I don't know if any of it has anything to do with your particular concerns, and I'm not sure how much of it has to do with my retrospective on the life of Aaron Schlossberg. But it reads like a Danielle Steel romance, so perhaps it will end up on an airport bookstore bestseller shelf.'

'Mind if I order breakfast first?' Jacobus asked. 'If I'm going to throw up it might as well be on a full stomach.'

Anderson asked if he could stay and listen.

'You mean you want a free breakfast,' Jacobus said.

Anderson sputtered an unintelligible response.

'I can see why Schneidermann likes you,' Jacobus said. 'Such a quick wit. Order whatever you like.'

Once the waitress departed, Jacobus asked Lilburn to bring him up to date.

'Under the guise of writing my *Times* piece,' Lilburn said, 'and per your instructions, I spoke to Elwood Dunster and some of the others who don't seem to like you very much. For the life of me, I can't understand why.'

Chase Anderson snorted beside him. Jacobus ignored it.

'As I haven't yet established a coherent narrative,' Lilburn continued, 'I will just read from my notes and let you glean what you may.

'You know Harold Handy, the music historian: *Short, compactly built. Late fifties, graying beard, elfin smile. An ebullient soul with monotone delivery. Acts as if everything he says is fascinating to him and should be to everyone else. Formed an alliance with Bronislaw Tawroszewicz. Unlike him in every imaginable way. Common hatred of Dame Sybil, who he views as pedant with no imagination.'*

Jacobus had no difficulty recalling that Handy found Sybil narrow-minded and that Sybil found Tawroszewicz incompetent. Still, Handy and Tawroszewicz seemed strange bedfellows.

'Go on,' he said.

'Dante Millefiori: *Tall. Magisterial. Big forehead. He and Schlossberg, something of an alliance if not warm friendship. Because (I think) they fed off each other's successes. Millefiori: kudos and engagements for premiering Schlossberg's latest; Schlossberg able to spread his musical seed with Millefiori as chief pollinator. Ergo, Millefiori agreed to supporting Tawroszewicz's tenure track efforts, but only as long as the latter remained subordinate in orchestral hierarchy.* Are you following all this? It's quite Byzantine.'

'You say Millefiori and Schlossberg weren't exactly bosom buddies?'

'My impression is that each of them had such a high opinion of themselves that neither could accommodate a second soul as an equal in such rarified atmosphere. Millefiori has a highly affected accent. Snooty, faux English.'

'Kind of like yours,' Jacobus commented.

'I have no accent,' Lilburn said, having learned over the years how to fend off Jacobus's gibes. 'I just happen to speak properly. Where Millefiori acquired his I couldn't guess for the life of me.

191

He's of Italian ancestry, clearly, but was born and raised in Indiana. Perhaps he wished to compete with Schlossberg, who had a great deal of that New York patrician dialect but without the sarcastic edge. But in case you were wondering, Jacobus, I should add that I perceived no overt ill will on Millefiori's part, just the ego thing so typical of you classical musicians. Touché.'

Jacobus had indeed been wondering. Conflict between two men with lofty self-images was not unheard of. Nathaniel had reminded him of that on numerous occasions.

'Here's where it gets distinctly Machiavellian,' Lilburn continued. 'I understand you've already spoken to Tallulah Dominguez and Alonzo Sumter. It seems the two of them approached Schlossberg, Handy, and Millefiori to make a deal. They would agree to support Tawroszewicz's tenure if Schlossberg, Handy, and Millefiori would go with them to Hedge and request Dunster be retired.'

Jacobus threw up his hands.

'I'm just the messenger!' Lilburn exclaimed. 'I gave you advance warning.'

Their breakfasts arrived. With his fingers, Jacobus found a piece of bacon on his plate. Unfortunately, he found his sunny-side-up egg first.

'What about Sybil?' Jacobus asked, wiping his fingers on the tablecloth. He didn't have much of an appetite, anyway. 'She made it clear she detests Tawroszewicz.'

'Fit to be tied. Irate. Irate that Tawroszewicz might get tenure and she couldn't do anything to prevent it. Mainly, I think it was that she can't brook being marginalized. All this wheeling and dealing and no one invited her to the table. And if you were wondering, she has no particular love for Dunster, either, as she has deemed his scholarly efforts lacking.'

'I sensed she feels that way about any musician who has actually held an instrument in his hands.'

'That may be a bit of an exaggeration, but I think essentially that's accurate. In fact, as an aside, that's how most of the academic faculty feel about the performance division. So much so it has officially been enshrined in conservatory policy.'

'Meaning?'

'Meaning that if an academic gives a performance it comes under the heading of "research," but if someone on the performance faculty were to perform the same music, no matter how seriously the program has been researched, it comes under the heading of "service."'

'Why should anyone give a shit about that?' Jacobus asked. 'Why waste time on semantics?'

'Because, as they say, time is money. "Research" is eligible for grants and "service" is not.'

'So you're saying that the performers are getting screwed?'

'That's what they seem to be claiming. But that's just a general gripe. Specifically, Dame Sybil felt it was a terrible disservice to the conservatory to give a quote-unquote "Paleolithic Neanderthal" like Tawroszewicz tenure. On the kinder, gentler side, she was all for Dunster retiring with dignity at a time of his own choosing.'

'But sooner rather than later?'

'Precisely.'

'So was the deal consummated?'

'You mean between the Jets and the Sharks? No. For one, it probably wouldn't have gotten very far anyway because Charles Hedge would certainly have countermanded any deal that reduced his ability to raise money. Dunster is on friendly terms with some of the conservatory's longtime major benefactors, and they would be disinclined to keep giving if Dunster were to be dismissed. And I must say, Jacobus, Dunster really is a nice man, your run-ins with him notwithstanding. Plus, he's got a wife, kids, grandkids. He's soft-spoken, knows his music.'

'Just a little tired after a million years of teaching?'

'It happens to the best of them.'

'Tell me about it,' Jacobus said.

'But the real catalyst for the deal falling through was Schlossberg's death. Just like when Yugoslavia fractured upon Tito's death, the moment Schlossberg was buried, the fragile Kinderhoek alliance disintegrated into so many baby Balkans.'

'There are two things I don't understand,' Jacobus said. 'First, why did Schlossberg support Tawroszewicz in the first place? I haven't heard one person say anything favorable about him, either musically or personally. The second thing is, it seems that before Schlossberg's death the two of them were buddy-buddy but since then Tawroszewicz has disavowed their friendship.'

'All of those I interviewed had precisely the

194

same two questions, and I'm afraid that I haven't heard any good answers. In fact, those two questions are about the only thing that everyone had in common. That and the computers.'

'Computers?'

'Well, not the computers themselves. But myriad complaints about having to do everything online now. Class rolls, grades, scheduling, payroll. Constantly updating their bios. You name it. I tell you, I am not unsympathetic. At the *Times* sometimes it feels as if journalism has simply become a means of providing employment for computer technicians. We don't talk to real people as much as we stare into the glowing monsters.'

'If everyone at the conservatory hates that computer crap,' Jacobus asked, 'why does the school do it?'

'Oh, I presume it's what Connie Jean Hawkins wants, and I suppose she convinced Hedge it was what all modern institutions need, and I imagine they got a grant for it. But over the last eighteen months it seems they've gone from dialup to Ethernet to wireless, and there have been an endless series of glitches.'

'The only word you just said that I understand is glitches,' Jacobus said.

'Well, it's the way of the world, I suppose. Though they may well be museum pieces by the end of the twentieth century, I still find the pad and the pencil to be the journalist's indispensable tools.'

'In your doodling did you write down anything interesting about Schlossberg? If I recall, he was supposed to be the subject of your interviews.'

'Most of it was simply corroborative. It was constructive to see his composing studio, courtesy of the widow Sybil. Curiously enough, between those two eminent musicians there was not one piano in the household. Speaking of museum pieces, she has her collection of clavichords and harpsichords and other keyboard dinosaurs, and—'

'Do you suppose that could be why they found him at a piano in the school practice room? Composing an opera on a harpsichord is like trying to roast a turkey on a Bunsen burner.'

'Good stab, Jacobus. But I don't think so. Schlossberg did all of his composing on his computer using a sampler with an electronic keyboard in his studio. It was an impressive array of technology. Besides, if he needed to use a piano, I presume he would have used one of the better ones in a teacher's studio. In any event, a piano would not have been adequate for *Anwar and Yitzhak*. Its scope is simply too vast. Sybil was quite forthcoming and showed me Schlossberg's unfinished score. It was quite ingenious how he integrated acoustic instruments and the human voice with computer-generated sound. His scores in the library are filed chronologically so you can see the progress of his creativity. Between them and his books on foraging, his work filled half the family library.'

'And what was in the other half, books on stomach remedies for each?'

'Jacobus, as someone of your keen intellect you should try to keep an open mind.'

'All right. I will.'

'You will?' Lilburn sounded genuinely surprised.

'Yes. But I reserve the right to say something is a piece of shit if I think it's a piece of shit. Meaning, if it has no discernible melody, no discernible harmony, no discernible rhythm, no discernible relation to the instrument for which is written, no discernible connection to our culture, and no discernible reason for existence other than to have received a grant from a group of like-minded esoteric pseudo-intellectuals.'

Lilburn offered a considered response.

'That seems reasonable,' he said. 'Let's leave it at that. But to answer your question, the other half of the library was Madame's. The books she authored, of course, but legions of early editions and manuscripts going back centuries. Monteverdi, Josquin, Purcell. Gesualdo, even! Composers of great genius whose music is heard all too infrequently. Imagine, the time span between some of those gentlemen and Vivaldi equals the time between Vivaldi and Aaron Schlossberg! What a collection! I must say it was awe-inspiring. Such history and such greatness. May I suggest that you have her show you around the library – just her half if you insist. Even if you can't see those scores, just being in their presence is something quite wondrous.'

Jacobus considered the possibility. He recalled that Sybil had invited him for a reading of her new book. As unappealing as that was, there was tempting ancillary potential. And he wasn't thinking of the scores.

'How is Madame feeling about Tawroszewicz at this point in time?' Jacobus asked. Of all the

197

simmering animosities, that one seemed closest to boiling over.

'Surprisingly, she's placed him on her back-burner. Now that Tawroszewicz will have to defend his tenure ambitions without Schlossberg's support, Sybil seems content to let him dangle at his own peril. He really doesn't appear to have much support anymore.'

'And what about Schlossberg's extracurricular activities? I heard gossip there was a time when the accompanist, Broder, had a throbbing heart for Schlossberg.'

'I haven't been able to corner Broder. She's booked all day, every day, accompanying the students for just about everyone's studio. I do want to talk to her, as she and Schlossberg over-lapped as students at NYU for a year. I'd like to fill out his younger days. But as for the gossip, it's just that. Gossip. Unsubstantiated. There's no way I could include any of that for a reputable publication.'

'How about for the *New York Times*?'

'Not even for them.'

Jacobus hadn't finished his breakfast, his appetite having deserted him. He had almost forgotten that Chase Anderson was still there. He hadn't said a word. To his credit, Jacobus thought. Lilburn was kind enough to pay for everyone's meal. 'The *Times* provided me a generous per diem,' he said. 'I'll consider this part of my research.'

Anderson helped Jacobus into the wheelchair. According to the doctors, it would only be a few more days before he could try walking on his own. Not a moment too soon.

'Who was Gesualdo?' Anderson asked when they were outside. 'Mr Lilburn sounded very impressed.'

'Gesualdo was a sixteenth-century composer with a highly chromatic sense of tonality. Almost futuristic.'

'Cool!'

'That's not the only thing that's cool. He's famous for chopping up his wife and her lover when he caught them in flagrante delicto.'

'Whoa! Did they catch him?'

'Yes they did.'

'And hanged him?'

'No, they didn't. You see, in addition to being a composer he was also a prince, which gave him immunity from prosecution. He went scot-free. Though it's said he spent the rest of his life in repentance.'

Seventeen

'Where to next, boss?' Anderson asked Jacobus.
Now he was calling him 'boss.'

'By any chance, did Ironsides have an assistant?' Jacobus asked.

'Sure did. I have a memory for detail. His assistant was a bodyguard who had previously been a delinquent.'

'You seem to be going in the opposite direction.'

'I get your gist, sir. But I have to say, what I just learned about music from you and Mr Lilburn was totally amazing.'

'So now you want to become a musician?'

'Actually, no, sir. You convinced me I'm going in the right direction.'

'Atta boy. Did you manage to find Lucien Knotts's professors? As part of *our investigation*?'

'Jeez! I totally forgot. It totally slipped my mind. I'm really sorry.'

'Good thing you have a memory for detail. What do you say we totally go to your computer and find out, since we have nothing better to do?'

They drove eastward on winding country roads. Anderson accelerated past intensely pungent dairy farms, slowed down to twenty-five in hamlets that often sported no more than a gas station and pizza parlor, and arrived a half hour later at the community college campus. Most of the buildings were of recent vintage and, in consideration of the limited financial resources of local government, were of utilitarian design with an emphasis on white, unadorned cinder block. As they passed the outdoor sports facilities, Anderson mentioned that the 4C baseball team had won the national junior college championship three years before.

'That's very impressive,' Jacobus said. 'Were you on the team?'

'Before my time. Only two-year programs here. Are you asking because I'm black?'

'What do you mean?'

'Like all blacks have to be athletes?'

'I don't know what you're talking about. My best friend is black and he can barely get his fat ass off the couch except to reach for potato chips.'

Anderson laughed.

'Well, I'm glad to hear that, because certain white folks have preconceptions about us.'

'Everyone has preconceptions about everyone else. White folks. Black folks. Old folks. Young folks. Teachers. Students. Most of the time they're wrong.'

'Most of the time?'

'Most of the time.'

They drove to the college library, which, with limited hours during the spring break, was about to close. Jacobus thought about preconceptions until Anderson pulled into a space at the parking lot. Anderson helped Jacobus out of the car and wheeled him through the heavy front doors, one of which closed upon his bad foot.

'Dammit!' Jacobus howled. 'I feel a preconception coming on and it has to do with intelligence.'

'Careful, sir,' Anderson said, 'or you might end up with two bad feet.'

They managed to get to the computer room without further incident. No one else was there. Anderson situated Jacobus in his wheelchair next to a computer table and turned on the computer. It hummed to life.

'Takes about three minutes to boot up,' Anderson said.

'Whatever that means.'

As they waited, Jacobus said, 'I'd assumed information about professors would be confidential.'

'It's supposed to be. But the school's spyware is way old and the firewalls and security systems they've set up are so easy to navigate around that anyone with half a brain can hack anything they want.'

'I'll keep that in mind,' Jacobus said.

Once the computer was operational, Anderson logged in to the college Internet system. Jacobus could hear him typing faster than Paganini's *Perpetuum Mobile*.

'OK. We've got it. Got his campus ID, courses with section and course numbers, his profs. You want to know his grades, too?'

'His teachers are all we need.'

'You know, I could even change his grades if I wanted to. But he got all As on his midterms so—'

'Just the teachers, please.'

'OK. This semester he's taking hotel management with Robert Windham, culinary arts with Arlene Shames, and accounting with Natt Considine. Name your poison.'

'Phone numbers?'

'Let's see. They have their office phone numbers here on campus, but not their home numbers.'

'So we can't get hold of them since they're on vacation?'

'Looks like it. Are we stuck?'

'Try them anyway. Maybe one of them will be in their office. If not, maybe they've left a contact number on their answering machine.'

'Good thinking, Mr Jacobus.'

'Thank you. I try to stay current with technology.'

Anderson dialed each of the numbers but with no luck. The best he could do was to leave a message to call his cellphone and hope that one of them would respond.

Jacobus had convinced himself that if he pushed himself, refusing to admit his energy level was on the wane, his 'not insignificant growth' would go away. He felt he had succeeded sufficiently for the day and told Anderson they had done enough for now.

When they arrived back at the inn, Yumi was waiting for Jacobus in the lobby.

'What are you doing here?' Jacobus asked. 'I thought you worked for a living.'

It was a line he had often used with Yumi, and one which typically evoked her laughing retort, 'No, I'm a musician,' but on this occasion her response was serious.

'I took the day off. I took the rest of the week off, in fact. It was only a pops concert, anyway.'

'I thought Harmonium's policy was to never play pops.'

'Times change. They need to raise money. Just like conservatories. But that's not what I'm here to discuss.'

'What is it, then?'

Yumi hesitated.

'I don't want to be rude, Chase,' she said, 'but I have to ask you to excuse yourself. I'll take over the wheelchair.'

Neither Jacobus nor Anderson knew what was up and both hesitated.

'Why don't you go see what else you can find out about Lucien's whereabouts?' Jacobus said to Anderson. 'Or make an appointment for me with Sybil Baker-Shmaker. Just do something for our investigation.'

Anderson politely acquiesced and departed.

'What's up?' Jacobus asked.

'I've booked a room upstairs,' Yumi replied, her last words until they arrived at the room. From the way the wheelchair swerved as she pushed him, Jacobus knew her mind, usually so orderly and focused, was distracted.

As soon as she turned the key and opened the door, Jacobus sensed a third presence, but he still had no idea what was going on. He heard Yumi sit in a chair next to him.

'Jake,' Yumi said, 'I've asked Mia Cheng to come here. I called Mia last night, as you requested. We spoke briefly, but from what she told me I felt we needed to meet face-to-face. Jake, you have to promise me that nothing we discuss here leaves the room unless we decide otherwise.'

Those were almost the same words he had used with Dr Simons about the growth on his lung and he had a feeling this news wasn't going to be much better. In all the years he had known her, Yumi had never spoken to him like that, had never issued an ultimatum, even when someone's life was in danger. There was an unaccountable coldness underneath the surface. Even her tirade against him after the aborted masterclass had been less ominous. What to make of it? There was only one way to find out.

'Yeah,' he said. 'Understood. Hello, Mia.'

There was no response.

'I'll start,' Yumi said. 'I think it will be easier that way. Mia told me that she and Audrey Rollins were sexually abused by Aaron Schlossberg. It was ongoing and—'

'Sexually abused?' Mia interrupted. 'Those are words they use in newspapers. Those are words that protect *him*! It wasn't sexual abuse.'

Jacobus stiffened. His hands flexed around the arms of his wheelchair. He heard Yumi shift in her seat.

'It was rape,' Mia continued. 'And he turned us into prostitutes.'

Jacobus pressed his right palm against his forehead, a hundred questions to ask. *An old man's lechery.* Yumi must have sensed that he was about to speak and placed a restraining hand on his arm. He kept his mouth shut.

'Mia, tell us how it started,' Yumi said. It wasn't an order. It was an invitation. Jacobus understood. If any voice would get the answers to the questions, it wouldn't be his; it would be

Yumi's, a soothing female voice. Secure, depend-
able, and sympathetic. In control.

'When we first got to the conservatory,' Mia
said, 'he had one of his parties. It was in the fall.
He liked to invite freshmen. He made us feel
important because he was so famous and we were
nothing, and even though the faculty were there
he paid more attention to us than to them.'

'Who do you mean by "we"?'

'All the freshmen. And he'd tell us about the
great music we would be collaborating on. That
was the first hook: "collaborating on." We were
special! To work with the great Aaron Schlossberg
as equals! He was so smooth. I need some water.'

Jacobus heard Yumi go to the bathroom sink
and fill a glass.

'Here you go,' she said, handing it to Mia. She
returned to her seat.

'Once in a while,' Mia resumed, 'he'd take his
"special students" out into the woods for foraging
parties. Not just girls. Boys, too. Everybody
wanted to be a "special student." He was just
grooming us. Then after the first year, he'd invite
us over to his house, to listen to music. He'd
serve us drinks—'

'Alcohol?'

'Of course! Like we were adults. And we would
discuss music, and he'd ask us our opinions.'

'Wasn't Sybil there?'

'For the innocent get-togethers, yeah. But when
she went out of town for one of her symposiums,
that's when he started showing us porn.'

'Did that make you uncomfortable?'

'Hell, yeah! What do you think? But he made

us feel like we were all in on this big adult secret. And he would talk to us like we were on his level. Like, "How would you describe the difference between adult films and art films by Polanski or Bergman?" As if we didn't know. But he kept it very intellectual. Very suave. You know his voice.'

Mia stopped.

'I'm glad he's dead,' she said.

And stopped again.

'Do you want some more water?' Yumi asked. 'Maybe this is enough for today.'

'No, no. You haven't heard the good part yet. That's when he started handing out the prizes. He'd make sure that the girls who stuck with the program got special consideration, like soloing with the orchestra or recording his newest master-piece. And then when you tried to be respectful and thank him for one thing or another, he'd give you a hug, and then next time he'd kiss you on the cheek, and the next time it was on the lips. He had the whole routine down pat. He was a real pro. He was such a pro that you almost felt like you were the one that wanted it and he was the one resisting temptation, and you'd feel guilty if you denied him. But it was my fault.'

'Why do you say that, Mia?' Yumi asked. Jacobus was surprised Yumi didn't disagree outright with Mia and make it clear it wasn't her fault at all. That the fault solely belonged to Schlossberg, the arch-manipulator. But he respected Yumi's instincts and trusted her ability to navigate the emotional minefield. She'll make an even better teacher than I ever was, he thought.

'"Give to get,"' Mia replied.

'What do you mean?'

'That's what my former parents used to say to me when they made me keep working after six hours of practicing. "If you want to succeed you have to give to get." Succeed at all costs. Do whatever it takes. Please the teacher. Give to get.'

Mia began to sob.

'They gave away my sister! I can't believe they gave away my sister.'

Jacobus heard Yumi rise from her chair and move to the bed, where Mia was sitting. She must have put her arm around Mia or done something to comfort her because Mia said, 'I'm OK. I'm OK.'

'This is a hard question, Mia, but to your knowledge,' Yumi asked, 'were there other students who Schlossberg abused?'

'You're making this sound like I'm at a trial!'

'I'm so sorry,' Yumi said, and she was crying now. 'It's hard to think of the right words.'

'Never mind. OK. He had a harem. We called each other Aaronites. Our funny little secret code-name. OK? When the cat was away, the mice would play. He had orgies at his house. And if a girl wanted out, sometimes he'd offer her more rewards but sometimes he'd make these threats—'

'Threats?' Jacobus was aghast.

'Not physical threats. Never physical threats. He was too smart for that. Subtle. Like not being sure it was the right thing for him to use his influence to get you into graduate school or a summer program. Or asking if you hoped you'd have your scholarship renewed. And when he'd finished harvesting graduating seniors he'd start

208

over again with a new crop of freshmen. His continuous supply of playthings.'

Jacobus asked a question even though he knew immediately he shouldn't have. 'But didn't anyone go to the administration? Didn't anyone file a complaint?'

'Against God? You're going to file a complaint against God? Aaron Schlossberg *ruled* the conservatory. What Aaron wanted, Aaron got.'

'That doesn't answer my question.' *Too harsh.*

'Jake!' Yumi said.

'OK. You want to know?' Mia said. 'I *did* file a complaint. In graphic detail. They said, "Thank you *so much* for coming forward," and that they would follow up internally. They were *so* concerned. They just wanted to make sure they got the facts right and got all sides of the story, and they'd issue a report. After two months they sent me a letter. You know what they told me? I hadn't presented any *physical evidence*. They told me *it was my fault*. My behavior was *inappropriate*. *My* behavior! It was a total whitewash.'

'Who is "they"?' Yumi asked. 'Who wrote that letter?' Those would have been Jacobus's next questions.

'Who do you think?' Mia replied, her voice edged with bitterness. 'Hedge.'

A silence fell upon the three of them. A clock ticked. A car drove past the inn. Down the corridor a door closed and the ice machine rattled. Normal life. It seemed far away.

'You called it off,' Jacobus said. 'Audrey Rollins didn't.'

'Yes, how do you know that?'

'She's the one who got selected to play "Spring."'

'Yeah.'

'Schlossberg must have heard about your complaint. That's how he knew you weren't going to be under his control anymore.'

'He knew before that.'

'How?'

'I bit. Hard.'

Eighteen

Jacobus didn't know what infuriated him more, Schlossberg's crimes or Hedge's cover-up. His instinct was to confront Hedge head on. To badger him until he confessed to having shielded a sexual predator. He knew, though, that his natural inclination in this situation would probably backfire and accomplish precisely the opposite result. Nathaniel often reminded him there were always two sides to a story and usually more. But even if there were a grain of truth to all this, a single grain, Hedge should be locked up. And what about Audrey Rollins? Where had she disappeared to? Mia had said that Schlossberg's threats were never physical, but Jacobus feared for her well-being.

'Have you been getting counseling?' Yumi, ever the sensible one, was asking Mia.

'My parents would kill me if I did,' she replied.

Jacobus was about to ask her why their approval still mattered to her after having disowned them, but Yumi pre-empted him by moving the conversation forward.

'But why would they?' she asked. 'After all you've gone through.'

'Because getting counseling means you're a failure.'

Jacobus was again ready to argue but suddenly realized that, much to his shock, until that moment he might have agreed with that statement.

211

'Don't worry about me,' Mia continued. 'What Schlossberg did to me makes me sick. But now he's dead. He can't touch me or anybody else anymore. I'll get over it. I'll survive.'

'What would you like us to do?' Yumi asked.

'I don't know. Nothing. I don't care. I have to go practice.'

'Sure, Mia,' Yumi said. 'Just call me if you need to talk. Anytime.'

Mia Cheng left the room without another word.

Jacobus and Yumi sat in silence, each waiting for the other to speak first.

'So what do we do now?' Jacobus asked.

'Kill him,' Yumi said.

'He's dead already,' Jacobus said, but he knew whom Yumi meant, and he knew she wasn't joking.

'Hedge. I could kill Charles Hedge. What he did is almost as bad as Schlossberg.'

'I'll be your accomplice if we include Connie Jean Hawkins, but let's wait until tomorrow. OK?'

Yumi called Chase Anderson to tell him that he could take the rest of the night off. Anderson reported that he had received two phone calls, one from Professor Schneidermann and the other from Professor Shames, Lucien Knotts's culinary arts instructor. Yumi handed her phone to Jacobus. Shames, Anderson said, would be happy to answer any questions Jacobus might have about Lucien Knotts, but since everyone was on spring break it wouldn't be possible to determine whether he had dropped out until classes started up again.

'And Schneidermann?' Jacobus asked.

'He has some information he wants to share with you. In person. I told him it might be too late for today.'

'Why the hell did you tell him that?' Jacobus barked.

'Sorry. That's just the impression you gave me.'

'Next time when you feel an impression coming on, just say to yourself, "Chase, maybe I should ask first." OK? Where did he want to meet?'

'He said he's babysitting his grandchildren at a miniature golf place just outside of town on Route 16. Family Putts. Can I take you there?'

'Yumi will. As she said, you've got the rest of the night off.'

Jacobus could feel Anderson bristle through the phone.

'Don't worry,' Jacobus added. 'You're still my number one assistant. I have an idea how I might need you for *our* investigation. But not quite yet.' That was as much reassurance as Jacobus cared to offer.

Yumi spotted Schneidermann sitting on a bench next to a five-foot-high, green ceramic frog that hid an internal plastic tube extending from its rectum up to its mouth, from which a carefully aimed golf ball could conveniently drop and land inches from the cup.

'Over here, over here, Mr Jacobus,' Schneidermann called. 'I'm glad you could make it to our tournament. So far, Yehuda is six under par and ahead by two strokes, but Ashira has been mounting a comeback since Pirate Cove. I understand from Mr Anderson that you've had a busy day. He has only the best things to say about you. Are you hungry?'

'Haven't had time to eat,' Jacobus said. All he wanted was whatever information Schneidermann had and then leave.

'You're in luck, then,' Schneidermann said. 'The reason I always sit at Froggy Hollow is because of the hotdog stand next to it. They make the best hotdogs in Cornwall County. And kosher! Why don't you and Miss Shinagawa go help yourselves and then we'll talk. And I recommend the hot sauerkraut highly.'

Jacobus took a deep breath. Contrary to his own nature, he understood that other people took their time. If he was going to optimize Schneidermann as a resource, he would have to let him proceed at his own pace. So he and Yumi bought hotdogs at Frank's Franks and returned to the bench, where they chatted aimlessly while they ate.

'I had a chance to speak to Doctors Pine and Dahl today,' Schneidermann said, finally easing into the subject at hand.

Usually, there was nothing Jacobus preferred to a good hotdog, but he found himself almost gagging on it. Whether it was because of the subject of doctors or whether it was because of his meeting with Mia, he didn't know. Whatever the reason, he finished it, though his stomach protested, simply because he didn't know how to get rid of it otherwise.

'What did the good doctors have to say?'

'In regard to Aaron Schlossberg's death, everyone, including Dr Pine's staff, followed protocol precisely. When the conservatory janitor discovered Schlossberg's body, he immediately called campus security. They in turn contacted the local police, who arrived on the scene expeditiously. The officer in charge called the hospital to find out the name of Schlossberg's personal physician, whom he then contacted. Schlossberg's physician was quite adamant that he had warned Schlossberg on more than one occasion that if he continued to pursue his wanton lifestyle in the face of his chronic diabetic condition he was risking imminent death.

'With that information, the officer contacted Schlossberg's wife, Sybil Baker-Hulme, and notified her that her husband had died. She consented to having the funeral parlor Kaplan and Sons transport the deceased to their facility.'

The cadence in Schneidermann's voice indicated finality.

'End of story?' Jacobus said.

'End of chapter. Because then I contacted Dr Dahl, the medical examiner, and told him of your suspicions. If you don't mind, I expressed them as my own concerns, since – and I'm not trying to be boastful – my name is known here and might carry some weight, and if I didn't express them forcefully then Dahl probably would have dismissed them out of hand. You see, his office is quite understaffed and overworked, and they are six months behind even with cadavers they know for certain to be victims of violence. Budget, you know.'

'And?'

'I asked whether he would consider exhuming the deceased and performing an autopsy.'

'And?'

'He said he would think about it, but I had the feeling he was just being polite. Unless we can present something more compelling, it is my opinion this case will go the way of so many others.'

Jacobus was torn. He was sure there was something more to be learned and knew what it would take for him to get at the truth, but at the same time he would never willingly betray a confidence, especially one so recently and painfully sought. Yumi had asked for his silence – had demanded it – and he had agreed. A deal was a deal. But it left him feeling utterly incapacitated.

He felt Yumi's hand pat his thigh. She whispered in his ear. 'I appreciate what you're thinking. Go ahead,' she said. 'It's OK.'

And so Jacobus told Schneidermann about Mia Cheng.

Nineteen

Thursday, April 2

Jacobus's day began with a deflating visit to Dr Simons to have his ankle examined. The verdict: the ankle had not yet adequately healed for him to resume walking. Dr Simons assured him it wasn't at all unusual to take this long, especially for someone of Jacobus's advanced age. The doctor said he hoped Jacobus was keeping up with RICE. Jacobus lied, and said of course he was. Simons asked, 'And what about the other thing?' Jacobus ignored him, even after Simons also asked if Jacobus had been suffering a loss of appetite.

After calling the inn, Moshe Schneidermann managed to find Jacobus at the medical center, which was in the same complex as the medical examiner's facility. Schneidermann had had a second conversation with Dr Dahl, who decided that after learning of Mia Cheng's experience, in context with the other suspicions Jacobus had raised, an autopsy was in order.

Jacobus's enthusiasm at Dahl's decision was quickly tamped down by Schneidermann, who told him that even though Dahl felt an autopsy might be appropriate he might decide not to go ahead with it.

'Why the hell not?' Jacobus asked.

'Because first of all, when Aaron Schlossberg

was discovered in the practice room he had already been dead for some time. I don't remember exactly how long they said. A day or two, at least. He has now been buried for a week and, by Jewish tradition, bodies are not embalmed. It is considered a desecration. But the longer it is before he is exhumed, the more difficult a revelatory autopsy will be. It might already be too late.'

'Then let's dig him up right away.'

'If only it were that easy. With few exceptions, Jewish law doesn't permit exhumation.'

'What are the exceptions?'

'To transfer a body for burial in Israel, or from a non-Jewish to a Jewish cemetery. Or if civil authorities demand an investigation into the cause of death. Or if the cemetery becomes inundated and remains underwater.'

'Are the sages forecasting forty days and forty nights of rain?'

'I'm afraid not.'

'What about civil authorities demanding an investigation? Isn't one out of four enough?'

'Perhaps, but assuming we manage the exhumation, we then encounter the problem of obtaining permission for the autopsies, which the religion does not permit except under the most extreme circumstances. Surely you're aware of that.'

'No, I was not aware of that,' Jacobus said, 'not being a practicing cadaver. What's the hangup?'

'Autopsies in general violate the principle of respect for the individual, both of the body and the soul. As with embalming, an autopsy is considered a desecration, but may be performed if it

218

may save a life. For example, if identification of the deceased's illness might cure someone who is still living.'

'Can the civil authorities demand an autopsy like they can an exhumation?'

'Yes. That is possible.'

'So get Dahl to tell Schlossberg's widow he's going to do a two-fer.'

'I don't think that's the best way,' Schneidermann said. 'She might resist and refuse consent outright. After all, she's still in mourning. If she contests it, then by the time Dahl does get official authorization, it could be worthless. Might I suggest a better way?'

As soon as Jacobus returned to the inn he called Sybil, following Schneidermann's instructions. He asked if she remembered that at the equinox party, which now seemed so long ago, she had piqued his interest in her new book. He asked whether, notwithstanding the recent tragic circumstances, she could conceivably be in any mood to satisfy his intellectual curiosity, since he would soon be leaving for New York City.

She had responded even more positively than he had expected.

'I would be perfectly delighted!' she said. 'The house is so very empty *sans* Aaron. I'm utterly at sixes and sevens.' She explained that the only course she had scheduled to teach this semester was a seminar on Baroque vibrato that met once a week, and naturally she had cancelled that week's class. And so on. 'Do, please, come for tea,' she concluded.

Which was how Jacobus and Yumi found themselves in Sybil Baker-Hulme's library. As Lilburn had described to Jacobus, on one side were the products of Schlossberg's creative legacy: the scores of his musical compositions and his books on foraging. The other side was Sybil's: books of her authorship and her collection of scores from centuries past.

Jacobus maneuvered himself as comfortably as possible in a leather armchair, elevating his injured foot onto a matching ottoman. Yumi, her ire at Schlossberg reignited by being in his library, was unable to sit. She paced fretfully. Sybil stood in the center of the room, a copy of *The Emergence of Mezzo Piano in the Late Baroque and Its Implications for European Society* in her hands like a prayer book.

For the next hour, Jacobus and Yumi endured a catechism on the 'moral rightness of historically informed performance,' and how the 'liberation of the human spirit' that was unleashed by the expansion of musical dynamics had, in a direct line from the concert hall to the royal chambers, led to the fall of kings and the rise of democratic institutions. Fortunately, Jacobus's eyes were invisible behind his dark glasses, so Sybil would never know that he had slept through half of the soliloquy. When she eventually came to the crucial point at which gluttonous European aristocracy had finally been overthrown by the irresistible power of music, Jacobus had jumped in before she could begin another.

'Fascinating!' he said. 'Utterly fascinating!'

Yumi, all too familiar with Jacobus's sense of humor, faked a cough and ran to the veranda.

Sybil, euphoric, floated on air to the kitchen. By the time she returned with tea and homemade scones, Yumi had regained her composure and was, at that moment, investigating Sybil's ancient scores.

'What in the world am I going to do with Aaron's collections?' Sybil asked. 'I suppose I should just give it all to the conservatory. They could certainly use it more than I, but then his shelves would be bare. I don't know if I could handle that. Life is barren enough as it is at the moment. But I shouldn't be maudlin. Should I? Stiff upper lip and all, we English! I can't tell you how much your visit has cheered me up. The two of you are just dears to come all the way here.'

'We can imagine how much you miss Aaron,' Yumi said, steering the conversation in the direction she and Jacobus had predetermined. 'He was such a . . . presence at the conservatory.'

'Indeed,' Sybil said, and she went on to relate some of their more glorious moments at Kinderhoek, rattling off the grand premieres, the intellectual adventures, the sumptuous parties.

'Aaron could get a little naughty, though,' she said.

'Naughty?' Jacobus almost jumped involuntarily at the word.

'Yes,' Sybil said. 'You know, all those rich foods. All the wine. If not for that, he might still be alive. But he had to live life his own way, and who am I to say he was wrong?'

221

It wasn't the kind of naughty he and Yumi were seeking to uncover, and it wasn't perfect, but Jacobus didn't know if there would ever be a more opportune opening.

'Sybil, do you know of anyone who might have wanted to harm Aaron?' Jacobus asked, who already knew of several.

'Why, no!' Sybil exclaimed. 'I can't imagine such a thing! Why do you ask such a question?'

Jacobus laid out all of the troubling inconsistencies, as he had with Schneidermann. He did it as gently as possible, but hoped he would be as convincing. He avoided any reference of Schlossberg's sexual predation. He didn't see what purpose that would serve at this point. And he didn't want to get kicked out before achieving what he had set out to do.

'This is all so strange!' Sybil said. 'So strange and so . . . My life has been turned upside down, and now will it be turned upside down again? But be that as it may. It's all too late. It's time to move on.'

'We – the county medical examiner, actually – wants to exhume Aaron and do an autopsy. So we – you – will know for sure. Have some closure. He'd like your consent, rather than having to order it.'

'Exhume Aaron! Heaven forbid! This is too ghoulish! Poor Aaron. He always said he wanted to be cremated. That would have put an end to this. And I was all for it. To have his ashes scattered over his precious woods. But it's his parents. They're Jews, you know. Orthodox. The worst kind. They're the ones who demanded the religious rigmarole. They would never agree to an exhumation!'

Yumi intervened.

'We were hoping you, as his spouse, might make the decision. As you say, Aaron didn't share his parents' beliefs. Dr Dahl says it's critical for an autopsy to take place as soon as possible for it to be of any potential value. What if you were to decide and then let his parents know after the fact? We were told that it would be permissible, in Jewish tradition, anyway, if civil authorities required it.'

'I'll have to think.'

Jacobus was about to say that time was not on their side, but Yumi was faster.

'Of course you do,' she said. 'Maybe we should go now and let you consider.'

Yumi helped Jacobus hop back into his wheel-chair. They thanked Sybil for her tea and her time.

'No!' Sybil said, as they were almost out the door.

'Why not?' Jacobus asked.

'I mean, no, I won't wait! Go ahead and do the autopsy if that is what must be done. Aaron's parents will no doubt be furious, but I'll handle that. I've gotten used to their feelings about Aaron having married a *shiksa*, so one more tussle won't make much difference.'

'I appreciate that,' Jacobus said and received a hug in return.

'Well, I understand that you've also got other concerns than Aaron. That poor young lady – his chamber music student – my mind's a bit of a fog, I can't remember her name.'

'Audrey?'

'Yes, Audrey. Elwood told me she not only withdrew from the program, she's actually gone missing.'

'Do you have any idea where she may be?' Jacobus asked.

'Heavens, no! It's terribly worrisome when someone disappears after another dies. I do hope she's all right.'

When they were back in Yumi's car, she said, 'I had a chance to look at Sybil's collection of old music. It's amazing.'

'So I've been told,' Jacobus replied.

'She even has a manuscript edition of the Four Seasons.'

'Impressive.'

'There was something interesting about it.'

'No doubt.'

'Not what you think.'

'What, then?'

'The score to "Spring"?'

'Yeah?'

'It's missing.'

Twenty

On the way back to the inn, Yumi dialed Moshe Schneidermann's phone and put Jacobus on. Jacobus informed Schneidermann of Sybil's consent to have Schlossberg's remains exhumed and autopsied, and told Schneidermann to call Dahl immediately, if not sooner.

'I'll call him immediately,' Schneidermann reassured Jacobus, 'but I can't guarantee it will be sooner.'

Jacobus then called Chase Anderson, who was at the community college, and asked him to invite Lucien Knotts's culinary arts professor for a quick chat. Finally, he asked Yumi to call Connie Jean Hawkins to set up an appointment with Hedge that afternoon. He knew if he made the call himself, Connie Jean would hang up on him.

At the inn, Yumi escorted Jacobus to his room so he could rest until Anderson arrived. Jacobus, for whom hygiene had never been the highest priority, nevertheless craved the shower he had been prevented from taking because of his fragile ankle. He certainly wasn't going to ask Yumi to assist him and settled instead for her handing him a wet washcloth.

'Don't forget behind the ears,' she said, and closed the door behind her.

Only with the knock at the door did Jacobus realize he had fallen asleep with the now cold washcloth in his hand. He quickly wiped his face with it and said, 'It's open.'

'How're ya doin'?' It was Anderson. He spoke somewhat sheepishly and Jacobus understood why. Jacobus had heard a second pair of footsteps, and they weren't Yumi's. He buttoned his shirt and sat up quickly.

'I'll survive,' Jacobus said. 'Pardon my appearance. Professor Shames, is it? I'm usually more sheveled. Thanks for coming all this way.'

'No problem. Plenty of free time with spring break. Chase explained one of my students might be in a pickle.'

'Maybe even a dilly of a pickle. It's more about his girlfriend who dropped out of the conservatory. We'd like to find her to talk to her, but it seems the two gherkins have escaped the barrel.'

'I wouldn't worry too much about Lucien,' Shames said. 'He's a little independent-minded, but he's a good student.'

'What do you mean by "independent-minded"?' Jacobus asked.

There was another knock on the door. This time it was Yumi. Jacobus did the introductions.

'Didn't mean to interrupt,' Yumi said. 'I just wanted to let you know we've got a three o'clock appointment with Dean Hedge.'

'I can't wait,' Jacobus said. 'In the meantime, Professor Shames was about to tell us about Lucien Knotts.'

'As I was saying,' Shames continued, 'he's a clever boy, but he follows a different drummer at times.'

'For example?'

226

'For example, in the retail food industry it's the law for restaurants to follow FDA regulations regarding what foods they may or may not serve to the public. It's to make sure public health and safety aren't compromised and also so that restaurants, which are held accountable, are less exposed to legal action if someone gets sick. It's for everyone's protection.'

'Lucien disagrees?'

'Not so much disagrees, but he seems to believe it's more important to serve food that's been grown locally without pesticides and insecticides for plant crops, or without hormones or feed fortified with antibiotics for meat.'

'And there's a problem with that?' Jacobus asked.

'There certainly is!' Shames replied. 'Here's an example: It's a lot easier for an FDA regulator to strictly supervise the production of corn if it's all grown the same way on a single ten-thousand-acre farm in Iowa and shipped under sanitized conditions than it is to have to supervise a thousand ten-acre farms scattered throughout New York and New England and have it delivered in the back of pickup trucks. Without oversight, how can you guarantee the food's safety?'

'Have you and Lucien argued about that?' Yumi asked.

'Yes, but on a friendly, scholarly level. I appreciate his passion, and it gets the other students involved. There are some groups here and there that agitate for local farming, but the future is in agribusiness. Only with agribusiness will we be able to solve the problem of world hunger.'

'Have Lucien's arguments about food ever gone beyond agriculture?' Jacobus asked.

'I'm not sure I know what you mean,' Shames replied.

'Well, before farming, humans were hunter-gatherers, weren't they? Has he ever talked about foraging, for example?'

'Why, that's very perceptive of you! Yes, he has! Glowingly!'

'And?'

'It's absolutely ludicrous, of course. Our course is on culinary arts. The focus is on creative cookery and even our discussion of agriculture is on the periphery of the curriculum. If Lucien wants to study caveman survival, we have an excellent anthropology department. Young people,' she said, as if that explained everything.

'Yes, young people.' Jacobus rubbed his sandpaper whiskers. He couldn't remember the last time he had shaved. He wondered why he even bothered, since every time he put a razor to his throat he took his life in his hands.

'Thank you, professor. You've been very helpful,' he said. 'I think I have to shave and get ready for another meeting now.'

'Before you go,' Yumi said to Shames, 'I've got an academic problem you or Chase might be able to help me with. Totally unrelated. It will only take a couple of minutes. Is that OK?'

'No problem,' Shames said.

'I got this email from our office manager,' Yumi said. 'It's about the scheduling of a tenure hearing, I think, but I don't understand what she's asking

228

for. It says, "Please go to H-T-T-P-colon-backslash-backslash-box-dot-Kinderhoek-dot-edu-backslash, and log in with your conservatory ID and password. Once you have logged in for the first time, Cbox will recognize your name so that we can invite you to see your folder with materials for the review. Please let me know that you have logged in to Cbox, and I can invite you to see your folder." I have no idea what any of that means.'

Shames laughed.

'They're doing the same hocus-pocus at the community college,' she said. 'Most of our faculty can't figure it out, either.'

'I think there's a computer in the hotel lobby,' Anderson said. 'What's your ID and password?'

'I don't even know!' Yumi said.

Anderson suggested that Yumi find that out at her meeting with Connie Jean and then he would be able to help her with the message. Yumi reasoned that she might as well just get the information from Connie Jean and avoid having to go through the whole exercise.

'Why do they bother with this shit anyway?' Jacobus asked.

'They're worried that someone could get your personal information that's stored on the computer files. Your social security number, your financial records. They could steal your entire identity.'

'I wouldn't wish that on my worst enemy,' Jacobus said.

Yumi invited Chase and Arlene Shames to join Jacobus and her for lunch, but Shames had to leave to prepare midterm grades for her classes. Regarding Lucien Knotts's whereabouts, she

229

suggested that on Monday, the first day classes resumed, Anderson should come to her classroom and see if Lucien was there. If not, then they could start to worry. 'Who knows?' she postulated. 'With the warm weather maybe they just went on a camping trip. It would be like Lucien to do something hippie like that.'

'Couldn't you just keep an eye out for Knotts yourself and let us know directly whether he shows up?' Jacobus asked.

'My classroom seats three hundred, Mr Jacobus,' Shames said. 'And I don't take attendance.'

Jacobus asked Anderson to return to the inn after driving Shames back to the community college and meet him and Yumi there after their meeting with Hedge. Then he and Yumi went for lunch at Chops to strategize. The daily special was pot roast. The thought entered his mind, which he immediately tried to banish, that he might never have another pot roast, so he ordered it even though he wasn't hungry. Why did that bastard Dr Simons have to mention anything about his 'not insignificant growth' if he didn't know what it was? He would die of anxiety sooner than he'd die from the tumor.

Yumi hadn't mentioned to Connie Jean that Jacobus would be accompanying her to the meeting with Hedge. They were banking on Yumi still being in the administration's good graces. As an adjunct, she had judiciously avoided becoming enmeshed in the full-time faculty's politics.

'I guess they trust me because I'm kind of an outsider,' Yumi said.

'And you seem so innocent,' Jacobus added.

230

At three o'clock they ascended the service elevator of the Lievenstock Administration Building, knocked on the door of Charles Hedge's office, and entered.

'What are you doing here?' Connie Jean said.

'I have an appointment with Dean Hedge,' Yumi said.

'I don't mean you. I mean him!'

'I've come to thank you,' Jacobus said.

Connie Jean seemed flustered.

'Thank me? For what?' she asked.

'For trying to prevent me from falling down the stairs,' Jacobus said, hoping he sounded honest. 'I appreciate it,' he added for good measure.

'Oh! Well, I'll just tell him both of you are here.'

'Thank you.'

'What it is you want?' Hedge asked after Yumi wheeled Jacobus in and seated herself.

'Has your office ever received any sexual harassment complaints?' Yumi asked. Though polite as ever, she was in no mood to waste time on subtlety.

Hedge chuckled. 'Most of the time the faculty work those things out among themselves. You know how musicians are. Like musical beds.'

'I don't mean faculty.'

'No? Who, then?'

'We have some very troubling news,' Yumi said. 'We believe one of my students was molested.'

'Oh, dear!' Hedge said. 'I can't believe anyone on our faculty would be involved.'

'Who said anything about faculty?' Jacobus asked.

231

'Well, I—'

'What is the conservatory's policy on sexual harassment?' Yumi asked.

'Zero tolerance! Absolutely. Ze-ro tol-er-ance!' he repeated with slow emphasis, as if that made it more definitive. 'We treat every accusation with utmost seriousness and conduct a full investigation. Any harassment whatsoever on the Kinderhoek campus is totally unacceptable. If a faculty member is found guilty of harassment, we impose strict penalties.'

'What penalties?' Yumi asked.

'The first offense, we issue a verbal reprimand; if there is a second, a written censure, which is entered into that member's permanent file; and the third time, the faculty member is dismissed.'

'What's your policy if a student plagiarizes?' Jacobus asked.

'Expulsion. There's no room for cheating at Kinderhoek.'

'So a kid copying a page from the biography of Luigi Boccherini is a worse offense than Professor Potentate groping a young girl.'

'Don't be absurd, Jacobus. There are levels of harassment. We've got it all spelled out in our policy statement. We would never—'

'We believe my student did file a complaint,' Yumi interrupted, determined to stay focused on their line of questioning.

'If she did, it would have been investigated,' Hedge said.

'How do you know it was a "she"?' Jacobus asked.

'Well, isn't it usually?' Hedge blustered.

232

'We'd like to see the file,' Yumi said.

'What file?'

'Of the investigation of my student's complaint against one of your faculty.'

'Not possible.'

'Why not?'

'First, because all records are fully confidential. Protects both parties. The mechanism we've put in place to handle sexual misconduct complaints stresses confidentiality. We want students to feel comfortable coming forward. If the students choose, the matter can be settled without the involvement of law enforcement. We investigate each case, which is heard by a special administrative committee. The findings remain confidential and are protected by privacy law.'

'How convenient,' Yumi said.

'I wouldn't take it that way,' Hedge said. 'And I don't appreciate your cynical tone, Yumi. It doesn't become you. Let's say someone accused Mr Jacobus of having abused a student,' he continued, sarcasm etched in his voice. 'Even verbally. Though such a scenario is so unlikely as to be almost ludicrous, if outside parties were to have access to such an outlandish accusation it could affect his pristine reputation. His career. At the same time, we wouldn't want the accuser's reputation impugned, either.

'Now, just for the sake of argument, if a complaint was in fact filed by your student, which is by no means a given – no, I don't mean to question your student's honesty – and if an investigation was in fact undertaken, then the conclusion must have been that harassment, in fact, did not take place. Otherwise, the faculty member would have been censured, and none of them have been.'

'So you're saying there's been no inappropriate behavior by any faculty members toward students?' Yumi asked.

'None that's been verified.'

'And even if there was, you wouldn't tell us?' Jacobus asked.

'That's correct. In accordance with the Family Educational Rights and Privacy Act, a federal law on the privacy of student records, Kinderhoek Conservatory is constrained from releasing identifiable information from a student's educational record to the public unless a student requests that the information be disclosed.'

'If my student gives her permission, then we can get the information?' Yumi asked.

'Let's cross that bridge when we get to it,' Hedge said. Then added, 'But my expectation is that she will decline that permission.'

'Why do you say that?' Yumi asked.

'Ask her.'

They had hit a stone wall. The meeting was a failure. Not wanting to leave empty-handed, on their way out of the office, Yumi asked Connie Jean for her conservatory ID and password so she could access her Cbox.

'Your ID is the first four letters of your last name followed by the last four digits of your social security number. I have no idea what your password is or anybody else's. You have to come up with your own. It just has to follow certain guidelines.'

'What guidelines?'

'You can find those on the faculty page of the conservatory website.'

'Do I need my password to access the faculty page?'

'Not necessarily, but it would be a lot easier if you had it.'

Jacobus and Yumi returned to the inn. Chase Anderson met them there after his hospital shift ended at eight p.m.

'What now?' he asked.

'You said there was a computer in the lobby,' Jacobus said.

'Yeah, but it's really slow. It's not even on Ethernet.'

'Where's there one that's on Ethernet?' Jacobus asked, as if he knew what Ethernet was.

'There's a bar and Internet café in town,' Anderson said. 'Van Winkle's.'

'Van Winkle's?' Jacobus asked. 'They serve beer there?'

'Thirty kinds. Their slogan is, "Get ripped at Van Winkle's."'

'I only need twenty. Let's go.'

At Van Winkle's, Anderson and Yumi worked on designing a password that satisfied the myriad requirements of the conservatory computer system. Jacobus ordered nachos grandes, mainly to keep Anderson happy.

'You want to check out Cbox now?' Anderson asked Yumi.

'No, I don't really care about Cbox,' Yumi confessed. 'What I want is for you to break into the conservatory files and find a report on Mia Cheng.'

'Without them knowing it's you trying to break in?' There was excitement in Anderson's voice.

'That's right.'

'Is that ethical?'

'Didn't you say you wanted to be a detective?' Jacobus interrupted, wiping the foam of a Sleepy Hollow Dunkelbier off his lips.

Anderson considered his answer.

'This might take a long time.'

'There's plenty of beer,' Jacobus said.

Last call had come and gone, and still Anderson had not managed to negotiate the extensive firewalls that had been erected around all the harassment report files.

'Let's call it a day,' Jacobus said. 'After midnight I turn into a prince.'

'No one will figure out it was me trying to get in,' Yumi said. 'Will they?'

'No worries there,' Anderson said. 'I went through enough back doors. You're safe. But you're not the only one who tried to get in.'

'Really! Who else?' Jacobus asked, suddenly no longer tired.

'Someone whose user ID is TAWR9122.'

'Tawroszewicz? What the hell?'

'You know him?' Anderson asked.

'Unfortunately, yes.'

Jacobus wasn't sure of his next move, but Yumi was ahead of him.

'Is it possible to get his password?'

236

'I already did. It's a simple one. F-r-#-1-0-P-R-I-X-!.'

'I don't know what F-r stands for,' Yumi said, 'but ten pricks? I can only imagine what that means.'

'You have a sick mind,' Jacobus said.

'From studying with you too long,' she replied. 'Do you have a better idea what it means?'

'No doubt the zero is the little kind. Combined with the one, it means "first" in French. It's *Premier prix*. First prize. That's what they call degrees when you graduate the Paris Conservatoire.'

Why would Tawroszewicz be interested in harassment files? Jacobus wondered.

'Did he get into the files?' he asked.

'Don't know.'

'Hey, pals.' It was the manager of Van Winkle's. 'We're closing up. I'll have to ask you to leave.'

'Ten more minutes?' Jacobus asked.

'Five.'

Once the manager was out of earshot, Jacobus said, 'Chase, can you use Tawroszewicz's ID and password to access faculty information?'

'No sweat.'

'Find his student evaluations. Everyone's told me they're great but everyone also seems to dislike him. Perchance, something is amiss.'

After their allotted five minutes, Anderson was still searching.

'Hurry up,' Jacobus said.

'I'm almost there. I'm almost there. Got it!'

'What do they say?' Yumi asked.

'They actually look pretty good,' Anderson

237

said. 'In fact, they all look good. He was telling the truth.'

Jacobus scratched his head.

'Read me one,' he said.

'Your five minutes were up five minutes ago,' the manager shouted to them.

'OK,' Jacobus shouted back. 'We're just about to go, but the young lady has to go to the bathroom first, all right? She's not feeling well. I think it was those nachos. Were they FDA approved?'

'Jesus! OK. Go ahead. But I've got to be back here at seven so give me a break.'

'Don't worry,' Yumi whispered to Jacobus. 'I'll give my nose a thorough powdering.' She patted him on the cheek.

'Read,' Jacobus said to Anderson.

'"Professor T is one of the good teachers I've ever worked with." "Mr T often compliments at us." "After two years with Professor Tavrosevich I always want to play in an orchestra again." "Sometimes I think I like playing the—"'

'Did you read all of that accurately?' Jacobus asked.

'Of course I did. Just because I go to a community college doesn't mean—'

'Down, boy! I'm not questioning your intelligence. I'm questioning the poetic license. What's your take?'

'Weird syntax.'

'My take, exactly.'

Twenty-One

Friday, April 3

The phone next to his bed woke Jacobus.

'Who the hell is it?' Jacobus grumbled into the receiver.

'Moshe Schneidermann. You sound a little hoarse. Are you feeling well?'

'What time is it?'

'Seven a.m. You did ask for sooner than immediately.'

'What are you talking about?'

'Last night, Dr Dahl received written permission from Sybil Baker-Hulme to exhume Aaron Schlossberg's body. It's Friday and he didn't want to wait until Monday out of fear the body would be beyond recovery. Also, Ms Baker-Hulme will have a difficult time as it is trying to placate her in-laws. If the body had been exhumed and defiled over *Shabbos* it would have been impossible.'

'When's the autopsy?'

'Today. Fortunately, we had a very cold winter so the ground temperature might have helped retard decomposition, but delay at this point could make the exercise pointless.'

'How long will it take to get the results?' Jacobus asked.

'Two weeks. Maybe three.'

'Jesus! What takes so long? Handel wrote the whole damn *Messiah* in three weeks.'

'Perhaps God was on his side. Dr Dahl will send tissue samples to the state laboratory. They will all require careful analysis, and as is the case with all public institutions, the laboratory technicians are overworked and underpaid.'

'Then just let me know what the results are when you can,' Jacobus said.

'I'm afraid I can't do that.'

'Why not? Don't you trust me? It was my idea to get the autopsy in the first place!'

'Calm yourself, Mr Jacobus. I'm not trying to keep anything from you. The fact is, even I can't get the results. By state statute – New York County Law 877, I believe – autopsy reports are only disclosable to three entities. First, to personal representatives, spouses, or next of kin. Second, with a court order, to anyone who is or may be affected in a civil or criminal action by the contents or anyone having a substantial interest therein. Or third, to certain state agencies.'

Why must getting to the truth be so difficult? Jacobus asked himself. Maybe there was a way.

'You tell Dahl that under New York County Law 877, as the personal representative of Sybil Baker-Hulme, he is hereby instructed to render unto me upon the conclusion of his autopsy the results of said autopsy.'

'Are you?'

'You can be damn sure I will be, but first I need to take a crap before Yumi gets here. She doesn't like it when my bowel movements keep her waiting.'

'Have a pleasant day,' Schneidermann said.

After Jacobus's breakfast, which was all of three cups of coffee and a half piece of toast, they went to hear Mia rehearse 'Spring' with the chamber orchestra at Feldstein Auditorium. Jacobus and Yumi sat at the back of the hall and off to the side so as to remain as inconspicuous as possible. He didn't want to make any more trouble if he could avoid it. Yumi assuaged his concerns, assuring him they were the only audience.

Their primary interest was to see how Mia had recovered from her tumultuous discussion with them. But it was also to take a closer look at Tawroszewicz. Chase Anderson's Internet search had teased Jacobus's curiosity. There were things he didn't understand fully, though he had his suspicions.

For the short amount of time Mia had had to prepare, her rehearsal of 'Spring' went remarkably well, especially considering the abnormal circumstances. Her playing was secure and clean, styled appropriately for Vivaldi, and reflective of the imagery of the music. It reminded Jacobus of the young Yumi, when she had first studied with him. And as with Yumi, he detected something hard as steel in Mia's playing that sought to conceal, to deflect attention, rather than to expose and connect with the listener. It had taken a murder and a stolen Stradivarius for Jacobus to unravel what had been under the surface with Yumi. With Mia he already knew, or thought he

241

did, and rather than being unsympathetic, he lauded her courage.

'Mr Jacobus,' came a voice from behind him. Snooty accent, Lilburn had said.

'Ah, Mr Millefiori,' Jacobus replied.

'Have we met?'

'No, you haven't had the pleasure.' Jacobus turned his head to the left to hear the man better. The orchestra on stage in one ear, Millefiori in the other. Stereo.

'Then how did you know it was I?'

'Regal accent.'

'Ah, thank you for noticing. And what brings you here?'

'To listen to Yumi's student. You?'

'To evaluate Mr Tawroszewicz. For his tenure review.'

'And so?'

'Sorry. That must remain confidential.'

'You were friends with Aaron Schlossberg, weren't you?' Jacobus asked.

'We worked a lot together,' Millefiori replied. 'His reputation was greatly enhanced when we performed his compositions on tour. We have one coming up in the fall and will premier what turned out to be his last completed symphonic work, *Cataclysm for Orchestra*. It will indeed be bittersweet.'

Jacobus tried not to cringe visibly.

'No doubt,' he said. 'With all that collaboration I imagine you knew him as well as anyone.'

'I should say.'

'Maybe even better than his wife.'

'Better than Sybil? Why do you suggest that?'

242

'In all the years you worked with Schlossberg, did you have any sense he was taking advantage of his students?'

'He did work them hard, and to my knowledge never paid them, if that's what you mean.'

'That's not what I mean. I mean improper sexual advantage and I mean female students.'

Jacobus heard Millefiori swallow several times before he responded.

'As I said, Mr Jacobus, some things must remain confidential. Some things are better left unsaid, especially unproven things. Now I must leave and work on this damned evaluation. Excuse me.'

'See ya,' Jacobus said. He heard Millefiori's footsteps quickly recede and turned his attention back to the rehearsal.

Unlike the previous orchestra rehearsal he had attended, this time Jacobus found Tawroszewicz to be circumspect, if not explicitly kind, in his comments to the students. He kept his badgering to a minimum and even offered what for him was a compliment: 'Not bad.' For once, he seemed more concerned with the orchestra than about his own grandiose self-image. The orchestra did, in fact, seem to sound better, and Jacobus wondered whether there was an actual improvement or whether the more positive atmosphere alone merely gave that impression. Or whether the two whethers were one and the same.

Vivaldi described 'Spring's' sparely orchestrated slow movement as: 'On the flower-strewn meadow, with leafy branches rustling overhead, the goatherd sleeps, his faithful dog beside him.' The only prominent part other than the solo violin was the harpsichord. Jacobus, sleep-deprived from a late night and early morning, related strongly to the goatherd and had to strain from nodding off. He pressed his sore foot into the floor, hoping that the pain would resuscitate him. To his pleasant surprise, far from causing him to cringe, the ache had subsided to a mere, dull reminder of his accident. Hope revived him, and he looked forward to being back on his feet and lying to the nurse about how he had followed her RICE instructions.

'That's what's-her-name, the accompanist,' he whispered to Yumi after a particularly tasteful arpeggio in the harpsichord. 'Right?'

'Lisette Broder?'

'Yeah. Her.'

'Yes. They had her play with the student orchestra because there aren't any harpsichord majors this year. How did you know?'

'It's the same realization of the continuo part when Audrey Rollins rehearsed with the orchestra and played at the masterclass. Broder said she had lost her part and was playing from a manuscript. Per tradition, in the manuscript Vivaldi would only have written the bass line, leaving the realization of the upper lines up to the creativity of the keyboardist, who in those days would often have been the composer himself. So for two different keyboardists to execute the realization exactly the same way would be as likely as Charles Hedge awarding me the Nobel Peace Prize. You think you can grab Broder after the rehearsal while I talk to Tawroszewicz?'

'Why?'

'Two reasons. First, she plays with all the students and is in all their teachers' studios. Chances are she can't help but overhear a lot of unofficial gossip. Second, she went to school with Aaron Schlossberg and maybe had a thing for him. Maybe she could shed some light on his youthful escapades.'

Their quiet conversation was interrupted by students stomping their feet and tapping their bows on their music stands at the conclusion of Mia's performance. Tawroszewicz thanked the orchestra and told them the rehearsal was over, which elicited even more vociferous cheers. Yumi wheeled Jacobus forward to the edge of the proscenium.

'I'm going to congratulate Mia first and then I'll look for Lisette,' Yumi said. 'I'll come back for you in a few minutes.'

'Ask Mia why she never reported Schlossberg to the police.'

'Now's not the time, Jake.'

'Is there a right time? Let's get it over with.'

'I'll play it by ear,' Yumi said, and left Jacobus.

Jacobus heard the stage emptying quickly. A vague residue of English Leather remained around the podium, but it could have simply been Tawroszewicz's olfactory doppelganger.

'Mr T, are you still there?' Jacobus asked.

'Ah, Mr Jacobus. You're brave man to still be at the conservatory. They told me Connie Jean tried to kill you.'

'Who's "they"?'

'It doesn't matter. You know. The grapevine.'

'Ah, yes. The grapevine. I, too, hear things

through the grapevine. I hear that your tenure review might not go so well now that your buddy, Schlossberg is out of the picture.'

'Those are the sour grapes you heard on the grapevine, maybe,' Tawroszewicz said. 'Schlossberg and me, we were never friends.'

'But at his party—'

'What does anything mean at a party? Will I say bad things about a man in his own house?'

'What bad things?'

Tawroszewicz laughed unpleasantly. It reminded Jacobus of the moment in *Othello* when Iago gets his hands on Desdemona's handkerchief.

'You should ask his wife that question,' Tawroszewicz said. 'Not me.'

'Ah, yes! The Dame Sybil. Isn't she supposed to narrate at your Vivaldi performance?'

'That's right.'

'So when is she going to rehearse with you?'

'As late as possible. Why waste rehearsal time?'

'Not the best of chums, either?'

'I am not the only one with whom she is not best friends. But I still have allies. And I will take my chances with tenure.'

'You've got your student evaluations.'

'I have another rehearsal to go to, Mr Jacobus.'

Jacobus heard the quickly receding footsteps echo on the stage floor. Tawroszewicz's brusque conclusion to their conversation confirmed his suspicions.

Other, more familiar, footsteps crescendoed in his direction.

'So?' he asked.

'I didn't ask her,' Yumi said. 'But I did tell her I wanted to talk to her in private.'

'All right. And Broder?'

'By the time I finished talking to Mia,' Yumi said, 'Lisette was gone. Another rehearsal, I guess.'

When they got back to the inn, Jacobus phoned Lilburn's room. There being no answer, he went to the desk to leave a message.

'Mr Lilburn checked out this morning,' the desk clerk informed him.

Jacobus had Yumi call him on her cellphone.

'Lilburn,' Jacobus said. 'I want you to find out if anything untoward went on with Schlossberg while he was a student at NYU. I also want you to find out if he and Lisette Broder played together when she was there, and if so, what was the extent of their relationship.'

'And by "untoward" you mean . . .?'

'As in raping women.'

'Dear me!'

'Might make a nice footnote in your retrospective.'

'I might be able to answer the second part of your request,' Lilburn said. 'I've got one of his biographies, *Resonance*, on my desk. But as for the first, I wouldn't know where to begin.'

'In that case, just the second for now. I've been trying to get a hold of Broder but she flits around here like a poltergeist. I'm hoping she can shed some light on his extracurricular activities.'

'All right. I've got to finish up this piece. It's turning out to be far more intriguing than I at first envisioned. I'll get back to you tonight.'

Jacobus's next call was to Chase Anderson.

'I'm sorry, Mr Jacobus,' Anderson said. 'I haven't figured out how to crack that firewall and I've got to go visit my mother in Plattsburgh this weekend.'

'When do you get back?'

'Sunday night.'

'Will you be able to find out if Lucien Knotts shows up to class on Monday?'

'Absolutely! I even found his photo ID online so I know what he looks like.'

'OK. Say hi to Mom for me.'

The last call was to Sybil Baker-Hulme. In the goriest detail his lurid imagination could conjure, Jacobus painstakingly described, step-by-step, how gruesome the autopsy was going to be. As soon as he was convinced she would have nightmares for the rest of her life, he told her that for legal purposes she needed to be present.

'I couldn't face that!' she cried. 'It's too, too horrific.'

Jacobus mentioned that the only way of getting out of it was by appointing a personal representative. Maybe she knew someone who had the stomach for it. Baker-Hulme asked if he would consent to be her appointee.

'After all, it might be one instance in which being blind is a distinct advantage,' she said.

Jacobus demurred. After all, he hardly knew the man. When she almost begged him, he grudgingly acquiesced. 'If it will spare you the discomfort,' he said.

'You're such a considerate dear,' she said. 'Just the thought of what they'll have to do makes me shudder. I'm going to Brooklyn, anyway – not that I want to – to break the news to Aaron's parents in person. I dread that almost as much as the thought of Aaron's autopsy.'

'How long will you be there?' Jacobus asked.

'Not a moment more than necessary!'

'Good.'

When Jacobus had learned of the growth on his lung, thoughts of mortality drove him to over-indulge in his passion for cholesterol. But now, he had had enough of Chops and Van Winkle's, and the thought of more encounters with the faculty at the conservatory café took away whatever appetite remained. So instead of lunch, he had Yumi take him to the hospital, where he exchanged his wheelchair for a fresh, tightly wrapped ankle bandage. The nurse thanked him for being the ideal patient.

'Come back soon,' she said as he departed. Yumi handed Jacobus his cane and helped him hobble around the hospital courtyard.

'Free at last! Free at last!' he said, gleefully tapping his cane on the sidewalk and poking it into beds of pansies. He even gave Yumi a peck on her cheek.

'I'm a new man!'

'Don't get carried away,' Yumi said.

'Why not?'

'Because you're about to walk into a statue of Dolly Cooney.'

Yumi drove Jacobus back to the inn, where he fought unsuccessfully against taking a nap. Was his energy dissipating? He had never thought about it. Maybe he'd been like this for years. Maybe it was his imagination. But even if it was for real, everyone runs out of steam when they get old. It was just natural. Wasn't it? Or was it something else. Something 'not insignificant.' Jacobus had a difficult time falling asleep.

He was awakened by a knock on the door, which by it's volume and rhythmic pattern he knew was Yumi's.

'Yeah. Come in.'

'Getting rid of that wheelchair and getting some sleep must have done you wonders. You look ten years younger,' Yumi said.

Was she lying? Just trying to make him feel better?

'Younger than what?' he asked. 'That's the question. What's up?'

'I spoke to Mia,' she said. 'She said that Hedge made her sign a nondisclosure statement saying she wouldn't go to law enforcement or talk about her complaint. If she signed, she'd continue to receive her scholarship plus be awarded a teaching assistanceship, which would provide her an additional stipend; but if she didn't sign, or signed and subsequently broke the agreement, she'd forfeit those benefits and be subject to being sued for defamation of both Schlossberg and the conservatory. The implicit threat was that it would ruin any future she had in music.'

'So she was paid off to keep her mouth shut.'

'It seems so. And she begged me to please not tell anyone but you.'

'Sometimes I wonder how many lambs we've

250

led to slaughter in the name of music,' Jacobus said.

Yumi did not offer an answer.

Schneidermann called at four thirty.

'Dr Dahl wants to see us,' he said.

'I thought you said the results would take ten years,' Jacobus replied.

'That's standard. I guess this situation is not.'

'Don't you have to go to synagogue soon?'

'It's spring break.'

Jacobus and Yumi met Schneidermann, who was waiting for them, at the conference room of the medical examiner's offices adjacent to the autopsy lab. Quiet, soothing music played over a PA. Jacobus traced his fingertips around the edge of the table at which they were seated. It was round. They chatted while they waited for Dahl. The sound was non-reverberant, like in a recording studio. 'Dead,' was the ironic adjective that entered into Jacobus's mind. A soundproofed room. He asked Yumi for more details. 'Not much to see,' she said, and described a room, window shades closed, that was spare but for two pots of artificial ficus trees and a few boxes of tissues on the table.

The connecting door from Dr Dahl's office opened and the doctor greeted them.

'Thank you for coming,' he said. He presented a form for Jacobus to sign that appointed him Sybil's official representative. Yumi helped him sign it.

'So this is where you meet with the families and break the bad news in a good way?' Jacobus asked.

'Yes, that's right. But I can't tell if the news I have for you is good or bad.'

'According to Professor Schneidermann, there shouldn't have been *any* news for a fortnight.'

'Ninety-nine percent of the time that would have been true, but indications were so clear to me that I can all but guarantee what the lab technicians are going to conclude. Frankly, I'm perplexed why the attending physician at the hospital didn't see the signs, but we can get to that later. I gather from Professor Schneidermann that you're already acquainted with the death certificate.'

'Yes.'

'Medically, the certificate is correct. Schlossberg did indeed die of renal and hepatic failure, from complications due to diabetes compounded by cirrhosis of the liver and advanced kidney disease.'

'So there's no case, then,' Jacobus said.

'I'm not sure what you mean by "case,"' Dahl continued, 'but you didn't hear what I said.'

'You said the certificate was correct.'

'Let me try to help,' Schneidermann intervened. 'Dr Dahl said *medically* correct. *Ethically* correct, maybe we're not so sure. What he's saying is that the certificate was the truth, but it was not the whole truth. The whole truth, which will be in the autopsy report, is that Aaron Schlossberg died from eating a poisoned mushroom.'

'Wait a minute! A lot of people ate poisoned mushrooms at that party,' Jacobus objected. 'And except for extreme cases of the squirts, no one was worse for the wear.'

'Yes, I heard about that unfortunate party,' Dahl said. 'It was in the local news. But I've

252

concluded from the symptoms and the follow-up lab tests that the mushrooms ingested by the guests were *Omphalotus olearius*. The common name is jack-o'-lanterns, and they're easily mistaken for chanterelles. They contain the toxin muscarine, which tends to cause acute gastro-enteritis soon after ingestion but without further toxicity. The common symptoms present as nausea, vomiting, and abdominal cramping as well as diarrhea. What you referred to as "the squirts." Are you following me so far?'

Jacobus grunted assent. Sybil had already told him that much.

'Good. Unlike his colleagues, however, Professor Schlossberg also ingested *Gyromitra esculenta*, what is sometimes referred to as brain mushroom, because to some people the convolutions on the mushroom's cap resemble a brain. They're also called false morels, because they closely resemble real morels – I personally think that's a more accurate name. And because morels are so sought after it's not beyond imagination that someone might convince himself that a false one was the real thing.'

'And false morels are worse than jack-o'-lanterns?' Jacobus asked.

'Far worse. They can be fatal. Not always. But at best they are quite dangerous. In fact, it wasn't until 1968 when we were really able to identify the chemical components of gyromitrin, which is the toxin in the mushroom. Its chemical name is acetaldehyde N-methyl-N-formylhydrazone—'

'Perhaps for Mr Jacobus that information is not essential,' Schneidermann said.

'Yes, cut to the chase,' Jacobus said. 'Yumi parked her car in a formylhydrazone and I don't want her to get a ticket.'

'Very well. Symptoms of *Gyromitra* poisoning occur within six to twelve hours of consumption, although cases of more severe poisoning may present sooner – sometimes only a couple hours after ingestion. Initially, the symptoms are similar to the ingestion of jack-o'-lanterns: primarily gastrointestinal, with sudden onset of nausea, vomiting, and watery diarrhea, which may be bloodstained. Dehydration may develop if the vomiting or diarrhea is severe. But then, dizziness, lethargy, vertigo, tremor, ataxia, nystagmus, and headaches develop soon after.'

'What are ataxia and . . . the other thing?' Yumi asked.

'Ataxia is gait abnormality,' Schneidermann explained. 'Trouble walking. Nystagmus are involuntary eye movements. It's sometimes called "dancing eye."'

'Yes,' Dahl continued. 'May I suggest that I finish my summary, and then you can ask all the questions you want? Otherwise, this might take a long time.'

'Summarize away,' Jacobus said.

'Thank you. Fever is a common and distinctive feature of *Gyromitra* poisoning which, surprisingly, does *not* develop after poisoning by other types of mushrooms. In most cases of *Gyromitra* poisoning, symptoms do not progress any further, and patients recover after two to six days of illness.'

'Sorry to barge in again, Dahl,' Jacobus said,

'but because of Schlossberg's diabetes, they did progress. Is that what you're saying?'

'Precisely. At least that is what I believe. In his case there was a less common phase of significant toxicity, including kidney and liver damage. This was evident upon my examination of Schlossberg's internal organs. As such, symptoms would have included neurological dysfunction, including seizures and coma, which would have developed between one and three days. The patient developed jaundice and the liver and spleen were enlarged. The lab will determine whether hyperglycemia – rising blood sugar levels – was followed by hypoglycemia – falling blood sugar levels. But liver toxicity was clear.'

Yumi's phone rang. She turned it off.

'Sorry.'

'Additionally,' Dahl continued, 'intravascular hemolysis caused destruction of red blood cells, resulting in increased free hemoglobin and hemoglobinuria, which led to renal toxicity and renal failure. Methemoglobinemia also occurred.'

Schneidermann interjected, 'This is where higher than normal levels of methemoglobin, which is a form of hemoglobin that cannot carry oxygen, are found in the blood. It causes the patient to become short of breath and cyanotic.'

'How do you know Schlossberg had shortness of breath?' Jacobus asked. 'He was already dead.'

'That may be presumed from his cyanotic state,' Dahl answered, 'meaning his skin and mucus membranes were blue and purple, which wouldn't have been the case otherwise. Frankly, I'm

255

surprised that didn't immediately send up a red flag to the attending physician.'

Jacobus recalled Chase Anderson's initial comments on Schlossberg's condition, that none of the other deceased diabetes patients had looked anything like Schlossberg. He had been right.

'Perhaps because his physician was being sensitive of Schlossberg's family's religious needs to bury him quickly,' Schneidermann said. 'Traditionally a Jewish burial takes place within twenty-four hours of death. Torah says, "You shall bury him the same day. His body should not remain all night." These days, that practice is no longer common except in Orthodox communities. Still, the funeral should take place as soon as possible following the death and never take place on *Shabbos* or holidays. So the fact that he had already been dead for two or three days . . .'

'This may be a stupid question,' Yumi said, 'but how badly did he suffer? At the end?'

'The terminal neurological phase would have concluded with delirium, muscle seizures and fasciculation – twitching – and mydriasis – pupil dilation – progressing to coma, circulatory collapse, and respiratory arrest. Death, when it occurs from ingestion of the toxin, usually takes from five to seven days after consumption. Because of Schlossberg's prior condition, I would say it happened much sooner. Not that that's much comfort. I think it's important to remember that death from ingestion of *Gyromitra esculenta* is uncommon, but with someone who had advanced diabetes, like Schlossberg . . .'

Jacobus finished Dahl's thought.

'It was a death sentence?'

'Unquestionably.'

'So you're saying someone killed Schlossberg with a poison mushroom?'

'Not in the least, Mr Jacobus! Not in the least!'

'Then what exactly are you saying?'

'Only that the manner of death on the death certificate probably should have indicated as "accident" instead of "natural." "Suicide" is possible but highly unlikely. It's difficult to imagine someone wanting to kill himself in such a manner, but there is neither reason nor cause to presume ill-intent.'

'Wouldn't you say, Fred,' Schneidermann asked, 'that the certificate should have indicated another option?'

'Not "homicide,"' Dahl said. 'There's no clinical basis for that.'

'No, not "homicide,"' Schneidermann said. 'But certainly "pending investigation" should be considered. Don't you think?'

'No. You were right the first time, Doc,' Jacobus interrupted. 'Either natural or accidental.'

'Why do you say that, Jake?' Yumi asked. She sounded perplexed.

'Don't want the good doctor to go out on a limb,' Jacobus said. 'Right, doc?'

'Well . . .'

'Look,' Jacobus explained. 'Schlossberg's family's going to be bent out of shape when they find out he's been dug up and Dahl made chopped liver out of him. His widow has gone through plenty. They want this show to be over. They've been grieving, they need to get on with their

257

lives, let alone having to deal with things like life insurance and all that bullshit. We now know how he died. An ill-fated fete, a lot of mistaken mushrooms passed around, and Schlossberg happened to be the unlucky schmuck to pick the blue ribbon. Case closed.'

'Mr Jacobus makes a valid point,' Schneidermann said.

'I'll think about it,' Dahl added. 'But accidental sounds right.'

'Who's going to notify Sybil Baker-Hulme?' Jacobus asked.

'I will,' Dahl said. 'Any more questions?'

There were none.

Yumi drove Jacobus back to the inn.

'Did you hear those symptoms?' Jacobus asked. 'Twitching, seizures, pupil dilation, dizziness. There's no way Schlossberg could have gotten from his house to the practice room. He couldn't even have gotten out his front door.'

'So then why didn't you want Dr Dahl to change his conclusion to "pending investigation"?' she asked.

'Because if he'd done that, the police would have to take over the case.'

'What's wrong with that?'

Jacobus pondered his response.

'Audrey,' he said.

'What about her?' Yumi asked.

Jacobus waited for it to sink in.

'You think she killed Aaron Schlossberg!' she said.

Jacobus shrugged. 'Think about this. What if

258

those two people I heard in the woods were her and her boyfriend, Lucien?'

'How would you know?'

'If we ever find him, if I hear his voice.'

'Hold on a sec,' she said. 'My phone's ringing.'

'I don't hear anything.'

'It's in my back pocket. It's on vibrate.'

The only phone Jacobus had ever owned was a rotary dial model. It would not have fit in his back pocket.

'I can only imagine how it feels,' he said.

'Hello,' Yumi said into the phone. 'Hold on.'

She gave the phone to Jacobus.

'It's Chase.'

'What's up?' Jacobus said. 'I thought you were going to visit Mom in Plattsburgh.'

'I had an idea.'

'Congratulations.'

'That was really exciting at Van Winkle's, hacking into the conservatory computers. So I got curious and went into the 4C Library files and found out what books Lucien Knotts checked out recently. Guess what?'

'Cut the crap. Tell me what you found out.'

'Among other things he checked out *Wild Living*. The big foraging book by Aaron Schlossberg?'

'So what? If you ask Sybil, she'd tell you the book was a bestseller. We knew that Schlossberg was an expert, and we knew from Professor Shames that Knotts was into foraging.'

'Yeah. But I went to the library and they had another copy. So I looked through it, and I was thinking about Schlossberg's party that Lucien worked at, and guess what?'

Just as Jacobus was about to curse at Chase for another "guess what," the answer came into his head.

'There's a chapter on mushrooms.'

'Not a chapter. A whole section.'

Twenty-Two

Saturday, April 4

Jacobus woke to an alarm clock ringing in the room next door and assumed it was morning. A light but steady rain slapped against the window. Mezzo piano. A historically informed rain. He started to get out of bed, but then realized he had no plan for the day beyond brushing his teeth.

He felt that the key to the puzzle rested with Audrey Rollins. To find her he needed to find Lucien, and to find Lucien he needed Chase's help. But Chase was in Plattsburgh visiting his mother and couldn't do a damn thing until classes started on Monday. What would he do with time on his hands for an entire weekend? With the rain, wandering outdoors was out of the question. A concert? That jazz guy, Sumter, had mentioned something about a jazz concert. If Nathaniel had been there, maybe. Jacobus nixed the idea and went to the bathroom to wash.

More talks with the faculty members? Maybe they could shed some light on Schlossberg. He dismissed that idea, too. Chances were he might divulge information he preferred to keep to himself.

He filled the sink, pointing his index finger vertically downward in it so he would know when it might overflow. He rubbed cold water on his face.

Plus, he was sick of conservatory politics. Of who was sleeping with whom. Of the ass-kissing for donations to construct a building as a monument to a family's wealth. Of the guerilla warfare between the academics and the performers. Of the character-assassinating whispering campaigns. Of making art a quantifiable commodity, a subordinate to the strangling effect of mindless computerization. Of the foraging of wide-eyed students by predatory professors in order to satisfy their almighty artistic ego. And libido.

Jacobus threw his toothbrush against the wall and heard it clatter somewhere on the tile floor. He should have waited until after brushing. Too late now.

Returning to his bed, he called Yumi from the bedside phone. Maybe she could drive him back to the city and he could spend a pleasant weekend arguing with Nathaniel over bagels, lox, and the latest Balkan atrocities.

'Good morning, Jake,' Yumi said.

'What are you doing today?'

'I'm in New York.'

'What are you talking about?'

'I didn't want to wake you. You seemed really tired. I'll be back on Monday.'

'What time is it?'

'Ten thirty.'

'Shit.'

'Is something wrong?'

'No. Speak to you later.' He hung up.

Next he called Nathaniel and was connected to his answering machine.

262

'You've reached the home of Nathaniel Williams. I'm out of the country until April twenty-third, but if you—'

He called his friend, Roy Miller, in the Berkshires in Massachusetts. He lived only an hour north of Kinnetonka Crossing. Maybe Roy would pick him up and he could spend the weekend at his house and visit with his dog. He hadn't been in contact with the Millers for over two months. They always liked to sit around and talk about things like steak and wood-cutting.

'Hey, buddy!' Miller said. 'How have you been?'

'Fine. How are things?'

'Grandkids here this weekend. All ten of 'em. Jesus! They don't give you a minute to breathe!'

'Ah. How's Trotsky?'

'Lovin' every minute of being the center of attention. They're all over him twenty-four/seven.'

'Great. How's my new house coming?'

'Last time I looked, pretty good. They're behind schedule a little. You know, long winter. But it's coming along. You'll like what they're doing.'

Jacobus couldn't think of anything to add.

'OK. See you.'

He got dressed with the intent of going to the lobby for coffee. He went to the elevator and pressed the down button, waited a few minutes and pressed it again and waited again. He heard someone walking towards him.

'Can I help you?' the someone asked.

'I've been waiting for the elevator the whole damn day,' Jacobus said.

'Oh. It's out of order.'

'Why don't they tell anybody?'

263

'There is a sign on it, sir.'

Now that he was out of the wheelchair, he could have taken the stairway, but instead Jacobus retreated to his room, fumbled for the doorknob, and closed the door behind him. Hours, or days, later, there was a knock on his door.

'What?' he called out.

'Housekeeping. Do you need your room cleaned?'

'No.'

'Tomorrow then?'

'No.'

'Don't you need anything?'

'Yes. To be left alone.'

Twenty-Three

Monday, April 6

The ringing phone woke him.

'I got him!' Anderson said.

'Who?' Jacobus asked. 'Who did you get?'

'Lucien! Lucien Knotts!'

'Knotts? Hmm. What Knotts?'

'Mr Jacobus, are you all right?'

'What do you mean, "Am I all right?" Of course I'm all right. All is right. Right is always right. What day is this?'

'Monday.'

'Time?'

'Nine thirty.'

'Morning?'

'Yes. Mr Jacobus, do you need some help?'

'Hold on.'

Jacobus dropped the receiver on the night table and, with his foot, found his cane on the floor next to his bed. He hobbled to the sink in the bathroom, turned on the cold tap, and stuck his head under the faucet. Without drying himself off, he returned to the phone.

'What do you mean, you got him?'

'Are you sure you're all right?'

'Yeah, yeah. I was just contemplating historically informed performance. Very deep. What's with Knotts?'

'Like we had planned. I'm outside his class and saw him go in. What do you want me to do?'

'When's your class?'

'Not till this afternoon.'

'Can you follow him without him seeing you?'

'Like Bogie?'

'Yeah. Just like Bogie. Call me back when you figure out where he's staying.'

Jacobus hung up and dialed Yumi.

'This your day to teach at the conservatory?' he asked.

'Yep. Back in town. How was your weekend?'

'Very relaxing. I might need you later. When do you finish?'

'Three. Unless my two o'clock student arrives late, in which case I'll finish early.'

'That's my girl. I'll be in touch.'

Jacobus cursed himself for the maudlin, self-pitying introspection that had consumed two days out of his life. He called for a cab and dressed hurriedly.

'Take me to an electronics store in town,' he told the driver.

'Circuit Boys OK?'

'Yeah. Fine. Whatever.'

Within an hour, Jacobus was back in his room with a portable cassette recorder and a serendipitous chopped liver on rye from Bialy Stock that his nose had led him to next to Circuit Boys. He took a bite of the sandwich, the first solid food he had eaten in days, expecting to demolish it in minutes, but no matter how much he chewed, he seemed incapable of swallowing.

Disregarding his lunch and unforgiving stomach, he turned his attention to the recorder. The simple device was a reasonable facsimile of the one Nathaniel had given him a few years before, so with a little assistance from the store employee he had familiarized himself with manipulating the five buttons: Play, Stop, Forward, Reverse, and Record. Taking one more tentative bite of chopped liver to bolster his fortitude, Jacobus began recording his observations on the matter of the curious death of famed composer, Aaron Schlossberg, beginning with the evening of Wednesday, March 18 and the 'Going for Baroque' symposium. Jacobus had bought a six-pack of ninety-minute cassettes along with the recorder. *That should be enough*, he thought.

Halfway through the second cassette, the phone rang.

'—don't – do!' Anderson said.

'What the hell are you saying?'

'Bad connection.' He repeated slowly. 'I. Don't. Know. What. To. Do.'

'Where are you?'

'Not far – Schlossberg – woods. Dirt road. If I follow, Lucien – know.'

'Will you remember where the road is?'

'What? Can't hear.'

'Will. You. Remember. Where. The. Fucking. Road. Is?'

'Yes. Don't need to shout.'

'All right. What time is it now?'

'Quarter of two. What – want me – do?'

'Go to class. Then have a milkshake on me.'

'Why?'

'That's what Bogie would've done. I'll call you later.'

Jacobus, too agitated to return to his dictation, hid the cassette recorder in a drawer under his underwear, where he was confident no one would be tempted to look for it. With Yumi about to arrive, he washed his face and changed his clothes so she wouldn't notice his standards for hygiene had sunk even further. He fidgeted until he heard her knock at the door.

'Where have you been?' he asked.

'Jake, are you OK? You look pale.'

'Why's everyone asking if I'm OK, damn it? Yeah, I'm OK. OK? What time is it?'

'Three thirty.'

'Three thirty? You said you'd finish at three.'

'My student arrived early and was prepared, so I gave her extra time.' Before Jacobus could bark his objections, she added, 'Just like you would have.'

Jacobus told her about his conversation with Anderson and they called him immediately.

He whispered, 'Can't talk. In class. Done in fifteen minutes. Meet you outside the library,' and hung up.

It took them a half hour to get to the 4C campus. They switched into Anderson's Gremlin, and drove back in the direction they came from, eventually detouring onto Sylvan Hollow Road, which led back toward the home of Sybil Baker-Hulme and the late Aaron Schlossberg. Jacobus sat in the front passenger seat with Yumi crammed behind him. About two miles before the house, Anderson stopped the car.

'Here's the turnoff,' he said. 'It's not really for cars. It must be an old logging road.'

'Why do you say that?' Jacobus asked.

'Just a guess. I've seen dirt roads like this before that just go off into the woods. I read that the WPA used to build logging camps in the thirties. I think that's why most of these trees look like they're less than fifty years old and why there's a lot of underbrush.'

'Can you drive this jalopy on that road?' Jacobus asked.

'Lucien was able to get there in his car, and he drives a Ford Pinto.'

'Let's go, then.'

Jacobus felt Yumi's hand on his shoulder.

'Wait, Jake. What if Lucien or Audrey are dangerous? And it's starting to get dark. What if we get stuck on this road?'

'"What if?" "What if?" All I've had for the last ten days are "what ifs". I need to start getting a "this is."'

'So?' asked Anderson. 'What do we do?'

'So let's go.'

The first hundred yards were passable, though still slick from the weekend rain. Then the road, or what was left of it, got rough. The Gremlin bumped up and down and jostled from side to side. Brush scratched at the sides of the car. Anderson expressed his fear of the disconcerting number of times the chassis landed heavily on boulders.

'Shit! Sorry. Shit! Sorry.' And on it went.

269

Anderson stopped the car.

'We here?' Jacobus asked.

'We're at a fork. I don't know which way to go,' Anderson said.

'Figure it out,' Jacobus replied. 'You wanted to be a detective. Get out and detect.'

Jacobus heard Anderson get out of the car or at least try to. The car door swung open and banged against a tree. Jacobus heard Anderson grunt as he slid out.

He returned after a few minutes.

'If we go left the road is dried out. If we go right there's a muddy area about twenty yards from here.'

'And you saw tire tracks past the mud?' Jacobus asked.

'Nope.'

'So then he must have gone left.'

'Yep. That's what I'm thinking.'

'Good work, Sherlock. Get back in.'

After bouncing along the left fork for another ten minutes, they arrived at a grassy clearing.

'I see a cabin!' Yumi said from the backseat. 'A few cabins. The edge of the woods. Over there.'

'And tire tracks in the grass,' Anderson said. 'Woo-hoo!'

After all the noise of their thudding drive, when Anderson turned off the car's engine they were blanketed by a startling, heavy silence. A 'No Trespassing' kind of silence.

'What now?' Yumi asked softly.

'Is his car there?' Jacobus asked.

'Don't see one,' Anderson said.

'Let's go take a look, then,' Jacobus said.

Anderson led the way across the field. Yumi, arm in arm with Jacobus, followed. His cane helped predict his next step. Usually it landed on solid, grass-covered ground. From time to time it stuck in mud and he had to yank it out. By the time he had gone fifty paces his shoes were thoroughly soggy. But for a few birds and a chattering squirrel, all was quiet. Was that a distant tree branch falling, landing with a strangely hollow echo? Jacobus's ears were on full alert.

Suddenly he stopped. Dizziness overtook him, combined with a curious sense of well-being. Was it from concentrating too hard? His knees began to buckle. He felt Yumi shift her position to support his weight. The haunting opening melody of the Brahms Clarinet Quintet entered his consciousness for no apparent reason. Anderson was by his side in an instant to assist Yumi.

'Jake, are you all right?' Yumi asked.

'I know this place,' Jacobus said.

'It reminds you of your home? Out here in the country?'

'No, no, no, no, no. I feel like I've been here. I feel vibrations.'

Two of the three cabins, overgrown with vines, were in a state of collapse. The third one, in the middle, was slightly better. Yumi and Anderson led Jacobus to that one. A pair of cracked, stone slab steps, no longer horizontal, led up to a low, uncovered porch that fronted the ramshackle cabin. Old floorboards, exposed to the elements for decades, flexed ominously under their feet. The accelerated speed of Jacobus's cane tapping reflected his lack of faith

271

in the porch's ability to support their weight for any length of time.

'Do you want to go back?' Yumi asked.

Jacobus's mind, if not his balance, regained its equilibrium, though the sense of having been in this place before persisted. He felt weak but was not in pain.

'No. I'm fine.'

'Let's get you inside and have a rest,' Anderson said. He knocked on the door. 'Looks like no one's here.' At which moment the front door creaked open.

It was Lucien Knotts.

'I think we've lost the element of surprise,' Yumi said to Jacobus. Her humor was her signal to Jacobus that she needed to know if he was OK.

'Hmm. No thanks to Sherlock,' he said, reassuring her.

'Can we come in?' he asked Knotts.

'Suit yourself.'

The inside of the cabin was stuffy, smelling of mold and mildew, and of vestiges of acrid woodsmoke. Uninsulated wooden floorboards amplified their footsteps and the tapping of Jacobus's cane. The cabin had retained the day's heat, and it was actually warmer inside than out, even though the windows – panes long gone – permitted air and flies to enter and exit at will.

'What do you want?' Knotts asked.

'To talk to Audrey,' Jacobus replied. 'That's all.'

'She's not here.'

'Yes, she is.'

'Ask your friends. This is a one-room cabin. Ask them if they see her.'

'She's here. First of all, when we were crossing the field I heard what I thought was a branch falling. But it wasn't. It was a wooden door shutting. Obviously it wasn't the front one because my friends had their eye on it. I also smelled the glorious aroma of eau de latrine when we were coming up the steps.'

'And second of all?'

'Second of all is that you didn't ask us who we were. You knew. Audrey must have told you. Tell her to come in from the outhouse before she gags in there.'

'What do you want with her? She didn't do anything.'

'Then she has nothing to worry about,' Jacobus said, which was his hope if not his conviction.

After a silence that was briefer than Jacobus expected, Lucien agreed.

'We don't have running water. You want a Coke?' he asked. 'Lukewarm?'

'Maybe later.'

Lucien went out the back door. Jacobus and Yumi sat in two rickety chairs, though how long the chairs would support them was questionable. When Lucien returned with Audrey, they sat on a tattered mattress on the floor. Anderson took a position by the back door in the event either Lucien or Audrey tried to flee, leaving Yumi to protect the entrance they had used.

'What do you want?' Audrey asked, echoing Lucien. She was more sullen, if that were possible, than she had been at the masterclass.

273

'I learned something interesting at that symposium a couple weeks ago,' Jacobus began. 'Were you there?'

Jacobus heard a commotion from the mattress.

'Wait!' Yumi shouted. Jacobus heard her jump from her chair, knocking it over. What had he said that was so distressing? Was Audrey going to attack him? He put his hands in front of his face to defend himself.

'I don't want to hear any more about that fucking symposium!' Audrey shouted.

'You don't understand!' Yumi said. 'Believe me. Lucien, tell her to stay.'

Jacobus sat there, not sure what to do next. If he opened his mouth again it could have ended things then and there, so he kept it shut and hoped. Lucien ultimately was able to convince Audrey to hear him out. Jacobus put his hands back down, folding them on his lap.

'What did you learn?' she asked.

'It was something Sybil Baker-Hulme said. I had never known it, and it took me a while to understand its significance. It was an answer to a question from her husband, Aaron Schlossberg, who, of all people, handed it to me on a silver platter.'

Jacobus waited for a response, but there being none other than the buzz of a confused fly trying to find the window opening, continued.

'Did you know that when Vivaldi conducted his orchestra at the orphanage in Venice, the performers had to play behind a metal grille so that the audience couldn't see them? That it was considered OK for girls to play music, to be the best orchestra in Venice, but *verboten* for them to perform in public? These days most people would consider that ridiculous. Going to a concert to hear music but not see the performers. But maybe they had a point.'

'What point?' Audrey asked. 'What does that have to do with anything?'

'The more I think about it, the more it seems to me that maybe it had less to do with modesty or women's subservience and more to do with actually protecting the girls. Girls who were just coming into womanhood but weren't familiar with the ways of the world. Girls who were easy prey to a man of influence or wealth. Girls who—'

'You've got it all wrong,' Audrey interrupted.

'Then why did you leave the school?' Jacobus asked.

'Because you humiliated me at the masterclass.'

'No, I didn't.'

'Yes, you did, Jake,' Yumi said, unexpectedly.

Jacobus was taken aback. He had almost forgotten about that particular confrontation. There had been so many since.

'Well, maybe I did,' he conceded. 'But it was only the result of your change of attitude from the party at Schlossberg's to the class. It was you who got the wheels rolling. And I think I know why.'

'You don't know anything.'

'Let me give it a whirl and then tell me if I'm wrong. You and Lucien were hired to help out at Schlossberg's equinox party. When you spoke to me there about the masterclass, you couldn't wait for it. I was impressed with your enthusiasm.

It was *you* who approached *me*, an intimidating, blind, old fart. You didn't have to do that.

'But then something happened, and I think I know what it was. Later in the evening, I heard two people, who I believe were you and Lucien, talking in the woods. The next day it was reported that quite a few of the partiers had gotten sick from eating bad mushrooms. And it was the same day of the masterclass at which you gave a convincing performance. I believe those two seemingly disparate events are connected.'

'Convincing performance? I thought you didn't like the way I played,' Audrey said.

'That's right. You played very poorly, much worse than at the rehearsal the day before, which was the first thing that made me wonder what the hell was going on. I believe you played poorly intentionally. But the performance I'm talking about is your acting performance. There in front of a large group of witnesses you manufactured a pretext to withdraw from the program that no one could argue with; even Yumi, who's nobody's sucker.

'So you dropped out and disappeared at about the same time that Schlossberg dropped dead.'

'He had diabetes,' Lucien said.

'Yes, he did,' Jacobus said. 'But that's not what he died from.'

'It's not?' Audrey asked. She sounded surprised. *Was she acting again?*

'No. He died from eating *Gyromitra esculenta*, and you can't imagine how hard I practiced pronouncing that.'

'How do you know that's how he died?' Lucien asked.

'Because our diligent, local medical examiner had him dug up and dissected. That's how.'

'Then it was an accident. He picked that shit himself.'

'Ah! The accident theory! Let me see if I understand this theory correctly. You think this expert on mushrooms – this gourmand who had written extensively about them – would pick just a single, exquisite morel only for himself, not show off and share it with his friends, and get it wrong to boot, fully aware that *Gyromitra* is among the most poisonous mushrooms in existence? And then, when he was at death's door, overcome with dizziness and seizures and nausea while his liver and kidneys were failing, instead of taking an ambulance to the emergency room at the hospital, he drove himself to the music building and seated himself at a piano in an unlit and unventilated practice room to work on his opera? Somehow, I'm not drawn to the accident theory. Having learned two important things since then, I think I've got a more plausible one.

'First, I learned that Aaron Schlossberg was a sexual predator.' He paused to let them acclimate to his awareness of this hidden knowledge.

'Yes, Schlossberg was a sexual predator, and you, Audrey, were one of his prey. One of his Aaronites. I don't know for how long, but from what I gather, it was ongoing. Yet, when I spoke to you at the party, a party in Schlossberg's very own home, your behavior strongly suggested you had learned to put that ordeal in the back of your mind, or at least thought his harassment was a thing of the past.

'The second thing I learned was that Lucien is a student at the community college, and not only is he taking a course in culinary arts, he's a devotee of Schlossberg's books on foraging. In particular, *Wild Living*.'

'A lot of people read his books,' Lucien said.

'Yes, but you were the one at his party, Lucien. I also learned that Schlossberg cultivated his relationships with his victims by taking them out into the woods on foraging parties. I can imagine how you felt about Schlossberg leading your girlfriend along the garden path. With your knowledge of mushrooms and with Audrey's help, you harvested a bunch of jack-o'-lanterns, which you knew would get everyone sick as a dog for a day or two. But that was only a diversion from the real deal, which was the *Gyromitra* for Schlossberg.'

'No.'

'You mixed it in with his squirrel stew or other creative concoction and served it to him, making sure that he, and he alone, ate it.'

'No.'

'You and Audrey, knowing you had your revenge, then moseyed into the woods and high-tailed it out of there. You decided upon a scenario she would fabricate at the masterclass, and she pulled it off to perfection. Almost.'

'No.'

'You keep saying no, no, no,' Jacobus said, with irritation, 'but I haven't heard a reason it shouldn't be yes, yes, yes.'

'If you're so sure,' Audrey asked, 'why didn't you go to the police?'

278

'Don't you get it?' Jacobus asked. It seemed so obvious. 'I'm on your side!'

'Why? Why should you be on my side?'

'I'll tell you why. When did you start playing the violin?'

'Five.'

'Just like me,' Jacobus said, though he was lying by one year. 'Kindergarten. While your classmates were playing with alphabet blocks, you were playing the violin. Think about that. Your parents paid thousands of dollars for your lessons and your violin. You busted your ass because you love music and love the violin. How many hours, Audrey? How many movies, how many dances, how many parties did you not go to with your friends because you had to practice?

'You're a talented kid, Audrey, but no genius. You're no prodigy. And by the way, neither was I, though Yumi might try to convince you otherwise. And you know what? I admire that more than if you were. Because it means dedication and hard work are that much more crucial when it's not easy. It means you didn't give up when that would have been an easy way out.

'So what happens? You audition to the conservatory that hundreds of other talented kids in the country are dying to get into, hoping against hope that you'll stand up to the competition and get in. And guess what? You're accepted. You can't believe it! You've made the big jump. Keep at it, and who knows, success may be just around the corner. The dream you've had since the time you learned to walk is in sight. Four more years of hard work and you'll be over the hump. Then

279

what? A career in an orchestra? Make a hundred grand a year and work with the greatest conductors? The greatest artists? Sure, but mainly it's so you can play beautiful music for the rest of your life. You can almost taste it.

'At the conservatory, you're assigned to work with the best teachers! World-renowned teachers! Teachers who will guide you! Teachers in whom you've placed your total trust! Your total trust.'

Jacobus's sigh told of a lifetime of disillusionment.

'And then you were betrayed. In Aaron Schlossberg's eyes, you were not a budding artist. You were not even a human being. You were a piece of meat. The hell with all those dreams of yours. He could care less. Schlossberg foraged for students like he foraged for his damned mushrooms. Schlossberg was a bastard and deserved what he got. That's why I didn't go to the police. Because if I were in your shoes, I would have killed him, too! I didn't go to the police because they wouldn't have been as patient with you as I am being right now. Yumi knows what a patient man I am. Isn't that right, Yumi?'

'We'll talk,' she said.

'I just wanted you to know, Audrey,' Jacobus finished, 'that I understand you.'

The floorboards creaked, but that was the only sound.

'Yeah,' Audrey said, finally. 'Some of it's true. But you're still wrong. We didn't do anything.'

'Tell me about it.'

'OK, you're right that he had sex with me,' she

280

said. She stopped. Jacobus waited and was inclined to say, 'Go on,' but held himself back.

'He made me feel guilty if I refused,' she finally continued, 'because he had gotten me some stuff to play—'

'Like the Vivaldi?' Yumi asked.

'Yeah, and his new piece. But after we did it I always felt disgusted with myself.'

'When did Lucien find out?' Yumi asked.

'Last year. I told him.'

'He and I got into a fight,' Lucien added. 'I hit him.'

'Did it end then?' Jacobus asked. 'Did he break it off?'

'For a while,' Audrey answered. 'But then he started again, like nothing had ever happened.'

'When was the last time?'

'The night of the symposium.' She laughed an unhappy laugh. 'He was raping me backstage while you and his wife and the others were talking about how important Baroque performance practice was.'

'That can't be,' Jacobus said. 'He was there in the audience!'

'He was and he wasn't,' Audrey said. To Lucien, she asked, 'Should I show him?'

Lucien said, 'I suppose. It's up to you.'

A moment later she handed Jacobus a piece of paper. It was twisted tight, like a candle wick. Jacobus unraveled it and tried to flatten out the wrinkles on his lap.

'Let me,' Yumi said. Jacobus handed it to her.

When she hadn't said anything for several seconds, he asked, 'What is it?'

'Audrey,' Yumi asked, 'do you really want me to read this out loud?'

'Yeah. I do.'

'*On the evening of Wednesday, March 18,*' Yumi read, '*Aaron Schlossberg, a faculty member of the Kinderhoek Conservatory of Music, pulled me into a utility room behind the stage of the Hiram Feldstein Auditorium of the Dolly Cooney Performance and raped me. The Baroque music symposium was going on onstage.*

'*As soon as we were in the room, he locked the door. It was dark. I said, "Please, no." He was taller than me and heavier, and he pinned me against the wall. I couldn't move my arms even if I wanted to, but I knew it didn't matter whether I resisted or not. It was always like that. He pressed his mouth on mine and pried my mouth open with his tongue. He pulled up my blouse, and when he touched me, it was repulsive and my skin turned to goose flesh. He unhooked my bra. His fingers were thick and slow, but he'd had lots of practice so it didn't take him long. He was distracted by applause when Sybil Baker-Hulme, his wife, finished her presentation, but only for a moment.*

'*Then he pulled up my skirt. I told him I didn't think we should be doing this and tried to press it back down. He said, "No worries," in that deep voice that he perfected that got so many of us in trouble. He kissed my neck. I looked away. Anywhere else but at him. He said, "Plenty of time," and reached between my legs. I cried out for him to stop . . .*'

'The shout that everyone heard,' Jacobus said.

282

'*Shh*,' Yumi said.

'*I froze when I heard more applause. I thought it meant the symposium was over. I told him again, "We shouldn't be doing this." He put his hand over my mouth. I couldn't breathe. He whispered into my ear, "You're exquisite," and started biting it. He unzipped his fly and grasped my hand, pulling it toward him. I closed my eyes. I thought I heard someone in the hallway. I said, "Someone's coming!" He said, "You're just nervous, baby. Relax. You'll enjoy it more."*

'*When he was finished, he said, "You're a doll," and zipped up his fly. He handed me a handkerchief. He said, "Here. Wipe yourself off." I asked, "Can I go now?" He unlocked the door, but he left first. I just stood there.*'

'That's the end,' Yumi announced.

No one said anything.

'Audrey, I know this is painful, but why are we reading this here?' Yumi asked. 'You asked Mr Jacobus why he didn't go to the police. I have the same question. Why didn't you take this to the police?'

'I was going to,' Audrey replied. 'But I – we – decided to take it to Aaron's house early the night of the party and show it to his wife.'

'Why her? Why not the police?'

'Because of who Aaron was. No one would believe he would do that to me. Because he's so famous. It would just be my word against his. I know what happened with Mia's complaint.'

'And what did Sybil say after she read it?' Yumi asked.

'She turned pale. I asked her if she wanted

283

me to leave, and she thought for a while. But she said no, she needed me for the party. She handed me the letter back and said she didn't have time for this now. We would discuss things later.'

Jacobus didn't want to doubt Audrey's account – the mention of the cry from backstage that had ruffled the assemblage seemed to fit – but there were things that still did not add up.

'But Schlossberg asked a question!' he exclaimed. 'At the symposium. How could he know what we'd been discussing on stage?'

'As soon as he left me, he went out into the auditorium. So he'd have an alibi,' Audrey said. 'He knew what his wife liked to talk about. He only needed a minute to come up with a question for everyone to hear. Aaron always planned an alibi. He called it his "P.D."'

'P.D.?'

'Plausible deniability. He was so slippery.'

'Can you tell us what happened the night of the party?' Yumi asked. 'Why did you agree to go in the first place?'

Lucien jumped in.

'Because I wanted to kill him.'

'No!' Audrey said. 'That isn't why we went. Lucien's just saying that. We had agreed because we wanted to show Aaron that nothing he had done would ruin our lives. That we could still be normal. To prove that even in his own house we were stronger than he was.'

That rang false to Jacobus, but he said nothing.

'Then it all went wrong,' Audrey continued. 'I was talking to you on the veranda about the

284

masterclass and then Aaron came and told me to clean up after Professor Dunster with Lucien. You remember that, don't you?'

Jacobus nodded.

'But I couldn't find either of them anywhere and was about to come back to you when his wife found me. She told me that the studio was a mess and I was getting paid to take care of it, not to hound the guests. So I went there, but it wasn't that much of a mess. I began straightening it up anyway.'

'Was anyone there?' he asked.

'Not until Aaron came in. It was like he knew we'd be alone there. For some reason he thought I had gone there to wait for him. He wanted to do it right there. I said no, but he grabbed me. I tried to shove him away, but he was so big, and he started squeezing me. And then Lucien walked in with Sybil. Aaron pushed me away and started yelling that I had entrapped him. I don't know what happened. Lucien and I were confused. It all happened so suddenly. We just got our things and left.'

Jacobus recalled that Schlossberg had been drinking heavily at the party. It was possible whatever minor restraints he had imposed upon his lust had been sufficiently loosened.

'Why did you leave out the back, through the woods?' Jacobus asked.

'I was humiliated. I couldn't look at anyone. I was sure someone must have heard the yelling.'

'And that's why you decided to drop out?'

'I couldn't face it anymore. I couldn't face going through with telling people about it. I couldn't face people looking at me. But what difference did it make? I couldn't have played any better, anyway.'

'So at that point, you'd decided to drop out,' Jacobus postulated, thinking out loud. 'But only when you heard people had gotten sick did you decide to actually disappear. And then Schlossberg died. You were afraid that after the scene with him, people would blame you and Lucien.'

'Yeah.'

Jacobus thought about that for a moment.

'You're not telling the truth,' Jacobus said. 'Either of you.'

'Yes, we are!'

'No. You can't be. Because everyone – his wife, the doctors, the authorities, his colleagues – everyone was absolutely certain Schlossberg died from diabetes. Natural causes! Not even an accident! No one had any idea he'd been poisoned. It never would have occurred to anyone to blame you for anything.'

Audrey and Lucien had no answer.

'It all fits,' Jacobus continued. 'It would have taken two people to haul Schlossberg, a big, dying man, away from his house. You could have done it a night or two after the party, waiting for Sybil to leave the house. She might have thought he had gone out for a breath of fresh air, trying to revive himself. Or to get some medicine from the drugstore. Who knows? Then, arriving at the vacant music building during spring break, you could easily have entered undetected, gone down the stairs or elevator, and deposited him in Room Nineteen. Sounds right to me.'

Still the two students were mute. Jacobus

waited. He would not be the one to break the silence.

'So, we thought if we told you everything you wouldn't believe us,' Lucien said.

'So far you've been about as honest as Richard Nixon, but try me.'

'We did put the jack-o'-lanterns in the party food,' Audrey admitted.

'Not we!' Lucien protested. 'I did it. Myself. Audrey didn't do anything. She didn't even know.'

'Well, that's very valiant of you. But why the hell would you do something asinine like that?'

'I just wanted to ruin his party!' Lucien said. 'That's all. He was always bragging about how great he was with his foraging and his parties. It made him feel so superior. I wanted to humiliate him. To make him feel the way he'd made Audrey feel. I thought using his own damn book would be a way to get back at him.'

'And when you heard he died you thought you might've killed him with those jack-o'-lanterns?'

'Yes. I knew they weren't supposed to be lethal, but then with his diabetes I figured maybe the combination . . . Anyway, that's the whole truth. We had nothing to do with the false morel. I swear.'

Jacobus was inclined to believe this story, because the one piece of the puzzle that had confused him – why Audrey had put on an act at the masterclass – was now explained. If she had had a premeditated plan to kill Schlossberg at the party, her act on the veranda had been Oscar-winning, and she simply didn't have

287

enough guile for that. She would have given something away. Now he understood the answer. At that point, she hadn't known Lucien had planned to sicken the guests.

Jacobus took a deep breath. He had been prepared to literally let them get away with murder. No one the wiser. Cause of death: ingestion of false morel. Manner of death: accidental. Case closed.

But now there was a new problem. If Audrey and Lucien hadn't murdered Schlossberg, then someone else had. And for what reason?

'How did you find this place?' Anderson asked, interrupting Jacobus's thoughts. It was the first thing Anderson had said since they had entered the cabin. 'I've lived around these woods for years and I've never seen it.'

Audrey laughed a bitter laugh.

'Aaron found it. Isn't that ironic? He foraged in this area a lot and just came upon it one day. It's only about a twenty-minute walk through the woods to his house. He used to take some of us out with him on his "expeditions." We'd feel really privileged. Then he'd bring us here. He told us, "only his special people." He said no one had been in it for years, so he cleaned it out and kept it for his little secret hideaway. Sometimes we spent the night. If I told him I wanted to leave, he'd laugh and say, "No one's stopping you," knowing there was no way for me to get home.'

'It seems a little weird and creepy,' Yumi said, 'that you would take your boyfriend to the place where your professor sexually harassed you.'

'I know,' Audrey replied. 'Pretty disgusting,

isn't it? But that's why I did it. I figured this would be the last place anyone would look for us, even if they knew it was here.'

'How did you find us?' Lucien asked.

Anderson started to answer. Jacobus interrupted him.

'Long story and not important,' he said. 'I understand students filed complaints against Schlossberg that got nowhere. Might any other faculty be aware of went on?'

'Maybe,' Audrey said. 'Who knows what they talk about? Maybe they like to brag about their trophies.'

'I have a question for Lucien,' Yumi said. 'At the party, why did you take Sybil to the studio where Audrey and Aaron were?'

'I didn't take her,' Lucien replied. 'She took me. She said we needed to go find Audrey because the party was almost over and we had to get the guests' jackets. We went through the whole house before we found them.'

'When the two of you entered the studio and saw Audrey and Aaron, what was your reaction?'

'I started shouting. I couldn't believe it. I wanted to kill him.' He paused. 'I suppose I shouldn't say that.'

'At least you're being honest. And Sybil's reaction?' Jacobus asked. 'What did she do?'

'I didn't notice,' Lucien said. 'I was too angry.'

'I remember,' Audrey said. 'It was a little weird. I'm not sure, but for a second I thought she smiled. Like Mona Lisa. Then she told us to get out.'

'So, what are you going to do now?' Lucien asked Jacobus.

'Not sure. But for the time being,' Jacobus said, reaching into his wallet and pulling out a handful of bills, 'here's some money.'

'For what?'

'You'll need a hamburger to go with whatever you've been foraging, and lukewarm Coke loses its appeal after the first case.'

He got up to leave, and Yumi rose with him.

'Do you want your letter back?' Yumi asked Audrey.

'No. I don't need it. I don't want it.'

'Audrey, you mentioned irony,' Jacobus said. 'There's another irony here. Do you know what this place is?'

'No. Not really. Just a cabin.'

'My young friend here thinks it was a WPA logging camp. It's a good guess. But I'm guessing he's wrong. I know he's wrong. Don't ask how an old blind man can be sure, but I can feel it.

'This is – this must be – one of the original Kinderhoek Settlement cabins. This is where World War II Jewish refugees, fleeing violence and annihilation in Europe, came for asylum. Where they came to play music together without fear. In this room, on this floor, in this quiet place, traumatized human beings played music to regain their sanity. To regain their sense of a future. I can feel their presence. I can feel the vibrations.

'Audrey, you're one of those refugees. You've escaped. You could have fled anywhere but you came to this place. You've survived. If you give up music, fine. But think about what it means to you first. Goodbye.'

Twenty-Four

Since Jacobus never did have faith in humanity, he couldn't truthfully say he had lost it. Jealousy, greed, lust, envy, resentment. Everyone picked at the scab of at least one, if not all of them. Always had. Always would. Nothing changes. What offense, what hurt – real or perceived – what pet peeve, might have provoked someone to murder Aaron Schlossberg?

Did he believe Audrey and Lucien? Maybe. He wanted to. College prank? Possible. When he and Nathaniel were college students, they had once poured a laxative into the fruit punch at a party at French House. *Snippy French majors. That'll teach them.* It was stupid and immature. He hadn't considered the possible consequences. Someone could have gotten seriously sick. Maybe someone had.

So it was possible they were telling the truth. But if Audrey and Lucien weren't the culprits, then who was? Sybil Baker-Hulme, who, like Gesualdo, discovered her illustrious spouse in a compromising position? Tawroszewicz, polar opposite of intellect and taste with Schlossberg, whose apparent friendship suddenly turned ice cold? Might Mr T have resented some conde-scending slight enough to feel the need to kill? Was there some issue over his tenure? Mia Cheng, with her tangled upbringing, who had reason enough? Could her controlled exterior have suppressed an inner rage that finally snapped? Dante Millefiori, the above-it-all whose success depended upon Schlossberg's celebrity? Hadn't he spoken of keeping secrets? Or any of the others. Dunster, Hedge, Handy? Consiglio even? After all, he had been the one who found him. The list went on and on. It could be any one of them. Or it might have been none of them at all.

'Need to rest a minute,' Jacobus said.

'We're almost back to the car,' Yumi replied.

'I said I need to rest.' He was short of breath. His brain was on overload as he considered the seemingly infinite number of possibilities. He wanted more than anything to sit down on the grass but didn't know how he'd get back up again. Or if he'd get back up again. 'Go on ahead without me if you want to.'

Anderson and Yumi waited with Jacobus in the tranquility of the woods on an early spring evening. It would have been an ideal day for a picnic, he thought, with thick-cut kosher salami sandwiches and deli mustard, and cold beer. An ideal day, if not for all the lying and the deceit. And the murder. *If not for that*. Easy to say. When was there a day in this world that was otherwise? So much for picnics.

'All right, let's go,' he said. They trudged to the car and drove off.

Halfway back to the inn, Yumi's phone rang. It was Lilburn. She handed the phone to Jacobus.

'Interesting tidbit,' Lilburn said. 'I've been doing my research on Aaron Schlossberg's NYU

292

days. I tracked down a copy of his graduating class's yearbook in their library. I must say, Schlossberg was much slimmer in those days. He cut quite a fine figure . . .'

'Cut the crap, Lilburn,' Jacobus said. 'Did you find out anything worth this phone call?'

'It's relevant, Jacobus. I traced the names of some of his fellow students from the yearbook. I started calling and got a few positive hits. I told them I was doing a Schlossberg retrospective for the *Times*, which is by no means untrue, so they were refreshingly forthcoming. Piecing things together, it seems that in the year he and Lisette Broder overlapped, they became an item. He wrote music for her and she played it. In the NYU archives I discovered a program in which she performed a piece of his called *Seductive Variations for Piano Alone*.'

'Remind me to listen to it the next time I—'

'For a few months the two of them were inseparable.'

'A few months? Until what?'

'Until Schlossberg did a month-long midyear project at the Royal Academy.'

'Ah!' Jacobus said. 'Let me guess what happens next. Lover boy returns to the Big Apple from the UK with a new, gleaming trophy on his arm: the charming, brilliant young duchess of historically informed performance.'

'Yes. You've hit the nail on the head. My sources told me that Miss Broder did not take kindly to being dumped in so public and unceremonious a fashion.'

A motive for murder? Jacobus wondered.

293

Maybe at the time. But why wait decades to retaliate? It didn't make much sense. And innocuous Lisette Broder? With her schedule, when would she even have time for murder?

Jacobus found himself about to be kicked out of Sybil Baker-Hulme's library.

'"Mona Lisa smile"?' Sybil Baker-Hulme railed dismissively. 'Is that what she said? Tell me, Mr Jacobus, what would you recommend? Tell me, Mr Jacobus, the proper way for a wife to respond upon finding her husband in the amorous clutches of a conniving hussy. What would you, Mr Jacobus, have had me do? Tear out my hair? Throw a vase? Faint? Would that have been the acceptable response?

'But that's not who I am, is it? "Mona Lisa smile," indeed! And why not? In its own way it *was* comic, the three of them entwined in their hopeless love triangle! Like a scene of a Handel opera, except of course Handel would have had gods and goddesses, not tawdry mortals.'

'Why do you say conniving?'

'Well, isn't that perfectly clear? A girl with such modest talent being selected over others with far greater qualifications to perform a concerto? Have you not heard the term "gold-digger," Mr Jacobus? It wouldn't be the first time a young woman used her body to advance her concert career. Is that not true?'

Jacobus could not deny it. He had often wondered at some of the questionable talent – not only women, either – who were getting plump, five-figure fees to perform with major orchestras.

There were enough stories. How much was true, he had no idea.

'Admittedly, Aaron sometimes let his penis influence his decision-making,' Sybil continued, 'but who benefitted the most, I ask you? Who initiated?'

'Why didn't you tell us any of this?' Jacobus protested, but he knew immediately it was the worst thing he could have said.

'Because it's none of your bloody business! Because my husband, whom I loved, has just died from a poisoned mushroom! Because . . . And such an *ordinary* girl. A girl threatening me with a one-page piece of crude, pulp fiction. A Trollope's trollop. Please leave. Now.'

When they got in the car, Anderson said, 'I guess that didn't go so well.'

None of it had. Before Jacobus had brought up the toxic subject of Audrey Rollins, Sybil also denied ever knowing that her dead husband and Lisette Broder had had a relationship. She even denied knowing Broder at all at NYU, and said that after joining the conservatory faculty Aaron had never mentioned her name except in the context of her position as staff accompanist. Sybil couldn't believe there was any truth to the 'fable' that Lisette Broder, 'of all people,' would have been attractive to her husband. And even if it were fact, and even if it were true that Lisette considered herself jilted, what did that have to do with anything?

'Only that the cause of your husband's death is suspicious,' Jacobus said. 'Do you think Broder might have wanted to kill him?'

'Mr Jacobus! Really! Suspicious? Murder? Lisette Broder? The medical examiner concluded Aaron's death was accidental. You were there, as I understand, as my surrogate. That is the end of it as far as I'm concerned.'

It wasn't the end of it for Jacobus. Not quite. It was then he asked whether Sybil was aware of the relationship between her husband and Audrey Rollins. He didn't want to call it what it was – rape – because he knew that wouldn't him get him very far. But it didn't matter. They were shown the door anyway.

Once more they tried calling Lisette Broder, and yet again all they got was her answering machine. Though it was getting late, Yumi suggested going to Stuyvesant Hall. Surely she must be in rehearsal with one student or another.

They found her in Room Nine. When Jacobus heard her and a student rehearsing the *Poem for Flute and Piano* by Charles Griffes, a piece of fluff he detested but which was for some reason a staple of flute students' repertoire, he wanted to abandon the plan, but Yumi assured him they would stop playing as soon as they opened the door. She was almost wrong.

'We have a senior recital coming up,' Broder said, 'and there's no time. I can't talk now.'

'Half hour?'

'I've got to practice "Spring" after this for the concert on Friday.'

She tried pushing the door closed on them.

'Tomorrow morning?' Jacobus asked.

Broder hesitated.

'Either now or tomorrow morning.' Jacobus made it sound like a final offer.

'Very well.' She checked her calendar. 'Seven a.m. Room Seven. I have a Haydn Trumpet Concerto at seven thirty.'

'Glutton for punishment,' Jacobus said to Yumi after Broder closed the soundproofed door on them.

Yumi dropped Jacobus off at the inn and immediately left for New York City because she had a Harmonium rehearsal the next morning. Jacobus was exhausted, but before going to bed he forced himself to record some more of his thoughts about the baffling case on his cassette player. He coughed up something into the bathroom sink that didn't taste good, and then probed around his chest to determine if he could feel any growths on his lungs. Not finding any, he fell into a deep sleep.

Twenty-Five

The next morning, promptly at seven a.m., Jacobus found Lisette Broder in Room Seven at Stuyvesant Hall. He found her dead. If not for his probing cane, he would have tripped over her body, which lay halfway between the door and piano bench.

Jacobus called Dr Dahl as soon as he could find a phone.

'Stay right there and don't touch a thing,' Dahl cautioned. 'It could be a crime scene.'

'Don't worry. I will not touch a thing.' Which was true, in a manner of speaking, because he already had retrieved all the music that Broder had left on the piano. Just a matter of syntax. While he waited for Dahl and the police to arrive, he sat on a wooden chair he found around the corner from the practice room, Broder's music in his arms, taking deep breaths to calm himself.

When the police arrived, Jacobus answered their questions as succinctly as possible. He stayed out of their way, waiting for Dahl to complete his work. He had a question of his own.

'Preliminary guess. Suffocation,' Dr Dahl said.

'Suffocation? Someone strangled her?'

'No. She wasn't strangled.'

'Then what?'

298

'I'm not sure. It's possible she suffocated if the ventilation had been shut off. If she had been here all night.'

'How can you run out of oxygen in a single night?' Jacobus asked.

'It's not so much running out of oxygen. It's the accumulation of carbon dioxide that's lethal. CO_2 is a toxic gas when the levels get too high – a mere five percent. In the poultry industry CO_2 asphyxia is a method used to humanely slaughter chickens. It's called CAS, or controlled-atmosphere stunning.'

'Lisette Broder wasn't a chicken.'

'Let me give you a human example: It takes twenty-four hours for a hermetically sealed room that's ten-by-ten-by-ten, or a thousand cubic feet, to be filled with a lethal concentration of CO_2 by a resting individual. Moderate activity will cut the time in half, and strenuous activity half again. A mere six hours. This room looks like about half that volume. If Broder had been practicing with great intensity and hadn't been aware what was happening, she might have realized too late what peril she was in. She could have passed out and then as the CO_2 level continued to increase from her breathing, it killed her.'

'So you think it was accidental?'

'What else is there to think? The door wasn't locked. She could have left anytime she chose to.'

'Had she turned off the ventilation?'

'No. The switch was still on.'

Jacobus remembered having tripped over the cord behind one of the modules.

'Did someone disconnect the electricity?'

'We checked that. It's still plugged in.'

'So how could she have died from carbon-dioxide poisoning?'

'It's my job to figure out the whats. The police figure out the hows. And in case you're wondering, this time we'll do an autopsy, but all indications are that's what happened.'

Jacobus wasn't buying it, but he kept it to himself. That the manner of death in Schlossberg's medical examiner's report remained 'accidental' was the product of his own persuasiveness, and he intended to keep his own counsel for the time being.

Schlossberg and Broder, both dead. Jacobus was totally perplexed. So many loose ends. He asked the police if he could leave. They had no objections. In fact, if he left it would be easier for them to continue about their business. As he rose from his chair, a voice he identified as the janitor, Sam Consiglio, addressed him.

'Mr Jacobus! The cops told me another one kicked the bucket. They want to ask me questions. How can this be happening?'

'Maybe *you* can tell *me*.'

'What do you mean?'

'You work around here. You mean to tell me you didn't see anything suspicious?'

'All I know's that when I left last night she was practicing here all by herself. And I don't have to be here in the mornings until seven thirty.'

'So how did she manage to stay all night? Don't you lock up?'

'Yeah, for the students. But faculty, they have

300

their special privileges. Got their own keys to the building. Not my idea.'

Jacobus sat back down. He drummed his fingers on the stack of Broder's music. Things began to become clear. He handed the music to Consiglio.

'Read me the names of the composers on all this music.' Consiglio rattled off one composer after another, which unsurprisingly included music Jacobus had heard at his masterclass.

'Felix Mendelssohn, César Frank—'

'Not Frank. Franck.'

'OK. Franck, Charles Griffiths—'

'Griffes.'

'Whatever.' He continued to pore his way through the dozen or so assortment of sonatas, concertos, and concert pieces. Finally, he stopped.

'That's everything?' Jacobus asked.

'I think so.'

Jacobus asked Consiglio to check to make sure. No, he might not pronounce all the names right, but he surely hadn't missed any.

Jacobus had had enough for one morning. He stood up to leave.

'You want me to put that chair back?' Consiglio asked.

'What do you mean, put it back? This is where I found it.'

'It's from the practice room.'

Jacobus had no idea why that chair was where it was, but Albert Pine, chief of police of Kinnetonka Crossing, did. Which was why Jacobus was sitting in a different chair, and an uncomfortable one at that, in the police chief's office.

'Why did you remove the chair from the practice room, Mr Jacobus?' Pine asked.

'I didn't. But if I had, what the hell difference does it make?'

'Because indications are that the chair was used to wedge the practice room door shut from the outside, making it impossible for the victim to open it.'

'What indications?'

'Abrasions on the carpeting outside the practice room and scratches under the door handle indicate the victim tried to open the door. Obviously, she was unsuccessful. Why did you need to see her at such an early hour?'

Jacobus was reluctant to explain the whole ball of wax. He had a feeling it wouldn't sit well with Pine that he had been conducting his own personal murder investigation. He was also pretty sure that if he unburdened himself to Pine, it would put Audrey and Lucien in serious jeopardy of being arrested. He was reasonably convinced they hadn't murdered Schlossberg. And, since they were in hiding, they could have had no connection to Broder's death. Jacobus was stymied.

'Broder was going to be performing in a concert this Friday,' he answered. 'The Vivaldi by Twilight concert. There's a violin student who's performing. I wanted to go over a few things about the part.'

'That's not what I understand.'

'What do you understand?'

'I understand from Professor Sybil Baker-Hulme that you expressed a keen interest in Lisette Broder's personal affairs. I understand

302

from the janitor, Sam Consiglio, that you were very inquisitive as to when and how faculty and students entered and left Stuyvesant Hall at night and in the morning.'

'What are you trying to say?' Jacobus barked.

'I also understand from Professor Elwood Dunster and others that you made it clear to anyone who would listen that you had no affinity for the music of Aaron Schlossberg. That in fact your aversion—'

'Are you saying that I killed Aaron Schlossberg and Lisette Broder?' Jacobus was dumbfounded.

'Maybe it's a coincidence that since you showed up on the Kinderhoek campus, both of them have died mysteriously. That you happened to be the one who found Broder's body, and that you were at the Schlossberg home the night he ingested a fatally poisonous mushroom.'

'If there's someone who's been eating too many mushrooms, it's you, Pine.'

'We'll see about that. But I do have to wonder why you have remained on school premises long after your dismal showing at your masterclass and your dismissal by the administration. Can you give me an explanation for that?'

'You've certainly been doing your homework in the past two hours, haven't you?' Jacobus said, beginning to understand. 'You and Lou Pine related, perhaps?'

'Brothers.'

'Go figure.'

'And he and I are very close. As a trustee on the conservatory board, he heard an earful from Charles Hedge about how you screwed up a ninety-million-dollar gift, and . . . well, let's just say my family doesn't keep secrets from each other. Until today I would have wanted you out of here, Mr Jacobus. But not now. Now I want to be close to you. Like my brother. Very, very close.'

'May I be excused now?' Jacobus asked. 'Or do you think I might also have killed Theodesia Lievenstock, too?'

Since he was at a loose end and probably under observation, Jacobus decided to go to the Lievenstock Music Library where it would be difficult to suspect him of subversive activity. He didn't want to remain there long and attract attention, so he cajoled the librarian into allowing him to borrow some cassette tapes of Aaron Schlossberg's music, convincing her that Sybil Baker-Hulme had requested them. 'Poor woman's still in mourning,' he said. 'His music makes her feel he's still with her.' From there he returned to the inn.

Jacobus did not consider Schlossberg's music to be beautiful, but the more he listened, the more he grudgingly accepted the fact that Schlossberg had known what he was doing. It didn't touch his heart, but it did awaken something in his brain. Whether his music would ever come close to giving Jacobus the same kind of emotional lift that Beethoven's did was a different story, but for the moment all he was searching for was simple guidance.

Schlossberg's most recent recording was an eclectic retrospective that included the *Seductive*

Variations. He had composed the piece in his pre-computer days, when real instruments played by real musicians were still in vogue. The performance on the tape was not by Lisette Broder, which was no surprise, but by Tallulah Dominguez, which seemed a much better fit. It was a strange piece, starting out in great complexity but ending very simply. Jacobus could make out threads of interconnected motivic ideas, but there seemed to be a great deal of random, superfluous material.

Being blind, he had no idea how many compositions were on the tape. When he turned it over to listen to Side Two, he was surprised to hear the voice of the composer himself. Spoken program notes. With a rich, persuasive voice like Schlossberg's, no doubt his producers felt it was a profitable marketing idea.

Schlossberg spoke in general terms of the sources of his inspiration. It was almost a verbatim repetition of what he had told Jacobus in person. How he loved nature and the forests; how Beethoven also loved nature and the forests; how he had evolved from acoustic instruments to synthesizers to a combination of the two. He also spoke about the individual pieces on the tape. What he said about *Seductive Variations* set off Jacobus's alarm bells:

'*The traditional musical format of theme and variations is for the composer to start out with a simple melody and then impress the listener with his versatility by reshaping the melody, going from Point A to Point B, etcetera, in any number of ingenious ways. Bach's* Goldberg Variations

305

and Beethoven's Diabelli Variations *are two of the greatest examples of this form.*

'But that's not how life really is, is it? In life we start out with seemingly infinite possibilities. Random and arbitrary possibilities. Which variations do we choose? How do we go from Point A to Point B in search of the holy grail? And what is our holy grail? For most people, it's love. But love of what? Along the path to love we are seduced by an assortment of possibilities: money, fame, possessions, power. Lust. Lust is perhaps the greatest seducer of them all. But when all is said and done, when we approach the opposite end of our existence, what is left – if we're lucky – is love. If we're not, we're left with nothing. In either case, we've gone from complexity to simplicity, opposite the traditional form of theme and variation. In Seductive Variations *I've followed the reverse fractals of nature's path.'*

Jacobus dialed the campus directory and was given the pager for Sam Consiglio, who immediately apologized if he had gotten Jacobus in trouble. He was just answering Pine's questions.

'No problem, Sam. But I have a question for you. You know what practice room Lisette Broder would've been in the night Aaron Schlossberg died?'

'That's a toughie. First of all, we don't know exactly which night he died, right? Second, it would've been on the sign-up sheet, and I get rid of them at the end of each week. And third, it was spring break, so there wasn't even a sign-up sheet. Especially being faculty, she wouldn't have needed to sign up anyway.'

'Good points. Hadn't thought of that. If someone did have that information, who would it be?'

'Connie Jean, I suppose. Once people sign up on the sheet on the door, I let Connie Jean know and she puts it into the computer. It's so that if anyone wants to change their time or cancels, she can arrange things. You could call her.'

'That probably wouldn't be the best idea, Sam. Think you might do that for me? Maybe tell her that Chief Pine needs to know and then get back to me?'

'I suppose I could do that. I figure I owe you one anyway. I'll give her a call right now.'

While Jacobus waited, he thought about the upcoming concert just three days ahead. Mia Cheng, not Audrey Rollins, performing 'Spring'. Someone other than Lisette Broder playing harpsichord. Sybil Baker-Hulme narrating the sonnet, in Venetian, while her arch-enemy, Bronislaw Tawroszewicz conducted the music. If audiences only knew what baggage musicians brought onstage with them.

Friday was also judgment day for Tawroszewicz's tenure review. Somehow all these disparate events and people were connected. The link seemed to be Aaron Schlossberg. Mia and Audrey, abused by him. Broder, his former, casually discarded flame. Baker-Hulme, the proud, cuckquean wife. Tawroszewicz, the . . . the what?

What was the bond that had held those two together? For a time, Schlossberg had been Tawroszewicz's sole pillar of support. Why? And why had Tawroszewicz disavowed their friendship

307

after Schlossberg's death? What was the solvent that in the end dissolved the glue?

Tuesday afternoon there was a scheduled chamber orchestra rehearsal. Jacobus didn't know what time it currently was. He guessed it was already afternoon. As soon as Consiglio called he would go to the rehearsal. He wasn't too interested in the music. More in the words. Not Vivaldi's. Tawroszewicz's.

He removed the Schlossberg tape from his cassette player and inserted his own, ready to record some new thoughts. Starting from the infinite possibilities and working his way to the simplest ones. Theme and variations in reverse. The phone rang. Jacobus pushed Stop.

'Mr Jacobus. Sam here. Yeah, well, I just spoke to Connie Jean. I had a tough time getting through. I got the impression that people in the office are running around like headless chickens over Miss Broder's death. Except for Connie Jean. You gotta believe she's a micromanager, but I guess this place would fall apart without her.'

'And so?' Jacobus prodded.

'Yeah. Turns out people could get into the practice rooms over the break only with her authorization. Some liability rigmarole that's over my head. Turns out Broder was booked into Room Nineteen.'

'Room Nineteen. Ring a bell, Sam?'

'Well, I'll be!'

Jacobus shuffled over to Feldstein Auditorium along the cobblestone path as quickly as he could without walking into a tree or giving himself a heart attack. He was so easily winded of late, which he attributed to old age and a lifetime of liverwurst. When he arrived at the auditorium there was no music to be heard. Footsteps approached.

'Excuse me,' Jacobus said to the footsteps. 'I miss the rehearsal?'

A young lady replied, 'It was canceled. Didn't you hear? Miss Broder died, so Mr T canceled it.'

'Know where I can find Mr T?'

'His office, I guess.'

'Might his office have a number?'

'Uh. Yeah, but I'm not sure.'

Jacobus hated asking favors but had no time to explore. The young lady, a viola student it turned out, agreed to accompany him.

Jacobus tapped his cane on the floor.

'Do you need me to, like, hold your arm or something?' she asked.

Jacobus almost replied, 'Not on our first date,' but caught himself. Though for decades it had been his standard response to that offer, it was not a comment he was comfortable with while investigating the murder of a faculty rapist.

Instead he asked, 'So, how do you like Mr T?' as they walked along the corridor.

'He's all right. I guess.'

'You guess?'

'He's weird.'

'The accent, you mean? East European?'

She laughed. 'No. He was always kind of mean. You know? But just this past week, he's been so nice. It's kind of creepy.'

'I understand he gets great student evaluations.'

309

'He does?'

Jacobus let it go at that. They passed a room from which a recording of dense orchestral music was emanating.

'Whose office is that?' Jacobus asked.

'That's Professor Millefiori. Do you want to go in?'

Jacobus considered it. Millefiori had more to lose from Schlossberg's death than anyone and nothing to gain. And as far as he knew, there was no particular connection between Millefiori and Broder. If he needed to see Millefiori he would do it another time.

'No thanks,' Jacobus said. 'But do you know what music that is? I've never heard it.'

'Oh, yes. That's Aaron Schlossberg's Third Symphony. We played it last semester.'

'That's the name? Third Symphony? Not *Calamari for Orchestra* or *Orsehay Itshay*?'

'I've never heard of those pieces. Did he write those, too?'

They arrived at Tawroszewicz's door.

'How are you spending your time now that they canceled the rehearsal?' Jacobus asked the student.

'I know I should be practicing, but I'm going shopping with my friends.'

Jacobus laughed. He thanked the student and knocked on the door.

'Yes. Come in.'

Jacobus entered.

'Oh, it's you. What do you want?'

'Just want to understand a few things,' Jacobus said.

'I'm busy.'

'I'll be brief. I was hoping to hear the rehearsal. You canceled it.'

'That was not my idea. It was Sybil's. We needed the rehearsal. She only has to talk.'

'Yet you agreed to canceling it?'

'My tenure review is Friday morning. I can't afford enemies.'

'But you have your excellent student evaluations. For example, "Professor T is one of the good teachers I've ever worked with."'

Jacobus heard a pencil drop.

'Strange syntax, don't you think?' Jacobus continued, after a pause whose length would have been uncomfortable for anyone else. 'I suppose that must have come from one of your typical semi-literate music students. Or maybe they were just in a rush. After all, who wants to waste time writing teacher evaluations on a computer when you can go shopping?'

'I don't know what you are talking about.'

'Hypothetically speaking, if one were to insert a negative in the evaluations to replace a positive, the syntax would be perfect. Try this one on: "Professor T is one of the *worst* teachers I've ever worked with." Here are some more examples, if my memory serves me: "Mr T often *yells* at us" instead of "*compliments*." "After two years with Professor Tawroszewicz I *never* want to play in an orchestra again" instead of "*always*." "Sometimes I think I *hate* playing" instead of "*like*." One might overlook the syntactical subtleties. If one were East European, for example.'

'Get out.'

311

'You gamed the system, didn't you?' Jacobus said. 'You dug into the school's computers. What's the word they use? Hack. That's it. You're a hacker. But hack has more than one meaning. Musically, you're also a hack. You have little to contribute except bullying the students, and you're doing everything you can think of to get tenure, except by becoming a better musician.'

'Shall I call the campus security?'

'I don't think you're going to,' Jacobus said.

'And why shouldn't I?'

'Because rigging the evaluations wasn't the worst part of what you did. One of your discoveries in your deep probes into the school's computer banks was a deep, dark secret about one of our illustrious faculty members. Wasn't it?'

'I don't know what you're talking about.'

'Yes, you've already said that. You were lying the first time and you're lying this time, too. You know all about the sexual harassment complaints that were written about Aaron Schlossberg. You know all about the reports and the whitewash and the—'

'He was a rapist!'

'Ah! So you do know! And you were a blackmailer! Schlossberg detested you, as do most of the other faculty members. You told Schlossberg what you'd found and threatened to expose him. I would guess he offered to pay you handsomely. But your price tag was something even more valuable: his support for your tenure. But at some point, he had enough, or maybe – amazingly enough – his sense of ethics got the better of him. He threatened you back and vowed to go public

312

and let the chips fall where they may. And that's why you poisoned him on the night of his party.'

Jacobus waited. Let Tawroszewicz call security now if he wanted.

The response was not what he expected. Tawroszewicz laughed. A tickle at first, which expanded little by little until his bellow filled the entire room. Jacobus thought Tawroszewicz might have gone mad.

'Now *you* don't know what you're talking about!' Tawroszewicz roared. 'Why would I murder Schlossberg? He was my biggest hope for tenure. My ace. I could not give up my ace. You know what I will have if I don't get tenure? I will have nothing. I tried twenty, thirty applications, auditions before getting this job here. "Sorry to inform you . . ." "After considerable deliberation . . ." Those were best answers. Mostly was nothing. If I lose here, who wants me? Twenty, thirty will be nothing. And once you are student conductor, you are *always* student conductor. Professional orchestras won't even look at you. You *smell* like student conductor. So where do I go, Mr Know Everything, if I don't get this job? I killed Schlossberg? You make me laugh. Go ahead. Arrest me. I laugh even more.'

Jacobus got up and left the room, listening to Tawroszewicz's howls echo through the corridor as he departed. Jacobus didn't care that Tawroszewicz thought he had just humiliated him. He had made some progress. He had learned something. He wasn't sure where it would lead, but the variations were spiraling back toward simplicity.

313

'Jacobus!'

Though the volume was raised, Jacobus immediately recognized the practiced monotone of Harold Handy.

'What finds you roaming these hallowed halls?' Handy asked.

'I heard about Lisette Broder. Wanted to find out what was happening.'

'Ah, yes. Poor Miss Broder. Dying suddenly is becoming quite the campus rage. The administration is fairly confounded, I'm telling you.'

'How so?'

'Why, ninety-million dollars so! Here they've planned all this hoopla to cajole the Feldstein progeny to fork over a large helping of their unearned fortune, and Aaron and Lisette have gone and ruined it. Hedge can't decide whether the show must go on or whether canceling it "in memory of" will bring the greater return, so for the moment he seems to be in a state of *rigor mortis*. Some of us hope it's just temporary.'

'And you. What's your take?'

'March 26, 1827.'

'Beethoven's death!' Jacobus said. 'What of it?'

'Exactly. What of it? One of the most dramatic deaths ever. The mighty Beethoven lay on his deathbed, unconscious for all everyone knew. His death rattle had gone on continuously for hours if we're to believe his biographers. But then, in midafternoon the sky turned unaccountably black, from whence was unleashed a supernal bolt of lightning and a violent clap of thunder. Beethoven opened his eyes and raised a defiant fist to the heavens!' Handy cleared his throat. 'And then Beethoven was no more.'

'I know the story.'

'Yes, but who cares? It's the music we care about, not Beethoven's death. If Charles Hedge were to raise his fist to heaven upon his expiration, who would care? And let's not forget that Beethoven was a schmuck during his lifetime.

'The moral of the story is, people drop dead all the time. How they die can be more or less creative – Lully put a baton through his foot while conducting and died from the infection – but chances are everyone's going to die one way or the other, sooner or later. The point is, Jacobus, the rhythm of life goes on. Music goes on. The vicissitudes of this conservatory, with all its warts, will continue to imperfectly churn out imperfect young musicians into the unforeseeable future, and then that, too will someday come to an end. After that, who knows? Maybe by that time Beethoven will have been forgotten entirely.'

'You're suggesting I pack my bags and go home.'

'Perish the thought! I've found you to be one of the most engaging minds to come across this campus in ages. You were a breath of fresh air at that symposium. I'm just presenting the big picture. Whether you decide to leave well enough alone is none of my business. All I'll say is I just think the wrong people chose to die. But what do I know? I'm just a music historian.'

What Handy hadn't mentioned, Jacobus noted, was the startling coincidence that Beethoven and Schlossberg died on the same day. Jacobus wondered if that fact might have given Schlossberg some solace in his last hours. He was reasonably confident Schlossberg would have preferred going out with a bang, as Beethoven had, instead of rotting to death, alone in a hermetically sealed fishbowl. Then again, maybe murder was poetic justice. But why hadn't Handy, the astute historian, bothered to mention the coincidence? Surely he must have realized it.

When Jacobus returned to the inn, he was intercepted by the desk clerk. He was in no mood for the distraction, having for a second time barked up the wrong tree in a looming forest of wrong trees. First Audrey, then Tawroszewicz. Who next? If he were wrong enough times and if enough people were murdered, there might be only one suspect left standing, and even then Jacobus wasn't sure if he'd get it right.

Once again a member of the Kinderhoek club had tried to humiliate him. Hedge, Connie Jean, Sybil, Al Pine, now Tawroszewicz. And for what? No one wanted him around. No one cared. Maybe Handy was right. Maybe he should just pack his bags and leave.

Even though he said, 'Don't bother me,' in a tone which meant it, the clerk, well-trained to deal with surly guests, persevered pleasantly.

'But, Mr Jacobus,' she said, 'you've received a postcard.'

'Postcard?' Jacobus asked himself as much as to the clerk. Who the hell would send him a postcard? Who even knew he was here?

'Read it to me,' he said.

'Sure,' she said.

Silence followed.

'Well, go ahead. I'm waiting,' Jacobus said.

'I don't know if I can read this. It's a little embarrassing.'

'Honey, I'm used to being embarrassed. A little more isn't going to kill me.'

'OK,' she said. 'But I'm just the messenger, OK?'

She cleared her throat:

'Dear Jake,

Greetings from Merry Old England. Just got done with some business in London. Looking forward to getting back to the city and whuppin' yo' white ole checkers ass. Fondly, N.

'I'm really sorry, Mr Jacobus. Shall I throw it out for you?'

Jacobus couldn't remember the last time he had laughed out loud.

'Nah, that's OK. I'll take it. I'll add it to my hate-mail collection. Tell me. What's there a picture of on the card? Spotted dick?'

'Let me see. It says, "*Margaret and Dennis Thatcher at the doorstep of the prime ministerial mansion, Chequers.*" She's wearing a—'

'That's fine,' Jacobus said. 'Very fine.' He pocketed the postcard and pulled out his wallet. 'Thanks,' he said, and gave the clerk a generous tip and thanked his friend Nathaniel from the bottom of his heart.

He went to his room, and while he showered

317

and shaved, he hummed 'Rule, Britannia.' He couldn't remember the last time he had sung in the shower, either.

'You still want to be part of *our investigation*?' he said to Chase Anderson on the phone.

'I'm pretty busy right now,' he said. He sounded doubtful. 'Exams. You know.'

'I'm about to bust the case wide open,' Jacobus responded. 'If you'd rather not be in on it . . .'

'What can I do?'

'I have a clandestine assignment for you. I need you to come here, pick up a secret envelope, and deliver it to Lucien Knotts without anyone but him knowing. Then tomorrow, he'll probably have a small package for you to deliver back here. Think you can do it? I hope that's not too much—'

'Sure thing. I have a late shift at the hospital tonight. I can drop by before. Seven thirty?'

'I'll be here.'

Jacobus continued to refine his taped narrative and added messages to Yumi, Nathaniel, and Roy Miller. He made a second, short recording on a separate tape, inserted it into an envelope, and sealed it.

'You're not looking very well, Mr Jacobus,' Anderson said when he arrived.

'You're not looking so hot, yourself,' Jacobus replied. Anderson laughed.

'It might take a while for Knotts to give you what I asked for,' he continued. 'Be sure to let him know how to contact you at any time. You can do that?' He handed Anderson the envelope that contained the taped message for Lucien Knotts. To sustain Anderson's enthusiasm, he added, 'It's of the utmost importance.'

'Whatever you say,' Anderson said. 'You figured out who did it?'

'I have. But if I divulge that information too soon, it may put more lives in jeopardy.'

'Gotcha! You can count on me. And, may I say, you've been great to work with.'

'You may. But then again, you may not. Now get the hell out of here.'

After Anderson left, Jacobus thought about going to get some dinner but his appetite seemed to have left him. In fact, he hadn't really felt hungry for weeks. What he did feel was tired. He went to the bathroom where he coughed up some more of whatever it was and, without undressing, went to bed.

Twenty-Six

Wednesday, April 8

Among the advantages of being blind is the ease of imagining oneself anywhere one wants. Jacobus was disinclined to leave his room at the inn. For one, he wasn't feeling particularly well, but mainly he was stuck there until Chase Anderson either called or arrived with the package. So all Jacobus had to do in order to be in his old home, which now existed only in his memory, was open his motel room window. Whether it was cloudy or sunny outside was immaterial. It was better he didn't know because it made it that much easier to imagine it was sunny. A fresh spring breeze carried the songs of chickadees into his room. Chickadees always buoyed his spirits. He pulled a chair over to the window and sat there, and very shortly he was lounging in his living room in the Berkshires.

It was the same with people. They were little more than voices to him. Sure, they each had their own unique scent, and once in a while he'd actually touch someone. A handshake here, an accidental bump there. Occasionally Yumi hugged him, which always felt good. Jacobus spent extra time reminiscing upon Yumi's English grandmother, Kate Padgett. Though he had only met her in person once and hadn't 'seen' her for years,

320

theirs had been as close to a serious relationship as Jacobus had ever had with a woman, but . . . He wasn't going to think about that.

He also never cared too much about whether it was day or night unless he had an appointment somewhere. If there was something he needed to do, he did it. If he was tired, which lately was more often than not, he would sleep. He had the luxury of spending hours on end to think without the distractions of visual images dancing in front of him.

In addition to the tape of Schlossberg's music, Jacobus had checked out *Don Giovanni* from the library. For him it was not only Mozart's greatest opera; he considered it one of the great operas, period. Plus, the subject – Don Giovanni's rape of Donna Anna and his ultimate descent into hell – seemed apropos at the moment. It helped him think. At the beginning of the opera, Donna Anna's father, the Commendatore, is slain by Giovanni as he is trying to defend his daughter's honor. At the end of the opera, he returns as a ghostly statue, daring Giovanni to take his hand. Giovanni, fearless in his arrogance, is too proud to refuse, but as soon as their hands make contact, Giovanni feels the icy hand of death. He sings: *'Who lacerates my soul? Who torments my body? What torment, oh me, what agony! What a hell! What a terror!'*

The chorus of demons responds: *'No horror is too dreadful for you! Come, there is worse in store!'*

Schlossberg, Jacobus thought, with his rich baritone voice, was the obvious Giovanni. Mia

Cheng or Audrey Rollins fit the role of Donna Anna, one of Giovanni's many 'conquests.' But who was the Commendatore in this plot? Jacobus asked himself. And though Schlossberg got what he deserved, were the killer's intentions noble, as were the Commendatore's? Or, more likely, were they the usual: jealousy, greed, ambition, or power?

The phone rang. It was Yumi. She asked Jacobus how he was doing. He said he was fine. Yumi said she was going to try to come up to the conservatory to hear Mia perform the Vivaldi on Friday night. She didn't mention anything about Lisette Broder. It sounded like she hadn't heard the news of her death. *Should he tell her?* He decided not to for the moment. She said maybe she could drive him back to New York after the concert because Saturday morning she had her first judo lesson.

'Judo?' Jacobus asked. 'Isn't that what matzohs are made of?'

It took her a moment to get the joke.

'Matzohs are just like your humor,' she replied.

'What do you mean?'

'Dry and tasteless.'

Jacobus laughed. 'Pretty soon your jokes will be as bad as mine.'

'As I always say,' she answered, 'I've learned from the worst.'

'Seriously,' Jacobus said. 'Why judo? Aren't you worried about your hands?'

Yumi explained that unlike many other martial arts, judo didn't require hitting or breaking things. It was like wrestling, but based more upon

322

balance and quickness than size and strength, and was a great way to stay in shape. If anything, it would be beneficial to her violin playing.

'But why? Aren't there other ways to stay in shape?'

'If you really want to know, it's because of what happened to Mia and Audrey. There are too many Schlossbergs in this world for my taste, and if anyone touches me against my will, I want to be able to break his arm.'

Jacobus thought about that for a minute.

'If you learn judo like you learned the violin,' he said, 'I pity the pervert who touches you.'

Yumi laughed and said she had to go to a rehearsal. She repeated that she would try to make it on Friday.

'Yumi,' Jacobus started, then stopped.

'Yes, Jake?'

'Nothing. I'll see you Friday.'

Sometime later, a knock on the door made Jacobus jump. He had fallen asleep. A second knock. Tentative. He had hoped it was Anderson, but it didn't sound like it.

'Mr Jacobus?' came the voice through the door. Mia Cheng's voice.

'Door's unlocked,' he called.

'I hope I'm not bothering you,' she replied.

'Of course not. Sit down. What's on your mind?'

'I'm thinking of quitting the violin,' she said.

'I know.'

'You do?' She sounded incredulous. 'How could you know?'

323

'I've known why ever since the first time I heard you play, though I wasn't sure what it meant at the time. Let me guess. You're thinking of quitting because you hate to play the violin. I'd go so far as to say you've always hated it. Because your parents forced you into it. Because you associate it with everything painful in your life. You rebel against the notion that just because you do something well – which, I have to say, you do very, very well – it means you *must* do it, and for all these years you've felt too guilty to admit to yourself that this is something you don't want to do. You've been the white sheep in the family but haven't realized it until now.'

'That's exactly how I feel! How did you know?'

'Because, honey, you're not the first one or the last to feel this way. It's all too common. But I must say with what you've gone through, I'm amazed that you've stuck it out as long as you have. You've got a long life ahead of you, and as much as some musicians may proclaim it, music is not necessarily the be-all and end-all. You've got a head on your shoulders and you'll find what you want in life sooner or later. Probably sooner. Feel better?'

Mia began crying. Jacobus hadn't intended that response but, since he was no good at comforting people, he just let her cry. Suddenly he felt her arms around him. She was hugging him, which made him even more uncomfortable. As he sat there, his arms at his sides, she thanked him profusely between sobs for being the first person in her life to understand. It was getting too personal for him.

'Have you told anyone yet?' he asked.

'No. Not even Ms Shinagawa. She'll kill me when she finds out.'

Jacobus thought about Yumi and her new hobby.

'No. I don't think she'll kill you.' *Someone else, maybe.* 'What about Friday?' he asked. 'You going to play?'

'I don't know. I can't decide. Should I?'

'Up to you, sweetheart. You don't want to let the rest of the orchestra down.'

'No, I guess not.'

Jacobus had an idea.

'On the other hand, if you could get someone to replace you . . .'

'I wish. But who?'

'How about Audrey? She's not as good as you, but she loves music.'

'But, she's out of the program. She's disappeared!'

'Maybe not.' Jacobus explained how Mia could contact Audrey and left it to her to make the decision.

Twenty-Seven

Thursday, April 9

Jacobus answered the phone.

'It's me, Chase. I've got the package. I can be there in about a half hour.'

'Today Thursday?' Jacobus asked.

'Yeah.'

'What time is it?'

'About ten. In the morning.'

'Good. Bring the package.'

It was going to be a long day. He quickly washed and dressed and organized himself, placing the tape recordings of his thoughts, some money, and an empty plastic hotel room laundry bag on the desk. He carefully placed the trash can next to the desk chair. He had barely sat down when there was a knock at the door.

'Come in. It's unlocked.'

Chase Anderson fumbled at the door. He was clearly excited by his undercover activities.

'Hand me the bag,' Jacobus said.

Jacobus was pleased that the paper bag was stapled shut, as he had instructed Lucien. He tore open the top of the bag and withdrew the requested item from it.

'You know what this is?' he asked, holding it up.

'A mushroom.'

'Not any mushroom. A *Gyromitra esculenta*!

326

A false morel! Here, take a close look.' He handed the mushroom to Chase and dropped the discarded bag into the waste paper basket next to him.

'No shit! This is the kind—' Chase said.

'That killed Aaron Schlossberg. Make sure you wash your hands before eating anything. Chase, I have a very important assignment for you. I want you to take this mushroom to Dr Dahl, the medical examiner at the Cooney Medical Center, and tell him to test it against the lab results that he should be getting any day. We need to corroborate how Schlossberg really died. Do you think you can handle that?'

'For sure. Can I put it back in the bag?'

'Take this plastic one,' Jacobus said, handing the laundry bag to Chase. 'It will keep the mushroom more sterile. No false positives or shit like that. I've got one other assignment for you that's equally important. I want you to take the cassettes and the money on the desk here. Mail the cassettes special delivery to Martin Lilburn, care of the *New York Times*. Use the money for the postage. I don't have the exact address. Can I trust you to get it for me?'

'No problem, Mr Jacobus. I'll get the address and an envelope and send it out right away.'

'You do that.'

'Is that all? I mean, is there anything else I can do?'

'Actually, there is. I've got an appointment this evening. Can you drive me somewhere? Somewhere not far?'

'I've got a class until six. I can cut if—'

'No, no. That'll be fine. Pick me up when you can.'

As soon as Jacobus heard the door close behind Chase, he reached into the trash can and retrieved the paper bag he had discarded. And then he waited.

The only question left was how merciful he should be. If he had been in Audrey's position, or Mia's, or probably any number of unnamed victims, he would have killed Schlossberg without any compunction whatsoever and not lost a minute's sleep. He would have slept better, in fact, knowing he had eliminated the worst kind of scum. The kind who, so enamored of their own greatness, feel entitled to prey upon the vulnerable, who only want to please.

A poor black man robs a convenience store and gets twenty years in jail, but a famous white professor who robs young women of their optimism, their self-worth, and their future gets what? A reprimand? No, not even that. A free pass. Jacobus would give him a castration.

If the system provided justice, Jacobus would have counseled patience. But the system only provided protection for the abuser and victimized the abused.

But wasn't the young woman partly *responsible?* they would ask. *Might she not have been at least* partly *complicit in their relationship? Didn't she accept favors willingly? Might the professor have misunderstood her intentions? We're just trying to understand. We must be fair. We're just trying to get to the bottom of this.*

'The bottom of this' is power. The power of

the professor over the student; the man over the woman; the dollar over morality. That's why he had hoped it had been Audrey and Lucien who killed Schlossberg. That would have been justice. *'The death of the great composer Aaron Schlossberg is a tragic loss to the world.'* Fuck him and fuck the world.

Jacobus heard a crash. He shook his head as if waking himself. He had overturned the desk. How had he done that? He was panting. He dropped to his hands and knees and desperately searched for the discarded paper bag among the broken desk lamp, which had become unplugged; the phone, whose complaining dial tone accused him of mistreatment; the dented trash can, which had been knocked over; the Gideon Bible, telephone book, hotel guide, and other miscellaneous disgorged contents of the desk drawer; and his indispensable cassette recorder. At last he found the bag underneath the desk blotter. He tried to set the desk aright but no longer had the strength.

He went into the bathroom and let the cold tap run over his head. He sat back down on the side of the bed and considered the source of his rage. It was justified, yes. But the intensity. Where had that come from? He knew the answer, though for his whole adult life he had tried to deny it, and rarely acknowledged it, even to himself.

'It' was his own victimization by a sexual predator when he was a little boy, a participant in the Grimsley Violin Competition. 'It' was when one of the judges, the renowned pedagogue, Fyodor Malinkovsky, offered him a great future in return for . . . favors. He had escaped the worst

329

humiliation when he gagged and vomited on Malinkovsky's legs. Of course, that sealed his fate regarding the competition, but not winning was not the wound that had never healed. 'It' never would.

So Jacobus had a dilemma. Schlossberg's killer had done the world a favor, in his view. But what if the reason for killing him was not to rid the world of a serial rapist but rather to replace one form of evil with another? That would not do. In that case, justice – if there were such a thing – would have to take its course. Jacobus would present the options. Where it would go from there was anyone's guess.

Jacobus waited for Anderson in the lobby so that he wouldn't see the devastation in his room. He wore his jacket though it was still warm.

'I've been invited to Sybil Baker-Hulme's house for dinner,' he told Anderson, when he arrived.

The bumps, the crunch of tires against crushed stone, and the discomfort of worn-out suspension reminded Jacobus of driving in Nathaniel's VW Rabbit over the dirt driveway that led to his house that was no longer there. Even the evening spring air, with the car window rolled down, had a similar, inviting freshness. But it wasn't exactly the same. And it wasn't Nathaniel in his Rabbit, Jacobus reminded himself. It was Chase Anderson driving his Gremlin along Sylvan Hollow Road.

The house he had lived in all those years – and which had stood for a hundred more before he had first set foot in it – now existed only in the memory of a blind man. What good was that? And when he was gone, what then? Who would remember the house? Who would remember him? In short shrift, neither would ever have existed. Maybe the scribes who wrote down all the *begats* in the Old Testament weren't totally worthless after all. Biblical Connie Jeans.

'Stay here,' Jacobus said, getting out of the car. 'Wait until she opens the door. Then take off.'

Jacobus began to walk toward the house. He stumbled when he stepped on an uneven slab of flagstone.

'You need help?' Anderson called.

'More than you can imagine. But stay in the car anyway.'

'When do you want me to pick you up?'

'I'll call you if I need you. You're a good kid.'

Jacobus resumed his approach and found his way to the front door. Having no idea where the doorbell was, he knocked hard. It was a big house, so when he heard footsteps coming from inside he breathed a sigh of relief. He felt the pocket inside his jacket yet again.

'Mr Jacobus!' Sybil Baker-Hulme said, more annoyed than surprised. 'What brings you here this time? I've had more than enough of you.'

Jacobus turned back to Chase Anderson, smiled, and waved. Anderson drove off.

'I heard you were distraught over Lisette Broder's death. I just wanted to come and commiserate.'

'I'm in no need of commiseration, Mr Jacobus. Especially from you.'

'Yes, I know how you must feel. But there's something I'd like to ask you to help me with

331

and, as you see, my ride is gone. Can you believe he just drove off like that? Young people these days! You wouldn't want me to walk home, would you? At night. It *is* night, isn't it?'

'Very well. If you must. Come in. You can call yourself a cab on your way out.'

He followed Sybil Baker-Hulme's footsteps into the library, though by now he could have found it on his own.

She offered him a drink with a voice cold enough to have chilled it. He was happy to accept a Scotch, no ice, which she placed on a small table next to the easy chair he sat in. Yes, a Scotch would be just right.

'Now, what is it you say you need my help with?'

'Just this. The score to *Anwar and Yitzhak* was not with your husband when he died. And the harpsichord part to Vivaldi's "Spring" wasn't with Lisette Broder when *she* died.'

Sybil laughed, but Jacobus noted its forced cadence. It spoke volumes. *How ridiculous,* it said, *but how true.*

'And is that supposed to mean something?' she asked.

'That's how I hope you can help me, because no matter how I go round and round with it, I always comes back to one conclusion.'

'And what conclusion is that?'

Jacobus held the glass of Scotch in both hands. With the fingertips of his left hand he tapped out the beginning notes of 'Spring' against the glass. *Such joyful music.*

'Come! Come! Out with it!' Sybil demanded. 'I don't have all night to dawdle.'

'I'm not sure how to say this in a subtle way. But what it means,' Jacobus said, almost reluctantly, 'is that you killed them both.'

Sybil laughed again, this time an augmented fourth higher. *The devil's interval. Any Baroque specialist would realize that,* Jacobus thought. *How ironic.*

'Surely—'

'Sorry. That wasn't fair of me to just drop that on you like that,' Jacobus said. 'Let me tell you a story. I'll start from the beginning. Maybe it'll sound familiar. And cut out the fake laugh. It's getting on my nerves.'

'I don't need to listen to this.'

'Oh, but you do! By the time I finish, you'll appreciate why.

'The story starts like this: Many years ago, a comely English lass – let's call her Sybil – is smitten with a budding, smooth-tongued American composer – let's call him Aaron. Aaron has no difficulty reciprocating her smittenness. It's his nature. The old story: boy meets girl, boy screws girl. They fall in love, get married, and live happily ever after.

'Except for one thing. When Aaron brings fair Sybil back home to New York, Sybil finds out there's been another woman in Aaron's life. Let's call her Lisette. Aaron says not to worry. She's yesterday's newspaper. So with hardly a blip, Aaron and Sybil return to their fairy tale existence, and Lisette finds cold comfort in being everyone's second string.

'Years pass. They're the perfect couple. Sybil and Aaron become celebrities in their fields.

333

They're highly sought-after both for their expertise and their personalities. And why not? They're both brilliant and attractive and have eminently persuasive voices in their own way. The lifetime faculty positions they accept from a renowned conservatory – let's call it the Kinderhoek Conservatory – are a dream come true. The sky's the limit. They're irresistibly *bon vivant*.

'The only problem, as Sybil soon finds out, is that even as Aaron gets older – a little gray around the edges, a couple more inches on the love handles – the women he's attracted to do not. In fact, they're students. Students at the conservatory. And it's more than a gleam in his eye or a charming penchant for pinching. It's what the older generation used to call philandering.

'Rumors about Aaron's proclivities spread among the conservatory community. What does Sybil do? She sees the danger. She doesn't want to see her whole wonderful ball of wax melt before her very eyes as the result of her husband's sophomoric behavior. What's more important to her, she asks herself? Her career and her celebrity, or her marriage?

'Sybil weighs the pluses and minuses. Maybe that's just the way men are, she thinks. Like the French. They all have lovers, don't they? It's Aaron being Aaron. It's in his DNA. And where's the harm? No one has complained, as far as she knows. So Sybil decides to tolerate, to forebear, knowing that her husband is having *affairs* with virtually any young piece of ass he can lay his hands on.

'A new character enters the story. Let's call him Bronislaw. Bronislaw is hired to conduct the conservatory chamber orchestra. Bronislaw is Polish without polish. His lack of musical style is anathema to everything Sybil has learned from her years of exhaustive research, and his boorish personality is repugnant to her, though for some reason the students give him positive evaluations. Aaron, strangely, also seems to have been won over by Bronislaw, and supports him in his effort to secure tenure. If not for Aaron, in fact, Bronislaw would be toast.

'Sybil simply can't fathom this. She can understand gullible students being impressed by a cretin, but Aaron? Warts aside, Aaron is a brilliant man whose musical standards were always light years ahead of anything Bronislaw would ever come close to achieving. Sybil remains in the dark, frustrated and angry.

'That is, until one day, by accident, Sybil finds Aaron in an amorous embrace with a student in a practice room. Let's call the student Audrey. Audrey plays the violin, and though she's pretty good, she's no prodigy. In a rage, Sybil says a lot of nasty things to Audrey, accusing her of seducing not only her husband but also Bronislaw as well, which Sybil has concluded must be the case because Audrey is sitting concertmaster of the chamber orchestra and doesn't deserve to be there.

'Audrey tries to defend herself, says it was Aaron who was the instigator and that it was Aaron who had asked Bronislaw to place her as concertmaster. And how could Bronislaw refuse, with his tenure in the balance? Audrey says that she, like all the other students, hated Bronislaw. That it was absurd for Sybil to even think she would sell her body to him simply for a month of sitting first chair in a student chamber orchestra. No one would do that.

'Even in her high pique, Sybil begins to figure out that something is going on that's not kosher. She becomes suspicious of those glowing evaluations Bronislaw brags so much about. She quietly speaks to other students, who all confirm what Audrey said. At least she was telling the truth in that regard. Everyone hates Bronislaw but the evaluations say otherwise. There can be only one answer to this riddle. And so Sybil confronts Bronislaw and, accusing him of somehow doctoring the student evaluations, threatens to report him to the administration, because in her mind he isn't even fit to replace Sam Consiglio as janitor.

'But Bronislaw is not the type to be easily intimidated. He says, "You might want to talk to hubby before blabbing to Hedge."

'And so Sybil does. And Aaron confesses that, yes, there had been some reports filed about him – nonsense of course, he says – about sexual harassment. Girls just trying to cover their asses. Whoops! Wrong use of vocabulary. But nevertheless, there are those reports, and Bronislaw somehow discovered their contents. How? Aaron has no idea. But there you have it, and unless Aaron supports Bronislaw for tenure, Bronislaw will blow it all up for them. There you go. Whole truth. According to Aaron.

'So it isn't the raping of his students that weighs on Aaron. It's those pesky reports. He would not like them going public. Definitely not. Nor would Sybil, who thought she was on the cusp of solving one problem only to find she now has another even bigger one: She has a husband who is a serial rapist being blackmailed by an incompetent she loathes. What to do?

'She could confront hubby head on. File for divorce. Turn him in. But she doesn't do either. She could expose Bronislaw for his blackmail, but if he calls her bluff and blows the whistle it will be the end of Aaron. At best, he'll be disgraced, his career down the tubes. At worst he'll end up in prison for a very long time. As a loyal spouse, Sybil would likely take some deep hits, maybe even lose her job and her stellar reputation. That part doesn't sit well with her. Not at all.

'But on the other hand, if Sybil does nothing, remaining mum with the knowledge of her husband's criminal behavior, Bronislaw might well get his tenure, and what's to say he wouldn't continue to hold the damning information over the couple's heads forever? Their lives would be hell.

'And that's when Sybil has the *aha!* moment: She'll kill hubby and, for all appearances, make it look like he died of natural causes! *The poor man's diabetes did him in. He should have taken better care of himself.* It was a stroke of genius! Dispensing with the rapist husband and getting the blackmailing colleague off her back in one fell swoop. Men! You can't live with 'em, but you sure can live without 'em. I'm paraphrasing Aaron here.

'But how and when to do it? That's the challenge. The devil in the details. Sybil comes up with a plan. At Aaron's famous spring equinox soiree, she'll mix in a little false morel, *Gyromitra esculenta* – I love saying that – into one of his artful recipes. She learns how to dabble in the dark arts of the wonderful world of poison mushrooms from *Wild Living*, one of hubby's own books on foraging, sitting right there on her library shelf. Ironic, isn't it? With his diabetes, she knows there's a good chance it'll kill him. Even if the medical examiner determines it was not his diabetes but mushroom poisoning that killed him, any reasonable person would chalk it up to a terrible, terrible mistake. Darn those false morels. The evil twin to the tasty, safe ones. Poor Aaron! Poor widow Sybil!

'Sybil savors the poetic irony of the plan. But then she has an even more brilliant idea, the result of some shrewd thinking on her part. What if, by some impossible odds, it is determined that Aaron's death is not from diabetes, not by accidental ingestion of the poison mushroom, but an intentional act? That someone did, indeed, put *Gyromitra esculenta* in his squirrel stew when no one was looking. Sybil would not want to take the blame, of course. Who would? But if not her, then who? Why, it would be that hussy: plain Audrey Rollins!

'When Sybil had thought the fling between Audrey and Aaron was a thing of the past she'd been willing, if not happy, to let bygones be bygones. After all, boyfriend Lucien had punched Aaron, Aaron had promised to mend his ways, and Sybil thought she had scared the girl away for good. But then she hears from her former rival, Lisette Broder, that Aaron just can't get enough of Audrey. Lisette reports the sounds of rutting she overheard while roaming the corridors of the Dolly Cooney Performance Building. While Sybil is expounding upon Baroque performance practice on stage at Feldstein Auditorium, hubby was pounding in a utility room backstage.

'In truth, had Audrey been a raving beauty Sybil might not have minded as much, but the fact that Audrey is plain and hubby *still* has the hots for her rubs Sybil the wrong way entirely. She decides she'll get back at Audrey Rollins for the humiliation the "affair" with her hubby has caused.

'So sly Sybil hires Audrey and her rash boyfriend, Lucien, to butle at the fateful soiree. She engineers a liaison between Audrey and Aaron, which Mr Testosterone believes will be an amorous one. At the precise moment, Sybil, under the pretext of having him clean up, escorts Lucien into the room to bear witness. Audrey and Lucien flee, but they are already trapped. If the authorities ever determine foul play in the death of Aaron Schlossberg, it will be pinned on Audrey and Lucien. In an amazing coincidence, as a childish prank, Lucien mixes nasty jack-o'-lantern mushrooms with tasty chanterelles, making half of the guests uncomfortably ill. They all recover, but, much to Sybil's delight, it puts an extra nail in Audrey and Lucien's collective coffin.

'To shed any doubt whatsoever about any potential involvement in his death, Sybil decides it will be more convenient for Aaron to die elsewhere. They always say the spouse is the prime suspect

339

and Sybil wants none of that. As Aaron's health precipitously deteriorates, she tells him she is going to be his Florence Nightingale and take him to the Dolly Cooney Medical Center. On the way, though, she makes a detour and deposits him at Stuyvesant Hall instead. As it's late at night during spring break she's confident no one will be there to see what she's doing or discover poor Aaron until it's too late. Unfortunately for her, Aaron is a big, burly man, and his dead weight – pardon the expression – is too much for her to handle alone.

'So before she leaves the house, Sybil calls her new confidante, Lisette Broder. As much as the two of them had been at odds with each other, they both have significant axes to grind with Aaron. And so Lisette, a genetically submissive sort, reluctantly agrees to assist the dominating Sybil. They drag the incapacitated Aaron along Sam Consiglio's slippery, newly waxed floor down into Room Nineteen, where Lisette had been diligently practicing, and leave him to die an ignominious and excruciating death. When the authorities find him, what other conclusion can they reach than that Aaron died while feverishly composing music until his last moments, like Mozart did with his Requiem? Even though Aaron fancied himself Beethoven.'

Jacobus took a sip of his Scotch. He savored its peaty richness and the fire that ran down into his belly.

'Are you finished?' Sybil asked.

'Not by a long shot, my dear. I'm just getting started. Did I mention that Schlossberg's murder was the perfect crime?'

340

'No. You didn't.'

'Good. Because it wasn't. You see, Sybil has already made several serious blunders. First, could Aaron have driven alone to Stuyvesant Hall in his condition? Impossible. But the fact was, his car wasn't even there. So how did he get there? Someone had to have driven him. Second, there was no music on the piano. What composer doesn't have music manuscript paper and a pencil while composing at the keyboard?

'And why, indeed, would Aaron be at a piano in the basement of Stuyvesant Hall? First of all, if he needed a piano, why use a second-rate student instrument when he could have had his pick of the faculty Steinways? Second, he did all his composing at home and not on a piano keyboard at all, but on his very sophisticated computer. In fact, the score to his unfinished opera, *Anwar and Yitzhak*, never left his studio. Things are suddenly not looking right.

'And they're not smelling right, either. Let's say – for argument's sake – that Aaron, on his last legs, managed to haul himself to Room Nineteen to compose. Why would he do it with the lights turned off? Only a blind man wouldn't turn on the lights. And the piano fallboard closed? That's even more of a head scratcher. And the ventilation turned off, too? Makes no sense. Maybe, just maybe, in the middle of winter that would've been overlooked, but it was an unseasonably warm spring break. That would have been very uncomfortable for Aaron, and when Sam the janitor discovered Aaron's body, it was even more unpleasant for him.

'What nails Sybil's coffin is the missing harpsichord part to Vivaldi's "Spring." Lisette had lost her Ricordi Edition part. An eagle-eyed violin teacher – let's call her Yumi – notices that the harpsichord part to "Spring" is also missing from Sybil's enviable library of Baroque manuscripts. Put two and two together, and you figure Lisette borrowed it for the chamber orchestra rehearsals. There's nothing at all sinister in that, except for the fact that Sybil had publicly disavowed having anything to do with Lisette. Why would she do that if she has nothing to hide?

'Sybil's missteps begin to conspire against her. One night, she receives a visit from a blind man – let's call him Persistent – who questions her about some inconsistencies in the story. An hour later she receives a call from Lisette, who frantically relates to Sybil that Persistent wouldn't take no for an answer. He is going to meet her the next morning and has uncomfortable questions.

'What to do? Things aren't looking good. The only one who knows what Sybil did to Aaron is Lisette. Sybil plans hastily. A little too hastily, it turns out.

'"Stay right there," Sybil tells Lisette. "We need to talk." She hurries to Stuyvesant Hall and finds Lisette in Room Seven. Sybil sees the Vivaldi harpsichord part in a pile of Lisette's music and realizes her error of having lied about not having anything to do with her. She takes the music back. That problem solved, at least. Now no one can connect the two of them. But in the end, it will do just the opposite.

'Sybil assures Lisette everything will be all right.

342

Sybil will take care of everything. Lisette returns to practicing, her back to the door. Sybil removes a chair and once outside wedges it under the door handle. She then disconnects the power from the wall outlet, cutting off the ventilation. At first Lisette thinks the light has simply gone out, but when she realizes the room is getting stuffy, she quickly understands the jeopardy she is in. Lisette is trapped. She tries the ventilation switch, but for some reason it's not working. She panics. But the more she panics the more toxic the air becomes with her own carbon dioxide. Lisette desperately tries to pry and pound open the soundproof door, but to no avail. She can't dislodge the chair that was wedged under the outside door handle and no one can hear her cries for help.

'When Persistent discovers Lisette's body the next morning, he also discovers that the Vivaldi harpsichord part is missing. For someone as conscientious as Lisette, it's highly unlikely she would lose something like that twice, especially a one-of-a-kind manuscript that belongs to someone else. Persistent recalled that Lisette told him she was going to practice it the night of her death, meaning it disappeared about the same time she died. So the most likely scenario is that Sybil, who had already made so many mistakes, took it back to try to erase any trace of their misbegotten connection.

'Whether she understood that critical error or not, Sybil used her redoubtable powers of persuasion with Hedge and company to make Persistent – who was already in their dog house – a suspect

343

in Lisette's murder. Can't you just picture her pouring her heart out over the callous killing of her bosom friend? And so soon after the death of her dear Aaron! It wouldn't take Lou Pine – the noted string-puller – very long to pass the message on to brother Al. But that was yet another nail in Sybil's coffin, because she did not truly know what she was up against with Persistent, who visited her two days later and told her his story.'

Twenty-Eight

Jacobus's mouth was dry. He took another sip of Scotch and smacked his lips. The whisky was almost gone. He let the flavor linger nostalgically.

'That's the story,' he said.

'What a splendid fairy tale!' Sybil Baker-Hulme said. 'I applaud you.' And she did. 'No wonder you are such a great musician. You have the most creative imagination I've ever encountered. But tell me, how does this fable end?'

'It ends however Sybil wants it to end.'

'Such as?' she asked.

'Turning herself in is one possibility.'

'Mr Jacobus, your naïveté is almost endearing. I don't think that's going to happen, because there are so many flaws in the story itself.'

'Such as?' he asked.

'Such as with regard to poor Lisette's death. You make the outlandish claim that after trapping her in a practice module I disconnected the ventilation system. But you're wrong, Mr Jacobus.'

'Am I?'

'You certainly are. There is no evidence whatsoever the plug was pulled.'

'And how would you know that, Sybil?' Jacobus asked quietly.

'Because . . .'

'Cat got your tongue? I'll tell you. Because after

345

you unplugged it you plugged it back in. After you watched as Lisette Broder begged to be let out of her gas chamber. After you waited for three or four hours and were sure she was dead. You plugged it back in and removed the wedged chair from underneath the door handle. But with so much to remember, it's no surprise you neglected to put the chair back in the module. It's the only explanation of how Lisette could have suffocated with the switch still on. And, face it, it's your pattern. The more you attempt to cover up, Sybil, the more you expose yourself.'

'Your theories are as empty as your musicianship,' she said.

I'm really getting under her skin now, Jacobus thought. He smiled to himself and waited.

'If, as you conjecture,' Sybil resumed, 'Aaron's dalliances were such common knowledge, why would he suddenly be susceptible to Bronislaw's blackmail? What Aaron was or wasn't doing with young ladies was hearsay. "He said, she said" kind of thing. If it did occur I would dare say it was consensual. Nothing could actually have been proved against him.

'Also, conservatory faculties, you know, are much like families. Warts and all. Yes, there's some truth in the notion that everyone might be ready to stab each other in the back, but they don't wash dirty linen in public because all of them, *all of them*, have more than their share of stained nighties.'

'Perhaps,' Jacobus said. 'But the dirt Bronislaw had was different than the run-of-the-mill gossip. It was hard evidence. It was documented proof stored in official files. If it had gone public it would have put an end to your marriage. In its own perverse way, I suppose it did. But it would also have ended Aaron's career and legacy, and put him in jail for a long time. The public humiliation of a trial alone would have killed him. It would also have opened a legal can of worms for the conservatory for covering up his crimes. And though I don't shed a tear for hacks like Hedge and Tawroszewicz, I've met a few good people here, and of course, there are the students.'

'Ah, yes. The sacred students!' Sybil said. 'The cavorting, sacred students. What makes you think one of them – let us call her plain Audrey Rollins – didn't kill Aaron? She, and many others according to your story, would have had ample motive. And Audrey had the means and opportunity as well, and disappeared at a most convenient time.'

'Audrey certainly made the story interesting,' Jacobus replied. 'But there were a few things that made her an unlikely suspect. First was Aaron's disposal at Stuyvesant Hall. Why? If they had poisoned him, why not just let him rot at home? But even if there were a reason she and her boyfriend had been planning on kidnapping him, they would had to have kept an eye on your house continuously from the time the party ended, just to make sure he was there to kidnap and you weren't there to witness it. Then they would have needed to track the deterioration of his health to make sure he was in such a weakened condition he wouldn't be able to resist, or once in the practice room, to escape. Second, according to Sam Consiglio and Connie Jean Hawkins, students were not permitted access to the building over spring break without special permission. Third, even if there was a connection between Audrey and Aaron's death, there was nothing to connect her to Lisette Broder's, especially since Audrey was still doing her best to remain invisible. Finally, I had a gut feeling that she was being honest and you were not.'

'So much supposition, Mr Jacobus! But if I hated her as much as you say, why would I have hired Audrey for that party?'

'That it was you and not your better half who hired her is certain, because he told me, himself, at the party. He did the cooking and you took care of all the other details. But you ask a good question. I asked myself the same one. Why? Why hire someone you hated and risk tawdry history repeating itself yet again? And the answer was: you *wanted* history to repeat itself!

'You had it all figured out. And you had to have planned it all in advance because false morels don't grow like dandelions. There's no guarantee you can find such a rare trophy on the spur of the moment.'

'Mr Jacobus. I say! What an ornate fabric you have weaved. A thing of speculative shreds and postulated patches. And you've fashioned it to fit so cozily!'

'Not that I believe a word of what you say, but I am going to ask you for a favor. Not for me but for the conservatory. All right, for me, too. It might seem to you as if I were trying to get away

348

with murder. But even if I were to go to trial I would have an excellent defense: the scorned wife, a husband who abused his position and preyed upon his own students. I could easily come out smelling like the proverbial rose. A heroine who saw a horrific wrong being committed over and over again and put an end to it, even at the peril of her own future. And believe me when I say I've got lawyers whose way with words could put Shakespeare to shame.

'Mr Jacobus, what's done is done. There's no going back. Let us move forward. Let us make reforms here at Kinderhoek to protect our young ladies. Let us make conservatory policies transparent and fair. But don't you agree that involving the police would bring everything down like a house of cards? What good could it possibly do? Consider the best interests of the students. And of music.'

'You know,' Jacobus said, 'I might have bought that if you had walloped Schlossberg over the head with a sledgehammer. I probably would've helped you do it. And it wouldn't have even bothered me that you tried to get away with it, either. After all, no one wants to rot in prison, especially when their mission is to proclaim to the world how mezzo piano liberated Europe.

'But I'm not going to let you off the hook, dear Sybil. Why? Because the reasons you killed him had little to do with righting a wrong. You stood idly by even after learning your husband had been raping young women and only decided to kill him when you discovered that Bronislaw Tawroszewicz was blackmailing him. By killing

349

him, you prevented Tawroszewicz from getting tenure. That was one motive.

'But, mainly, you killed him to get revenge upon a young woman. If all else failed, you were all too ready to pin the crime on Audrey Rollins, an innocent human being who had already been victimized by your husband. You even planted the idea in my head that she had killed Schlossberg when you so subtly and innocently asked me about her well-being.

'You would have been content to see Audrey Rollins and Lucien Knotts behind bars forever for the crime you committed. More than content. Delighted. And then you murdered Lisette Broder for no other reason than to keep her from talking. To think that you were trying to entice me with your new book at the same time you knew you were about to murder your husband. You talk about Shakespeare, Lady Macbeth.'

'You sound so bitter, Mr Jacobus. So very bitter. I begin to believe your setbacks in life have clouded your rationality. Your desperate need for validation, both personally and professionally, is so very, very great. I'm saddened by it. I really am. The brilliance that once was, gone so far astray. I must ask you, why have you come here this evening? What are your intentions? To make me grovel? To plead for mercy?'

'By no means.'

'Then what?'

'To give you an opportunity to make amends. I've sent a tape recording to the *New York Times* reporter Martin Lilburn. It is essentially word-for-word what I've just laid out. If you surrender

350

to the authorities, I've told him not to print it. If you continue to deny it, you'll have hell to pay and you won't get back any change. Lilburn will be waiting to hear from me.'

Sybil laughed.

'How melodramatic! If only Aaron had been here to write an opera about it. *The authorities*, whom I presume you to mean my dear friend Police Chief Albert Pine, suspect me of murder as much as they understand Pythagorean tuning. The only possible result of Mr Lilburn's exposé would be a lawsuit, which he would lose. Mr Jacobus, I've done my best to discourage you from rash and futile action. I must now remind you to consider the fact that you do not have a shred of proof I had anything to do with either murder.'

'I'm aware of that, Sybil. Which is why I've told Lilburn that if you prevent me from coming forward with the truth, he should print it immediately. On the tape I told him that you had invited me to dinner and that I suspected it was your intention to kill me with a poison mushroom. You would then cover up the murder to make it look like an accident, as you've done before.'

'What a laughable fairy tale! Dinner? Killing you? Is that the other possible outcome you alluded to? Turn myself in or kill you? Please, Mr Jacobus! How absurd!'

'But you're wrong, Sybil. If you don't turn yourself in, you *are* going to kill me.'

'Truly? Let me understand this correctly. I . . . am going to kill . . . you?'

'Yes. You will kill me.'

'Mr Jacobus, your musical imagination comes as no surprise, but it appears I never gave you enough credit for your cloak-and-dagger fantasies! I'm not sure how I'm supposed to play my part in this game, but might it have something to do with your trusty tape recorder that you've hidden in your jacket?'

'What tape recorder?' Jacobus asked. The surprise in his voice was real.

'Why, the one you used to record the fairy tale you sent to Mr Lilburn. Don't think I haven't been aware that you've been wearing your shabby jacket since you arrived, even though the evening is warm as midsummer. And that bulge inside which only a blind man could fail to see. Sorry for the insult, but it's true. There *is* an advantage to being able to see, after all. Mr Jacobus, I don't know what kind of a simpleton you take me for, but I realized your intent from the moment you crossed my threshold. You've been trying to elicit a confession from me on your tape recorder and I'm sorry to say your childish scheme simply is not going to work.'

'That's what you think is in my jacket? A tape recorder?'

'Well, if not, then what? Please show me that I'm not correct. Put your cards on the table. If you're man enough.'

'Very well. If that's what you want.'

Jacobus pulled the small, brown paper bag from inside his jacket. From it he extracted a small object. He held it out so that Sybil could see it clearly.

'You will recognize this, Sybil. *Gyromitra esculenta*. False morel. The same kind of mushroom you used to murder your husband. No one knows I have it. I'm going to eat it now. It may kill me. It may not. Either way, there will be no doubt who served it to me on a silver platter. Maybe in the delicious steak-and-kidney pie you prepared for the occasion. Like Lilburn, the young man who dropped me off here also believes you invited me for dinner because I told him you had. He saw you, and no one else, greet me. Once I eat this mushroom, it will give credence to everything I said on the tape. The police *will* find my body here. There *will* be evidence. There *will* be the corroboration from Lilburn and Anderson. There *will* be no other possible explanation of my death. You *will* be arrested, tried, and convicted. Whether they also convict you for the murders of your husband and Lisette Broder won't matter very much because paying the price for my murder *will* be sufficient. Once I eat this mushroom, Sybil, my life will be over, but so will yours.'

'There's no evidence I made dinner for you.' All the bravado of having the upper hand had disappeared. It was replaced by cold, desperate calculation.

'After you poison me,' Jacobus pursued, 'you'll do your damnedest to clean up after yourself. You're clever that way. And a fine housekeeper.'

'That's not a real false morel. You're faking!'

'I don't think so. This is your last chance.'

'You're a madman. You wouldn't dare!'

As a musician, Jacobus had always been intrigued

by how many disparate thoughts the human brain was capable of processing in a single instant. He could be totally immersed in a late Beethoven string quartet while simultaneously wondering what he would have for dinner after the performance and which students he hoped would cancel lessons in the upcoming week.

Now, he was similarly impressed with how many thoughts circled his brain in the twinkling of an eye: *Will Mia perform 'Spring' tomorrow, or will she have convinced Audrey to return? Will Mia give up the violin entirely as she said? Will their futures be scarred from their experiences with Schlossberg? How could they not?*

What about Hedge? Will he get the ninety-million dollars from the Feldstein fortune? Is the conservatory 'Going for Baroque' or just plain going broke? Lousy pun. Has Hedge been covering up Schlossberg's mysterious death as well as his sexual crimes? Yumi did interrupt that whispered meeting among Hedge, Cooney, Dunster, and Dr Pine when they were supposedly mourning Schlossberg.

Did Connie Jean really try to push me down the stairs? Will Tawroszewicz get his tenure or be booted out of the school? Will Dunster retire? Will Handy take over the helm from Sybil? What will become of all the others? And that good kid, Chase Anderson? Will he become a detective or a medical assistant? I fooled Anderson. As far as the kid knows, there was only one false morel in the bag, and that one went to the lab. A mere diversion so that neither he nor Knotts could know my real purpose.

354

Would the 'not insignificant growth' on my lung have killed me anyway? Doesn't matter now.

Those were questions he'd never know the answer to if he ate the mushroom. Not that he cared all that much. It wasn't as if those kinds of things only happened once. The human soap opera had been going on since apes started walking upright, and no matter when he died he'd always have a nagging curiosity about what would happen tomorrow. There would always be unanswered questions, no matter how the current story ended. But that couldn't be helped. That's just the way things were.

And Schneidermann! What would he think of me killing myself in order to incriminate someone else? 'On one hand, Mr Jacobus, such actions are highly objectionable. Suicide is considered by many a desecration of God's work! On the other hand . . .' God's work! Where the hell has He been all these years?

Will Trotsky miss me? Probably not. And Nathaniel and Roy Miller. I'll miss playing checkers with Nathaniel. Maybe they'll miss me. I told them on the tape not to. And Yumi – dear Yumi. I told her I hope she gets a black belt in judo. Break those fuckers' arms.

I really do want to hear 'Spring.' Oh, well. Just another concert.

'Oh, yes, I would, Sybil,' Jacobus replied, and popped the mushroom into his mouth. 'King me!' he proclaimed.

'King me?' Sybil asked.

'Nobody be whuppin' *my* white ole checkers ass!' Jacobus cackled.

355

The mushroom didn't taste particularly good. It didn't go very well with the final drops of Scotch he used as a chaser. He dropped the glass and heard it break on the wooden floor. The mushroom was slightly bitter and fibrous, and he had to chew longer than he expected. He wondered whether eating it raw increased or decreased its potency. Maybe he should have cooked it. *Lucien would have known. Schlossberg would have known. Too late now. False morels, Sybil and I. Will tomorrow's Vivaldi by Twilight concert go on at all? Will Sybil be reciting Vivaldi's sonnet? In Venetian? Smiling pompously? I think not. Last damn symposium I'll ever attend.*

Jacobus loved silence. You would think a blind man would be afraid of it, but he loved the silence. Even more than music at times. It liberated him. At his old home in the Berkshires the silence had been so deep, so profoundly deep, especially at night, that he could hear his own breathing and nothing more. He would hold his breath in order not to disturb it.

Jacobus had won his final game of checkers. He sat back and waited and smiled. *Stirred by the festive tones of rustic pipes, nymphs and shepherds lightly dance beneath the verdant canopy of spring.* So much for nymphs and shepherds.

The days would be getting longer now. Jacobus thought he heard a light patter at the window behind him. Or was it inside him?

'Is it raining?' he asked.

Author's Note

My primary goals in the Daniel Jacobus series have been to write entertaining stories, provide a glimpse into the multi-faceted world of classical music, and give lay readers a good beginners' listening list of some of the world's greatest music. I've generally shied away from wading into political or broad social issues. When I started writing *Spring Break* I knew it was going to take place in a music conservatory and that a murder would be committed over some bone of contention, of which there are enough to make complete skeletons. I hadn't determined who the victim or murderer would be, or the motive.

But as I worked through my rough draft, those question marks became clear as, one after another, institutions of higher education became the subject of front-page headlines in highly publicized cases of sexual violence on their campuses. It didn't matter whether it was a major Ivy League university or a church-administered one. Sexual harassment remains a doggedly tenacious epidemic in our general culture, and no less so on college campuses where, literally, one is presumed to know better. With the setting of *Spring Break* already established, I felt compelled to address this issue head on.

When drunken frat boys and campus sports heroes rape female students, we wring our hands but chalk it up to bad upbringing or aberrant behavior or extra testosterone or the reason-numbing effects of binge drinking. We decry it but can, to some degree, understand it. But when such crimes are committed by revered university professors, how do we explain *that* away? Misunderstandings? If a professor can't discern the difference between right and wrong, who can? Is it that difficult?

We cringe in disgust when Catholic priests are exposed for abusing children. We are outraged when male-dominated cultures of so-called Third World countries relegate women to second-class status. We recoil in horror when marauding mercenaries in Africa rape women as their reward and as a tool to terrorize the populace into submission. Why is it, then, in our supposedly advanced democracy, we continue to tolerate sexual violence on college campuses? To claim we don't tolerate it is simply denying the reality. The abuse persists, administrations continue to place the prestige of their universities ahead of the well-being of their own students, and the justice system continues to bend over backwards to protect the rights of the accused to the point of victimizing the victims. Why is it we do not demand change? Is it because we're in a state of denial that 'the greatest country in the world' may be no better than the lowest of the low? I don't really have answers to those questions. I wish I did, but what I at least *can* do in *Spring Break* is provide food for thought.

Acknowledgements

I've spent many a year on the faculty of various educational institutions, so I have a pretty thorough sense of how that end of the music business works. But there were two critical components of *Spring Break* I didn't know much about: the best way to kill someone using mushrooms, and what happens to murder victims after they've been offed. Searching the Internet, I became very confused about the differences between death certificates, coroner's reports, medical examiner's reports, and autopsy reports. Nor was I confident I could figure out the difference between a coroner, a pathologist, a forensic pathologist, and a medical examiner simply from *CSI* reruns. The solution was to contact Utah's chief medical examiner, Dr Todd Grey, at the University of Utah Medical Center, a stone's throw from my house in Salt Lake City. Dr Grey, who has since retired, kindly set aside time for me in his intensely busy schedule for a revelatory meeting in which he explained all these things and patiently answered my redundant questions. Having been thus enlightened, Daniel Jacobus was ultimately able to piece together who killed the unfortunate Aaron Schlossberg.

Regarding the mushrooms, I was able to take advantage of the best kind of person-to-person research: that which is done when the source of the information one needs is one's own offspring. My son, Jacob, a PhD student in evolutionary and ecological biology at Cornell University, provided me with crucial insight into the nature of certain poisonous mushrooms and the various ways one could kill people with them. Walking through the woods with Jake has become a fungi-spotting adventure. I couldn't be a prouder parent.

Thanks, too, to my intrepid agent, Josh Getzler of HSG Agency, who is diligently on the prowl seeking new platforms for my work. To my editors, and the team at Severn House, with whom it has been a pleasure to 'make the rough places plain.' And finally, to my wife, Cecily, and daughter, Kate, whose moral and critical support means so much.